The
ATHEIST'S
BIBLE

———

The
ATHEIST'S
BIBLE

SHALOM
CAMENIETZKI

thistledown press

Library and Archives Canada Cataloguing in Publication

Camenietzki, Shalom, 1939-
The atheist's bible / Shalom Camenietzki.

ISBN 1-897235-16-X

I. Title.

PS8605.A478A84 2006   C813'.6   C2006-903731-0

Cover and book design by Jackie Forrie
Typeset by Thistledown Press
Printed and bound in Canada

Thistledown Press Ltd.
633 Main Street
Saskatoon, Saskatchewan, S7H 0J8
www.thistledownpress.com

Thistledown Press gratefully acknowledges the financial assistance of the Canada
Council for the Arts, the Saskatchewan Arts Board, and the Government of
Canada through the Book Publishing Industry Development Program for its
publishing program.

Canadian   Patrimoine
Heritage   canadien

Canada Council   Conseil des Arts
for the Arts   du Canada

ACKNOWLEDGEMENTS

The author would like to thank *The Cormorant, Novella,* the *Prairie Journal, paperplates,* and *Green's Magazine* for publishing stories included in this collection. The *Dalhousie Review* and *Parchment* granted me much needed support and recognition by each publishing two of the stories included in this book.

Susan Ioannou, a Canadian poet, has masterfully edited the early versions of my writing and in the process taught me the nuts and bolts of writing fiction in English.

John Lent edited the final versions of my stories and provided much clarity, insight, and support.

CONTENTS

To Kerstin,
    my sweet Penelope
        you wait
and
  wait
        whenever
        I roam
        the black continents

The Star Of Childhood Memories

For a fifty-two-year-old man, it feels less embarrassing to write about my nanny than to tell others I'm still in love with her. My friends strain and squint, puzzled, when I tell them how Maria stands out as the most inspiring figure in my life. Deep in my heart I know they expect me — a portly, greying psychologist — to credit my parents, my analyst, or one of my teachers, as the wellsprings of my character. I do insist that Maria is the key for understanding me in depth, but my colleagues reply that I overstate her influence on me.

At cocktail parties in Toronto, where people chit-chat about Italian restaurants and private schools, I do bring up how Maria, the only nanny I ever had, overshadows my life, even today. And from the reactions I get, you would think I had mentioned indelicate stains in my shorts! People mouth, "Oh, really?" and roll the conversation over into a new topic. Not that I try to be difficult, but working mothers have left — to re-fill their glasses, they said — when I stated that mostly Maria, and not my mother, forged my talents. The example I usually give for Maria's impact on my personality is my good habit of calling a spade a spade.

The first memory to slip from the mists and silences of my infancy is of Maria. In a once-flowery blue dress, she is standing barefoot on our shaded front porch, holding a two-year-old naked me in her arms. It must have been a summer morning in Rio de Janeiro: droplets of perspiration already shimmer on her forehead.

"Candy, candy," I wiggle in Maria's bony hands, and wave a frantic goodbye at my short and plump mother. Mamãe sports a blue suit with brass buttons, a frilly white blouse, matching blue shoes, and a black leather purse. She's leaving for work, and doesn't stop. Instead, as she walks away, she turns her head and waves goodbye. Whenever this scene comes back to me, I get the eerie feeling it repeats itself often.

At that time, it surprised me that people called Maria "black" because her face was not the colour of the black beans we ate at noon, but brown like the hunks of *rapadura* she dropped in her coffee. She smiled often, more often than my Jewish parents ever did, and two rows of gapped teeth twinkled behind her lush lips. I wondered then if I smiled at Maria because she smiled first, or did she smile because *I* smiled at her? I began to sort out this chicken-or-egg puzzle only years later, when I learned the word "simultaneity."

Because my mother had an "interesting office job" in downtown Rio, Maria took care of me the whole day. As far back as I can remember, playing "Horse" was our favourite game. First, Maria got down on her hands and knees, her smiling face turned to watch me clamber onto her back. As she galloped along the walls of the living room, I swayed back and forth, my hands clutching the neck of her dress. "*Oba! Oba!*" I screamed, and my bare heels spurred her on. When she puffed to a stop, I slid off. My turn. I threw myself on all fours and scurried from one corner of the room to the other.

"*Oba! Oba!*" she slapped my bum, to make me go faster and faster.

We played the game a dozen times — or more. Too soon she announced, "I have to look at the beans on the stove" (that was in the mornings). In the afternoons she said, "Your mother is soon home. I have to fix dinner." Even before I turned two, I concluded that adults — even my Maria — didn't have much stamina for play. They needed a lot of breaks.

While Maria worked around the house, I played with Little Horse. My inseparable toy stood only five inches tall, but boasted a thick mane and a long tail, and his glass eyes shone a lovely brown. I held him all day long, and his wooden back and neck had grown *very* dark. At night he slept under my pillow, and it was out of the question for me to stay in bed, even with the lights on, unless I felt his legs poking the back of my head. In the daytime he basked in my adoring eyes. I hugged and praised him a lot. I was his sweet, loving nanny.

One morning, as I played in my room with Little Horse, I called out to Maria. No reply. I called again, louder. Desperate for the sound of her voice, clutching Little Horse, I wobbled up from the floor. In a cold sweat and a stomach in knots, I toddled in and out of all the rooms. "Maria! Maria!" I begged.

"*A-yim, A-yim,*" I heard her singing.

I followed the echoes of her voice. In the far corner of my mother's bedroom, I found my queen on her knees, reeking of gasoline and wax. She leaned on her left hand, while her right rubbed in the pearl-white wax with a rag. A white cloth hid most of her black, kinky hair. Maria raised her head, and with her upper sleeve wiped her moist brow. She smiled. Her black eyes glinted, so soothing, so sweet.

"Your horse is just a little one," Maria stressed. "A big horse, a real one, pulls wagons full of vegetables, fruit, or bags of rice. When they pooh, they lift their tails up and to the left. They're so clever that they pooh and trot, *at the same time*, and the green droppings fall down and roll on the cobblestones."

I gaped. Her magical stories about things happening at the same time left me as awe-struck as the mystery of she and me smiling *at the same time*. What other wonders loomed beyond the entrance to our side street and the vast shade of the ficus trees?

It happened on Friday, the day before my third birthday.

Once I stopped fussing and emptied my glass of warm milk, Maria went to my room to get the hairbrush and comb. As far as I can tell, this sequence — warm milk, fussing, combing — had taken place every morning of my life since I was two months old, when Mamãe, I'm told, hired Maria.

Maria returned to the kitchen and, humming the same wordless song I heard every day, brushed and combed my hair at length. After setting the brush and comb on the table, her fingers rested on my head, gently. My hair and scalp told me her fingers were coiling three curls: a big one on top, and a small one on each side. The brushing and combing had felt a bit like a chore, but her fingers now sent waves of delight down my neck. I chuckled, but not enough to interfere with her work. She played with the curls for a while longer, to savour, I imagined, the twists and turns of fingers through hair. I knew we were done when her wistful tune stopped.

"Let's look in the mirror," she suggested.

We walked to my mother's bedroom, and inside the armoire, in the mirror, I saw three little curls framing a round face, two brown eyes and a thick, short nose. High above me, Maria's chocolate-brown face smiled, pleased that the curls, *her* curls, stood up without any pins. Only my romping in and out of rooms would later on flatten the fruits of her work.

On that Friday, a sultry afternoon of a long, drawn-out summer, Papai came home from his store earlier than usual. Playing with blocks beside my bed, I heard him say a brief 'hello' at the entrance, then go straight to my brother's room. The door closed, and soon I heard some muffled chuckles and whispers, too blurred for me to follow. Papai and Samuel, my brother, excluded me from conversations at times, so I went on building my block truck.

Mamãe, who left her work on Fridays at noon, must have been in the kitchen telling Maria what had to be done now that the Sabbath was only three hours away. The keen smell of gefilte fish floated through the house, subduing the scent of the chicken in the oven and the aroma of carrots stewing with raisins and cinnamon sticks. A white linen cloth, stiff and shining from the iron, would be stretched out on the dining room table. Two tall candles, their wicks already lit once, would be standing in silver holders, like soldiers at attention, waiting for my mother's blessing.

"We are going out, the three of us," Papai announced at the kitchen entrance.

"In this heat?" asked Mamãe who, like Maria, kept me indoors on hot afternoons.

"The boys are going for a walk," Papai sounded cheery. "We'll be back in an hour."

"An hour? Well, keep the little one in the shade, as much as possible." Mamãe meant me, of course; my brother would soon be fifteen years old.

Outdoors, a white ball of fire still torched our neighbourhood. I squinted hard, and the dusty air scorched my nostrils.

"We are going to the barber, for a haircut," Papai turned to me, as we walked our empty side street, my left hand in his right. "You will be three years old tomorrow, and I want you to look like a boy, a real boy." He stopped and stared me in the eye, as if to stress the importance of that moment. "When you were a baby, your long hair and curls looked just beautiful. Your Mamãe and Maria still want to keep them for a while. But I'm your father, and I've decided that from today on, you'll have short hair, just like Samuel and me."

"I never had curls, my whole life," said Samuel. Walking two steps ahead, my skinny, bespectacled, always clever brother bragged about something I didn't quite understand. The more we walked, the scarier the scene became, so I asked no questions.

"Going to the barber is a surprise. I'm glad Mother didn't suspect anything when I said we were out for a walk." My father smiled, proud of his ruse.

They took me to a barber shop on Rua Pereira Nunes, where the streetcars ran, and Maria and I shopped for groceries. "In downtown Rio," Maria's voice now played in my head, "there are some *really* big boulevards. One of these days we'll take the streetcar and have a look." Above the entrance to the shop, a green awning carved a square oasis of shade in the blinding sidewalk.

"Good afternoon, *senhor* Ari. I see you brought me a new customer." Inside the shop, the white barber, a stocky, half balding man, rubbed his hands. His trim, sloping black moustache made his face look fierce.

"I want him to have a short cut, like a boy, Ademir," my father sounded firm. "His *baba* still rolls his hair into curls."

"I know what you mean, *senhor* Ari. These black girls are really nice to the kids, but, after a while, they behave as if they owned our children." The barber studied me up and down, amused, and went back to sharpen his razor on a long strip of leather, the blade flipping from side to side. Papai sat next to me, reading a newspaper, while Samuel chose to wait in the street, under the awning. In public my brother behaved as though he had never met me before, but at home he kept reading me stories, even when I didn't ask.

Two big globes lit the shop and cast a sallow tint on everyone's faces. Overhead, a large, sluggish fan turned and blew warm air down my face. The place reeked of lather and aftershave, and the background scent of talc carried me back to our bathroom. There, Maria powdered me after showers, and I giggled — perhaps too much so — when she rubbed my crotch with her fine, scented dust.

The barber's chair tilted back, and a customer lay flat on it, an apron covering him to his knees. His cheeks and neck had vanished under thick lather, while his closed eyes and the upturned corners of his mouth suggested the man was having a sweet dream. Ademir, holding the razor between his right thumb and a bent finger, startled me when he took the blade to the man's neck. Bending close to check, he cleared a strip in the lather and wiped the blade on a pile of paper tissues. The barber continued to shave in silence, unsmiling, absorbed in this ceremony for males.

"It's soon your turn," Papai gave me a pat on the head. He must have seen me biting my nails and wobbling up for a better angle at the man before me. I felt relieved when the customer sat up and, the apron removed, got to his feet, smiling at Ademir.

"It's your son's turn, *senhor* Ari."

I saw the barber place a wooden board across the arms of the chair. Then he bent down, tweaked my chin with his thumb and finger, and asked for my name.

"*Kha-yïm*," I bleated. It hurt me that Ademir was taken aback at the sound of my name, a smile curling the corners of his mouth.

"It's a Hebrew name, Ademir," my father explained. "I called the boy after his grandfather, who passed away just before the war. Actually, the name means 'life' and sounds quite pleasant in our language."

"I'll get used to it, *senhor* Ari."

Ademir held me high in the air, my head close to the lazy fan. He cooed a few times, twisted me left and right, then sat me on the board. The apron he tightened to my neck covered me like a blanket and more. The mirror showed a familiar face, its hair now long and flat this time of the day. Samuel had walked in to watch the operation. Papai stood on my right.

Twice Ademir snipped in the air a long, lacklustre pair of scissors that made a zipping sound. Five quick strokes on the top and sides, and a lot of hair disappeared from my head in the mirror. On the real apron and chair, some flimsy strands of black hair clung to the white cloth, unsteady, as if they would blow away in a moment. The barber wasted no time and trimmed behind my ears and neck.

"I don't use the razor on kids, *senhor* Ari. They wiggle when you try, and I hate to nick them by mistake."

"This is a fine haircut, as is," my father replied.

The mirror showed a new version of myself: a smaller head, a higher forehead, two even more anxious eyes. Is that what a real boy is supposed to look like? I was not at all impressed; the reflection struck me as scrawny, frail.

"Tomorrow you'll get a real tricycle, a big one," Papai told me on our way home. "Your friends will stand behind your seat, and you can take them for rides on the sidewalk."

"And I'll put a bell on your right handle bar," Samuel followed up. "I already got one, for you." I stroked my head and the short hair felt creepy.

I still have found no words to describe the little something that had slipped out of my life and would never come back.

"Mamãe and Maria have stopped boiling the gefilte fish," I muttered when we arrived home. The smell of fish had mellowed, and now I savoured my favourite, the aroma of prunes and other dried fruits that had stewed for hours. Their backs to us, the women were still bustling in the kitchen, hurrying to put the last touches to the meal.

"Look, Rivkah," Papai said.

Mamãe turned around, drying her hands on a towel. Her brown eyes glared and four fingers capped her mouth. "What have you done, Arieh?" This was my father's Hebrew name, but only Mamãe ever used it. My father surprised me, he didn't mind at all when people mangled his first name.

"That's his first hair cut. Now he looks the three year old he'll be tomorrow."

Maria took off her apron, tossed it on the counter, and walked out of the kitchen. Soon, the door to her quarters slammed. My mother's puzzled eyes begged an explanation, because Maria always prefaced all her answers with "*Sim, senhora*" or "*Não, senhora.*" I turned to follow my nanny to find out how she was feeling, but my father barked, "Go play in your room." A bit later I heard him order Samuel to his room, too.

About an hour later, when I came out of my room, it was dark. I saw Mamãe wearing the white apron Maria used when she brought plates and vessels from kitchen to table, back and forth. Mamãe blessed over the candles with a muffled voice. Her cheeks glowed, and I sensed that she felt very angry.

The four of us ate in silence, even my talkative father. I looked around the table. Maria's absence cast a shadow on my plate, the tablecloth, the walls. My heart had sunk. Was she in her room? What was she doing? I wondered, but didn't dare ask aloud. Clearly, Maria was not to be mentioned. My head rested on my left hand and I glanced in despair at the morsels of chicken on my plate. Sooner or later Mamãe would nag at me to finish my plate. Friday's roasted chicken had never been my favourite dish, and I mumbled to myself prayers for a painless way to gulp down the pasty ball in my mouth.

"You should have told us you were going to the barber," Mamãe broke the silence.

"No matter what, I don't think a maid, *uma empregada*, should decide how our son looks," Papai half closed his left eye. Two upright lines between his eyebrows deepened.

"Maria cares a lot about Khayim's appearance. If you'd told us about the haircut the day before, she wouldn't have been hurt." Mamãe cocked her head. She looked down her nose at Papai, as if she had knocked him out of the argument.

"I took the trouble of closing the store early to make a point: he isn't a baby any more," Papai waved his hand at me. "And to tell you the truth, the boy spends too much time with Maria, anyhow."

"Are you criticising *me*? Every time we have a problem, you drop hints about my work, or about me not spending enough time at home."

Samuel stood up, still chewing the last bite of dessert.

"Aren't you staying for coffee?" My mother's tone of voice implied he should.

"I'm sorry to eat and run like this, Mamãe, but my friends are waiting."

After coffee, Papai removed the dishes, while Mamãe tied on Maria's kitchen apron, the dark blue one, to rinse the plates and pans.

I tossed in bed that night, studying the ceiling, the pictures on the walls, and each one of my toys on the floor. Sleep, however, refused to come. I propped up my pillow, but my worries kept me awake. What had happened to my Maria? Where was she? Had she left me? I hadn't seen her eating anything since lunch time. Her empty tummy, I imagined, was growling and aching.

Despite the closed door, I could hear from the living room the muted voice of the radio announcer dropping names I had heard before at dinner time: Churchill, El-Alamein, Hitler. Sleep stubbornly refused to come, so I decided to take a risk and see my love.

I slunk out of bed and walked to the door. I turned the handle so softly it made no sound at all. The corridor to Maria's quarters was dark at my end and the other, but I had to cross a long swath of light from the living room. I heard the clear voice of the radio announcer and pictured my parents on the sofa, listening to the news, slices of lemon swimming in their cups of tea.

I tiptoed up the corridor, a huge heart pounding in my chest. I had almost crossed the stretch of light, when Mamãe rose from her seat and ambled up to me.

"What happened? Is the radio keeping you awake? Tell me, Khayim, I'll turn it off".

I stood flat on my feet, no longer a burglar.

"And where are you going?" Still peeved, Papai sat on the sofa and watched me from behind a lowered newspaper.

I squinted back. "Maria."

"We don't know where she is," he said. "And if she's still with us, she may be asleep." His comment disturbed me; it had never entered my mind she would ever fall asleep before me.

Mamãe bent over and kissed me. "If she's in her room, you can play with her. But you have to be in bed soon. Tomorrow is your birthday party. You need a good night's rest."

In front of the door to Maria's quarters I stood and listened to the silence. With my shoulder, I pushed on the door. An inch-wide column of light shone ahead.

"Maria?" I held my breath.

"Come in, love. Don't just stand there."

She sat on the white cover of her bed. Her quarters were an elongated cubicle, and the window, on my right, was too small to let in the evening breeze. Three walls were white, unadorned, but on the fourth, a bare, unstained wooden cross shone two feet above the head of her bed. In the centre, a naked bulb hung by a cord from the ceiling.

"I was praying," she stood up. I must have looked puzzled because she added, "to God." Now, this name sounded familiar! She often exclaimed "Thank God" or "My God." "Dinner?" I asked when she sat down again. Maria nodded, and despite my attempts to engage her, she gazed at the floor, sullen. I leaned on the side of her bed and racked my brain to find something that would take her bad mood away.

Palm down, I stretched out my right hand to play one of her favourite games. She pinched the back of my hand, I pinched the back of hers, she pinched mine again. When she said "now," we tossed the pile of connected hands high in the air, then threw ourselves into each other's arms. We played the game a couple of times, but now her hugs felt limp, her kisses too dry.

I did not give up. First I wiggled myself onto her lap, then kissed her cheeks and put my arms round her neck. She didn't draw back when I blew air in her ear, but remained listless, no matter what I tried.

"I should've known better." Her fingers stroked my hair. "I'm just a maid, *uma empregada*. I can't make decisions about your hair." She fell silent again. "And one day, your *baba* will kiss you goodbye, I'm afraid."

"Em-pe-ga-da," my lips and tongue struggled with the twice heard polysyllable.

"It's late," she helped me to my feet, "time you go to bed. Tomorrow you'll get a tricycle. It'll be a wonderful birthday." She kissed me good night on both cheeks, then led me back to the living room.

Mamãe tucked me in a second time. I lay awake, all over again. The ceiling and the walls loomed darker now. I barely made out my toys on the floor. I wondered what awful things I must have done, because in just one day Mamãe, Maria, and my father — even my brother — got upset. I remember feeling so sad that I had to talk myself to sleep: Maria hadn't left me, after all. Tomorrow I could get on with being a three-year-old boy.

This may sound unbelievable, but the star of my childhood memories ran a very tight household. No departures from routine were allowed — ever. Mornings meant porridge steaming in my bowl, and it was useless to appeal her rule on finishing the white, gooey stuff. Daily I scooped the cinnamon and sugar off the top, and, to make her happy, gulped down two spoons of the flabby substance. Lips sloped down, I snivelled and whimpered, probably looking like a mask of tragedy. Maria caressed my neck, she muttered *meu coraçao* — my heart — but her right eyebrow stayed just a little bit up, until I scraped clean the bottom of my bowl.

Breakfast finished, she hummed a soft samba, to celebrate, I imagine, the still young morning; a day of sweet routines lay ahead. First, her match lit the gas burner. It boomed once, the same bass of the giants in the stories she made up for me. Little flames streamed out of endless cavities and moulded a blue crown with a black hole in the middle. On top of the flames she rested a glistening aluminum pot, to cook the black beans she and I ate every day, except on weekends and Jewish holidays.

While I rode my red tricycle or played with Carlos in the backyard, Maria waxed and polished our wooden floors. All the while, the blessed scents of her slow-cooking beans, meats, onions, garlic, sausage, and seven spices wafted in from the kitchen and lifted my body and soul higher and higher on the steps of a ladder to heaven.

"A-yim," she mispronounced my name again, "It's noon now. Your beans are soft."

Ravenous, I sprinted all the way to the table, because she almost never handed out any snacks. My right hand clutched the spoon, ready to throw myself at the beans, the rice, the blackened meats.

She ladled vast helpings of her homemade manna onto a bed of steamed rice. At the end of the meal, I felt so blissful and drowsy, that more often than not she took me in her arms and carried me to my room. My after-lunch naps were long.

At three o'clock, when Maria stopped wiggling her butt to the *sambas de amor* from her favourite radio program, we got ready for our daily walk. Even if puddles dotted the streets, she still helped me every day into a starched sailor's outfit smelling of dew. (My wardrobe, I assume, must have been home to five or six such uniforms, including caps with foot-long, black ribbons fluttering down the back.) Before I swung the front door open, she urged me, "Stand still, *meu coraçao*," while her thumb and finger slid up and down the crease of my pants. She spat saliva the size of a mothball onto the brush, to lend my buckled shoes a clear, limpid shine. Only then we darted down the steps of the front porch.

Maria owned only one good-looking, white taffeta dress, which she wore for our strolls. She always wore white low-heeled shoes, for she stood quite tall and bent a bit forward. A *Kreeme*, a warped one, I vaguely remember someone — probably my father — whispering in Yiddish once.

While we strolled side by side — I refused to hold hands in public — I breathed in her afternoon aroma, a blend of mild Palmolive and the odours of woman-after-bath.

Walking on the sidewalk, we came across throngs of mothers, nannies and children in their finest garb. All girls wore short, pink dresses, and boys wore sailor suits, high fashion in the forties. I glanced at my Maria from time to time, to show her off, the most appealing, best smelling woman in the neighbourhood.

Every time we stumbled upon empty cans on the sidewalk, their lids tilted up like visors, my right toe itched to kick the cans so badly that tears welled in my eyes. And to this day I'll swear there is no music as rousing — not even Shostakovich's Ninth — as the sound of a well-kicked can, rattling away into silence. But Maria tapped my shoulder. In my best shoes and clothes, can-kicking was out of the question, no matter how hard my sighs courted the cans.

On evenings and weekends I had an easy time with my mother. Her tired, long face forever mirrored the guilt of spending fewer hours with me than Maria did. Almost every day Mamãe bribed me with new toys or sweets. I loved my Mamãe. With her, I never had to finish my plate. My spoon on the floor, or a few short-lived whimpers got me off the hook. After dessert, I rode my tricycle indoors for hours, imitating car horns at the top of my voice. I cycled in and out of all the rooms, except for Samuel's. My brother kicked me in the ass if he ever caught me breathing near his treasures.

More often than not, I woke up surprised to find myself in my room. Who had carried me to bed? How did I get into my pyjamas? The night before I didn't wash myself, undress and crawl into bed. I'd played as late as I wished, and lay down to rest on the sofa only when my legs began to hurt, tired.

My heart tells me my first memories just don't add up. Early images of Papai and Samuel almost never flash in my mind. My intellect points out that even if Samuel locked himself in his room or spent some evenings outside our home, I should have kept at least a few traces of him. And even if my father kept his furniture store open late, six evenings a week, a child's mind should have registered a few lasting pictures. What happened? Did I inadvertently or unwittingly expel these two figures from my private Eden — well, some of the time — and never let them come back? But instead of hunches, hopeful leads or answers, I hear only the echoes of echoes rumbling in the distance.

Clearly, I recall my fourth birthday. Green and yellow streamers, the colour of the Brazilian flag, spilled from the corners of our dining room, climbing up again in the centre to join the lamp above the table. Mamãe and Maria tied white and blue balloons, the colour of the Zionist flag, to the back of each chair in the house. Carlos, four kids from our side street, and two cousins of mine came to the party.

When Mamãe brought in my chocolate cake with four pink, skinny candles burning on top, only the mothers sang "Happy Birthday." We kids sat around the table and looked at each other puzzled and pained, our chins and white shirts smeared with brown icing. The crowd turned cranky, and it grew increasingly painful for me to sit at the head of the table, embarrassed. Glass after glass of *guarana* tumbled down, and puddles the colour of amber stained the white tablecloth. Wistful, I noticed how nobody finished their slices of birthday cake.

But Mamãe never got upset at the uproar and mess. Twice she clapped her hands. "Time to play outdoors," she announced. On the way out, my guests howled like hungry coyotes and wolves.

Mamãe just smiled at me. "Did you enjoy the cake?"

Soon after that birthday, a mystery began to haunt me: what did my Maria do after dark, while I slept? Where, and with whom, did she spend her evening hours? In the afternoons, while I napped, she washed dishes. Then, hidden in the cool shade of our neighbour's avocado tree, she smoked a cigar in the backyard. I knew she occasionally took a nap, because several times I'd woken her to play. Maria prayed at bedtime, but I wished to get hold of more precious clues to her life at night. Of course, I could have posed a few direct questions, but they struck me as being too delicate. Week after week I procrastinated, till it became impossible for me to ask.

For comparison, I kept track of how other members of my family spent their evenings. After dinner, my sleepy mother listened to the radio or read the newspaper. On warm nights when I abandoned my overheated room and moist pillow, I would find her sitting at the dinner table again, poring over papers. Did my Mamãe ever take a break from her work?

From my bedroom, I often overheard my parents speaking Yiddish. Whenever I squinted my way into the living room, I found them sipping cups of hot tea. They never dropped sugar cubes into their drink, but balanced the cubes on the tips of their tongues. "That's the way my family did it, in Poland," Mamãe had explained. "It keeps the taste of tea."

With the war still raging in Europe, my parents almost never mentioned their families in my presence.

It was no mystery, really, how Samuel usually spent his evenings. Right after dessert, my brother, now sixteen years old, rushed to the living room and planted his feet by our metre-tall radio. Bent over, he brought his left ear close to the speaker, and rocked back and forth from the waist, the way we Jews pray. His eyes stayed wide open throughout the local and national news. But as soon as the announcer reported on the Red Army advancing in eastern Europe, he closed his eyes and rocked slowly, in bliss. If there was no news from the eastern front, he stopped swaying at once. Furious, he paced the room.

"Brazil is a fascist dictatorship!" Samuel yelled and raised a fist. "They don't want the masses to know about Stalin's victories!" In the middle of the room he came to a standstill and mumbled, his forefinger wagging at an invisible audience — rehearsing a political speech, it appeared.

Amused — and smug — I had watched my brother's love for Stalin for months. On the eastern wall of his room, above his bed, Samuel nailed a photograph of a dour, unsmiling man with a high brow and rope-thick moustache, who didn't look people in the eye. Once or twice a week Samuel brought home a couple of red carnations or roses. First he crossed the stems, then lovingly gazed at the flowers. After smelling them, he pinned the roses or carnations to the wall, right below the picture of his sweetheart in a faraway land. Rarely had I witnessed Samuel enjoying his love affair in my plain, homely ways. Flowers sniffed and pinned, he never succumbed to Stalin's own fragrances, the way I smelled my Maria, many times a day.

Lately, my skinny, restless, myopic brother had refused to wear glasses. At all times he looked cross-eyed, as if startled out of a dream. Once Papai commented that both Stalin and Hitler bore ferocious moustaches — the hallmark of intellectual lightweights. For days Samuel scurried red-eyed about the house. This barb, I believe, must have hurt a lot, since my father was a very smart man. In his youth, before he had gone into business, he had spent three years learning the Talmud and commentaries in Poland. "Not all my fingers," he used to say, "are needed to count the men who beat me in a game of chess."

As clear as an oboe solo, one evening flows from the recesses of my memory. I was about four, and it must have been Friday because two candles had burnt past midway. Mamãe turned to my father at the head of the table.

"Last night, Arieh," she said in Yiddish, "I turned off the lights at eleven thirty. Samuel wasn't home." Her low voice breathed despair.

"Where were you?" Papai barked. Between his eyebrows, two upright lines sprang to life.

"I hung around the gate with my friends." Samuel replied in Portuguese, to be on the safe side. "I forgot to look at my watch. I'm sorry." He blinked and fidgeted in his chair. The "gate" meant the entrance to our side street.

"He's not telling the truth, Arieh." Mamãe raised her voice, in Portuguese. "He's going to political meetings. How will he be able to concentrate at school?"

My father's stern face gave Mamãe a chance to finish her piece. Usually, Samuel hollered that she meddled in his life.

"And what were *you* doing at the gate?" My father turned curious. "That's where maids hang around with *namorados*."

My heart beat faster.

"I was talking to friends," Samuel shrugged. "That's all."

"Friends? What friends?" My father's eyes brightened, his air of authority vanished. "I bet you guys were ogling the couples doing whatever they were doing." He smiled shiftily. "Was Maria there?"

"Oh, no," said Samuel. "I've never seen her with a man, anywhere. Have you?"

"She is tall and gawky," Papai chuckled. "It'll take her a long time to find a man."

I blushed. I wanted to hide.

Mamãe brought her forefinger to her lips. In a loud voice she turned to Papai and Samuel. "The roast is very good, isn't it?"

Desperate, I prayed to God that Maria didn't hear anything. My father laughed, tilting his head back, his Adam's apple jutting out. "Never mind, Rivkah. Samuel is soon a man. Some things you just can't read in books. Let the boy learn about real life at home."

"Not many men like a skinny ass," Samuel laughed, encouraged.

"Ugly women look like machos," my father hammered the verdict.

Roaring, Samuel slapped the table.

I reached for my glass of *guarana*, but it wobbled and tipped over. Highlighted by the wood beneath, an amber river streamed across the table cloth, towards Samuel.

"What's going on?" my brother hollered. "I swear Khayim spilled the *guarana* on purpose." He flung his chair back, and jumped to his feet, wiping his pants with a napkin.

Scared, I stood up.

"And now, look what you did." My mother's voice soared, "You got Khayim upset." Her hand flailed back and forth, from Papai to Samuel.

My father stopped smiling. "Just a joke, we meant no harm."

A joke," Mamãe hissed in Yiddish. "How can you say something so gross when Maria's in the kitchen? And in front of the boy?" Her nostrils swelled: rarely had I seen my phlegmatic mother so angry. "You just wait, Arieh. You and I will have a little talk about all this."

"What is there more to talk about?" Papai said.

"Enough. Be quiet. You've done a lot of damage already," she said. Bending over, chin almost brushing her plate, Mamãe told Samuel, also in Yiddish. "Is this the way you Commies treat working-class women? *Shame on you!*"

Samuel turned white and withdrew into his chair. He too couldn't handle my mother's sudden anger.

Mamãe stood up, folded her napkin and patted it flat on the table. She walked to my chair, and took my willing hand. On the way to my room I licked my briny tears.

"Nothing but a stupid joke," Mamãe said later, as I stood by my bed. She knelt down and hugged me. "You know Maria likes you so much, she's so good to you."

Was Mamãe feeling guilty again? I wondered.

She unlocked her hug, and wiped the tears off my cheeks. I lay on my bed, facing the wall.

"Too early to go to bed," Mamãe spoke softly. "I'll read you a story. You'll feel better." She untied the laces and pulled off my shoes. "Please, turn over. Look at me," she implored, but still stunned, I continued to gaze at the wall. Her hand cupped my shoulder to roll me over. I sat up.

Mamãe read from *Robinson Crusoe*, but occasionally raised her eyes to watch mine. I stopped sobbing, but barely listened. I worried, instead. Was Maria crying in her room? I dreaded she would *never* recover from the two monsters' mean blows. And she'd done them no harm at all!

Are you feeling better?" Mamãe asked at the end of her story.

"Yes," I muttered, but a finger of shame stung my cheeks. I'd listened to the first twenty words. Maybe less.

Once in pyjamas, I began to hiccup. Every few seconds the loud and frightening hiccups exploded. My chest and shoulders shuddered.

"Do you want a lemonade?" Mamãe asked.

I nodded, and she headed for the door. "I'll ask your Maria to make one."

Bewildered, I began to cry again. Mamãe had acknowledged that another woman, a maid, could better settle me down.

Soon Maria strolled in, and the scent of the freshly squeezed lemon filled the room. Not a grain of pulp floated on top.

Maria eyed me up and down, while my mother, two steps behind, stared at me with tear-drenched eyes. Sipping the sweet potion, I stole a glimpse at Maria. Her eyes and tight cheeks betrayed no inner storms. Yet, vertical lines appeared in the gap between her eyes. To calm the two women, I gulped down the lemonade, and stretched out in bed.

"I'll see you in the morning," Maria waved good night from the door.

Mamãe bent down by my bed. "Next weekend," she hummed in my ear, "we'll spend a whole day at the Zoo, as we did a year ago."

"Two years ago," I uttered, half-asleep.

Later, I awoke as if a hand had yanked me up by the hair. In the darkness, feverish thoughts kept me alert. What is a *namorado*? How can she find one? Where could *I* get her one?

As I tossed in bed, the initial question returned: how did Maria spend her evenings? Right away, other questions came up. *Why* didn't she spend time at the gate like other maids?

And what, precisely, did couples do at the gate? Why did Papai laugh when Samuel said she *couldn't* find a *namorado*?

I sat up. Eyes adapted to the darkness, I made out the ceiling lamp, the curtains blowing by the window, the silhouette of my tricycle on the floor. The walls and ceiling glowed, as if painted the minute before. Unannounced, my father's laughter and Samuel's roar bounced off the walls and ceiling. My forefingers plugged my ears, to block out the monstrous sounds. I gritted my teeth.

"*Can't* find a *namorado!*"

I repeated this horrible phrase so many times that I began to have doubts. Had I heard it in the dining room? Or just now, lying on my bed? Maybe I'd not heard it at all? Maybe I just needed to close my eyes and fall asleep again? Forget such stupid words!

Still, my face and scalp were boiling. Painfully alert, I counted and recounted the spokes in my tricycle's wheels. I sat up. Wave after wave of shame flowed from every pore. The room became unbearably hot. There was no escape.

Where in the world could I find her a man?

Despite the pain, it didn't occur to me to walk to my mother's room and cry, "Help, help." The darkness, the silence in the house, the body heat befuddled me. My thoughts rioted in all directions. But not even for a second did I doubt it was my inalienable duty to make Maria feel better.

When a sleepless night seemed almost certain, a name flashed into my mind: Manuel! — a short, skinny black man in clogs and frayed clothes. About once a month Manuel came to our side street to sing the latest sambas from a booklet he held. At the end of his throaty performances, his fans yelled "bravo!" and "bis!" The older boys whistled.

Manuel bowed, then smiled. Working his way through the audience, he sold booklets to those who could read. Others, like children or Maria, rewarded him with fresh fruit, a slice of bread, or a glass of cold water on a hot day.

"Manuel!" My scream shattered the silence and cleared my thinking.

Leaning on my elbows, I knew he was a good match. Maria laughed during his tours to our street. When he departed, they waved good-bye and smiled. Made for each other, no doubt. She would be happy. I slid under the cotton blanket and surrendered to sleep.

"You're quiet this morning," Maria commented when I showed up for an early breakfast. "There must be a reason."

My eyes latched onto the table, to avoid hers. "Manuel!"

"Manuel?" She wiped her hands on her apron and drew closer. "Did you dream about him? Don't be afraid. Tell me the dream."

I stole a glance: she'd knitted her eyebrows. "Manuel! You . . . the gate . . . the whole evening!" On my bed, I'd prepared a much better speech. But her body rose one foot away. Only those words left my lips.

Her eyes quivered, one tenth of a second. "But my love," she bent down and kissed my hair. "Manuel's already married. He has six children. They are poor. They live in a *favela*." She gazed at the window, then eyed me. "I'd rather stay with you and your parents. It would be awful, plain awful, for me to marry a poor worker, and live again in a shack."

"But if you find a *namorado*," I blurted out, "I still want to live with you!"

"My love! I'm not going anywhere. I'm in school. It takes time to learn to read and write."

"School? What school?"

"Night school. Three times a week, after dishes. When you're a big boy, I'll get myself a job. Maybe a clerk, in a store. I don't want to be a maid for the rest of my life."

I stared at her, less anxious, less jealous.

She planted a moist kiss on my nose. Her breath smelled of coffee. "Don't worry. The day I have to leave, you'll be the first one to know."

I listened, but couldn't quite trust words. They had bruised me the evening before, and I felt fearful, even of her.

She straightened up. "You look very tired, Ayim. You don't have to finish the porridge. Just three, four spoons more."

"But thank you, Maria!" I lit up, amazed.

She went back to her work in the kitchen. The rest of the house was silent; my family hadn't stirred yet. I rolled my tricycle into the backyard. Carlos was not out yet.

Against a pale blue sky, the sluggish leaves of our neighbour's avocado rustled in the morning breeze. Hidden in the dark branches, a lone, unseen bird piped. It stopped in mid-song, shy.

A vise clamped my temples. My eyes burned. My jaws ached. I must have clenched them in a rage for hours. Too tired to ride my tricycle, I toddled into the shade and collapsed on a bed of leaves and dry branches. Looking up, I caught sight of pale blue, jagged slivers of sky shining through the foliage.

My eyelids felt heavy. I kept them closed longer and longer. In front of me, Maria's face flashed on and off: her dignified face the night before, and her forgiving face that morning.

It didn't bother me that I'd failed as her matchmaker. But I craved sleep, and a chance to forget how my own brother and father had hurt me and my innocent nanny. I prayed for tears to soothe my eyes, and for dreams to relieve a sadness in my heart.

As years add up to decades, and the decades ring up a half-century, memories of Maria deepen my own insights into the essence of caring. But were I to write a book, and especially a book that sold well, on the altruism of young children, it would be quite difficult to get referrals from my greying, rotund, stolid colleagues. My fellow psychologists, almost without exception, swear that altruism is an acquired taste, like the love of Schoenberg's music. Perhaps some teenagers — but certainly not children — are ready to appreciate such subtleties. For so egocentric are children — my professors droned, and I, wishing to graduate, pretended to agree — that even for a moment they could not conceive of enhancing the well-being of anyone but themselves.

I would be spared no mockery and, behind my back, be pitied as a closet amateur, if I went public on my nanny's teachings. Her actions — not her words, mind you — have for decades inspired me to see how humans of all ages care for others deeply, and, at the same time, are inevitably self-serving.

Maria and my family introduced me to these tangled issues on an unbearably hot afternoon. Our lunch dishes were stacked to dry on a folded-out wooden rack. To my right, Maria hummed a wordless tune and with a wad of steel wool polished her aluminum pots to a sheen.

"Chemistry! Chemistry!" I trumpeted. Standing on the kitchen stool, my right hand clutched a small corked bottle. A second corked bottle bobbed up and down in the water of a steel bowl, which I'd set on the marble counter.

"What *are* you doing?" She approached my lab, suspicious. "And why is the gas burner on?"

The evening before, Samuel, my seventeen-year-old brother, had monopolized the dinner conversation and made my parents shake with laughter. In great detail he had told how *seu* Perelmuter, his chemistry teacher, heated a glass tube until yellow fumes billowed out the top, like a mushroom. The room began stinking of rotten eggs. The students snuffled and plugged their noses with forefingers and thumbs.

"The class turned into a matinee at the movies," Samuel smiled, triumphant, as my father wiped the tears that had gathered in his eyes. Murderously jealous of all the attention my brother was getting, I twisted and turned in my chair.

"The guys jeered and whistled," my brother carried on. "The girls shrieked 'Help! Help!'" The teacher, my brother said, folded his white handkerchief down the middle, and tied it at the back of his head. "*Seu* Perelmuter," Samuel wore a deadpan face, "looked just like a train-robber."

Oh, well. The real story was that Samuel took his chemistry course *very*, *very* seriously: a good grade would certainly help him fulfil his dreams of getting him into medical school. Already in kindergarten, my brother made it known he would be a doctor when he grew up. And even I must give him credit for having no second thoughts whatsoever on the matter of his vocation. Samuel — and there was both pride and anxiety in the way my parents told this tale — had battled with meningitis and asthma as a kid. He'd spent more time flat on his back than playing ball with his friends. Nevertheless, it got boring for me to hear my brother, an ardent lover of Lenin and Stalin, boast, time and again, how he would become a pediatrician and treat the children of the proletariat for a token fee.

"Hand me the bottles!" Maria's tone of voice left no room for pleading. "One bottle has nail polish," she established after uncorking it and sniffing. "The other one is empty. Jesus, what *are* you doing?"

She was right. I'd stolen nail polish from a bottle in my mother's dressing table. "It's an *experiment*," I showed off my new word, right hand stretching for one of the bottles, which she moved out of my reach.

"I'm pouring the nail polish back. Don't you dare move till I return."

Quickly, I wrapped a kitchen towel round the bottle's neck. I twisted the bottle left and right in the gas flame, the way I visualized the Chemistry teacher doing it. When I dipped the heated bottle into the water in the bowl, a muffled sound reached my ears. I let go of the towel, and, to prevent my cracked bottle from disintegrating, tussled with it in the cold water.

A dull pain cut across the back of my right hand, as a red and shapeless jet mingled with the water. I raised my wounded hand out of the bowl and gazed at two open lips in the middle of a red pool. A slender, off-white bone shone through the wound.

"Maria!" I screamed, in terror.

In she ran. "*Meu Deus!*" she clapped her hands, "Ayim, what have you done?" Maria picked the towel from the floor and slit its edge with a knife. The cloth shrieked as she ripped a long strip off and rolled it round my bleeding hand, tight. In a hurry she helped me into my shoes. Her purse hung on her left shoulder when she locked the door to our house from outside.

"Let's rush, love, before they close the doctor's office," she muttered as I waddled down the stairs of our porch.

I blinked into the *mormaço*, the silent, white, flaming afternoon outdoors. Other families, I cried, must be still sitting at the table. Where was my Mamãe? At her office? On the phone? I dragged my feet, whingeing about the bare bone and the gore, even if her bandage covered it now. It scared me to death even to think what *they* — I couldn't attach a picture to their anonymous faces — would do to my hand.

"Hurry, love, hurry." She tugged at my other hand, but I felt so sad, and so scared, that my legs just wouldn't obey. She halted and, without a word, lifted me high up. And for whose sake, I still ask myself today, did she take me in her arms like her baby, making me feel less afraid, less fragile?

Maria began to run, and I heard her clogs beating the pavement, each of her steps shattering the silence anew. In a while she was panting, and a crooked old man with a black walking stick stopped dead on the pavement, to let us pass, safely.

"How's . . . your hand?" she asked, her throat rasping like an old pump. My mumbles didn't quite reach her ears, apparently. She went on, puffing, "It'll be . . . all right . . . don't worry . . . doctor . . . in a sec."

In front of the doctor's house Maria set me on my feet. She caught her breath, wiped her wet forehead, smoothed down her fading yellow dress. She knocked on the door. We waited.

"*Doutor* Almeida is on house-calls," a grey-haired white woman in a baby-pink robe leaned her arm on a door jamb. Her voice, nasal, sounded as if she was snorting through an old telephone. "And we're going out afterwards. He can't see any patients when he's back."

"But the boy's bleeding." Maria was panting, still.

"Where's his mother then?"

"She works, downtown."

"Oh, I see." The woman eyed me as though she had just got hold of an essential clue. "What's your name, *menino*?"

"Kha-yim," I stressed the last syllable.

"Jews," the woman sighed. "Oh well. These days a lot of women, not only *gringas*, take a full-time job. Sooner or later, kids get hurt at home. My husband sees it, everyday." The woman made me feel awful, a flawed creature that deserved nothing but guilt and shame for being there.

The woman pointed at the fierce sun. "Take the streetcar, to the First Aid. Anyone will tell you where to get off." She pulled in her robe. "*Nega*, do you have enough money for the streetcar?"

"Yes, *senhora*."

By the curb we waited and waited. Thinking about it now, the street felt as though a lens had converged the sun's rays to scorch the Earth. Time and again Maria bent forward, to stare at the street. "Only a few streetcars run this time of the day," she muttered, indignant. Almost no cars passed by. Their drivers, I told myself, were taking a nap.

It must have been a long streetcar ride, because I woke up in her lap, my forehead moist. We got off and, my knees and ankles feeling like melting butter again, walked along a shaded lane. She stopped by a building with an ambulance parked in front and groomed my hair with her fingers. In a room smelling of iodine and perspiring bodies, a nurse in white coat told Maria to take a seat and wait for our turn.

We sat on a wooden bench, and, to my left, an emaciated black man hunched forward, the toenails of his muddied, twisted-in feet scratching the floor. His tattered clothes and body stank of urine and filth. Once in a while the man slowly opened his eyes, then locked them again. In terror, I snuggled up to Maria.

"It's our turn," Maria woke me again.

Anxious, I followed her and the nurse to a room that reeked of gauze and alcohol. A tall, balding man in a white coat sat on a chair and gestured at a swivelling, white stool. Maria stood behind me, her hands on my shoulder.

"What's your name, *menino*?" the doctor asked.

"Ayim," Maria answered for me. I didn't mind, so petrified I felt.

The doctor began unrolling Maria's towel strip, each layer stained with larger and larger coins of blood. Pain struck only when he pulled out the last piece of cloth, and a brittle clot shimmered on top of the wound. I held my breath, relieved not to see the lean bone.

"We'll have to stitch it up. It won't hurt," the doctor said, and I, of course, didn't believe a word.

The doctor doused a cotton ball with peroxide, and was taking it to the wound when Maria's moist hands shielded my eyes. Did she do it to allay my fears or for her own well-being, I still wonder.

The cool, moist ball swabbed the back of my hand, around the cut, then went at the wound itself. I tried to jerk my hand back, but someone gripped my wrist, tightly. A needle pierced my hand, I cried and begged them to stop; still, they went on working in silence, the needle groping in and out of my skin. What about the bone? I dreaded even to think.

"Gauze, please," the doctor muttered.

When Maria uncovered my eyes a clean white cloth wrapped my right hand. The first thing to enter my mind was whether sickly Samuel had ever sported such a neat little bandage, narrow enough to let my fingers bend.

"Come back in ten days, to remove the stitches."

"Yes, *senhor doutor*."

The *mormaço* had abated as we headed home, and the sun, like a strawberry now, hung just above the dark red tiles of the two-storey houses. On the now crowded streetcar, Maria remained dour, even when I tried a conversation about a two-toned car that passed by. As alert as if I'd just woken up from a good night's sleep, I waved my bandage up and down in the air. It took a while before a red-cheeked woman — it was still hot and humid — bent forward and turned to me, "*Menino*, what happened to your hand?"

"He cut himself; it was an accident," Maria answered for me, curt, and I felt anxious at once. I never knew what to do when she was in a funk.

Our front door stood wide open. "Where have you been?" Mamãe screamed as soon as Maria and I, in tow, stepped in. "I came home from work, blood was on the kitchen counter, water on the floor! What have you done to my son?" She held up my hand and showed it to my father, who had just rushed in, from the living room.

"What happened to his hand?" he bellowed, and I got even more scared.

Maria waited a while before she said, "Ayim cut himself with a piece of glass."

"You left him unsupervised," My mother screamed again, and I began to cry. "We can't have you. He's not five years old yet, and you left him unattended."

"And why the hell didn't you call me at the store or leave a message with a neighbour?" My father lowered his voice, now mean and cold.

"I . . . can't write . . . when I'm in a hurry to the doctor's office." Maria, pretty angry, bit her lower lip.

"After what happened, we can't trust you any more. You're fired." Mamãe said.

Maria didn't apologize for anything.

"You'll get two weeks pay," my father added. "You're allowed to use our phone while you look for a new job."

At dinner Mamãe sat close and, spoon by spoon, fed me like a baby. I cooperated in gulping down a tomato salad, a chicken leg with rice, several slices of bread and butter, and a mashed banana.

"What a horrible day. No wonder he's so hungry," my mother eyed Papai.

Samuel's myopic eyes ogled me with annoyance now that I was hogging all the attention.

All the while I visualized my *baba* wasting away, as the sick man I had seen languishing in the waiting room. Hungry and thirsty she would limp up and down the streets during the *mormaço*. Open wounds and unspeakable pains would come over her, and she would die by the curb one night, all alone. As I swallowed my last spoonful of banana, boiling tears — of injustice, I suppose — gathered under my eyelids. Rage began eating me up inside. I prayed for a huge Negro to come into the dining room and, with a fork, pluck out the eyes of everyone in my family.

"Do you want sugar and lemon juice on your avocado?"

"Yes, Mamãe," I answered, compliant.

Despite the sweet and sour oily cream of avocado filling my mouth, I felt my belly shrinking in pain — like Maria's empty stomach, I imagined. I swore to help her.

The last spoon of dessert over, I slid out of my chair and, officially on my way to the washroom, stuck a forefinger down my throat. In four or five fits I threw up my entire dinner on the carpet, not on the wooden floor, just the way I must have planned almost from the start.

"What now?" My father raised his voice. Samuel got up and stood nearby, to catch a better look at my vomit.

Eyes and forehead strained, Mamãe wiped my mouth with her napkin. Three or four times her hand patted my forehead, as if searching for a fever. Then she bit her lower lip and took me in her arms. A few minutes later she bathed me and tucked me in.

In a cold anger I stretched out in bed and brooded on the ceiling. She looked at me for a few moments, her head bent down. "Forgive me, please forgive me," my mother begged. I did not look at her even once.

"I made a terrible mistake." Now, on the verge of crying, she sounded pitiful. "I saw the bandage on your hand and felt very bad. I know, it's very hard on you. Every day I leave you behind, with her, when I go to work. Please," she held my wounded hand, "I already told Maria she'll stay on as long as she wishes." I closed my eyes and felt tears well up in the corners.

The day Maria took me to *doutor* Almeida to remove the bandage, a pearl-white scar, an inch long and a quarter of an inch wide, shone against my tanned hand.

"We must take good care of our boy," Mamãe told Maria when she came from work in the evening, "the scar may never disappear."

Maria wore a frozen mask, and I felt rotten inside. What a rotten, mean kid! I'd stolen nail-polish, broken bottles, made people angry, had to see doctors back and forth — and all for a few crumbs of attention!

Maria fondled or kissed my scar whenever we sat down to play. "The scar isn't very nice," she would say, wistful, "but your hand is beautiful, still."

"You can pinch the scar, any time you want," I tried my best to cheer her up.

One morning she whispered a secret. While asleep, my scar rotated, clockwise; after one year, when it completed a full circle, the scar would disappear. My hand would be as good as new. For weeks I vetted my hand by the window as soon as I opened my eyes in the morning; but the slothful, lazy, indolent, do-nothing scar never moved at all.

This was the only lie my nanny ever told me. Did she do it out of kindness, to soothe me, or to feel better herself? I want to believe I've long ago forgiven her, as memories of her fib make me smile, just the way *she* used to smile: for her sake and mine, at the same time.

"What's your mother tongue, Khayim?" I've been asked in Toronto, where only two of the countless languages spoken close to the tallest of all towers, boast official status.

"Yiddish, of course," Mamãe would have answered, without a thought.

This assertion carries a grain of truth, as all her endearments and words to her sons were expressed only in *her* mother tongue. From early on, I'd learned to accept my mother's lacklustre eyes and long face after a day's work at the office. She never kicked up a fuss, as many housewives would, when Samuel and I fostered our own brand of bilingualism by firing back in Portuguese. Thus, my heart rebels, I could not have spoken my first words in a hybrid of Hebrew and German.

The first sounds out of my lips, I suspect, were the tuneful phrases to explode from Maria's mouth. Every few minutes she spluttered "*Nossa Senhora!*" — Our Lady! — or "*Meu* Jesus!" And so spontaneous were these words that each, I believed, had a life inside her chest; from time to time her exclamations needed a breath of fresh air and stepped outdoors, for a stroll. To me, *Deus*, Jesus and *Nossa Senhora* were inner parts of her body, not unlike the beads of sweat her arm wiped off her brow.

Once I began to talk, my parents told me with a snigger, I too exclaimed "Jesus!" and "*Credo!*" at all hours of the evening. How amusing to hear a kid with a name like Khayim cry out like a Catholic! They begged me and begged me, I remember, to sound like Maria. They laughed, and wouldn't hear enough of it. And too many times was I carted in my oversized pyjamas into the living room, to entertain friends of my family with my version of her prayers.

Before long, the praise turned to shame, for Maria's words and music became rehearsed, a lifeless act. One night, standing at the centre of our well-lit living room, I shook my head and sealed my eyes and my lips. My parents coaxed me to perform, and two aunts moaned in protest. Still, nobody since has heard me parrot the words that thrived inside my nanny's chest.

But it was Maria's cooking, not her prayers, that brought forth the warmest citations from my mother. On Friday evenings, with few exceptions, Maria served Gefilte Fish on a leaf of lettuce, each portion bathing in clear broth. (In the old iceboxes, the broth cooled, but never jellied.) A carrot ring crowned each slice, and the ground meat overflowed its enclosing skin.

"The student surpassed her teacher," Mamãe commented once, alluding to Maria's learning the intricacies of Polish-Jewish cooking while labouring in my mother's hot kitchen.

But the master never tasted her own Rosh Hashanah honey cakes. Honey — Maria's grimaced in pain, as her hand rubbed her belly — irritated her bowel, badly. Still, on the eve of the holy day, my nose informed me her cake was rising in the oven. (I played no rough games with Carlos that afternoon — for fear of soiling my navy-blue suit in our back yard). More and more, the scents of walnuts, cinnamon, butter and cloves wafted through the entire neighbourhood, like messengers of an irresistible faith. With growing vehemence, the aromas proclaimed a sweet, new year — not only upon the Jews in their dry-cleaned clothes, but upon their Catholic neighbours, too.

Weeks after Rosh Hashanah — I must have been in Hebrew kindergarten — I dropped in for a sip of water. Who, for the first time, did I find sitting at the jacaranda dining table with Samuel, but Maria, her apron off? Forefinger on an open book, Maria haltingly muttered numbers, as if in pain.

"You may sit with us if you want, but you have to be very quiet," Samuel told me. Turning to Maria, he pointed at her book. "Nine times eight," he lowered his voice, "minus seven equal . . . " he waited. She looked up, her eyes tremulous.

"Sixty five!" he gave away the answer, smiling.

Maria's face darkened, and wrinkles rose between her eyebrows. She studied her book, then eyed Samuel. Her face lit up, and she smiled, thankful.

My heart raced in alarm: this was not their first encounter! I blamed myself for playing too many games in our side street. What else, I worried, was going on?

Early afternoons were a good time for Maria's private lessons. From five to six, three times a week, her teacher cudgelled his brain under *seu* Bandeira, *his* tutor in Math and Physics, the way many therapists consume high doses of therapy. Now in his final year of high school, Samuel was so fearful of failing the entrance examinations to medical school, that he surprised me and my parents by locking himself in his room at night, to do homework.

The year before, he'd spent almost every evening at underground political meetings. These were difficult times for my parents, who brooded over untouched cups of tea at the living-room table. Not even radio broadcasts of Nazi Armies being smashed in Europe would shake off their grief over their untoward firstborn.

"What have we done?" Mamãe would sigh, as if waiting for her indictment to be served.

"I have no idea," Papai replied, his sad eyes peering beyond the wall. "Since 1920 I've been a Zionist, and now I feel betrayed. Yes, betrayed. How do we tell even your best friends we have a commie at home?."

"It'll be all right, Arieh. It's just a stage he's going through. When they win the war, he'll get over Communism." Evidently, Mamãe believed in stages, the unyielding mechanisms that governed the lives of her children from the inside.

To allay my gloom, I would anxiously sneak into Samuel's room. I riffled through book after book. They contained no coloured pictures, only drawings of disgusting things, such as frogs being nailed to a desk, their open eyes begging for mercy.

It became impossible for me to relax when Samuel winked at Maria as she served dinner. Were there secrets between them? Such signs of intimacy worried me so much that I cut out all afternoon games in the street. Instead, I chaperoned Maria from the beginning to the end of her lessons. I checked her reader and Math book, too, but found no clues that would lull my impotent jealousy. Why was Samuel all of a sudden fooling around with *my* nanny? And why was he working so hard to help her with numbers?

I breathed some relief when the Math lessons ceased, and Samuel began reading from big-lettered leaflets he brought along. Soon Maria read longer and longer sentences from his leaflets. But droplets shone on Maria's forehead, and an unsteady forefinger escorted each of her words, no matter how well her voice flowed.

They worked hard on her writing, too. At first Maria clutched her pencil until her finger pads shone, chalk-white. Gently, Samuel's fingers would pat hers, and his voice, like a doctor's, would lilt, "*sossega, sossega*" — calm down.

My heart warmed to my brother, so loving a teacher. As though floodgates had opened inside, some tender feelings Samuel rarely showed were flowing now. I loved him, at that time, for helping Maria.

"What you guys see is just the beginning," Samuel boasted at dinner. Tears of excitement glinted behind the glasses he was wearing, since he'd metamorphosed into a candidate for medical school. To the last bite of my dessert, he bored me by ranting about maids and workers reading underground leaflets and, before long, rising against their class enemies, the fat cats.

"It's just around the corner," he shook his forefinger, threatening the fat cats around the table. "Our revolution is just

months away. Nothing under the sun will remain the same."
His vehemence and my parents' fearful, frozen faces gave me
goosebumps.

A few mornings later, Maria commented, "Looks like the
Allies will win the war before long. I'm praying for it to be
over even before the *Carnaval*."

Recently, she had begun reading the newspaper, her finger
no longer shaking across the narrow columns. How proud she
stood at the grocery store, her forefinger off the paper while
reading her shopping list! "One kilo of sugar, one bar of
laundry soap, two kilos of black beans." Her voice would rise,
as clear as my mother's silver dinner bell. On rainy afternoons
she no longer made up tales of wolves chasing bad boys;
instead, she read me stories from my mother's books.

"Do you want me to teach you a Hebrew song?" I offered
at the end of such a story. I was aching to teach her *something*.

"No, thank you, not today," she said. "Some other time,"
she added, thoughtful, "after I take the tests."

"Tests? What tests?" I asked in alarm. My brother spoke of
tests as instruments of torture, lying in wait.

"The teachers ask you to read and write and play with
numbers. If you do right, they hand you a paper saying you're
an educated person." She raised her chin, in anticipation of
something precious.

Weeks later she announced we were going out, in the
afternoon.

"And where are we going?" I asked. It was one of those
hot days she did not allow me in the backyard, until the
mormaço had passed away.

"You don't know this place. We haven't been there before.
It's only a few streetcar stops away."

Why is she so secretive? I asked myself.

"When you wake up from your nap," she went on, "take a shower, please, and put on your navy-blue suit."

"Not the suit, Maria! Please, it's too hot!"

"I know, love, it *is* hot. But still, I'd like you to wear it. For *me*." Puzzled, I watched her lowered eyes, this being the first time she ever asked me to do something for her sake.

When I opened my eyes, she stood by my bed, smiling, her white taffeta dress tightened at the waist by a slender black belt. Her white, freshly dyed shoes glistened against her brown skin.

After my cold shower she helped me into a suffocating outfit: a starched, white, long-sleeved shirt and long, blue pants. I dreaded even to think how hot it would feel in the street. She knelt down to knot my red tie and tighten my blue suspenders.

"I'll carry your jacket. It's still hot outside," she said. I breathed in relief.

Under a still high sun, we made our way to the streetcar stop. Wave upon wave of torrid air spewed into the flaming streets, as if an oven door had been flung open. Maria's large, white straw hat kept her face in the shade, elegant.

Within minutes we alighted and walked in the shade of tenement houses lining both sides of the street. Unlidded garbage bins gave off a nauseating stench of rotting tissues and putrid vegetables. Everywhere I looked coloured shirts and sheets hung out to dry. On narrow sidewalks and cobblestones a host of skimpily dressed, barefoot children played soccer with a ball of rags.

She halted by a house not much bigger than ours. Steps of cement led to tall, double doors of brown-stained wood.

"What's this, Maria?"

"My church," she said, and bent down to adjust my tie and suspenders.

"A church? Is this a church?" I asked, incredulous. My father would raise hell — no, kill Maria — if he ever found out I'd set even my toes inside a church. Right there and then I decided not to tell.

"You can't talk loud inside the church."

She helped me into my jacket, then took my hand in hers. We walked up the stairs, and past the wooden doors. My face felt cool and dry. Inside, the church looked very dark, except for a small altar that glowed in the light of a few candles and a bare bulb, overhead.

She let go of my hand and, chin to her breastbone, genuflected to the altar. Standing upright, and more dignified than I'd ever seen her, she crossed herself. My hand in hers again, we walked slowly down the aisle. By the third pew Maria stopped and nudged me in first. After she bent legs to the kneeler, her fingers quickly covered her ankles with the hem of her dress.

Kneeling so close that my pants brushed her dress, I stared at her in astonishment and fear.

"Let me pray. Then I'll tell you why we're here." She closed her eyes and joined her palms. Under her wide-brimmed hat she murmured, solemn.

All around, the other pews were empty. The sides of the church remained very dark, even after my eyes had adapted to the humble light. Ahead, a blue, worn-out velvet runner covered the altar, some of its golden fringes missing — like my front teeth, I thought.

Behind the altar rose the small statue of a black and barefoot, skin-and-bones man fastened to a wooden cross. His chin was planted on his shoulder, and his locked eyes and twisted mouth signalled overwhelming pain. I gasped. In the dim light, the statue of Jesus dressed in a loincloth reminded me of the sick man who sat next to me in the waiting room of the First Aid station.

"I promised you'd be the first to hear," her whisper ripped my reveries. "I passed the tests. I got a job with the railway," she spoke quickly. "In about two weeks, I'll be a cashier."

Her eyes turned pensive. I panicked. "But you'll be living with us, won't you, Maria?" I whispered back.

"No, I'll be renting a room, not far from work. But don't worry, I'll come and visit you. You know I like you very much, don't you?" She bent her head and kissed my lips, softly.

"Please Maria, please, don't go." I fought back my sobs. Samuel's face flashed across the scene. I hated him, he'd taught her numbers. I pictured myself tossing a pot of boiling water at his face.

"I'll help your mother look for a maid. I've talked to Laurinda, a friend of mine. She'll start the day I leave." She fondled my cheek. "Your birthday is coming up soon — "

"I don't care!" my shout reverberated in the church.

"Ayim," she squeezed her eyelids in disapproval, "we better pray now. Pray. He'll listen. He always listens to children." She turned to the altar.

"But what do I tell him?" More than desperate, I was whispering again.

She eyed me. "Tell Him how you feel, tell Him what you want. Don't worry, your prayer will be heard." She blew air into my ear. "I've brought you up to be white and black inside, rich and poor, Jew and Catholic, at the same time."

"But I don't know what to say," my eyes watered.

"Go ahead, love, pray. Ayim," she paused, her face stern. "It'll hurt when I leave, but it's time for me to go." Her eyes locked on the altar.

I joined my palms in front of my chin and closed my eyes. "*Deus*," I whispered and halted in fright. Was I praying to the right person? She'd forgotten to say! I opened my eyes, but she was still in her prayers. It wouldn't be right to disturb her.

"*Senhor* Jesus." Anxiety rushed over me. What a huge risk! What if I'd addressed the wrong *senhor*? But I forced myself to continue. "If Maria leaves me, it'll be very, very hard. You see, she took care of me all my life and I . . . I . . . like her very much." I sobbed a few times, softly. "It'll be awful . . . if she leaves me."

I wiped my cheeks. "All I want, *Deus* and *senhor* Jesus, is for Maria to stay with me." I slowed down, scared I'd done the wrong thing by mentioning *Deus* before Jesus. "No, I really don't mind if she works for the railway," I whispered a wee bit louder, to sound mature. "My mother works, too. I know how it feels."

The knots in my stomach were tearing me apart. I inhaled deeply. "But If Maria lives with us, instead of renting a room, I'll be good. I'll stop biting my nails. I'll never, never fool around with my brother's things."

Feverishly, my confused mind searched for an offering that would appease her *senhores*, so distant, so silent. "If you want me to, I'll come here and pray. I know how to get here, I do. I hope you won't mind if I show up in short sleeves and canvas shoes."

Maria was still absorbed in her prayers. I closed my eyes like her, and vowed to be honest with Jesus and *Deus* and the whole world. "If Maria stays with me, I promise not to bring marbles to Shul on Saturdays. I will not lie to my father that I need to pee, and then play in the backyard with the bad boys."

"Did you say your prayer?" She was smiling, and I nodded. Maria stood up and crossed herself. Hand in hand we walked up the aisle. Past the doors of the church, the city still blazed, white. My hands shielded my eyes from the stunning light.

Still, I took in the black outline of Maria's hat and her long neck, as graceful as a swan's. Her pointed nose and the fleshy lips that kissed me so many times drew a sweet, most lovely silhouette on the blinding sky. This is my last memory of her.

The next few weeks were the most eventful time of my life. Maria left and Laurinda took her job. Soon after, I started grade one, and, to celebrate my sixth birthday, my parents threw a big party. Maria, I'm told, came by to visit me three times, once before the party, twice after. My brother got drunk — like a dirty Goy, my father hissed — and danced in the streets with a broom, the day he began medical school. Soon after, he was thrown in jail for a week. Two plainclothes policemen beat him up for his subversive political activities while calling him a dirty Jew.

I've heard many tales about those heady days, and the family album preserves the fading pictures of all characters, doing their best to smile at the camera. But all these stories leave me indifferent, as if they happened on some other, cold planet. A clumsy hand, I feel, erased that time from the black-board of my memory, and just a few specks of chalk glitter on the plank floor. Angry, and perhaps more unforgiving that I'm ready to admit, I still bang my head against walls that others cannot see.

Yet, in childlike whispers I still pray, "One day I'll be whole again, with her."

On Sunday afternoons, in Toronto, I take long naps. I wake up in a daze, with fragments of dreams hovering over the surface of my mind. Quite often I remember dreams about Maria and my childhood. My heart is filled with *saudade* — that untranslatable Portuguese word that loosely means a painful longing, a deep pining for a person, a home, or one's past. I pine for Maria and remember my halcyon days with her.

Months ago, I decided to translate my longings into action. I paid a visit to the priciest private investigator in Toronto, Mr. Neil O'Hara. Mr. O'Hara was tall and paunchy. His hair was cropped short, and he wore a navy blue suit and a white shirt. He talked in a business-like fashion as he laid out the terms of his work for me. Any similarity of that private eye to the characters I have seen in movies and television programs was utterly superficial.

Excited, I told him about Maria. He asked details, and I poured out all I knew about her life and background. It turned out, to my surprise, that I didn't know her surname, her place of birth, and birthday. I had no idea where she worked after she left my parents' home.

Mr. O'Hara leaned back in his chair. "You're giving me too little information about Maria, doctor. It'll be a lot of work to find her."

He surprised me. I had wallowed so much in my memories of Maria that it had never dawned on me that what I remembered was insufficient for a private eye hired to find her. I leaned forward. "Make an effort, Mr. O'Hara. It's very important for me to meet her."

"Is she a relative?"

"No," I replied. "She was what Brazilians call my *mãe preta*, my black mother. She raised me. She is the most important figure in my life after my wife and children."

"I'll see what I can do. There isn't much to go by. To get started, I need a retainer of ten thousand dollars."

Over the next few months Mr. O'Hara called me every month to report on the progress of the case. In fact, he let me in on leads that went nowhere, on dead ends in the investigation, on information that led to no further clues. After eight months on the job he invited me to his office and let me know that he was closing the file, as he saw no chance of ever finding Maria. "She may be dead or she may have moved away from Rio. Brazil is a huge country. We have no clues about where she ended up." He signed a check on the little money that remained from the retainer.

I felt devastated. My fantasies of holding her in my arms and kissing her kinky white hair went up in smoke. I would never again feel on my cheeks the hands that had caressed me so many times. Her lips, I fantasized, were still as lush as I remembered. To introduce a grain of reality into my daydreams, I imagined an overweight woman with wrinkles in the corner of her eyes and mouth. I had planned to visit her in Rio and shower her with gifts. I had even calculated that if I worked an extra hour a week, I could support her financially. Life in the Third World is so cheap when you deal with Canadian dollars!

None of that would ever happen. My Maria would forever be the stuff of dreams, memories, and fantasies, as intangible as characters from children's tales. It occurred to me to allay my grief by perpetuating her in a novella, a paean to her kindness and caring. Yet, all the words I wrote paled in comparison with the *saudade* that filled my heart.

THE MAN IN THE COFFIN

The headache flung him back into the moist pillow. In a moment he opened his eyes and through a haze saw Mamãe sitting on his bed.

"Time to get up for school, Jaime." Her hand patted his forehead, then hurried down his face and chest. "But Jaime," she cried out, "you're all wet. A fever! You're running a fever!"

A week of bedrest, however, and three illustrated books by Monteiro Lobato, a pile of comics, a trunk of rock candy and one aspirin, three times a day, as *doutor* Francisco Machado prescribed on a house call, put Jaime back on his feet. But another fever struck shortly after he returned to school. For a week Jaime twisted in bed, whimpering about headaches and the suffocating sheets.

"I know," his mother consoled him. "It's *awful* to lie in bed at the beginning of summer."

"Worse than the illness, Mamãe."

"It'll be all right, son. The newspapers said the Allies will enter Berlin, by April. Just imagine, Jaime," her voice rose cheerily, "this horrible war over just when you begin grade two."

"And the summer, Mamãe. Will we be away from Rio?" He feared they might.

She sucked in her lower lip. "I'm not sure we can afford it this year. Your Papai said these days his store is as empty as a soccer field on a rainy day."

Weeks after the mercury in the thermometer no longer glistened past the 37 mark, Jaime still looked pale, like a Sabbath candle. Mamãe shook her head. Several times a day his booming coughs made Mamãe sprint to the kitchen, from which she returned with a glass of mineral water vibrating in her hand, as if a sacrament.

Whenever Jaime coughed, Mamãe drew a deep breath and held it — forever, it seemed. Her almond-shaped face blanched, and her unblinking eyes belied such terrors that as soon as a fit had peaked, he croaked, "I'll be fine, Mamãe, just fine." Jaime relaxed a tad only after her chest had heaved down. Crazy. He was driving his Mamãe crazy!

Mamãe battled his illness with cough syrup, a recipe she had unearthed in her home health manual. For hours the potion simmered on top of the stove, its sweet-and-sour stench of licorice haunting all corners of the flat. So thick was the final preparation that Mamãe held the bottle upside down, until the black, pin-thin column of goo eventually filled up a soup spoon.

"Swallow it, Jaime," his mother begged. "It's good for you."

"Yes Mamãe," he sighed respectfully.

Jaime locked his eyelids and, in desperation, pinched his nose, too. Still, baby snakes slithered up and down his spine long after he'd swallowed it.

"Jaime," she said one afternoon, "we're going to the homeopath."

"Going where, Mamãe?" he asked, wondering what she had up her sleeve. His soccer buddies were knocking at his door less and less. In the vestibule Mamãe told them she felt sorry, but Jaime wasn't well enough to play outdoors.

"It's a small pharmacy," she waved, implying there was nothing to worry about. "We'll take the streetcar."

"Didn't Papai say it's time I see the doctor?"

"Sure, Jaime, but you're still coughing a lot. Let's give *seu* Pereira, the homeopath, a chance, too. I'm told he makes very good cough medicines."

Dark, cool and dry inside, the pharmacy was a wood-panelled, room-size store. Two yellow globes overhead gave off a soothing light, and the queer odours of herbs and syrups reminded Jaime of an air-conditioned movie theatre.

Mamãe chatted with a white-haired, wizened man — *seu* Pereira, he overheard — whose liquid eyes smiled at Jaime from above a pair of silver-rimmed glasses. Meanwhile, Jaime ogled a metre-tall flask inside a glass case. Filled with sea-blue water, the shapely bottle glowed like something magical, out of a comic strip.

"What did you get?" Jaime asked, as they stepped into the blinding, blighting heat of the street.

"Bath salts. We'll start tonight."

"*We*? We Mamãe?"

"I'll keep you company, Jaime. *Seu* Pereira said to soak every evening, for half an hour. At least."

At bedtime, the bathroom smelled like vinegar. He wore his blue swim trunks while soaking in the warm water of the tub. At this stage of his life, nothing would have felt more embarrassing than Mamãe having even a peek at his water-shrivelled *pipi*. While Mamãe perched on the low, white, round stool from the kitchen and read from *Stories From The Orient*, a library book, his hands skimmed the surface of the water, and his head, like a slow, inverted pendulum, swayed left and right.

"Jaime," Mamãe banged the book on her knees. "Stop it! The floor is sopping wet." The long ceremony, the odours, and her whining voice made him so angry he barely resisted the urge to jump to his feet and yell, "Shut up! Drop dead!"

He'd, of course, yelled meaner, more obscene words in the street. But as he sat in the bathtub, speechless, his fury abated, and he felt guilty, unbearably guilty, for wishing Mamãe dead. "What if I'd yelled that I hate her?" he asked himself in anguish. He pictured Mamãe's pained eyelids narrowing to a thin line. Her heart, he imagined, would break with a pop, like a wine bottle being uncorked. So he turned his head to the wall, and scanned the grout greying between the white tiles.

"How's the *mikveh* going?" His father's parted lips and raised eyebrows appeared at the door, mocking.

Mamãe stared past an imaginary mirror.

Papai shook his head as if in despair, and in a moment his face disappeared. Jaime heard his father scuffing his slippers in the corridor leading to the living room.

"*Mikveh*? Jaime giggled. Just the sound of some Yiddish words made his tummy wiggle. "What's a *mikveh*, Mamãe?"

"A Jewish ritual bath," she blinked, solemn. "Your late grandmother Leah went to the *mikveh* every Friday. Not just to wash her hair and skin, mind you, but to feel better inside, in her soul." She slammed the storybook shut, and stood up. Her pursed lips signalled she would not delve into the meanings of the *mikveh* and the soul that evening.

Later, in his bed, the odours of soap and vinegary vapours came back to life, and Jaime felt sick. The memory of his mother's fragrances also made him shudder. Hopelessly alert, he listened to the cars rolling by in the street. He remembered his father saying, "The traffic in Rio never stops, day and night."

Will I ever fall asleep? he asked himself, breathing deeply.

He writhed in bed with the unshaken certainty he would cough to death one day. Pale and devastated, his parents would raise the edge of the sheet covering his corpse, and stare at his blue face, now as cold and stiff as a tile.

"A *morte!* A *morte!*" he muttered.

Jaime closed his eyes and took a deep breath. He then relaxed his legs, arms, and belly. He drained his body of all sensations by making sure his chest, cheeks and lips did not stir. A dozen times or more he had rehearsed how it would feel to be dead.

It didn't work. Again and again a black dome hovered under his eyelids. He always felt *something*.

A streetcar rattled by, and he opened his eyes. The wall next to his arm glowed two shades lighter than moments before. He made out the gauze-like curtains blowing to and fro at the window, then the little rug by his bed. Time came to a halt; his body would never cool off.

"For the rest of my life," he murmured, in despair, "I'll toss and toss on disgusting, moist sheets."

"I'm going to the bathroom." Jaime regretted saying it, even before the words left his lips. A baby. Still broadcasting every bit of news to his mother. He set his Monteiro Lobato book on the floor, pulled down his pants, then adjusted his bum to the white, cool seat. In the early-morning light, the corners of the bathroom lurked mysterious and soothing. Window open, the air felt less humid, too. Mamãe had taken a bath: traces of Palmolive and her *eau de cologne* filled the air. He revisited ten pages, but his bowels were not in the mood.

Bored, he stood by the window and watched a sparrow perched on the telephone cable between his and the next apartment building. The bird inclined its neck, and began to preen its chest in a frenzy. Moments later, a diminutive beak emerged from under brown feathers, as the bird paused to catch its breath. After glancing around, the sparrow sprang into the thin air, and, beating its wings, flew away, free. The abandoned telephone cable rocked back and forth.

"*Destino. Destino.*"

He learned that word while Mamãe had read him the story of Akhmad, a young merchant from Baghdad, who'd made his fortune in spices and tea. Akhmad's parents had arranged for him to marry Fatima, a *beautiful* girl, Mamãe stressed. But lo and behold, right in the middle of the wedding party, Akhmad's pants had slid down to his ankles.

"What?" Jaime sat up on his knees and toes. Mamãe? Reading stories like that?

Akhmad felt *so* ashamed, Mamãe continued, unperturbed, that he fled to Calcutta. There, Akhmad started wheeling and dealing in spices and tea, and in twenty-five years became the richest Muslim in India.

Though very wealthy, Mamãe raised her eyes from the book, Akhmad felt many *saudades*; he pined for his parents and five brothers. So one day he took a boat and later a carriage back to Baghdad.

As Akhmad approached his hometown, he stopped the carriage at the top of a mountain because a magnificent stone bridge that did not exist when he was a young man had caught his attention.

"Driver," Akhmad asked, "when did they build that bridge?"

"Oh," the driver chuckled. "They finished it some ten years after Akhmad's wedding, when he got caught with his pants down."

Mamãe closed the book, and gazed at Jaime, silent.

He gasped. "But *why?* Why Mamãe? *Why* did Akhmad lose his pants? And why did he go back to Baghdad?"

"*Destino*, son, *destino*." Mamãe smiled, her sad eyes very dim. "Awful things happen, things that people don't want to happen at all. Like your cough." Lips fluttering, her eyes glinted behind a film of tears. "Or my bad nerves."

She paused. "Jaime," Mamãe kissed his temple, lightly. "Your Mamãe," she breathed on his ear, "lost two babies before you came along." The book on the floor, she lifted him from under his armpits. "It's really not your fault," she whispered, "that I worry, that I love you too much."

A blood stain the size of a coin glimmered on Jaime's pillow case. He meant to scrub it off under running water, as he had cleansed smaller stains, but, unexpectedly, Mamãe stepped into his room, and yanked the pillow out of his hand.

"Jaime, did you . . . " her right hand darted for his forehead, "did you cough this morning?"

"Raquel," Papai strode into the room. "Please, go lie down," his hand cradled her elbow. "The whole night you sat up in bed. Relax. The boy will be all right."

"Please," she turned to his father, "I feel even worse when you *tell* me to relax. Jaime," she lowered her voice, a mere whisper, "get dressed. We're going to the doctor."

"The boy'll be fine," his father stepped back. "Just stop fussing and calling 'Jaime', 'Jaime', 'Jaime', every time you open your mouth. It's *very* irritating!"

"And what about school, Mamãe?" Jaime bleated.

At last Mamãe blinked. "First, we'll find out why you're coughing blood."

The waiting room of *doutor* Francisco Machado smelled of iodine, peroxide, and gauze. It lacked curtains, as Mamãe had remarked on a previous visit, and the December morning light bounced off the dazzling, gloss-painted white walls. On the wall to Jaime's left, a striped, pink-and-white poster depicted the muscles of a hairless human being with glaring, black eyes. Below the tummy, a bundle of muscles converged into a flat triangle outlining a phony crotch.

Across from Jaime sat a three or four-year-old boy who wouldn't take his eyes off the floor; the boy's lower lip twitched. Leaning over him, a black woman — the boy's nanny, Jaime thought — whispered in the boy's ear. "Any moment," Jaime told himself, "this little kid will bawl and whine." Jaime resolved to tough it out, and, after jerking his head up, straightened his spine.

Mamãe became involved in a magazine she'd brought along. Jaime read and re-read the captions of his Captain Marvel comic, but almost nothing at all registered with him. A dizzying anxiety simmered in the pit of his stomach.

"*Sanatorio*, Mrs. Cuschnir," Jaime imagined the doctor's soothing voice. "Jaime is very ill. He must get into a *sanatorio*, in the mountains. It's dangerous to live under the same roof with him."

"How long, *seu doutor?*"

"Two, three years."

"*Sanatorio*," Jaime repeated, almost aloud.

Days before, on a particularly warm night, when all the doors and windows at home had been kept open, he'd overheard his mother's voice, almost as clear as a radio announcer's. "In a Swiss *sanatorio*, in the high mountains, he'll get over the cough in a matter of months."

"But the store, Raquel, the store!" His father had whispered, louder than Mamãe. "It's almost empty! I've plenty of time to read all the ads and editorials!" After the clatter of a truck, he resumed. "And what about the war, woman? Even if we could afford a spa, how do we get him to Switzerland now?"

After a while she answered. "You have to find a way, Bernardo."

"Find a way?" Papai shot back. "I hope you don't mean *right now!*"

In the waiting room, the doctor stood by the open door to his consulting room and nodded, once. As Jaime shuffled by, he glanced up at the doctor's hairdo, which Mamãe disliked immensely. "The man's over forty," she had complained, "and his brillantined brown hair shines. How unnatural! How vain!" She had raised her palms in despair. "Even on late house calls, every one of his hairs lies in its correct place!"

At the doctor's request, Jaime stuck out his tongue as hard as he could. The doctor shone down his patient's throat the same kind of Eveready chrome-coated flashlight Jaime kept in his closet. He didn't ask Jaime to take off his shirt, nor to simulate a cough.

"The blood came from his mouth," the *doutor* pronounced, still standing up. "When he's nervous, Jaime seems to bite his cheeks. A bad habit. I wouldn't worry much about the stain."

"But what if it's a rare disease, *doutor*? Something hard to diagnose, unknown to science . . . " Mamãe challenged. At home, Jaime had heard Mamãe rehearsing her rebuttals to Papai or the doctor as she washed dishes or darned socks.

"*Minha senhora,*" the doctor's voice rose. "I've already told you. Jaime doesn't have tuberculosis, asthma, or even bronchitis, if that's what you're afraid of." He marched to his chair, and sat behind his desk. "You seem to be at the end of your rope, Mrs. Cuschnir." He leaned back, and joined his palms in front of his Adam's apple. "Take my word. A month long rest, away from Rio, will do *you* and Jaime a lot of good."

"You make it sound so easy, *seu doutor.*" Mamãe rose to her feet, the toss of her chin ordering Jaime to stand up. "Have a nice summer, *doutor.* We'll be looking for a poor man's solution."

A few days later Jaime was very glad to spend the afternoon playing cops and robbers with his pal Carlos Alberto — "Gazoberto." Mamãe asked Gazoberto's mother to keep an eye on Jaime: she had made an appointment with Rabbi Feldman in his Shul, downtown.

"And what did *your* Rabbi tell you?" Papai asked, but only after dinner, as he stirred his demitasse of coffee with a spoon.

"Rabbi Feldman is a *very* nice man, Bernardo," Mamãe sipped her coffee. "And he's right. We'll all feel much better in our hearts and souls if I bless the candles on Fridays, and keep a kosher home." She banged her demitasse on the saucer. "For God's sake, Bernardo, don't smirk! Your son's health is in jeopardy!"

"And . . . " Papai faked a deep sigh, "I assume your rabbi asked for a donation to some *Yeshiveh* in the Holy Land. Money and religion always stroll hand in hand." Time and again, his forefinger and thumb rubbed one another. "How much money did you give him, Raquel?"

Before Mamãe replied, Jaime began to laugh, hysterically, until he coughed twice, lightly.

"Use your head," Papai continued, but only after Jaime's fingers wiped the tears from his eyes. "Didn't the *doutor* tell you and the boy to spend the summer away from Rio? What's the point," he shook his head, "of running bills if you don't follow his recommendations?"

"Come on, Bernardo, we can't possibly afford a month's vacation for two! A war's going on!" Mamãe stood up, and, in anger, stacked Jaime's plate on hers. "People are living on bread and beans. Nobody's buying new shoes!"

"We'll borrow some," Papai answered, softer. "For a three weeks rest. And in March, when kids go back to school, I'll introduce new lines of canvas shoes and clogs. Raquel, *please*. For once, just give your pessimism and worries a break."

Papai pushed back his chair, and ambled to their bedroom. He came back soon and sat on his chair, where he worked with a pencil and a pad he had brought with him. Humming, he jotted down a column of unavoidable expenses: train fare, cabs, pocket money, room and board in a hotel. Jaime pushed back his chair, and stood by his side.

Papai bit the end of the pencil, while his fingers stroked Jaime's cheeks. He erased and corrected a couple of figures, then read the total.

"Raquel," he blared, "we can afford three weeks for Jaime and you in some quiet place. Not Poços de Caldas or São Lourenço!" He dismissed the idea with a wave. "These two are out of the question! Just posh places for the rich!"

"What about *two* weeks in Lambari?" Mamãe sat down, her eyes glittering. "A quiet town, good mineral waters. Some Jewish people we know spend the summer there, every year."

"Take it easy!" Papai tossed his head left and right, cheery. "I'll not go bankrupt if you and Jaime spend *three* weeks in a modest hotel."

Mamãe turned around the pad, and her eyes flitted up and down the column of figures. "Jaime needs a couple of pants, a few shirts, new shoes. I'll be fine with one new outfit. Simple."

Wide-eyed and pensive, Mamãe slowly moved her lips, as if conversing with herself. "There's absolutely nothing to lose," she let out at last, "by keeping a kosher home. Bernardo," her voice rose, "tomorrow morning I'll scrub the ice-box with hot water. Then I'll set up separate milk and meat sections."

Papai stared out the front window, but no cab had arrived yet. He strode to the flat's entrance, swung the door open, and, despite some clumsy bumping into the jambs, hauled two pot-bellied suitcases out.

"We haven't left home yet, and your Papai is missing us already," Mamãe remarked from her green chair. Above her plucked eyebrows, a white straw hat with an oversized rim was tilted to her right, smartly. The fluttering corners of her brown eyes studied a hand-held mirror, checking her thin nose for powder.

From his brown sofa Jaime watched his mother's face, unfrazzled for once. Half-smiling, he pictured his mother as a wealthy lady who had travelled in all five continents.

"Ar-khen-tee-na," he chuckled.

His parents had spent their honeymoon in Buenos Aires, and by her bedside table Mamãe boasted a silver-framed picture of the two of them laughing in front of a fountain, forefingers pointing at the camera. Business had been bad since then, and on some Sundays his parents ventured only as far as the city buses would take their picnic basket, crowded with sandwiches, a black Thermos with coffee and a bottle of guarana for Jaime.

"The flat is getting hot," Papai's head popped in the door. "Let's wait in the street."

"He's afraid the cab driver fell asleep at the station," Mamãe murmured.

It was a bright and muggy February morning outdoors. Standing on the sidewalk between his parents, Jaime hated more and more the idea of spending three weeks away from his friends in Rio. His right hand brushed the dark brown hair off his wet brow, and he felt humiliated that his arms and legs glowed as pale as newsprint in mid summer. All around, the starched, new white shirt Mamãe had made him wear for the trip was getting doughy and sticky, driving him crazy. He would gladly swap all his possessions for the pleasures of running his nails up and down his sides. But nothing, he shook his head, nothing made his mother's voice rise in indignation like the sight of people scratching — even their foreheads — in public. Twice Jaime's angry heel kicked the curb, horse-style. He compromised: only two decorous elbows chafed his sides.

Nervously, Papai shuffled his feet by the suitcases, his white Panama hat pushed to the middle of his crown. By eight-thirty the sun was already dazzling; Papai's right hand sheltered his squinting eyes. He wore the light brown suit and matching green-and-brown tie Mamãe had suggested — no, had told him — to put on.

Jaime clenched his jaws, because he didn't wish the world to see how much he despised this docile man, his father, who only an hour ago had mumbled, "Yes Raquel," when Mamãe had ordered him what to wear. Eyes watering, Jaime blamed his own insane shirt more on his father than on Mamãe. Spineless. Why's Papai so spineless?

"Here it is," his father's elated voice sliced through Jaime's anger.

A black cab stopped by the curb. The driver moaned "*Oba!*" each time he lifted a suitcase into the trunk.

In the front seat Papai stretched out his legs and smiled, evidently pleased with his command post. His forefinger pointed ahead. "To the railway station."

A long row of black cabs parked at the entrance to the station. Papai supervised as a porter transferred the two suitcases to a dolly. In a brightly lit hall, which Jaime deemed larger than a soccer field, passengers huddled in long lines by small ticket-offices. There were no children in sight; only adults hurried to and from the dark tracks lurking in the back.

"It's getting late." Papai pulled out two black-on-green tickets and held them high, on show. "I'm running ahead, with the porter."

Passengers and porters with their dollies raced down the dark track. The air reeked of burning coal, soot, and steam. The bare yellow bulbs they met every few steps made all faces glow, like golden masks. To Jaime's right, a train whistled in agony, and some twenty meters ahead Papai waved, urging them to hurry. Mamãe's heels clicked and clicked on the track.

Jaime began coughing into his fist. He stopped on the track, and from his back pocket drew a white handkerchief. The folded, square layers of cloth capped his mouth and chin, but barely muffled the sound of the cavernous fits. At the end of one particularly long cough he wheezed and crimsoned like an old smoker, one hand pounding his chest.

"We'll be late, son, let's go," begged Papai. He had run back and nudged Jaime's shoulder.

They stopped at the third wagon of their train; ahead, a locomotive was blowing off an almost vertical white plume. Once inside the wagon, Jaime turned and watched Mamãe raise the hem of her white cotton dress three inches or so, and walk up the steps.

Inside the dark second class wagon, the porter — with the help of Papai — managed somehow to cram their suitcases into the luggage rack overhead. After his father tipped the porter, Jaime sat by the window.

"Please write every day." Papai stood in the aisle and hung his head down. "Otherwise I may worry." He chuckled.

Jaime wondered whether Papai poked fun at himself or at Mamãe.

"I left some meatballs and rice in the icebox." Mamãe removed her hat, and not once, but twice, shook her hair into place. "But you can eat out, too."

"Restaurants?" His father shrugged. "Who am I, Rothschild? The way business is going?"

Papai's loud voice made Jaime feel embarrassed again: the other passengers in the wagon were watching the commotion.

A whistle shrieked. Papai bent over, hurriedly hugged Mamãe and gave her a kiss on the lips. He hugged Jaime. "Do what your mother tells you, son. Write," he whispered, "and let me know how you and Mamãe are coming along."

He rushed to the exit. Jaime, now on his feet, watched until his father appeared on the track, where a steward in navy-blue uniform and brass buttons slammed the door of the wagon shut. Hesitant, the train began rolling off, and Mamãe stood up, too. They waved back till the train veered to the right, and the brown figure with a white hat vanished.

On the way to Lambari, as the slow train whistled wistfully inside a half-hour long tunnel, Jaime fell prey to a bad coughing spell. Though an attendant had filed through the car and slid down the window sashes, soot sneaked into the dark space lit only by wan bulbs; a few clandestine sparkles twirled above the passengers' heads, hit the black ceiling, and died instantaneously.

For hours the train stopped by a grey, peeling railway station that made Jaime think of an abandoned doghouse.

"The war is fouling up everything," Mamãe grumbled. "The world is going to pot."

As they waited, group after group of skinny, barefoot children in tatters huddled below the open train windows. Their enormous black eyes stared up at the passengers. Now and then one of the children raised a square basket of raspberries for sale.

"Were they poor before the war, Mamãe?" Jaime whispered.

"Yes, Jaime. They've always been poor." From her purse she fished out a scented handkerchief and patted his moist forehead. "*Destino*, son, *destino*," she sighed. "There's very little they can do to change their lot. It's very sad, Jaime, but these people will live in poverty. All their lives."

Most windows at their hotel, a mid-size house, were dark when they arrived late at night. The cab driver toiled to steer their suitcases through a sea of chairs surrounding a long dining table already set for breakfast. Up a flight of stairs, their landlady showed Mamãe and Jaime their dark, almost bare room: an armoire, two twin beds separated by a table with a dim reading lamp and, facing a large window, one chair by a small desk.

At once Jaime felt relieved: Mamãe would spend nights three feet away! Had they shared a bed, their bodies would inevitably touch. He would hear her breathing, in and out. How, Jaime had asked himself in the train — and even at home — could he possibly escape the smell of her night cream, the same acrid odour of new leather soles? And what if she kept a vigil? He would not feel free to toss in bed to reduce his anxiety, because *he* would ask himself endless times, "Is Mamãe worrying?"

As soon as the landlady left their room Jaime stretched out on his bed. "It feels just like a hammock," he commented, smiling. "No chance at all of falling out of bed in the middle of the night."

Next morning, when Jaime looked out the open window, he noticed small patches of blue sky enclosed by thickening banks of clouds. The air felt cooler, purer and crisper than in Rio.

For his first stroll in the park, Jaime was made to wear another starched, itchy, cotton shirt. Blue suspenders pulled his navy-blue pants up, almost a whole inch above his navel.

Mamãe emerged from her long session in the washroom down the hall in yesterday's new hat, a creme-coloured dress and white gloves to her wrists.

Walking by Mamãe in the shade of majestic ficus trees, Jaime glanced, very annoyed, at the raspberry-red tiled roofs of the two-storey brick houses lining both sides of the street. All his life he'd lived in a tall apartment building surrounded by tall apartment buildings; until this very moment, he never gave even a passing thought to the variety of roofs in the world. What? Come all the way from Rio to see some porous, old roofs?

At eye level, neither streetcars nor children on bicycles rolled by. "What," he puzzled, "does a small town like Lambari offer a kid from a big town like Rio?"

In a while Jaime caught sight of the park's black ironwork fencing in trees, sprawling lawns, shrubs, roses and carnations of many colours. Close to the open gates, Mamãe stopped by a kiosk and bought tall drinking glasses with handles, "Lambari" printed green on yellow on them.

Inside the park, they sauntered along a paved cement trail. No children in sight. In a moment, an elderly couple with empty drinking glasses held by stiff fingers doddered toward Jaime and his mother. Like Mamãe, the old woman wore a white straw hat pushed to her right. The ruddy-faced man sported a Panama hat, a white linen suit and white leather shoes. Ravaged by wrinkles, the husband's face much resembled his wife's, as if old age had conspired to make them indistinguishable. The couple hobbled forward, and Jaime asked himself, "Does this couple care what direction their stroll is taking?"

"Don't turn your head back, Jaime." Mamãe hissed.

"The fogeys can't see what I'm doing," he whispered back.

"Still, Jaime, it's unkind to stare at old people."

"But Mamãe, what are they doing here?"

"The fresh air," she sighed, "and the mineral water make a lot of people feel better."

He chuckled. "Isn't it about time they died?"

"It's human nature, Jaime." Her voice rose, sharp, and more didactic than usual. "It may appear absurd, Jaime, but people do all they can to prolong their lives. It's an 'ins-tinct'," she minced each syllable. "We have no choice in the matter."

Other elderly couples — dressed in white, tall glasses hooked on their little fingers — walked by. The men, especially, amused Jaime, as most of them shambled like wounded crabs, leaning on trembling canes or clutching their wiry wives by the arm.

After a brief stroll, the porous cement of the trail gave way to a polished stone Mamãe called "marble." Stairs led to a round, enclosed forum with four separate fountains in the centre. Mamãe stopped by fountain number three, which her guidebook recommended for most children's ailments. She rinsed Jaime's glass, then stooped to fill it with water gurgling from one of four spouts shaped like swans' heads.

In a moment Mamãe handed Jaime a glass of effervescent mineral water that smelled almost like the vinegary, homeopathic salt baths back home. Boiling inside, Jaime slowly supped the medicinal liquid. Did Papai and Mamãe borrow a fortune for this? He swallowed, then gritted his teeth. Did he come all the way from Rio just to make him drink some stupid mineral water they could buy at any corner store? And why the hell, he felt like spitting the nauseous liquid from his mouth, would free water from a fountain make him feel better than Mamãe's prayers? He narrowed his eyes and pictured himself breaking a corner of his glass on the fountain and slashing an anonymous face and arms. His eyes grew moist, as a tide of impotent fury took over. *Why*, he shook his head, *why spend money to sleep on sagging mattresses?*

Mamãe eyed him softly. "Finish your glass, Jaime," she said in *doutor* Machado's soothing voice. "It's good for you."

Treatment over, they strolled on. After a time Mamãe relaxed enough to sit on a green, wooden bench and converse with the captions and pictures in her magazine. More than bored, Jaime sat on her bench, two feet away. The clouds had lowered and turned a shade greyer. No wind was blowing, and his stiff, oversized shirt smothered him like a wool blanket. An urge to do something mischievous, reckless, outrageous took possession of him.

Jaime closed his eyes and pictured Gazoberto, his pal down the hall. They hide in the shade of a mango tree, the best place to pee on a hot day. They stretch high on their toes, and in seconds two arches of piss cross each other in mid air. Their own rain generously flogs the dead leaves on the ground, till the foaming, unholy waters begin to stream down, slowly.

"Shame on you, *vagabundos*!" A woman Jaime cannot see hollers from the nearest house. Without shaking, Jaime tucks his *pipi* back into his pants. Ahead of Gazoberto he runs into the sunlit alley, giggling.

"Why are you smiling, Jaime?" Mamãe asked, the magazine on her lap.

"Oh," he blushed. "Nothing. Nothing important."

But a nasty itch, the precursor of his coughs and convulsions, began to grate the bottom of his throat. His right finger blocked one nostril, and, to disguise the strain, he inhaled, softly. Mamãe turned a page of her magazine. The sore in the throat died down in a while, but a restless void now pestered his whole being. "I'm going for a walk," he said as he jumped to his feet.

"Now?" She raised her chin, and eyed the sky with appre-hension. "It might rain, Jaime, and I didn't bring your jacket."

"It's just a passing cloud," he made a cheerful toss with his head.

"There, Jaime," she stood up, pointing. "Don't go outside the side-entrance to the park. And don't be long. If it starts raining, come right back."

Capering along the winding trail, he vowed not to look back, not to confirm his suspicion that his mother's eyes were riveted to his back. Solitude, he felt, could be a real treat.

Outside the open gate to the park he saw a cocoa-coloured man donning a huge straw hat that appeared absurd now that the sun had completely disappeared behind the darkening, lowering sky. Stripped to the waist, the man's moist back shone like a clear windowpane. The worker stood knee-deep inside a ditch, shovelling red-brown soil into a mound by the sidewalk. Jaime walked close and looked down. As if desperate, an earthworm was burrowing its coiled body into the mound.

"What are you doing?" Jaime ventured, standing by the ditch.

"What am I digging?" the worker poked his shovel into the ground. He raised one eyebrow, amused. "Beats me, *menino*." He bent down and picked up a rope interrupted by two knots. "They told me to dig a ditch down to here," his fingers clasped the lower knot. "And then this long and this wide," he cradled the second knot.

Obviously enjoying his audience, the man smiled and large, gapped teeth showed. "And what about you, *menino*? With those cute suspenders, you look like you've just snuck out of church. Did you finish your prayers?"

"Wrong!" Jaime made an ugly face. "We're Jews, from Rio!"

"Rio?" the ditch-digger let out a cat-whistle. "I suspected you're not one of our local weeds. Tell me, *menino*, is your Papai or Mamãe looking for a gardener? Or a handyman? I'll do anything to land a job in Rio." He winked, conspiratorial.

"We live in an apartment building," Jaime laughed. "No need for help."

"Too bad." Chuckling, the man spread his hand on his chest. "For me, I mean. *Carnaval* is just a couple of weeks away, and I had hopes you'd find me a place to stay."

Jaime turned to his right. Skies of pewter hung just above the park's black fence and, on the other side of the street, scraped a row of red-roofed townhouses. Down the street, an old, brown, nodding horse with oversized shoes pulled a dray that rattled each time its wheels grappled with the cobblestones. A wreath of white carnations lay sideways between the horse's ears, as if dropped there in a hurry. Two thirds of an unstained pine coffin occupied the length of the dray. The rest of the coffin jutted out, obscene.

Heart pounding in his chest, Jaime gazed in terror at a tall young man, whose black pants hardly covered his bare ankles. Scuffling by, the young man embraced a squat woman veiled and dressed in black. Right after her, two boys in brown pants and white shirts, one about Jaime's age, the other a couple of years older, stared at the coffin, transfixed, as they filed by. About a dozen adults in black suits and black dresses marched at the end of the cortege, each to his own beat.

Feet and ankles muddied, the worker climbed out of his ditch and stood by the curb, stiff. He hung his chin down, the straw hat now concealing his bare chest and one arm. As soon as the last man in the cortege passed by, the worker donned his hat. Almost playful now, he hopped back into his ditch, and resumed the shovelling of soil onto the sidewalk.

Jaime bent down, and whispered, "But . . . who died?".

The worker stopped digging. He grinned, and two rows of Chiclets teeth twinkled. "Who's getting buried? Well, the man in the coffin, of course," he chuckled. "Didn't you see, *menino*? He was a man, not a woman. He left a widow behind." His eyebrows darted up and down, as his finger pointed at his ditch. "And that's where they're dumping the man in the coffin." The worker plunged his shovel into the bottom of the ditch, and in a moment a mound of soil surfaced on top. "Back to work," he mumbled.

Jaime slapped a hand over his mouth. Left arm flat on his belly, he bent over, and laughed his head off. Breathless, in pain, ecstatic, he sucked air back through his mouth. Behind his locked eyes, the worker's teeth shone whiter than in real life. "The man in the coffin" rang in his ears, brutally mocking the absurd fogeys in the park, his mother's inane water rituals, her never-ending worries.

"So silly," Jaime laughed, tears streaming down his cheeks. A picture in a book flashed through his mind: a band of penguins standing on ice — stiff and formal and pompous. "Full of it, adults are full of it," he chortled. "They make me laugh. Make no more sense than . . . " Jaime stopped laughing for a moment, and pondered, " . . . than raindrops poised on a window pane. Dumb! No better than the ditch-digger."

"The man in the coffin" rang again in Jaime's ear — louder, more irreverent.

"A *morte, a morte*," Jaime answered, giggling at his own fears. He coughed, lightly.

"What happened?" Behind his back, he heard Mamãe, alarmed.

He turned, and her handkerchief wiped his cheeks. "Jaime, why are you crying, Jaime?" Breathless, Mamãe scrutinized Jaime's face, the worker toiling inside his ditch, the black figures disappearing at the end of the street.

"I'm fine, Mamãe." He sobered up. "A funeral passed by and the man said . . . " He pointed at the worker, but the whooping laughter came back.

"Are you all right?" She reached for his forehead, but drew back her moist hand, almost disappointed. "Did you cough?"

"No, not really, Mamãe," he lowered his voice because an elderly couple was approaching. He wouldn't embarrass his Mamãe in the street.

The darkening clouds suggested rain, and Mamãe urged him to hurry back to their hotel. Inside the vestibule, the smell of pinto beans cooked in much garlic and meat made his nostrils swell with pleasure. Mamãe led the way into the dining room where only adults were having a meal. The people at the table smiled, but Jaime felt exposed, on show for aging fogeys. Carefully standing away from Mamãe, he captured the scents of boiled rice, and fancied a plate of steaming beans ladled on a bed of rice and sprinkled with cassava flour.

"Jaime isn't feeling very well," Mamãe told the landlady. "We'll have lunch upstairs, in our room, if it's not too much to ask."

Once in their room, Mamãe insisted that he change into his pyjamas. "We're having a nap, after we eat."

Three soft knocks on the door, and the landlady ushered in two sets of stacked aluminum pails with lids. On a second trip, she laid on the desk a tray with plates, silverware, a green bottle of water and glasses.

Jaime sat on his bed and, as Mamãe showed him, set a plate with rice, beans and meats on his thighs. The lukewarm food tasted good. Spoonfuls later, and without warning, "the man in the coffin" jingled in his ears. He spat out a mouthful, as a loud laugh escaped. His plate slid off his knees, and the mostly brown food cascaded onto the floor.

Mamãe stood up, glaring, and grabbed his shoulders. "What now?"

He wished he could honour his mother, but another gale of laughter shook him.

"Jaime," she nudged him toward his bed. "Lie down. At four, we're going to see a doctor."

"But Mamãe," he tried his best to choke the laughter, "there's nothing wrong with me."

"Stop laughing, for God's sake!" Mamãe yelled. "It's weird!"

As an itch was gathering in his throat, he stretched out in bed. Head turned to the wall, he reflected for a time, then sat up. "Mamãe," he said sweetly, to make peace. "I just remembered the worker saying the man in the coffin was the one getting buried. That's all. Would I lie to you?"

"There's absolutely nothing funny about a funeral," she replied, scowling. "Nothing. Lie straight, Jaime, relax," she begged. "We'll see what the doctor has to say."

"What if he tells *you* to calm down? Do we pack our suitcases, and take the first train back home?"

Mamãe stretched out on her bedcover, clothes and shoes on, and raised her magazine.

Exhausted from throttling his laughter and the itch in his throat, Jaime scanned the hairline cracks on the wall, to see if he could make out faces or animals.

An ominous cough began assembling in his upper chest. He sucked in his belly, and in a moment broke out in a cold sweat. With a thumb he blocked one nostril: Mamãe, he swore, wouldn't hear a thing. The pain was awesome, but he decided to get tough. This time he would strike back, give his cough, *a morte* and his stupid *destino* at least one good punch in the nose.

Jaws clenched, he rolled onto his back, quietly. In a daze, he trained his gaze at the ceiling lamp. Tears rushed to his eyes, and soon rolled down into his ears. Just when his chest was about to snap, he clamped his neck with two fingers and thumbs.

When Jaime regained consciousness, his chest and neck ached badly, but it didn't feel as though he'd cough for a while. By degrees he recognized that his mother was nodding off, her magazine open on the floor between their beds.

Jaime sat up and looked out the window. A timid blue patch, the shape of a lion's head, rose from behind thinning clouds. For a second or two he held his breath, then exhaled, triumphant, free. If Mamãe had not been asleep, he would have clamped two fingers with his lips, and whistled sharper than a locomotive before a tunnel.

"But . . . when Mamãe wakes up," he murmured, "she'll take me to this Lambari town doctor." He shrugged. "Afterwards, we'll stroll in the park, and, if he's still working, I'll have a look at the ditch-digger." He shook his head vehemently, not to laugh loudly and wake up Mamãe. "Of course," he giggled, "we'll sip mineral water for free."

"But before I go to bed," he took an oath, "I'll write Papai a letter."

In silence he rolled out of bed, and, standing by the window, stared at the sky growing blue in places.

"Dear Papai." Searching for words, he scratched the back of his head. "There's, really, no need to worry," he mumbled. "My cough is not as bad as it was, back in Rio. I'm not worried about my *morte*, and Mamãe stopped talking about our *destino*. She is doing just fine."

Noah And The Dove

The door to my office closed behind Silvia. I stared out at Saint Clair Avenue West as it gleamed through the branches of black, leafless trees. An old, swaying streetcar clattered by. Slow-moving car after slow-moving car rolled along, too, spluttering salt-and-pepper slush on the curbs. Here and there, bent-over men and women — probably trudging in or out of their therapy sessions — gingerly stepped onto sidewalks buried under downtrodden snow. Black and dark green winter coats blotched the bleak landscape illuminated from below.

The old building where I and eight other therapists plied our trade was eerily silent. I felt a lump in my throat. I could hear myself breathing. The encounter with Silvia had left me tired, irritable, empty, vulnerable to both shame and gratitude — what my students' textbooks call "the blind spots in one's personality."

"Hi Doctor Goldblatt." The taped voice had quivered like a child begging for a beating to stop. "It's Silvia, Silvia Zongaro. Remember me?"

The tape whirred on. I waited.

"Till May ninety-two I was in your Wednesday group. Actually, for two and a half years." Long pause. "Is it okay to have a twenty-five minute session?" Longer pause. "You see, right now I'm unemployed, and you psychologists are *so* expensive. And, Doctor, please, as soon as possible, *please*. Area code 416 586 8734. That's my home number, after seven. And . . . yes, thank you doctor. I —"

My answering machine, the size of a record player, let out a beep.

While my fingernails tapped the desktop, I played back her message. I thought over those many months. I played it back again.

That evening I called Silvia from my home and offered to see her the next day, on my lunch break.

"*Thank* you, Doc, but *thank* you," she breathed into the phone.

I put the receiver back in its cradle, got up, and headed for the basement. It was as musty as ever. At the bottom of the poorly-lit staircase I knelt under a bare bulb dangling at the end of a twisted brown cord and pulled out the bottom drawer of the almond, third lateral filecabinet. My forefinger sped through tightly stacked charts, halting near the end of my confidential records.

Zongaro, Silvia. I slid her chart out.

Standing up, I riffled through the enclosed letters and hand-written notes. How's Silvia doing these days, I wondered, my gut shrinking into an aching baseball, my shallow breathing not entirely unpleasurable. Whom — or what — would I meet tomorrow? Patient? Disciple? Friend? Acquaintance? Any queer combination of the above?

Sam Katz had made the referral, by phone. "Hi Irv. How's the family?"

"Very well, thank you. And how's everything with you?"

"Just fine. Do you have an opening in one of your groups for a borderline woman?"

A borderline? Again? My fingernails dug into the smooth skin of my neck. "Depends, Sam," I shot back. Why didn't they ever send the wealthy, nice, neurotic babes from Forest Hill my way?

"The patient," he went on, "is twenty-nine, with a Fine Arts degree from York. She swallowed rat poison, then slashed her wrists. Spent — one sec, let me check my notes — *five* weeks in our unit. A boyfriend of two years — he repaired computers, wrote plays in the evenings — left her for a friend."

"His friend or her friend?"

"No, Irv. *Her* friend, a woman. Also a painter. My patient's parents — they're from Friule, very Catholic — had predicted that it would never work out with a Jewish guy."

"So why are you sending her to *me*, Sam?"

He didn't answer.

I waited.

His silence was obnoxious.

"Was she in therapy before?"

"Sort of. First year in college she swallowed a bottle of aspirins, then for a few months saw a counsellor-schmoun-sellor. Irv," his voice rose, "she's workable, *really* psychologi-cally minded. This is not a dump, Irv." I heard him inhale. "Her family owns a restaurant, on College. They agreed to pay for her therapy until she's back on her feet."

"Still living with her parents?" I hooted.

"No! She has her own apartment. Irv," he insisted, "bottom line, the girl is likeable. I feel for her."

"Is she on medication?"

"Perphenazine, six milligrams, at bedtime. I'll follow her, once a month."

Puckering my lips, I glanced at my appointment book, an Emmentaler cheese of openings. Jessie, my eldest, needed a second set of orthodontic braces; I'd promised her and Harvey a horse and riding lessons.

"Sam? Are you there? Okay. You can give her my name."

"Thank you, Irv. The patient is Silvia, Silvia Zongaro.

The basement light was poor. Did I need to read page after page of my own scribbled comments? I sighed. Even if I were twisting and tossing on a wet mattress in a nursing home, the name "Zongaro" would still conjure black, intense, liquid eyes in a taut Modigliani face without powder or rouge.

Eyes closed, I visualized Silvia's oversized sleeves wiping her tears: the slow, absent-minded motions of someone unconcerned about tears gathering on her pointed chin. Waiting and waiting for her turn to share her feelings on Wednesday evenings, she chewed her lower lip white. Shame? Rage? Both?

Now, standing under the bare bulb in my dank basement, a twenty-five-year-old professional habit — or compulsion — made me imagine stern-faced colleagues looking over my shoulder, whispering in each other ear, "Is our Irv performing all the rituals required by the code of conduct?"

Compelled, I studied Silvia's chart as a line-by-line editor would. The first entry, verbatim notes on a greening, lined page wrested off a spiral pad, stated that I had first seen Silvia on September 4, 1989. The black ink of my extra-fine fountain pen had grown pale — almost purple-blue. Incomprehensible in places, the minuscule lower-case letters ran into each other, more like a student jotting down his mentor's caveats than a seasoned therapist's observations. My enormous capital letters did not amuse me. Did I come across also as detached? Self-important? Imposing? Preachy, perhaps?

No, surely my notes were written for *my* benefit, *my* private consumption. Unless an irate ex-patient charged me with malpractice, no one would ever set eyes on my inelegant *oeuvre*. "Some writers," I mumbled aloud, "are much better protected than others."

My December 22, 1991 entry was one of the longest. "Patient set a large, square package wrapped in brown paper on my desk. Insisted that I open it only at home. Refused to discuss what messages she was sending me and the group. Said that what she felt was too personal, perhaps her art could express. Got a lot of confrontations, became upset, yelled, cried, left the room, came back, apologized, saying that a timid light had begun to shine at the end of her tunnel."

In a flash, that last session before Christmas break came back: nine pairs of peregrine eyes watched how I'd react to the flat, five-by-three-foot ribbonless gift. Behind closed lips I nibbled the tip of my tongue, praying, "Please, almighty God, don't let me blush!" (Words of gratitude, Hallmark cards, and Christmas gifts inflame my cheeks, I've been told too many times.) In the charged room, eyes were unblinking and nostrils flared. Glancing around, at long last I smiled. "Thank you, Silvia, thank you. I feel flattered."

A long silence.

"I understand what Silvia is trying to accomplish." Larry, to my right, got me off the hook. He loosened his pretty, red-and-blue silk tie. It pleasingly clashed with his grey pin-stripe suit. "But isn't the gift," he pointed, "some sort of a bribe?"

"Here you go again, Larry," Nancy fired, and in mock despair cuffed her cropped white hair. "Only head stuff ever comes out of your mouth." She slapped her belly. "Why the fuck don't you, for once, tell us how do you really feel? How do you *feel* about the gift?"

"And what about you, Nancy?" Bob, the group's most senior member (four years) bellowed.

Session over, the entire group filed out of my office in dead silence. Relieved to escape unscathed that week, I exhaled. "I'll cross the bridge when I get there, in two weeks."

Minutes later I slid the heavy gift across the back seat of a cab, compelled by Silvia's wishes that I open it only at home. Eager to avoid lengthy explanations to my wife that would only prolong my devouring curiosity, I clumped down the narrow stairs through the side entrance, inadvertently ramming one corner of the huge gift into one wall, then the other, until I reached the basement.

"Holy Moses!" I murmured. "How damn clumsy can you get?"

Panting, I set the flat gift on the basement's cement floor. As my heart fluttered in pain and pleasure, I removed pieces of transparent tape, then, like a nurse unrolling bandages, tore off layer after layer of khaki-coloured wrapping paper.

In a silvery frame was a glass-covered picture drawn mostly in charcoal and white. Instantly I recognized the hull of a wooden ark and, in the background, cages with pairs of giraffes, elephants, ostriches. Gripping a flat-headed hammer, stood a white-maned, white-bearded Noah, a robe flowing to his ankles. Next to Noah, by the ark's small window, hovered an oversized dove with an olive branch across its black beak. White paint glimmered on the space between Noah and the dove to signify, I assumed, a bond between two figures eyeing each other with affection.

The bottom right corner of the glass had cracked, apparently while I had descended the stairs. White, ugly lines like a miniature, skeletal fan ripped the glossy skin.

Why *did* I have to rush down the stairs? I hated — no, despised — my clumsiness and greed. My cheeks burned. I shook my head and vowed to finally put down on paper — after Christmas, or by February at the latest — my theories of shame and gratitude that I'd been developing since my second year in graduate school.

Sighing, I stared down at Silvia's file. I had to take matters in stride. Yet, I couldn't resist. One by one I reviewed the turning points in her personal history and treatment. One note in particular caught my attention: in Silvia's eyes, her part-time job in a nursing home had been as inspiring as her art work.

Bending down again, I squeezed her chart back into its alphabetical place. With precision, I reconstructed in my mind the members of my Wednesday group from nineteen eighty-nine until Silvia left.

I smiled, recalling face after face: Larry, Nancy, Bob, Silvia, and others who had long departed from my life. What had happened to these people? Where were they now? My chest began to hurt. My breathing grew harder. And where had the last ten, fifteen, twenty-five years of *my* life gone?

I had no idea.

"Good morning," I said, the day I met Silvia on my lunch break, as she had anxiously requested on the phone.

Right ankle planted across her knee, she was reading *Psychology Today* in the waiting room. After closing the magazine, she raised it a bit, then abruptly let go. *Psychology Today* flopped on a messy pile of glossy magazines on a side table.

Silvia cocked her chin. "It's noon now, Doctor G." She stood up.

Smiling, I shook her moist, cold, bony hand. Her eyes had grown dim. Her cheeks were pale and sunken. Nights without much sleep. What had prompted her to call?

She wore the same long, grey winter coat, but more discoloured and frayed. Soon I'd find out, were there gaping holes at the elbows?

"Same place?" She asked and wended her way towards the green, thickly carpeted staircase to my office.

"Uh, huh," I snorted.

Midway up the staircase, she turned her head back. "Every time I see my dentist, I lie down in a different room. Pity you're not a Freudian, Doctor G. Right now, I could make use of a couch."

Two steps below her, I stared at the soiled snow and translucent ice buttons dangling from the bottom of her loose, washed-out jeans. Soon the ice and snow would melt down, onto my Swedish rya rug.

She opened the door to my office.

"Make yourself comfortable," I said, motioning her inside what had been a bedroom in a Victorian mansion converted into therapists' offices.

"I'll keep my coat on." She shrugged lightly, her contralto barely audible. "I feel cold and, besides, I won't be long." She perched stiffly on one of my green leather sofas and, gazing all around the room, sniffed a few times, as if surprised. After a while she pronounced, "Fresh dyes. When did you get the two loveseats?"

"About a year ago."

"Strange," she sighed. "In my mind I had enshrined a room with rust-coloured, corduroy sofas. Now it's in green leather."

"Do you have some feelings about my room?"

She lifted one brow and eyed me.

Was she irritated, I wondered. Disappointed? A blend of both?

"Some things never change," she murmured, as if in afterthought.

For a while we said nothing. Getting too close, Irv, too quickly. Lay off! Slow down your breathing.

The silence was a palpable membrane. I straightened up in my chair. "Some things never change," I ventured softly. "Like my questions?"

Eyes watering, slowly she turned her head and stared at the window. As in the past, her cropped, greying temple disclosed a minute, delicately carved ear.

A streetcar rattled by.

I tried again. "What are you thinking about?"

In slow motion, Silvia turned her face in my direction. Cheeks glinting with tears, and oblivious to the box of Kleenex resting on the sofa's arm, absent-mindedly she took a crumpled, grey handkerchief from her coat pocket. She dabbed her eyes, then concealed her handkerchief in a girl's tight fist.

"Last week I was laid off." She avoided my eyes and gazed at her soaking boots and the blurred, white line above the once-black soles.

My rya rug was still dry.

In a moment she resumed. "They're closing the nursing home."

"The same one, when you were seeing me?"

She cocked her head. Silver beamed in her teary eyes. "You remember, eh?" She nodded, then blew her nose into her handkerchief. "Yeah, I painted in the mornings, then worked in the afternoons and evenings." She drew in much air. "The owners sent a memo to the staff saying that the nursing home was losing money." Tears shone on her chin, almost loose. "The old folks will be shipped to other homes around the province."

She stared at her knees, one sleeve wiping both cheeks dry. "I've known some of them for years! They won't survive the move. I know!"

"But what about you?"

She pursed her lips, unmistakably angry. Her sleeve sponged her eyes, then her cheeks. "But I do have somewhere to go, Doctor G." Her voice grew louder.

Her narrowing eyes began to pierce mine. "You remember when I told you in group you're not Doctor Perfect, but you can live with my rage?"

I couldn't recall those words, but nodded twice.

Her cheeks quivered behind a fresh film of tears. "My parents never talked about *their* rage. They forbade me, can you imagine, *forbade* me to have strong feelings, good or bad." Her eyes gauged the impact of her words on me. She leaned forward and raised her fist. "Just listen, doc," she yelled, making my heart beat even faster. "I *am* in a rage! Hate them! Could kill somebody!"

She leaped to her feet and stared down at me. "You know, and I know! The old folks will die in a matter of weeks. Months, at most!" She snorted back her tears. "And, Doctor G, I don't want to hear any fucking horseshit from you right now!"

By now my breathing was so shallow that my entire torso ached. "Let me in," I urged, one hand motioning toward my chest. "Tell me more. You look so hurt."

Damn! Wished I could take back the last few phrases. Superficial horseshit. Good luck no students or interns were watching behind a one-way mirror.

She watched me warily. My heart hammered.

"*Nothing!*" Her scream brought back memories of howls that had terrorized her group and me. "I know, I know, Doctor G.! Sooner or later you'll ask me what is it *I* can do about it. You're *so* reasonable, Doctor, so realistic. Fuck it!"

She flung a glance at the window, then turned, staring me in the eye. "They gave me one afternoon, can you imagine, just *one afternoon*, to say goodbye. I did. To only half my frightened folks. Some of them cried, cold fingers clutching mine. You know old fingers. They don't easily let go."

I nodded and nodded.

Tears streaming down her cheeks, she stamped a few times, then sat down and leaned back on the sofa.

We brooded.

She sighed deeply.

"Did you feel you have to help the old folks the way I and the group had helped you?" I asked.

She slewed in her seat. "Maybe. I'll think about it." She raised a forefinger and smoothed her lips. "What about the other guys in the group?"

"Nobody you know is still there."

"Guess you won't tell me more than that." A kinder light shone in her hard eyes. "Confidential, eh?"

"Mmh, mmh."

"And the picture I gave you? Still have it?"

"Of course. In my study, at home."

Her face softened. "I see."

"Silvia," I leaned forward, "I never told you I had to change the glass on the picture. I cracked one of the corners."

"But it *was* cracked."

Stung, I sat up. "I thought *I* did it."

She turned her head sideways, eyes still watching mine. "All this time you thought *you* broke it?"

"Yeah." I prayed not to blush.

She leaned back, crossed one thigh over the other, then uncrossed it again. Eyes level with mine, she watched my face as if for the first time. "But you . . . you thanked me again the week after, in group." The corners of her lips curled in anger. "You didn't say a word about the glass, Doctor G. Not a word! You're *so* polite. And shy! Terribly shy!"

My scalp and cheeks felt hot. "I am." My voice escaped lower than I had wanted. "Sounds like you've just discovered something about me."

"You look so awkward!" she hissed. "A little boy caught with his hand in the cookie jar."

To bide time, I pinched my chin with a thumb and a forefinger. The silence in the room felt unbearable.

What felt like hours passed before I found something helpful to say. "Silvia," I exhaled, exhausted, "have you learned today something that you didn't know before? Something about Noah, let's say?"

"Yeah. A lot!" Up and down she inspected me. "For two and a half years I heard your pep talks on venting feelings on the spot. And you? You didn't even acknowledge *your* fantasy of breaking the glass!"

"Disappointed?"

"But of course!" She raised her head, more than indignant. "I'm paying fifty dollars to find out you're not the person I remembered."

In January my fees had gone up. This, however, was not the time to bring up my raise. I waited.

Soon she turned her head to the window sill. "My time is up."

"You still remember where I keep my clock?"

"Some things never change, Doc," she crooned. "You yourself agreed with that statement."

I leaned forward. "I'm on my break, Silvia. You may want to stay a while longer."

"No. I can afford only half a session in Angst Alley."

I spoke softly. "I can get coffee from the staff room. No problem."

"It was very kind of you to see me right away, doc." Unsmiling, she nodded slowly several times. "Thank you. I mean it."

A red-hot ice pick lodged in my belly: is that the way *I* nod?

She went on, "I really don't want to take more of your time." She stood up, then wiped her right hand on her coat. When I shook her fingers, they felt warm.

"If you don't mind," she said, "I'll mail you my cheque next week."

"That's okay."

I stared out at St. Clair Avenue. Another streetcar clattered by. I mumbled aloud, "Patients enter my life in agony, and then take off." How many people got close to me and, long months later, shortly after their life became tolerable, cheerily announced that I was no longer needed?

I turned up my empty palms. Carpenters left desks behind, writers wrote books. What the hell did *I* have to show? Where were the thousands of soothing phrases I've stitched for others to wear? What had happened to all my work?

Wistful, I fondled the gifts adorning my window-sill: a cricket cage from China, a pen stand, polished Alberta stones, two Inuit carvings, a hand-made Teddy bear — bits of evidence that I'd been of help to some.

"But people pass my name around," I tried to allay my self-doubts. "Some, like Silvia, even come back for more —

whatever *that* is." My arms and hands shivered. "I can't be all that bad."

My office, it seemed, reverberated with the million of words I'd uttered to pacify — or knock sense — into people who hardly ever listened to what their friends told them.

"Facts!" I challenged Ben, a member of an imaginary group. "You're giving us the facts, not your *feelings*." Bitter, I smiled. Probably other therapists used and abused the same lines that *I* overused.

On to the challenge I went again. "Ben, we haven't got to the *root of your problem!*" The most quoted cliché in clinical circles. Shaking, I laughed and laughed.

What if my next door colleague overheard my laughter? "Relax, Irv!" I breathed deeply. "Take it easy, man."

In my mind, I jotted down the first lines of a self-pitying, Tchaikovsky confessional: "After twenty-five years, my lateral-file cabinets contain some thirty thousand lines of prose I'm not proud of. Is that all?"

It amused me to think how in my grandparents' days, hordes of ministers and rabbis in black dispensed almost the same snippets of wisdom for which I was princely paid. And long before those wiseacres, medicine men and paid prophets thrived, too.

Therapies come and therapies go. Still, human miseries remain more or less the same. Is our suffering nurture or nature? Exhausted, I cast my vote for Mother Nature.

I slid the sash window up, the corners of its windowpane adorned with powdery snow flakes. Arctic air punched my nose and cheeks; outdoors, dovish snowflakes were tucking the trees, roofs, sidewalks, and street under a clean, fluffy eiderdown. Tweaking my shaking chin, I prayed for the day warm tears would soothe my cheeks.

The Atheist's Bible

DYING OF LIVER CANCER UPSTAIRS, Dad slept only three or four hours at night, ate one skimpy meal a day, and edited his *Atheist's Bible*, an annotated anthology of philosophers from the ancient Greeks to Sartre. Every hour his old printer roared and rattled to life, giving Mom and me a start. Would he rest, we wondered, or resume his feverish work?

His crimsoned eyes gave off a queer, bleary light. His sucked-in cheeks glowed like sallow candles. Secretive and withdrawn, he wouldn't tell how much morphine maintained his mad schedule.

Mom toiled in the garden —— "to keep my sanity," she muttered. In the evenings she nodded off on the living room sofa, an open book and her reading glasses nestled on her chest. Anxious, gloomy, but excited, I crammed for my finals in philosophy. Fumes and the scents of freshly mown lawns wafted through the windows. Shrieking kids played street hockey until after dark. In the dead of night, only my father's tramping up and down the staircase, or a lonely cat meowing outdoors, disturbed me.

"Thank you for your comments," Dad told me one evening. He was referring to my written feedback in the margins of his two-inch thick manuscript.

So far, I'd held back my resentment about his treatment of Freud's theories. He'd even written a special introduction about Freud's influence on psychiatry, a distinction not accorded to any other thinker. Why did he give so much space to his idol at others' expense? But what was the point of confronting a man with only weeks to live? What significant passages could he revise, what chapters rewrite?

Dad's dogged commitment to his book pissed me off. His project had been completed, but pig-headedly he strove for editorial perfection. What for? No more than fifteen hundred copies of his book would ever be printed. Only three or four reviewers would read his book from cover to cover!

He had lost much weight. His pants hung awkwardly from his tightened belt. His shirts floated above collapsed shoulders. Months before he had fainted at his hospital office. The chief of pathology forbade him to come back. In retaliation for his forced retirement, whenever he wasn't writing he tottered up and down the staircase, a declaration of being alive.

From behind my closed door I'd hear Mom on the upper landing asking, "But Joel, how *are* you feeling?"

"I've been better, I've been worse," he'd say. At other times he'd answer, "Okay," or "Not too bad."

I gritted my teeth. Herr Doctor was not happy with a well-edited, *finished* manuscript on his desk! Why wasn't he saying goodbye to his family? Why not be honest, grieve his approaching death? With weeks to live, why did he have to polish each sentence into glimmering Carrara marble?

One night I woke to my shoulder being shaken. I blinked to avoid the eye-piercing ceiling light.

Mom stood by my bed, her robe untied. "Wake up, Marvin! Wake up."

Muscles aching, I rubbed my sore eyes. I'd been typing till two in the morning. "*What?* What now?"

"Your father threw up blood. He flushed it down the toilet, but I saw small stains on the floor."

I sat up. "What do you want *me* to do, Mom? He doesn't want any fucking help. He wants to write till he croaks."

She tied up her robe. "Maybe he should see a psychiatrist."

"A shrink? Sorry, Mom. He'll kick the bucket before the Prozac kicks in."

"No! No pills! I meant for him to talk to someone, get things off his chest. He's so lonely, so scared."

"Where the hell is he?"

"In his study."

I knocked on his door. No answer. I decided to sidle into his fortress, now barely lit by a reading lamp on his desk. On his computer monitor, black double-spaced lines crowded the off-white screen. "C:\WP51\BIBLE.34" shone in the bottom left corner.

I leaned closer. The thirty-fourth version of his book? Was he psychotic?

Behind me, Mom turned on the ceiling light.

"I was trying . . . " he raised his head from the pillow, "to fall asleep . . . " A twig of coagulated blood spread from one corner of his mouth to his neck. Red stains the size of cookies glimmered on his pillow. Blood on his shirt, too. Slowly he sat up. "Take me to Toronto General."

He stayed in the hospital for two days. We visited him every evening. He lay canted in a tall bed with a manual crank. Against the chalk-white sheets and pillow his brown eyes glittered. His face had grown so papery that his Auschwitz-survivor cheekbones were about to pierce the skin. The nose, enlarged and crooked, seemed ready to collapse. His kindling-thin fingers rested on a blue hospital blanket.

He stared at us. "They want to give me chemo. Do they expect me to ignore the side effects? No way. I can't write if I stay in this joint. I've more important things to do."

"We brought you a few pages, pencils, and erasers," Mom cajoled him. "You can work right here." Her hard look urged me to intervene, but I shrugged

Dad signed himself out of the hospital against medical advice. "I got a couple of fresh ideas," he said, sluggishly climbing the stairs to his study.

He didn't come down for meals. My furious, frightened mother took soup and pureed vegetables to his desk.

Every so often his printer rattled.

Despite the ambience of doom at home, I sang and danced when a form letter from New York University announced that I had been accepted to Graduate School in philosophy. My studies would start right after Labour Day.

The next morning, as I scanned the "Help Wanted" section of the *Toronto Star*, a van parked by our driveway. A delivery man in a brown shirt and pants toted a large manila parcel. He strode to our front door.

The bell rang. I opened the door. "Doctor Kleinberg is ill. I'll sign for him."

The man handed me a blue ballpoint pen. As I signed the clipboard, I yelled above the noise of the printer's machine-gun patter, "Dad! There's a parcel for you!"

"Be down in a minute," he shouted back. "Put the parcel on the coffee table."

One hand clutching the rail like a toddler, one step at a time, he eased down the staircase. Once he set his feet on the main floor, he doddered to the glass-covered table. His eyes glinted. "Please bring me a butcher's knife."

In two surgical strokes he scalpelled open the brown tape around it and tore off the wrapping paper. From inside the box his gaunt, trembling fingers eased out a pewter urn shaped like the Stanley Cup. He removed the lid, bent forward, and examined the inside.

Mom came into the room. He handed her the urn. She clutched it with her hands. "But Joel, what is *this*?" she asked, more angry than curious. She turned the vessel all around. "I can't believe it! Why *are* you doing this to us?" She banged the urn to the floor. Tears rilled down her cheeks. "I can't take it any more! I'm going for a walk!"

"Pat!" Dad raised his cavernous voice. "Let me explain!"

She headed through the vestibule and slammed the front door shut.

I scooped up the urn. Its walls were thin. It weighed less than a pound. Close to the rim an engraving proclaimed, "Here Lies An Individual." A smaller engraving announced, "Joel Kleinberg, 1942 – 1994, Editor of the *Atheist's Bible*."

Had he lost touch with reality? Was he oblivious to the people who cared about him? "But Dad!" I yelled. "How the hell could you do that?"

"Do what? What's wrong? Don't I deserve to choose my own tombstone?"

"Dad! You decided to be *cremated*!"

"You got it, son. What *is* the problem? Why can't your mother and you respect my last wishes?"

"But Dad, Mom likes traditions, like candles on Fridays, fasting on Yom Kippur. Her parents were Orthodox. A cremation would crush her."

He picked up the lid by its knob and pounded it onto the urn. "Look, Marvin, I'm not interested in sentimental rituals that cost an arm and a leg. I got my urn for one hundred and forty dollars, engraving and tax included."

"That's it!" I muttered, a futile attempt to curb my fury. "You didn't consult us! Mom is right. You don't give a shit about us."

His stoical mask fell. "Selfish!" he barked. "Inconsiderate! Selfish! I'm sick and tired of hearing about my selfishness. This is the only death I'll ever have!"

Scared and disbelieving, I crawled to the wing chair. I sat down.

He picked up his urn and eyed it lovingly. He smiled. "My unveiled tombstone!"

"But what about us?"

"No problem. I'm leaving behind a million dollars in life insurance, the house is paid off, five hundred grand in RRSPs, a lot of good IBM stock."

I shook my head. We were both *pretending* this was a man-to-man talk. We raised our voices, traded passionate words, shoved arguments down each other's throats. But we belonged to different worlds. His eyes were set on the impenetrable continents of nothingness. He wished, above all, to be recognized and remembered as a brilliant scholar. His tenacity at the end of his road struck me as inhuman, outrageous, bizarre.

My world stood uncharted. I bobbed between undergraduate and graduate schools, between Toronto and New York. Who the hell was I?

The spark in his eyes died down. "I know Mom and you will grieve after I go. But I'm not trying to put a lid — no pun intended — on anybody's feelings."

We glared past each other in silence, avoiding eye contact. A car rattled by, probably interrupting children from playing tag. "Please, Dad, *please*. We're worried. You're unable to see what you're doing to yourself."

"Look! I led a pretty conventional life. At the end of the line I'm dying in an unorthodox fashion. Is that so hard to take?"

"Yes!"

His expression grew tired. He looked grey. "Please bear with me. In a few days it'll be over."

"How much morphine are you taking, Dad?"

"A lot," he replied, embarrassed. "But it gives me more quality time than the goddamn chemo ever would."

"And the book?"

"I'll never be satisfied! But when I meet my maker, you'll find on my desk a printed draft and two sets of backed-up disks."

My heart raced. Meet my maker? What was behind his atheist's front? I got up and laid my hand on his shoulder. "Would you like me to say Kaddish after you?"

His mocking eyes gazed into mine. "Thank you, son, but no, thank you. Not at all. Freud and Sartre were my Rabbis. They taught me I need no prayers before and after I go."

Two nights later he stood on the landing and shouted, "Marvin, please come up!"

He led me into his study. By his computer stood the swivelling chair and an upholstered stool from his bedroom. "Sit down," he urged me. "I want to show you something." From his bookshelf he pulled out an old, black volume and handed it to me. He lounged on his chair as I inspected the book. The barely gilded letters on the front cover were still legible: "Holy Bible". The right bottom corner bore a faint inscription: "Placed by the Gideons."

For the first time in my life I riffled through a King James' Bible. There were lines in several languages, including Hebrew. More than puzzled, I waited.

"That's how my project got started, fifteen years ago," he said. "I was in Montreal to read a paper at a convention I didn't feel like attending. After my presentation and several particularly obnoxious questions from the audience, I felt immensely tired. My friends went for dinner in Old Montreal, but I didn't join them. An overwhelming need to be alone took over. The idea of hearing a human voice gave me goosebumps. In my hotel room I disconnected the phone and turned off the light. I lay in bed like a mummy. Mesmerized, I listened to the air conditioner whirring.

"There was no past, no present, no future. I undressed, crawled under the blanket, but couldn't fall asleep. Out of the blue a thunderbolt made me sit up. 'Who the fuck are you? Who the fuck are you?' It was not a hallucination, but an unrelenting inner voice asking me who was I.

"At last I answered, 'A pathologist.' I presented the evidence: medical school, four years of residence, written and oral exams, a paper almost every year. All this didn't shut up the voice."

He stopped and drew in his breath. "The interrogation went on. 'Who the fuck are you?' I've no idea how long it lasted. I begged the voice to let me sleep!"

He massaged his belly. "Frantically I searched for something to read besides professional articles. When I opened the top drawer of the bedside table, I found this Bible."

"You mean, you *stole* the Bible?"

"Yeah," he managed to smile. "The rest of the evening I read the passages recommended when feeling afraid, anxious, backsliding. Next day I woke up at noon, the Gideons' Bible open on my chest."

I brought my chair closer. "What did you get out of it?"

"The realization that *some people* have a book to read when they feel awful. What could a godless Jew read?"

He eased himself up. "Back in a sec," he said, and left the room.

I closed my eyes. He was popping more morphine.

Minutes later he returned, his sparse hair combed, the face seeming less wrinkled. He sat down. "I'm a doctor," he resumed. "I believe in science, in biology. None of this watery horseshit about 'I *think*, therefore I am.'" He glared at me, as if I had authored the dictum he hated so much. "I think only as long as my brain is alive! For *twenty-five* years I've been a pathologist. Not even *once* have I come across what you airy-fairy philosophers call soul, or any such crap."

I patted his knee. "Relax, Dad. We're not going to solve all these problems today."

He glanced at my hand. "The body just *is*. At the end of the road it fucks up, but it's all we have to go by. Birth, death, and everything in between are blue skies patched on and off with black clouds."

I nodded. He desperately wanted me to remember him and each one of his arguments. I felt sad. Once again, that thick mist between us.

"Ostensibly," he said, "I edited my little Bible to collect the classics in the field. Personally, I didn't want to hear questions about my feathery identity."

The room had grown darker. An aroma of roasting chicken floated up from the kitchen; there would be pasta and tossed salad, too.

He stared at his computer for a moment. He eyed me. "Contempt," he turned and eyed me, "I've come to realize, is the root of my atheism. Contempt for the masses that yearn for prophets who will tell them how to live; contempt for navel gazers who preach that death and dying have a meaning. Meaning outside the boundaries of a living body? Marvin! There are more fools than sand in the sea!"

His dry eyes and knitted brows spoke of a lonely man. Would he poke his neck out of his shell and share his terrors with me?

No.

"Dinner time!" Mom called from downstairs.

"Dad," I said. "In your book you've given a lot of space to Freud. Come on, a Jew, a doctor, eh?"

"Oh, no! He was the most quoted writer in this century. Except for a lethal dose, he refused to take painkillers. He wanted to stay lucid to the bitter end."

"Did that inspire you not to take chemo?"

"Yeah. We atheists have no recipes for a long, happy life. But we die without sentimental lullabies about a loving Big Daddy up there."

Dad and I had no further heart-to-hearts. A few days later he cascaded down the stairs and was taken to a hospital. Hours later he died.

He was cremated, but Mom insisted we sit shivah. She crouched on the living room sofa, crying without tears. Relatives, friends, neighbours, and Dad's colleagues paraded by us, mumbling their sorrow. They patted me on the shoulder. They whispered words of comfort. I bit my tongue. The condolences crowd didn't know how infuriating my father had been, as he sat upstairs by his desk, writing and dying.

Days after his death, the funeral home delivered the pewter urn with his ashes. I set it by the fireplace. That same afternoon I mailed the last version of his manuscript to Mr. Castlefield, the literary agent my father had hired. I kept one backed-up diskette in his study, another in Mom's safety deposit box. Now that his printer no longer clanked and clattered upstairs, the house sounded eerily quiet. Mom and I never entered his study.

Three months later, during the Christmas vacation, Mr. Castlefield was in our house, sitting on the sofa Dad had liked. The balding, bespectacled, heavyset agent rubbed his pink hands. Bearing good news, or just warming his palms? "I'm happy to let you know that Joel's book was accepted for publication." He shot glances at Mom and me. He waited for his words to sink in. "He'd have been very proud." He wore a professorial mask. "Yale University Press, however, wants some changes. First, the title has to go. Too offensive, too controversial. It'll raise eyebrows. They want something like, 'Atheism: An Anthology'."

"Hell no!" I blurted out. "Out of the question!"

"Let Mr. Castlefield talk," Mom said.

"Also," the agent went on, "the publisher wants to omit some annotations. The book is scholarly and well-edited, but it's too subjective, not critical enough of certain writers."

"Come on, that's his legacy!" I butted in. "Fifteen years he worked on it! We'll look somewhere else."

The agent exhaled, impatient. "It'll be the same everywhere. The book is excellent, but the title and some passages are too provocative."

"Marvin," Mom turned to me, "why are you getting so worked up? We're talking about minor changes."

"No way, Mom! We're not changing the title or the tone of the book." I stood up and walked to the fireplace. I lifted the urn with Dad's ashes and handed it to the philistine agent.

He scrutinized the urn. He pursed his lips. He mumbled, "Is that why you don't want any changes?"

"Over my dead body!" I stared at my mother, furious. "How could you even think of another title? At the end, the book was everything — his life, his passion."

"Do I know that," she replied. "No need to rub it in."

A week ago, Mr. Castlefield sent us another of several letters. After two years, North American publishers had refused even to cast a glance at the book. Now, The World Of Ideas, a Dutch publisher, had agreed to bring it out, unchanged, provided that the author's estate bought two thousand hard bound copies in advance.

Two thousand? In advance? Mom and I looked at each other.

These days, we are busy compiling a list. Two thousand libraries will be mailed *The Atheist's Bible* free of charge.

THE CONFORMIST

SITTING BETWEEN THE SILVER-HAIRED MATRON and a young, busty, brunette woman, he peered out the oval, diminutive window. On the horizon, cotton clouds marred a copper-and-blood early-spring sunset. Were the plane's glittering wing and motors made of aluminum or silver?

As flight attendants in black suits and white blouses served trays of beef with miniature bottles of red wine, the young woman broke the ice. "Hi," she said. "I'm Aviva Harari. I'm going back home after two *wonderful* years in Toronto."

"I'm Neil. I live there."

She sighed. "I was an *au pair* with a really nice family in Forest Hill. They've two girls. The oldest, Sarah, is six years old. Anna will be four in June."

He nodded to the rhythm of her speech.

"In the mornings I drove the girls to day care. Then we played in Hebrew. Their mother, Mrs. Levine — she's a busy family lawyer — came home at six and cooked dinner. After hours I took Psychology at York, but back home I'll double major in English and Hebrew. I'd like to teach high school one day."

His mouth twitched. The girl's chatty staccato was a touch guttural. She couldn't pronounce "the," but said "de" instead.

He noticed her teeth were chalk-white, and her smile cute. "I'm a pathologist," he replied. "I'll read a paper in Tel Aviv."

"How *nice!*" She scrutinized his face. "Are you Jewish? No offence, but you don't look Jewish."

He laughed. "Yep. I'm a blond member of the tribe. My parents keep kosher, but I'm secular."

She tucked a strand of chestnut-brown hair behind her ear. "How long will you be staying in Tel Aviv?"

"Three days. I've heard the water there is chilly this time of the year, but I'm used to the lakes in Ontario."

"Are you married?"

"I have two daughters, fourteen and eleven. Good kids. No drugs. No alcohol." He paused. Had he revealed too much? "My oldest already had her bat mitzvah. The youngest is still under her Rabbi's thumb."

"I understand how she must feel. Well, I'm twenty-two, but I don't think about water under the bridge. You see, my mother died nine years ago."

"I'm very sorry to hear that."

She heaved a sigh. "My dad is a painter, in Tel Aviv. Three years ago he remarried, but my stepmother and I didn't get along. Same old story. So I got my job through an agency. Then there was Christopher, my boyfriend for a year. He offered to convert, but I wasn't ready to commit."

As the last of the supper trays were cleared away, an attendant rolled down a silvery screen. They were about to show *The Firm*, a movie he had seen with his wife.

Aviva adjusted her earphones, gazed at the screen, and moved her lips as if to concentrate better. He tried to read his thriller, but his mind wandered. He felt like continuing their chat. It was so easy to confide in a total stranger he'd never see again. His wife was right: he had always been too quiet.

He should, she niggled, sound more welcoming than just mumbling "Okay, okay," whenever his acquaintances called.

But he felt he could live with his limitations, even if stand-up parties were hard on him, and he sipped his gin and tonic as if it were Tabasco. Yes, he was scared of chatty women cornering him.

He went through life dissecting tissues, studying them under a microscope, projecting slides onto screens, writing non-fiction that only white-coated colleagues and coroners read. An anti-social character. A loner. The only reason he dragged his feet to the movies was to escort his wife. Mostly at her instigation, sex took place on Sunday mornings, when the girls were away. Afterward they read *The New York Times* in bed.

Aviva took off her earphones. "You're not watching the movie? It has a convincing story line, really good actors, not much action."

"I prefer subtitled movies. They keep me focused, and I don't think about work; I'd rather go on enjoying our conversation." His face turned hot. Was he flushing?

"I love your trimmed beard. Does your wife complain it's ticklish? I would."

Was she hitting on him? His creamy dick came to life. He turned to fondle her cheek, but his elbow banged the seat ahead. He glanced around. Did the old woman see him make a pass?

The lights in the plane dimmed. A chestnut glow emerged. Both of them turned off their overhead pot lights. He looked ahead and pictured amber lights in a foggy night.

She stood up. "I'm going to pee."

He stood up, and his silver-haired neighbour wobbled to her feet, muttering something unintelligible, as if resentful. As they hesitated in the aisle, he watched Aviva amble toward the lavatory, her legs bowed like a horse rider's. He wished she'd soon return. They'd sit in her corner and share a claustrophobic intimacy of arms and knees.

The old woman turned to him. "D'you know when we'll land in Tel Aviv? We left late. Not that I'm scared of flying, but I'd rather have my feet on firm ground."

He wondered about her accent. Upper New York State? The Midwest? He'd better not ask lest she bombard him with details. What a drag! Were it not for her, he'd raise the partition between him and Aviva. They'd have room to stretch out on three seats. He'd have her to himself, bask in her undivided attention.

He walked down the other end of the aisle to the lavatories and waited for his turn. Soon he stepped into a cubicle smelling of cheap eau de cologne and lemony floor cleaner. Fluorescent lights went on. He fantasized the one-man washroom being spacious enough to accommodate both Aviva and him. Why not crawl out of his cave, live it up with the big-tits, thick-thighed girl with whom he had been rubbing arms and knees? How unfortunate they wouldn't be able to stand up face to face and make love! He sighed. Fooling around in this closet was out of the question. He peed, flushed, and squeezed himself back out into the aisle.

It disappointed him that Aviva wasn't in her seat. The old woman was nowhere in sight. She must have gone to the lavatories down the other side.

When Aviva came back and slid her legs between two rows of seats, he avoided ogling her butt and thighs. What would the next instalment of their in-flight romance be?

She sat down by the window. He perched next to her. Unfortunately, the old woman came back. She canted her seat as far as it went, and closed her eyes. He wished she'd fall asleep soon.

"Did you pee?" Aviva asked.

He nodded.

He pushed a button in the partition between them, then raised it. An attendant soon approached and handed them teal wool blankets. They covered themselves. He took a deep breath, held it for a moment, then tickled her hand. She puckered her lips as if about to say something. He tickled her again. This time she tickled his wrist and forearm very lightly. He groped for her hand and held it. Her fingers felt limp. What a constricting love nest! He visualized himself crawling inside a knee-high cave.

Under the blankets he fooled around with her juicy inner thighs. Her hand stopped him. "What do you want, Neil?"

"You."

"I think you just want to play with me."

He felt her breast but in the process banged his elbow on the seat ahead. A dull pain. She winced and hit her head on the plane's wall. "Ah!" She exclaimed.

His elbow stood in the way when he tried to slide his hand under her T-shirt. She grabbed his arm and set his hand on his lap.

He turned his head to assess whether his neighbour had heard him breathe in desperation. In indignation the old woman might holler, "Quit molesting the girl, you jerk!" An attendant would order him to sit in a crewmember's seat. Rows of passengers would stand up to watch who were the perverts having sex under wraps.

He wondered what to do next. He hesitated for a while, then overcame his inhibitions by rapidly unzipping his fly. "I'm dying to get a hand job."

"Forget about it! I enjoy it only in a relationship. Otherwise it's just a game."

He pushed his blanket away, slid down the partition between them, and turned on his pot light.

She laughed. "Are you going to read now?"

He nodded.

"My, my, you look so hurt! But let's cut out the kiddie stuff, Neil! Why don't we sleep together in my dad's house? I still have my old bedroom there."

He enjoyed his skin breaking out in goosebumps. But soon he pictured her father, a man not ten years older than himself. What would he think about his daughter picking up a middle-aged man on her flight home, then sleeping with him under her father's roof? And when the guest had left, the host would catch sight of disgusting, floury stains on the sheets. He'd grimace. Even if a world away, the guest would condemn himself for defiling Aviva. Yes, he knew she'd been around, but nevertheless he'd feel guilty and embarrassed. "What would your father and stepmother think?" He asked.

"I don't care. I don't owe them any apologies. Let the witch think whatever she wants. She's not my mother."

"Two nights with you would be terrific. Unfortunately, I have to leave my wife a phone number at the hotel. She'd be terribly hurt if she got a private number." He reached for her cheek. "I'm sorry, Aviva."

"Why can't you call your wife late at night? It'll be early morning in Toronto."

He felt he was blushing. "It was lovely to touch you. Sleeping together in your father's home is another matter."

"Why don't we spend two nights in a hotel?"

What? Touring Tel Aviv with a chubby girl on his arm? What would his colleagues think? "I can't stay with you. Too many obstacles."

"Have you forgotten your toothbrush at home? What's wrong with two no-strings-attached nights? I thought I turned you on."

"Sorry, but I'll remain faithful to my wife."

"I won't beg you, Neil. You'll go back home as pristine as tundra," she chortled. "Have you been in this predicament before?"

He resented "predicament." He stared at the magazine rack and his knees. Two nights with such a lippy chick? He knew he was uptight, but it bugged him all the same that she was poking fun at him. Why not just tell her that she was not his type?

She had covered her mouth with her hand as if about to cry.

"I'm sorry," he said. "I like you. When you come to visit friends in Toronto, we'll go out for dinner. Just friends."

She removed her hand from her mouth and waved as if he were a whiney mosquito. "Fooling around was okay, right? I was just an appetizer, eh? Not good enough for an affair?"

His throat thickened. He panicked at the thought of not soothing her. What if she hollered, started a scandal? "I lost my head. Got carried away."

She mumbled, "Now I want to sleep."

He switched on the pot light overhead. He tried to read, but the sentences whirled and wandered. He puzzled over what the characters were saying to one another. He closed his eyes. The girl had gone out of her way, offered herself. He'd chickened out.

He turned off the light, took off his shoes, massaged his swollen feet, tried to fall asleep. In a moment he realized he, too, was upset. His world, he felt, was as puny as an ant's, his life a tidy catalogue of boring, lukewarm events. He knew she'd have fanned fresh air into his stale cubicle.

Something similar had happened before, he thought. In Pre-Med he and Sally had many common interests. Sex was fabulous. He'd surprised himself when he'd invited a *shikseh* for a Sunday brunch at his parents'. He'd reassured them she was just a friend.

But she insisted they move in together. "No, Neil, I'm not pregnant. I just want to know where we're at."

"I need space, Sally. I'm not ready for a commitment."

She'd dumped him.

In a matter of weeks he'd begged her to reconsider. He'd proposed.

"I want to think it over, Neil. Trust is like a match. After it's gone out, it's hard to rekindle it. I suspect you changed your mind because I pressured you."

"But you come first, Sally. I'll never ask you to convert. Our children will go to public schools."

She'd taken him back.

He'd told his parents he'd marry her. "No! She isn't pregnant."

Next Friday Mom had lit two candles and blessed them. A black scarf had concealed her hair and forehead. Blood-shot, swollen eyes. She must have cried for days, as if already mourning him. Dad had worn a black skullcap over a milk-white face. As if fighting back tears he'd poured the wine and blessed it. He'd broken hunks off one of two lustrous, braided loaves of bread, had dipped them in salt, passed them around, and blessed them in a dying voice. Both of them had worn what-have-we-done-to-deserve-this masks.

For a week he hadn't slept a wink. For a month he hadn't been able to concentrate on his studies. He'd lost ten pounds. He'd gathered moxie, and over lunch told Sally, "I can't abandon my parents. It'll kill them." He'd stared at the chequered tablecloth. "I love you, Sally, but the Jewish way of life flows in my veins. I can't lie."

Days later she'd mailed him a Jewish Bible translated according to the traditional Hebrew text. More guilt.

From then on he'd dated only Jewish girls. He'd staved off self-criticisms but every morning the mirror had reflected a hunk of mediocrity. After a year, the dust had settled. Sally's elongated face, deep navel, and thin thighs had receded into the background. He'd forgiven himself.

All at once the ceiling lights in the plane exploded. He blinked and rubbed his eyes with numb palms. He heard the motors roaring.

Aviva was sitting back, eyes closed. Was she avoiding the light or still sleeping?

Breakfast was served. They ate in silence. He asked her what was the matter.

"I'm tired. I wish I'd slept the whole night."

He felt castrated now that she was denying that something meaningful had passed between them. He took a deep breath. Two girls had despised him. Would Aviva discard him like a soiled Kleenex?

Why the hell was he so calculating? Why was his life as safe as Canada Savings Bonds? Why not get his hands dirty or lose control once in a blue moon? Something pinched his heart. He was glad the flight would be over soon.

When the breakfast trays were cleared, the captain announced in English and French they'd land on time. It was drizzling in Tel Aviv. "Please fasten your seat belts."

He looked over her shoulder and saw white apartment buildings of all sizes with television antennas on top, trees, black streets, and cars of all colours.

The plane was inclining, losing altitude, searching the designated runway. Engines roared. Touchdown. It felt like the plane went over a bump. It taxied along the tarmac and came to a stop.

Aviva removed her backpack from the overhead luggage compartment. She walked down the aisle ahead of him. He thought of a crowd lining up for a blockbuster movie. It bothered him that she didn't look back even once.

They reached the tarmac. The daylight dazzled him. Fumes and hot air assaulted his nose. He blinked.

The drizzle had stopped. The sky was overcast and the breeze warm, like Toronto in mid-June.

In a squat terminal they stood in line to have their passports checked. Would there be hassles? After all, Israel was a Mediterranean country.

They headed toward a wide hall with revolving conveyor belts. In minutes they were disgorging suitcase after suitcase. He grabbed his green one. In a moment they'd say goodbye. Should he hug her?

He missed her already. He regretted that he'd not sleep with her. Like a snake he'd have shed a skin, have fun, no longer tethered to the pole of mediocrity.

She grabbed a beat-up brown suitcase. He strode towards her. He halted. "Aviva," he cried out.

She turned to him, studying him as if for the first time.

"I'd love to be with you tonight. And the next."

"Go fuck yourself, you spineless wimp!" She strode away.

His heart pounded. His breathing was shallow. He headed to the sliding doors. He waited for a cab, feeling stunned and empty, alone and lonely. He had taken advantage of her. Insulted her. She was right. He was a slime-ball in search of a hassle-free life. Already he regretted what he hadn't done.

Much of the next day he was busy reading his paper at the convention. Right after he finished answering the questions from the floor, he rushed to his room, heart pounding. Fortunately, he remembered Aviva's surname, Harari, and that her father lived in Tel Aviv.

The phone operator spoke good English. She counted twenty-six Hararis in the Tel Aviv area code. Though Neil begged her, she wouldn't dictate their phone numbers to him. He got hold of a telephone directory, grateful for the eight years he'd toiled to learn Hebrew.

Dialling in desperation, Neil connected with eight Hararis, both men and women who told him they were sorry, but they had no young relatives called Aviva. He left detailed messages to other subscribers with the same surname, explaining that he would be in Tel Aviv only two more days, and the matter was extremely urgent. In the evening and the whole next day he watched television in his room, panicking at the idea of missing a phone call if he went to the beach.

The people that returned his calls didn't know any Aviva. He stayed in his room, hoping that a miracle might happen and he'd get in touch with her. He got a few more calls, but the apologies irritated him. He had no clear idea of what he might tell Aviva, except to say he was terribly sorry. He'd beg her to give him a second chance. He didn't leave his room until it was time to take a cab to the airport, all the while hoping that he'd hear from her.

Once inside the plane, he sat by the window and felt lonely. Next to Neil sat an elderly couple who spoke Hebrew and paid no attention to him. The fantasy that he'd meet Aviva inside the plane dissipated. He missed her, and a wave of sadness descended upon him. In his mind he could hear her yelling that he was a spineless wimp. A rigid guy, he added, a conformist.

THE WINNING TICKET

AT LAST, MY TURN IN LINE ARRIVED. I handed over my ticket to the squat, bespectacled, East Indian woman at the vendor's counter, confident that this time it contained the set of winning numbers. Looking bored, she pinched the small printout with her forefinger and thumb and as indifferent to her surroundings as a butcher carving meat, brought it under the blood-red light of a small scanner.

Her face lit up. "Oh, my God!" Her voice rose well above her customary whisper. "You hit the jackpot!"

My heart raced. It was just the way I'd fantasized it hundreds of times.

Her husband rushed over. A much taller East Indian, he wore monster eyeglasses that shone less than his bald pate. "Oh, please," he sputtered, "let me take a picture of you holding the ticket — here, beside my wife, against the background of our kiosk."

"What? Oh sure, sure," I said, shaken at how the entire scene playing itself out was a colossal *deja vu* or, more exactly, the fulfilment of a recurring dream. Why not make the vendors happy too? Let them share in my joy, celebrate my victory.

The man rummaged under the counter and produced an enormous Polaroid camera. Smiling and giggling, his wife and I posed, holding between us the fulfilled dream of millions of Canadians. The flash went off. As the woman exclaimed to two passers-by — "It was our kiosk that sold him the grand prize!" — the camera buzzed. In a few moments, it ejected the photograph. In the already discoloured picture, an unphotogenic me was dazedly trying to smile, while the East Indian woman flashed her teeth and threw her head back as if she were the winner.

I was on my lunch break. Despite the urge to rush downtown and at once take possession of my prize, I decided to pass by my office and tell George Dunbar, my lanky, taciturn manager, that I wasn't feeling well and was heading home. Why antagonize the boss before I knew exactly how much I had won? You never knew how long you might have to depend on your superiors. Better behave as if you still respected them, even though your bank account had swollen immensely.

For weeks the newspapers had carried stories about the accumulating Super 7 Lottery, stoking people's dreams of kingly retirement in Florida, Provence, or both. I knew that week's prize stood at thirty-five million dollars, the largest ever in Canada, but was not at all sure, at that point, what my share of the treasure would be. Perhaps I had won only a couple of million. That was a limited amount and cautious me reasoned that it wasn't the right time to tell George Dunbar to stuff my joyless job. "You see, George," I'd announce only if I won a much greater sum, "my trips around the globe preclude me from coming to work."

I wrote my bank password on the blessed piece of paper, folded it, and buried it deep in my pocket. A wave of paranoia washed over me. What if one of the passers-by had witnessed the commotion by the kiosk? What if someone was following me, intent on knocking me down and stealing my ticket to boundless comfort? I froze, looked around, and saw a tall man leaning against a column. His chocolate-coloured hands held a spread-out *Toronto Star*, which concealed his face and chest. He wore scruffy jeans and more-grey-than-white running shoes. Panicking, I felt sure he was hiding behind the newspaper. As soon as I let down my guard he would grab me, knock me unconscious, and steal my ticket.

Brushing people aside, I ran up the stairs leading to the entrance of the mall. At the top, I stopped, caught my breath, and despite my pounding heart, slowly, ever so slowly, peered in all directions. The dark-skinned man with the newspaper was nowhere. Nobody seemed to be tailing me. The safest thing to do, I told myself, was to hop into a cab and tell the driver to take me to the lottery office on Bloor Street.

Outdoors, the grey, overcast sky hung low over my head, and the gloom intensified my fear of being robbed. I crossed the street and approached a line of taxis parked by the curb. I opened the door of the first cab, settled into the back seat, and gave the driver my destination. It reassured me that he didn't react at all when he heard the address. Could I be so lucky that he didn't grasp that his greatest dream was burning a hole in my pocket?

As the driver navigated our way downtown, it occurred to me that I would have felt much safer if I'd told my wife about the prize. Even better, I should have asked the lawyer who had helped us buy our townhouse to meet me at the lottery office when I dealt with the authorities. I am, basically, a shy man who often doesn't know whether to keep my hands inside or outside my pockets. The prospect of collecting the prize and dealing with the media ambushing the winners scared the hell out of me.

I paid the cab driver. No, he didn't seem aware of my plans to collect a fortune. I wended my way to the lottery office and halted at a long counter. "May I help you," asked a pale, blond woman with long, maroon nails.

I wished I had come with my lawyer, since anxious me couldn't decide whether or not to hand over my ticket. What if she claimed mine wasn't a winner? What would I do if she vanished? Call the police? I had no evidence to support my claims for millions except for a slip of paper with the magic configuration of numbers.

Hand trembling, I lent her the decisive piece of paper, which she placed under a scanner. She covered her mouth with her palm, then let out a scream. "Congratulations! You're the only winner! Please step inside. The manager will issue you a cheque."

The details of what happened next are still a blur because of my excitement. I recall a bald, all-smiles, moustachioed man in a blue suit and red tie handing me an oversized cheque with my name and, black on white, the sum of thirty-five million and no/100 dollars. Delirious, I began to hum the Ode to Joy. I did, after all, get hold of the money without the help of either my lawyer or my wife.

I also remember a bevy of reporters surrounding me with tape recorders and cameras. They fired questions which in my frenzy of being super rich, I could answer only in monosyllables. As they pressured me for details, something to excite their audiences, I uttered words that later on, when I saw myself on television, surprised me a great deal. "Keep up the fantasy of hitting the big prize," I said. "Nurture the dream, work on it, imagine yourself raking in the loot. Don't feel discouraged if you're not rewarded right away. Play the lottery, and let your fantasies rule you. Don't try to control them."

Despite my excitement and confusion, it occurred to me while being interviewed that I would never again have to report to George Dunbar. Instead of tedious programming at my workstation, I would spend my days travelling the six continents, to include Antarctica. Between cruises I'd meet with investment advisors for three-Martini lunches, or sit down with representatives of charities to determine wise, tax-deductible donations.

For a whole week Elaine, my wife, my two boys, and my whole family celebrated my good luck. We emptied bottles of champagne as if they were soda pop. Next, we pondered where to live. We considered buying a big house downtown, but these plans fell through when a gust of paranoia overcame me. I remembered how two newspapers had published long stories about me, including my picture, full name, and home address. Elaine and I had appeared on local and national television and had, to my chagrin, become household names. I became so fearful of my family being kidnapped for ransom that I hired two bodyguards to escort the boys to school. Like shadows, the bodyguards accompanied us wherever we went. They slept in one of the bedrooms in our small townhouse, while the boys bunked in another.

"It's terrible," Elaine constantly complained, "to have strangers with us day and night. I want us to have a home, not a fortress with guards. Snap out of your worries, Mark! Stop going to psychiatrists and popping pills! You have to get back to what you were before you won the big prize."

After months of complaining, Elaine finally had her way: I fired the bodyguards and bought us a five-washroom penthouse equipped with the latest surveillance gadgetry. Every room in the condo had video cameras and alarm equipment, all well-concealed. Despite the pills and the precautions, I tossed and writhed in bed, listening to every real and imagined noise. The lack of sleep tortured me, and I imagined masked gangsters kidnapping my entire family at gunpoint. In the next frame of this scenario, I gave in to their demands for cash and didn't call the police. When you are very rich, you don't beg for help. You pay through the nose and feel smug about it.

This also may sound unbelievable: I had money problems with my family. After I cashed in the bonanza, Elaine got into the habit of buying new clothes and accessories every week. "We can well afford it," she said. "Why not enjoy our money? Would it make you happy if we kept it in the bank, untouched?"

"Of course not," I said. "But we must keep things in perspective. We can't just spend and spend, as if there's no tomorrow. It's a moral issue."

"Next I'll hear about the millions starving in Ethiopia."

After much wrangling, we compromised: Elaine agreed to a budget of ten thousand dollars a month for personal expenses. This didn't satisfy me since I maintained that one ought to be prudent even if one had plenty of cash. Elaine claimed that it was my rigidity talking. I had not, she said, let go of the old days of limited spending and maximum savings.

I tried my philosophy on my kids, and had nothing but failures to report. Jim, my oldest, got so incensed at the idea of being given an allowance of one hundred dollars a week that he got a job flipping hamburgers. He worked after school until ten at night and paid for all his own expenses. His schoolwork suffered, and he resisted my repeated urging to work less, study more, and accept my allowance. "I want to be my own man," he insisted. "I can do without your godamn money." Martin, his younger brother, wanted to follow in Jim's footsteps. He argued he couldn't wait until he was sixteen and got a job at McDonald's. He too wanted to pay his own way.

Since redeeming the winning ticket two years ago, I had incurred a remarkable number of losses. First to go were my friends at work. The day I came to say goodbye to them and to George Dunbar, I was initially greeted with loud exclamations of merriment and congratulatory comments like, "Please don't forget us now that you live a life of leisure and have nothing to worry about."

No worries, eh? Little did they know what I went through every night.

Within weeks it turned out that my friends at work were trying to forget about me. Having plenty of time on my hands, I invited them for lunches and after-hours drinks. My calls went unanswered. It didn't take long for Elaine to come up with an intriguing explanation. "They are so envious that they don't want to meet you at all. They'd rather stew in their own bile than see you in a triumphant mood."

"*What* triumphant mood? I hardly sleep at night!"

"But you exude prosperity. Your eyes tell the world that you belong to the Wealth and Leisure Club. Your buddies feel it, and they seethe with resentment."

"It can't be!" I said. "They are my friends! We go back many years. Of course, some of them conceded that they envied my luck. They even asked for tips on winning the lottery."

"Don't be so naïve! Your so-called friends are angry! You climbed a giant mountain and in the process left them behind, in the valley. Accept it, Mark, they don't want to deal with the feelings you evoke in them."

It was hard to admit that she was right. However, soon I realized that, except for Fred, my old friends from high school and university had also stopped calling me. It was time I acknowledged their blend of envy and anger, rather than wallow in superficial astonishment. As for Fred, he and I went out for dinner a few days ago. As we sipped our cappuccinos, he looked embarrassed but, anyhow, hit on me for a hundred thousand bucks. "A loan," he said. " I'll use my townhouse as a collateral."

"Fred," I said, "we've been friends since grade five. That's a long time, man. Still, I don't want money to come between us. Why don't you get a loan from your bank?"

He smiled embarrassedly and asked the waiter for our cheques. When I told Elaine the incident she said I shouldn't be surprised if I don't hear from Fred again. "He wanted an interest-free loan. You refused to play his game, and he feels resentful." She heaved a sigh. "Things have changed dramatically, Mark. Now that we're very rich, I also feel that my old friends are avoiding me. As I said before, I bet they feel envious or angry — probably both."

"What are we going to do for a social life?" I asked, anticipating loneliness and isolation after Fred too didn't answer my calls.

"We'll hang out with our kind of people: wealthy folks, globetrotters, philanthropists, people of leisure."

Easier said than done. Despite the many gala dinners and balls promoting the cause of every imaginable organ or disease, I made no new friends. Several times a week I went out wearing my tuxedo. Still, I remained miserably on the sidelines, not really enjoying myself. I missed my old friends, and I envied Elaine, who had managed to connect with a number of women. When my mood was down, I called myself a wealthy nebbish.

Except for charities asking for donations at dinnertime, nobody called me. I no longer picked up the phone, but instead, let the answering machine take messages. Though I was supposed to enjoy my boundless leisure, the fact was that daily I racked my brain to figure out how to spend my time enjoyably. I didn't miss my boss or my old job, but when I sat down to dinner, I missed the old feelings of competence and accomplishment that came after a day's work at the office.

Nowadays, twice a week, when I'm not travelling or stuffing envelopes as a volunteer in some obscure community agency, I meet my stockbrokers in their offices. They've offered to make house calls, but I'd rather kill time travelling back and forth. The brokers talk and talk about the fate of my stocks and rattle off reasons why I'm still not making twenty percent a year on my investments. They chatter incessantly about Tom, Dick, and Harry, the managers of mutual funds who look after my easily earned money. As they babble on and on, my mind wanders, and I fidget in my chair because I feel no affinity to people I'll never meet in person. Still, it troubles me when sooner or later the brokers suggest that I make changes in my portfolio — changes that bring them hefty commissions. I feel so guilty about having made a fortune without working for it that I don't stand up to the chatterboxes.

Quite often I think about the man who was reading the newspaper in the mall the day I found out that I'd hit the jackpot. What if he had robbed me? How would my life have turned out without my millions? I'm sure I would have grieved the loss of my fortune for a long time. I would have had no choice but to toil and moil at the office and put up with George Dunbar nagging and chiding me. The whole year long I would have pined for my hard-earned three-week vacation with my in-laws in Mississauga. But each day I'd look in the mirror and see a hassled man who, nevertheless, had tried his best to live in dignity.

FOR MONTHS I HAD BEEN OGLING the tall, pretty young woman from afar. An eight, on a scale from one to ten. Perhaps even a nine.

My heart beat faster whenever I saw her standing at the entrance to the office building where I had my law practice. Blood rushed to my face every time I saw her perched on a chair at the smoky snack bar on the ground floor. As I passed by, I tried my best to beam a smile. Some of the time she noticed me and smiled back. I felt like singing.

I'd first noticed her in the fall. Now, in springtime, almost daily she wore short leather jackets over miniskirts and matching panty hose. The sight of her shapely thighs filled me with sharp pleasure.

One Friday afternoon I stepped into the elevator alone. It stopped on the second floor. Who but my darling entered, wearing a green dress to her knees. I looked her in the face. She smiled. Ivory-white teeth gleamed behind maroon lipstick. Cosmetic dentistry. Must have cost an arm and a leg.

"Going home?" I asked.

She nodded.

The elevator came to a stop. In slow motion the doors slid open. I let her out first and escorted her to the building's entrance. Once on the street, she stopped and turned to me. "Have a good weekend."

"You too. By the way, I'm Marvin Cohen."

"I'm Gail."

I put my hand forward and shook hers. I raised her limp fingers and kissed her hand. Looking up, I gazed into her eyes. Her left eye turned inward, a bit cockeyed. I consoled myself that the defect only added to her charm, rendered her accessible, human.

It was only months later, when the dust of this and other events settled, that I delved into the meaning of my out-of-character conduct. Was my impulsive kiss a reflection of a life crisis? Were repressed passions bobbing to the surface? Did I plant a kiss to show off what I'd absorbed from black-and-white movies?

She covered her mouth with her hand and laughed. Was I the first man to kiss her hand in public? Was she basking in the power of her charms? Was she delighted to witness one more instance of devouring desire? As of today, I've concocted only such flimsy hypotheses about her motives. Passions, I've learned, exaggerate the significance of cues, even of mere signs of civility.

She said goodbye, then swung about. Her thin ankles turned me on, as I correlated them with firm breasts. My ears were on fire. I'd stood only a foot away from my icon, even touched her! And more than once she'd flashed a smile. We'd exchanged a few words. How melodious was her voice! I had, no doubt, fallen madly in love.

The trees in bud cast a transparent lime-green veil against the blue sky. By the stone wall of a nearby building red tulips struggled to emerge from their leafy straightjackets. The chilly air probably crimsoned my cheeks. Despite the car fumes assaulting my nose, I felt invigorated, optimistic, inspired. The girl's compliance and attention on the sidewalk had thickened my blood, thinned my saliva. I told myself I'd have a wonderful weekend.

I barely slept that night. Well after midnight I left my bed. Liz, my wife, is a light sleeper, and I didn't want to wake her. She would have urged me to stay in our bed. In the darkness I traipsed to our spare bedroom and stretched under the bed cover. I turned on the reading light. I found it impossible to read or lie still. My excitement reminded me of boys and girls in the days before television who turned feverish the night before a circus came to town.

That weekend, time crept more slowly than a crab. I raked manure over our greening lawn and trimmed leafless rose bushes. I hummed Shostakovich's Ninth. Liz, a researcher in pediatric neuro-psychology, commented, "You're working in the back yard more enthusiastically than ever. Has something happened?"

"Spring is in the air," I answered.

It surprised me that she'd commented on my exuberant mood. In those days we lived like roommates, two streetcars passing by each other at predictable times. We made few demands on each other. In the evenings she wrote or read papers in her study, while I prepared for court cases in mine. Every hour she hit the fridge for a scoop of ice-cream, and had gained much weight. I went to bed by midnight, she retired two hours later. Every morning I woke up early, and she slept till nine o'clock. Whenever I approached her for sex, she kept me waiting until she finished reading an article. After years of simmering anger, sex happened only on birthdays, our anniversary, and New Year's Eve.

On Monday I took my coffee break at ten-thirty. Gail wasn't in the snack bar. I had a second cup, all the while eyeing the entrance. She arrived by eleven and sat in the smoking section. She sipped her coffee slowly and smoked, rounding her graceful lips. Her mouth barely touched the cigarette.

I slid my necktie left and right and stood up. I strode to her table. Luckily, a chair beside hers was available.

"How was your weekend?" I smiled despite my fears of being ignored. I'd have felt miserably rejected.

She blew smoke aside. "Lots of fun. And yours?"

Her hair was shinier than on Friday, her lips pink. She wore no rouge or mascara, and her cheeks glowed white. "I thought about you, was dying to talk to you. How old are you, Gail?"

"Twenty-one."

"I'll be sixty-two in the fall."

She stood up. "Sorry. I have to be back at the office."

"When is your next coffee break?"

"About three."

I tailed her as she walked to the door. My throat and lungs hurt from the snack bar's smoke. I'm allergic to it and was about to cough. Once again I fell in love with her pretty legs majestically sculpting her green tights. Her narrow hips suggested it'd be hard on her to give birth to our first child.

Fortunately, the elevator we boarded was empty. I raised her fingers to my lips. "Your hands are absolutely lovely," I said.

"Thank you," she replied. "You remind me of a father figure charming his secretary. An office romance." She flashed a pretty smile at me.

I kissed her hand and wrist. She offered no resistance when I rubbed my lips on the marble-smooth, hairless skin of her forearm. I eyed her. She looked amused. I wondered if she harboured even a fraction of my passion.

Even before two-thirty I waited for her in the smoking section of the snack bar. The disgusting smoke irritated my nostrils.

As she sat across the table I asked, "What do you do for a living, Gail?"

"These days I'm a filing clerk." She looked aside, as if collecting her thoughts. "It's okay. It pays the rent. How about you?"

"I'm a lawyer. I write a lot of letters. Really boring stuff. Do you have a boyfriend?"

"Not these days."

I bent forward and stared her in the eye to look self-confident. "How about dinner some time next week?"

"We'll see."

The matter-of-factness in her voice stung me. I drew back. Was my darling a spoiled young girl?

My hopes and passions re-awakened when, at my request, she gave me her phone number at work.

I tossed and twisted in bed that night. I fantasized about Gail's bedroom, the lamp by her bedside table casting a soft, mellow light. Her naked body glowed white. She spread her legs. I lay between her thighs, a timid teenager learning the intricacies of lovemaking. At first she thrusted to a slow beat, and despite my efforts I barely kept in synch. Our sweat and breath mingled. I felt overwhelmed by her moaning, her mounting desperation.

Next day we had coffee only in the afternoon. I told her I had once written a memoir, *Remembrances of An Only Child*. Published in my high-school yearbook, it was an account of excruciating loneliness and painful embarrassment at being asked whether I missed having a brother or a sister. Most days my father, an accountant, came home at nine-thirty, when I often was already asleep. He had dinner at a quarter to ten and sex at ten fifteen. Then he watched TV and drank till one. My mother, a volunteer for Hadassah, came home at five. During dinner she bored me silly with long-winded tales about the lives of her friends. Right after dessert she parked by the phone and gabbed even after I went to bed.

"I've written countless volumes of legal papers," I said. "My memoir was my only expression of real feelings."

"Was it well received?"

"My English teacher encouraged me to submit it for publication in a magazine for young writers. I regret I didn't. But at the time I was too ashamed to broadcast to the world how I felt. How about lunch tomorrow?"

"People will talk."

That comment irked me. I was putting out all I had, and she was barely reciprocating!

On Wednesday I had a court appearance and didn't see my *belle*. Wednesday nights Liz and I babysit Jennifer, our son's two-year-old daughter. As usual, we helped her spoon down her dinner. Shortly after, Liz and I took her to the bathtub. There, she frolicked with floating plastic boats and bubbly foam.

I looked at Jennifer's naked little body. In a flash her flat chest and puny genitals disappeared, and I hallucinated Gail's pubic hair. She lolled in the tub, skimming the frothy water. Her pear-shaped wet breasts glistened. Her firm auburn nipples jutted above the water level. I massaged her back and breasts, then fingered her tight, moist vagina. My cock was so hard that it hurt.

"Hand over the towel, Marvin." Liz startled me back into reality. "You seem so distracted, so self-absorbed! For days you haven't spoken to me. At nights you toss in bed. What's going on?"

I shrugged. "Nothing."

"Whatever is brewing, it's making me angrier by the day. I don't know how much longer I can put up with your crap."

It took me a long time to fall asleep that night. Masturbation was out of the question with Liz next to me, highlighting articles on neurology and neuropsychology. In the last few years, the post-mortems of mice's brains had become her passion.

Gail had stormed into my life. All day I daydreamed about her. To quench my thirst, it would have been enough to caress her long legs. I'd feel younger, animated, vigorous, creative, a kid writing his memoirs.

On Thursday morning, at eight-thirty sharp, I called her. No answer. At nine on the dot her phone rang and rang. My impatience mounted. I felt a whiff of anger and left a message on her answering machine. "Gail, please call."

Every few minutes I searched for messages. Only hours later we talked. She agreed to have coffee downstairs.

The smoky snack bar didn't bother me much as I waited for her. But my heart palpitated, and my palms were cold and moist. She entered the snack bar and poured herself a cup of coffee. Smiling, she strode toward my table. It occured to me that she was a crowd pleaser who would smile at anyone under the sun. I probably was no more than a recent acquaintance, an ageing gentleman who spied on her and became ecstatic whenever he kissed her hand. Was I a toy, or a curio, in her eyes? Perhaps a dreamer, an eccentric, an old fool?

"Have you heard of *Death In Venice?*" I asked as soon as she sat down and lit a cigarette.

"Venice? That's Italy, right? I'd love to learn Spanish and work in Mexico."

"They made a movie out of it. It's the story of a middle-aged writer, a man, who falls madly in love with a beautiful boy. He never says a word to him, just ogles him and his family from a distance. At one point he gets a barber to make him up so that he'll look young and appealing."

She turned her head and blew out smoke. "How old is this story?"

"Around World War One. The long and the short of it is that the writer dies of a heart attack when the boy leaves Venice."

"You've written a memoir and tons of letters. Afraid you'll die of love, eh?"

"I hope not. How about dinner tonight?"

"I've a date."

Her words stung me. I thought she belonged to me. One day, I'd dreamt, she'd accept my invitations, allow me to delve my tongue deep into her mouth, feel her breasts, fondle her inner thighs. Away from the dinky snack bar I'd bask in her beauty. I'd no longer share her with clerks and receptionists.

She had inspired me. I'd rewrite my memoirs and update them. I'd dedicate the book to her. It would be published, reviewed, recognized. Friends and colleagues would congratulate me. I'd feel accomplished. "Who's he?" I finally asked, feeling hurt and jealous.

"Friend of a friend. I just met him at a party. He's thirty-nine. I like older guys."

"What are my chances?"

She smiled. "How old are your children?"

"Thirty-two and thirty. A boy and a girl."

She stubbed her cigarette in the ashtray. "I have to go."

Next day I called her first thing in the morning. I got her office's receptionist. Gail would be back after lunch.

I called at twelve-thirty. She wasn't at her desk. I left a message. She called me after two.

"How about a coffee break in my office?" My voice quivered. My secretary will brew a fresh pot."

"But what about smoking? We can't open the windows in this building."

"Don't worry. The air conditioning will suck in the smoke."

"I can't promise. Have a lot of work to do."

"Please, Gail, please. Suite 507. I'll wait in the hallway." I waited over an hour.

Once she arrived I showed her the way to my study. First we went past Jane, my platinum-haired receptionist, who was attentively filing her nails. Shirley, my middle-aged secretary was transcribing a letter. She took off her earphone as we passed by. Her wide eyes expressed amazement at the well-dressed young woman ahead of me. In those days I saw too many bedraggled victims of car accidents who bored me stiff with their tall tales about rapacious insurance companies and icy-hearted doctors.

"Sit down," I said. "We'll have coffee in a moment."

She perched on the edge of a love seat. She looked around, nodding lightly, seemingly impressed by my spacious, professionally decorated study. She leaned forward and lit a cigarette. I sat across from her on a wing chair, a coffee table between us. I handed her an ashtray I'd brought from home and bent forward. Her ivory face glowed as if illuminated from within. Through her chive-green blouse her breasts were sculpted pomegranates. She had crossed her thighs. Her knees resembled smooth half spheres. I wished she'd lie down on the love seat. I'd perch on my knees and lick and fondle her from forehead to toes.

I stood up. "I want to show you something." I strode to my desk and from a drawer pulled out a yellowing reprint. "My memoir." I handed it to her.

She glanced at it. "Is that it?"

"I'll update it, write about my university years, bring to life the colourful characters I've met in my career. I'll devote a chapter to you."

"How about your wife?"

"She's okay. We had fun when we were young. She spent five years at home with the kids, then resumed her career. She's a researcher."

Shirley brought in the coffee and the cups. She lingered in the room as if to verify she wasn't dreaming about me entertaining a pretty girl at work.

Soon Gail stood up. "I have to go."

I put forth my hand and held the tip of her fingers. I kissed her nails and knuckles. In a moment she drew back and strode to the office door. I followed her. When I tried to touch her hand in the hallway she asked me not to kiss her in public.

"Are you embarrassed?" I asked.

"I like you, but I don't want people to get the wrong idea."

"May I walk you to your office?"

"No. I'll call you one of these days."

"I can't wait that long."

"Please, Marvin. You're going way too fast. Let's just be friends, eh?"

She turned about and strode toward the elevator. Slowly I walked over to my study and looked out the window. The sky was dark gray, the sidewalk wet. Under black umbrellas pedestrians hurried. A screeching streetcar made a right turn into St. Clair Avenue East. I felt devastated.

Who was I? What was I? Until now I'd led a very conventional life. A good student, a good lawyer, a good enough father and husband. No affairs, no drugs, very little booze. One trip abroad every year. A small circle of friends. Half a dozen dinner parties a year. A life as predictable as a cuckoo clock.

Gail had hit me in the gut, and my innards were on fire. No matter how hard I tried, things would never be the same again. It dawned on me that now, by the window, I was undergoing an irrevocable change.

I craved blue skies, a warm sun, inspiration.

I turned about and strode to the reception area. "Shirley," I instructed, "I'll be away from the office for a while. Please file all messages and refer new cases to Stan Greenberg, my old partner."

"Where are you going, Marvin?" She asked.

"Europe."

Once at home I announced to Liz that I was taking time off to write my memoirs in Venice.

She smirked. "Is this a quest for your after-sixty true self?"

I didn't answer.

"I won't be waiting for you, Marvin. Once you leave, that's it. I'll start divorce proceedings right away."

Next day I took a plane to Rome, then travelled to Venice by train. The following morning, still numb from jet lag, I rented a small apartment in a yellow boarding house fronting on a malodorous canal.

Shortly after unpacking I began to write. Paragraphs and pages flowed, as smooth and gentle as the skin of a sleepy lake. In a few days I had on my desk a good draft of my first year at university.

One late afternoon, after a long day of writing, I went for a stroll. The sun was still shining on the streets, the canals, and the orange and pink walls of nearby houses. As I ambled leisurely, I crossed a bridge that reminded me of a scene from the movie *Death in Venice*. In that scene, as an epidemic raged in the city, the infatuated middle-aged writer came across much lime on the ground. The stark white of the powdery disinfectant clashed with the blackening water of the canals. I smiled. Though I too was in love, perhaps even infatuated, I didn't have the end of life on my mind. Thomas Mann's connections between sexuality and death struck me as poetic, but a bit overwrought. At that time, my creativity was at its peak. I craved life and accomplishments, and any thoughts about death would have felt alien to me.

Next morning I called Gail. I got her answering machine. Two hours later I called again, only to hear her recorded message. It devastated me to think it might take me many days before I'd have a chance to get hold of her.

At long last we connected. "I'm in Venice," I said.

"What are you doing there?"

"Writing my memoirs."

"And what about your practice?"

I felt hurt. She sounded so pragmatic, so cool. Didn't she realize what she'd meant to me, how she'd changed my life? "I'll see you back in Toronto."

I'd lost her. The magic had evaporated. My eyes were moist. I hadn't cried since my mother's funeral. It was only days later, when I felt less raw and vulnerable that I commented to myself that a *shikseh* had impassioned an ageing Jew, then dropped him.

Nine months later I was back in Toronto, my book halfway done. Liz had sued for divorce. My children were angry with me for dumping their mother. The idea of resuming my work as a lawyer gave me goosebumps. I fantasized about freelancing for newspapers and magazines, writing about the arts, politics, life.

Early one morning I called Gail. "What about lunch?"

"My boyfriend would go nuts if he found out about you."

"Is he the guy you went out on a date?"

"Yes. Sorry, Marvin, but I can't see you again."

"Please, Gail!"

"I have to go, Marvin." She hung up.

It hurt terribly. I stood up, paced the room, and began to rearrange the books in the shelves, aware of my attempt to ward off pain. I feared that if I cried, I would cry until I turned into a puddle of tears on the floor.

I began to pace once again until a voice inside my head suggested that I talk to someone. It occurred to me to keep up with the Jones' and call a psychologist. As I looked up the Yellow Pages for a doctor close to my office, it dawned on me that it might take days or weeks to see a designated sound-board. I needed to talk right there and then.

I called Stan Greenberg, the old friend from high school who had covered my practice while I stayed in Venice. His secretary, Marsha, let me know that he was unavailable until the afternoon.

"Please, Marsha," I said imploringly, "tell Stan to call me as soon as he's free. It's urgent."

I sorted out all my books, then went for a brisk walk. Despite my efforts to forget Gail's rejection, my breathing was shallow and painful. I walked fast, but still felt like crying.

After lunch I sat by the phone and waited for Stan's call. After what seemed like an eternity and a half, we connected. "What's up, Marvin?" he asked in the comforting voice of a lawyer who had dealt with countless troubles in his long career.

My throat felt thick. "Stan, she . . . she left me!

"But Marvin," he said avuncularly, "she left you months ago, when you were in Venice."

"No, Stan," I hollered. "Not Liz! I'm talking about Gail, the woman I'm crazy about!"

"You mean the girl with the pretty legs?"

His summation felt like icy water on my boiling face. I squeezed the receiver. "Yes, Stan. But she meant *a hell of a lot* to me! Don't put her down! Don't invalidate my passion! Because of her I turned my life around!"

He fell silent, probably waiting to hear what else was troubling me.

"Stan," I whispered, "can we get together? After work? I need to talk!"

"Sure! How about at eight, at Brownes Bistro? It's a quiet place." He lowered his voice. "But Marvin, you sound . . . what's the word . . . distressed? How about seeing a therapist? I've heard good stuff about Jack Moldofsky, the red-haired psychologist who does legal work. He really helped my brother."

"I'll be all right, Stan. Don't worry! I did a lot of thinking while I waited for your call. Remember my *Remembrances of An Only Child*? Sounds lonely and self-pitying, eh? But it looks like I'm finally coming to terms with my loneliness! Gail and my life in Venice helped me. I'll tell you over dinner."

My Look-Alike

I FIRST FOUND OUT ABOUT HIM THIRTY YEARS AGO. As I sat on the floor of an Israeli army truck, my olive-green jacket barely warding off the winter chill, I was starting my four-day vacation, and all I wanted to think about was women and sex. As I dragged on a cigarette, a slim, moustachioed corporal clambered onto the truck. He sat down facing me and stretched out his legs. He studied my face, as if something unmistakable had caught his attention. "But how are you, Yuval?" he asked. "What's up?"

"But I'm Ron Lifschitz," I laughed.

"Strange," the corporal mumbled. "I could have sworn you were Yuval! You look like identical twins, two drops of water! The same brown eyes, thin nose, narrow forehead, and thick lips. He and I went to high school together, in Bat Yam. Last I heard he was still in the Air Force."

"Give your Yuval my regards. Tell him I look forward to meeting him in person."

Israel is a very small country, not much bigger than the Greater Toronto Area. From time to time, people who knew Yuval chanced upon me. They let me know that after two and a half years of military service he'd spent months cruising the bars in Europe. "Discovering which city had the sexiest women," a woman friend of his told me.

At that stage of my life, my look-alike posed no threat to my sense of self. He evoked only amusement, curiosity, and a vague feeling of being flattered by all the attention bestowed upon me. Were we really that close in appearance? Could I, with some coaching, play the role of Yuval, and vice-versa? Would I turn on the same women he did, or did our personalities differ so much that they wouldn't find me sexy?

A couple of years after I was discharged from the Army, my balding professor threw a party for his undergraduate students at his home. I approached a particularly good-looking student who stood alone by the window, a glass of orange juice in her hand. She was peering at the greening buds in the garden and other manifestations of early spring in Jerusalem.

"Hi! I'm Ron. I'm in Doctor Yariv's seminar on Kant."

"I'm Ednah. Haven't we met before?"

"This is my third year in philosophy. I haven't seen you around." I looked down. She wore a cream-coloured miniskirt and blacktight leggings.

"I put most of my efforts into psychology," she said. "I want to be a psychotherapist. It's so hard to find a job with a degree in philosophy."

"I want to teach it at the university." I didn't want to mention yet that I had worked hard to average above ninety so that my slot in graduate school would be guaranteed.

She canted her head and said with a lopsided smile. "*Now* I remember where I've seen you before! With Naama. Are you still dating her?"

"I'm not Casanova. I would have remembered your friend."

"I swear I saw you with her. You were in Haifa at the time, studying electrical engineering. You told me you're from Bat Yam."

I felt deflated. A whiff of anger took over. Him? Again? Here I was, getting to know this attractive woman and Yuval's long shadow was slithering like a snake between the two of us. What a nuisance! I felt as if Ednah and I had been sitting on a couch watching a movie when her roommate had butted in, and the evening's charm vanished. Damn him!

"It must be Yuval, my look-alike."

"Do you know him?"

"What for? Israel is such a small country. Sooner or later I meet people who tell me all about him." I leaned forward, eyebrows raised. "What is my Cain up to these days?"

"Last I heard he wanted to study abroad."

I felt so pissed off at Yuval The Interloper, his deeds and plans for the future, that I couldn't act calmly enough to get her last name and phone number. What a pity! What a lovely smile! Such pretty legs! And a student of psychology! Must be quite bright. Unfortunately, I gave her up because of an unknown character whose only relevance to my life was that people mistook us for one another. They thought I was playing parlour games or hiding my true self.

Four years later, I was standing in the Paris Metro, reading *Haaretz*, when my gut warned me that someone was observing me closely. I turned around. A man about my age, wearing eyeglasses and a well-trimmed moustache eyed me intently. I looked into his black eyes, but the impolite stranger didn't blink.

The train came to a stop. The doors slid open, passengers left, new faces showed up. The doors closed, and the train rolled smoothly on its rubber wheels. "It's you, Yuval, isn't it?" the man said in Hebrew. "I haven't seen you since our years in the Air Force."

Yuval? Again? Persecuting me in Paris? Were there no safe havens on Earth?

That was my third year of graduate studies at the Sorbonne. I had little course work left. My thesis advisor already had a couple of chapters of my doctoral dissertation on Hegel's conceptions of self and identity. I lived modestly on a scholarship from the French government. I didn't work on Sundays, and was on my way to pick up Aline, my fiancee. We had tickets for a pantomime.

"I've never met you in my life, mister. And my name is not Yuval."

"Amazing," he said, "absolutely amazing. You look just like Yuval, and you dress casually, just like him. I last saw Yuval in London." The man paused, as if weighing in his mind how much he could trust me. "After his MBA, he got a job with IBM. Something to do with computers. At the time, he was thinking of getting a job in New York, where he said the action really was."

"Tell your friend that his look-alike has a job offer from Tel Aviv University. If things work out, I'll settle down there."

"I'll let him know. The more I look at you, the more similar the two of you appear. Even your voice bears some similarity to his. Unbelievable!"

I thought of Yuval living in New York and me in Tel Aviv. The geographical separation suited me just fine. Somehow, it reminded me of the Pope, who in the 1490s drew a line on the map to divide the seas between Spanish and Portuguese explorers.

I would live in the east, my look-alike in the west. We'd never meet, thank God.

Maybe from time to time a stranger would stare at me, wonder aloud about our similarities, but I would never have to confront Yuval face to face. If a stranger mentioned him, the intrusion upon my sense of self and the disruption of feeling at home with my accomplishments would last only a few moments. At worst, they would bother me for a few days, but my life would resume where I'd left off. If Yuval gave me ants in the pants every few months, that was nothing to worry about. No reason to adjust my life to suit him. He was, essentially, a fluke, a cloud that periodically hid the sunshine, casting a brief shadow on the ground. He marked where and how my life stood, whenever total strangers made our paths cross.

If my identity was the stories I told myself about the ups and downs in my life, then my look-alike was a persistent disruption of my identity. That's what I told myself. But to my increasing annoyance, repeated encounters with people who knew him made me realize how much he threatened my uniqueness, even if oceans and continents separated us.

After our marriage, Aline and I moved to Tel Aviv. My position at the university was good, and we lived in a comfortable apartment. I had numerous old friends. But Aline dreaded the young soldiers with guns that she met everywhere. During the two years we stayed in Israel, people died or were injured in several bomb attacks. The rumours about an impending war never ceased. Aline lost sleep, anticipating the day our future children would be serving in the army.

With the help of my thesis advisor, I got a teaching position in Lawrence, Kansas, a small town smack in the middle of the Bible Belt. Faculty and students from outside the state grumbled that the air in the unending prairies was very clean, but sex, by local standards, was deemed dirty. The theatres never showed foreign films. On Sundays most people flocked to church; others drove to nearby man-made lakes to operate their motor boats.

Aline and I socialized a great deal on the weekends to fill up the many stretches of free time. One summer afternoon, as we attended a barbecue with other faculty and wives, I noticed a tall, balding man grinning from ear to ear every time he cast a glance at me. More intrigued than annoyed, I decided to approach the smiling machine.

"Hi." I put my hand forward. "I'm Ron Lifschitz."

"Really?" The man wiped his mouth with a napkin, then pumped my hand. "I'm Bob Clarke. I was sure you were Yuval Lev."

I froze, angry and impatient. Even in the boondocks, after all these years, I couldn't shake off the burden of my look-alike. Like a reoccurring nightmare, he intruded on my peace of mind and left residues that were impossible to ignore.

He continued. "I just spoke to Yuval a couple of weeks ago, in New York. At the time people were talking a lot about him." He sized me up and down, as if I were on sale. Any moment, I expected, he would reach out and open my mouth to check out my teeth.

He bit his lip. "I can't tell you how similar the two of you look. It's mind-boggling!" He leaned forward. "Only when I look at you up close, I realize that Yuval has a slightly receding hairline, and his belly juts out more than yours. When I first looked at you, I wondered why a financier like Yuval would choose to hide in, of all places, a small town in Kansas."

"He's a financier now?"

"He tried his hand at big business. He came up with an idea for a software company and got many people to invest in it. The business went bust, and lots of investors lost their shirts." He looked me in the eye, gauging the impact of his words. "He recently went into hiding to avoid the investors' wrath. There are a lot of gun-toting guys with some nasty questions looking for Yuval in New York. I've heard talk of lawsuits and fraud charges." He raised his eyebrows. "If I were you, I would stay right here in Kansas, until the worst blows over. You and Yuval are so similar! Somebody might mistake you for him and take his anger out on you."

"Thank you for the warning. I've no intention of going to the Big Apple in the foreseeable future."

"Good for you! Hard to tell what his creditors might do, if they got hold of you."

At first, that conversation made me angry and afraid. Yuval's conduct had become a threat to my integrity, and my sense of self was at stake. After a while, it infuriated me how our physical similarities had set limitations on my freedom of movement. Was I to avoid New York indefinitely? What if I wanted to attend a conference there?

I was totally innocent of any wrongdoing. Still, my life was no longer determined by my choices and decisions but, instead, it also depended on superficial physical traits. They might have led some angry people to think of me not as Ron, a peaceful prof, but a hated man they wanted dead.

After many years in Kansas, my publication list included two books and several chapters on Hegel, plus two dozen articles. Aline and I had two sons who had already celebrated their Bar-Mitzvahs. We both decided it was time to leave Lawrence for a big city in the north. I had been born and bred in Tel Aviv, and she had spent her youth in Paris. Together we both pined for the opera, the ballet, and foreign movies. We missed the excitement, the bright lights, and the fumes and perfumes of big-city living. The University of Toronto offered me the most attractive position, and I took it. We bought a modest duplex within walking distance of the campus.

Months after we were settled, my chairman invited us for dinner at his home. The hosts and guests stood in the living room, sipping sherries and Camparis. A stubby man with a trimmed white beard approached me. "I'm sorry, but I forgot your name."

"Have we met before?" I asked, puzzled.

"Yes, a few months ago, at the Rices. You have a Hebrew name which, I'm embarrassed to say, I find hard to remember."

"I'm Ron Lifchitz. The first name is Hebrew, the last one is common among Jews from East Europe."

"I'm Bruce Wilcox. If I remember it right, you're in the software business."

"No, I teach philosophy at U of T."

"That's amazing. The gentleman in the software business had a Hebrew name and looked just like you. The same height, the same complexion, a similar hairdo. He was a bit heavyset, though."

"I suppose his name was Yuval. I've heard about him for decades. What is he up to these days?" I regretted asking, but a deep-seated curiosity had overcome me.

Bruce laughed. "Funny that you ask. Right after he told me he was in the software business, he added that he has the biggest outdoor swimming pool in Mississauga. He even bragged that it costs him five hundred dollars a month just to heat it. He talked about money in a very direct and explicit way. Un-Canadian, eh?"

"Yes. Back home guys rub your shirt with a forefinger and thumb and ask you how much it cost. But did you say he lives in Mississauga these days?"

"Yes. Do you know his last name?"

"Lev."

"You could easily find his phone number on the Internet."

At home, Aline told me that during the dinner I had looked absent-minded and been much quieter than usual. Indeed, my thoughts had raced back to my chapters on Hegel. What was a sense of self, I had ruminated, but striving for continuity and relative stability in one's own and others' eyes? Wasn't it a pivot around which all experiences revolved? Yet, Yuval's intrusions were disrupting my feelings of being a continuous self.

Although I had uprooted myself from Israel, lived in Paris, Lawrence and now Toronto, I was still a husband, a father, a son, a brother, a neighbour, a longstanding friend to many in several countries. I had worked very hard to publish in my field and become a full prof. I could look in the mirror and congratulate myself on a list of accomplishments, and be myself.

My look-alike threatened all that. He was a constant reminder that a sense of self was not carved in stone, but like a cork at sea, bobbed up and down. If people could easily take me for somebody else, weren't my persona and achievements fragile? After each allusion to Yuval's existence, I was forced to confront myself. I emerged feeling fluid and evanescent.

Next day, I called Yuval at home. He had an unmistakable Israeli accent. When I told him in Hebrew who I was, he laughed, claiming that in Israel people had approached him, thinking he was me. No, it had never happened in New York or Toronto.

"Do you mind if we meet?" I asked. "People tell me we're so alike. I'd like to see it with my own eyes."

"No problem. Why don't you drop by my place next Sunday? We can sit around the pool or take a dip. Whatever you want."

"I just want to talk and swap impressions."

"That's fine."

His house was in a suburb of Mississauga. Skinny young trees dotted the large properties, as I drove by rows of monster homes with lush, manicured lawns in front. Many of the houses peered into the street from behind rows of white, massive Corinthian columns that made me think of

Canadianized plantations. It was a pleasant summer afternoon, but the streets were deserted, people probably watching TV or frolicking in their backyard pools. I felt both amused and disgusted by the lifestyle of the *nouveau riche*.

After I banged the heavy brass knocker twice, a bespectacled young woman in shorts and bare feet opened the door. First she covered her mouth with her hand, then giggled merrily. "*Abba*," she turned around and hollered, "it's for you. Your look-alike is here." A monumental carpeted staircase curved some twenty feet behind her.

Yuval wore a yellow golf shirt with a logo and short pants that exposed legs hairier than mine. He was my height, but his beer belly jutted out. He was, indeed, very similar to me, though my hair is thinner and greyer than his.

He shook my hand vigorously. "The two musketeers finally meet," he said in Hebrew. "Let's drink to that. What would you like? Just ask. I have a very well-stocked bar."

"I'll have orange juice."

"Like back home, uh? Nothing alcoholic, eh?"

He led me into a vast living room with mammoth off-white suede sofas. I perched on a love seat, and he sprawled on a three-seater. We talked and talked, but the spotlight was on him. Shamelessly he hogged centre stage, telling me story after story about his youth in Bat Yam, his service in the Air Force, his studies in Haifa and London, his work in New York and Toronto. Occasionally, I inserted bits about my past and present life.

He didn't mention any problems. No regrets saddened his upbeat chatter. He came across as optimistic as a beer commercial. Like me, he was a wandering Jew whose children grew up in the mazes of malls, rock 'n roll, videos, American TV, and the drug *au courant*, and yet he was in denial. "We're migrants," I felt like telling Yuval. In fact, I wanted to shake him and shout, "Why not face it? We're citizens of the world who feel at home nowhere!"

"You want another drink?" Yuval asked. "I got some Chivas Regal – better than the old Israeli orange juice."

I hated Yuval Lev! His patter bored me stiff, and his barely concealed smugness angered me. He was as infuriating as bad poetry, and I regretted driving thirty kilometres to spend time with such a self-centred bore. For decades, his existence had threatened me, and now my accumulated rage was coming out. I pictured myself aiming a loaded gun at his forehead, ignoring his raised hands and cries for mercy and compassion. The next frame showed blood stains and gobs of brain splashed on his sofa.

I leapt up. "I have to go!"

He stood up, his forehead furrowed. "What happened, Ron? We were having such a good time."

"Shut up, you nattering son of a bitch! I've had enough of your crap!"

He approached me. "Relax, Ron." His hand reached out to my arm.

I pushed him back as hard as I could. He tottered, nearly losing his balance. I made a fist and raised it. He winced, shielding his face with his arm, obviously terrified of what I might do. It felt good to see my enemy abject and humiliated in his own home.

I ran to the entrance and yanked the door open. I didn't bother to bang it shut. Once in the car, I pressed the gas pedal hard, and the tires screeched. I drove at high speed, furious at the cars that slowed me down. After parking, I went straight to my study and didn't say a word until dinner.

Only after a couple of days, did my rage abate. I'm not one to wear my anger on my sleeve, and the outburst left me upset for weeks. From time to time, I've felt flashes of guilt for having assaulted someone I'd just met face to face in the privacy of his home.

Now I'm resigned to the fact that he and I live within short driving distance. Occasionally I'll hear about him. People will mistake me for him, and for days I'll feel that my accomplishments are negated. It can't be helped. However, no longer will I cringe or feel threatened. My look-alike, I've learned, is about as potent as eczema. It flares up once in a while, but unfortunately doesn't get cured.

THE TRANSFORMATION OF HARVEY KLEIN

WEEKS AFTER HARVEY KLEIN TURNED SEVENTY-SIX, his wife Sarah leaned across the dinner table. With swollen fingers she combed her short, silvery hair and stared Harvey in the eye. "What I need," her veined hand fondled the air as if outlining small waves, "are spiritual, heart-wrenching, *meaningful* experiences. That Rabbi Feldman lives in his head."

Harvey raised his bald pate and extended the palms of his thin, gnarled hands. "But the Rabbi is a scholar, Sarah. He isn't big on feelings."

"C'mon, Harvey. From the pulpit, he talks down to the congregation as if we were kids. And the services at his Beth Shalom?" she rolled her eyes in mock despair, "just opportunities for women to show off their latest dresses, hats, and jewellery. I'm sick and tired of Rabbi Feldman."

Harvey straightened his spine. Whenever his wife of forty-seven years declared she was "sick and tired," changes became inevitable. Recently, she trumpeted that she was sick and tired of toiling in the garden and scraping the snow off the car without Harvey's help. Lo and behold, three months later they were living in a condo with a heated garage.

He'd stopped standing up to her years ago, when his premature ejaculation had begun. At the beginning he read books, saw sex therapists, tried herbs and medications — all to no avail. For a couple of seconds, the damned thing sputtered like a leaky faucet even before penetration. Sarah got angry, called him selfish, and no amount of apologies appeased her. She refused to give it a go, and their love life consisted of brief, loose hugs and dry kisses on the lips. "I won't get aroused in vain," she said, and he stopped protesting. Over the years he turned meek, shy, crestfallen, and unassertive. When he felt down he called himself king of the hen-pecked Jews.

While in pursuit of meaningful experiences, Sarah called the Toronto Jewish Information Hotline, talked to friends, read brochures. Finally, she decided to try Yedidei Shabbat, friends of Sabbath, a spiritual group that met on Friday evenings in the home of Aaron Weiss, its founder.

"All I'm asking," she said, "is for you to accompany me to the first meeting. If you don't like it, you can always go back to your Rabbi Feldman and his Shul."

"Friday is fine. I don't go to the office." He still worked several hours a week as a chartered accountant for technophobic old Jews who preferred handwritten summaries of their businesses to computerized reports. After leisurely going over their returns, he spent time schmoozing over cups of coffee about their children's accomplishments and the prodigious talents of their grandchildren.

Since Harvey knew nothing about the customs of Yedidei Shabbat, he played it safe in a long-sleeved white shirt and a tie; it was, anyhow, too warm to wear a jacket. Sarah looked smart in trim black pants and a silky red blouse.

Aaron Weiss greeted them at the door, dressed in a short-sleeved plaid shirt, scruffy jeans, and Birkenstock sandals. He was a paunchy man with a thick, scraggly moustache and untrimmed grey beard — about forty-five, Harvey estimated. After giving them tight hugs and moist kisses on both cheeks, Aaron led the way to the basement. On the way down, Harvey took off his tie and buried it in his pocket, already embarrassed by the effusiveness of a total stranger.

By the entrance to the basement was a nearly closed door. Inside the brightly lit room he saw pink tiles on the wall and a green towel on a white rack. He exhaled, reassured. It felt good to know where the washroom was: his enlarged prostate drove him to pee frequently. It would have embarrassed him to ask an obvious, revealing question in the middle of the ceremony. People might think he was irredeemably old, a decrepit coot.

They entered a basement lit only by candles. It smelled of sweet incense and coffee. Despite the near darkness, he saw a dozen men and women sitting on the carpeted floor, their heads covered. He and Sarah were by far the oldest in the room. He had a bad back, and the thought of sitting on the floor for a couple of hours troubled him. He visualized physio-therapy, lying once again on a narrow bed covered with white paper, his ankles attached to a traction machine. He prayed the spiritual ceremony would be reasonably short and cause no spasms.

After introductions to the group members, another round of moist kisses followed. He and Sarah sat on the floor, surrounded by a sea of legs in jeans and feet in sandals. He thanked God for finding a spot where he could lean his back against the wall.

Aaron Weiss passed around stapled pages with texts in English and Hebrew. Harvey subtly weighed the bundle on his palm and ruefully concluded that it would be a long, long evening. How many times would he wobble to his feet to go pee?

The Friends sang blessings in Hebrew. A young woman with fleshy, glimmering cheeks and a bulbous nose — probably in her thirties — read poems about love between friends, community life, spring in Israel. In his heart he thanked her for reading in English — his command of Hebrew consisted of dozens of phrases he remembered from his bar mitzvah. They helped him navigate the oceans of the Sidur, the prayer book. "But," he pondered, "what in God's name has this kind of poetry to do with Friday services?"

As if on cue, the group sang animatedly a string of Hebrew songs he couldn't identify. Occasionally, a song was sprightly, and they clapped hands to the rhythm. Sarah, to his surprise, joined them with the fervour of an old-timer enjoying herself. He, on the other hand, missed the hymns he had known since childhood. He longed for his chair in the Shul. The upholstery there was thin, he couldn't plunk his bum into it, but the back provided firm support. Moreover, from time to time the congregation rose and then sat down, good opportunities to stretch his legs. Now he worried that he would come across as gawky and ungainly when he rose to his feet to go to the washroom.

Aaron Weiss dissolved his reveries when he introduced the evening's speaker, a skinny, intense-looking girl with a thick brown braid resting on her shoulder and pita-flat chest. She could easily be my granddaughter, thought Harvey, who was not particularly curious about her topic, Kabbalah and Feminism. He tweaked his nose, thanking God that as far as he remembered, feminism had only been around since the sixties; it was scary to think that the girl might attempt to survey over a thousand years of Kabbalah.

He half listened, knowing that Sarah, once at home, would insist on a rehash of the evening; he'd be expected to say something intelligent about the program. He cupped his chin in one hand and, to combat his boredom, looked closely at each group member. One of the women sitting across the room, near the table with the coffee urn, surprised him: she had a very attractive face. How come he hadn't noticed her before? Had she come late and sat down while he was engrossed in his back and bladder?

He stared, rapt. The pretty woman listened to the speech spellbound, as if drinking every word. Despite the poor lighting, he concluded that the belle had chestnut, if not black, eyes. Her ginger-coloured, frizzy, thick mane brushed her shoulders. She sat with her legs gracefully beneath her. He couldn't tell her age in the distance separating them.

He gazed, mesmerized and already enamoured, breathing shallowly, his heart filling his chest. It startled him to think that his persistent stare might lead the woman to perceive him as childish, intrusive, sacrilegious. She'd recoil. Fearful of rejection, he turned his head the other way: Sarah was absorbed in the presentation, unaware of the storm inside him.

When the young woman ended her speech, he too clapped hands, then wobbled to his feet. His buttocks and lower back felt sore and frozen. He found his way to the washroom, making efforts not to dodder. When he re-entered the dimly lit room, the group was happily singing how blissful it was for sisters to sing on Shabbat, a song unknown to him.

He sat down again. Now the members stretched out their arms and embraced one another. Sarah enthusiastically joined the fold. Without asking Harvey's permission, two overly-eager youngsters grabbed his shoulders. Yedidei Shabbat, he concluded, obviously enjoyed physical affection. But their hippie rituals didn't move him. He'd rather welcome the

Sabbath sitting at the head of a table with a white linen cloth, fine china, and two tall, glimmering silver candleholders. His two daughters, their husbands, and four grandchildren would listen attentively to his blessings. They all would sing traditional Ashkenazi songs welcoming queen Shabbes — not some Sephardi-Israeli "Shabbat".

After more singing and readings, Aaron Weis blessed the wine and passed around the silver cup. In a few moments, the entire group stood up and together broke a challeh, a braided white bread. At long last, Harvey thought, the ceremony was over.

The pretty woman was standing by the coffee urn and cakes, waiting for her turn to pour herself a cup. Excited, he stood behind her. After filling his cup, he introduced himself.

"Michele Halperin," she said, "but all my friends call me Mickey." She put forth her delicate, elongated hand with no bulging veins. Her fingernails were unpainted, lovely. Her papery cheeks and loose jowl suggested she might be sixty or a bit more.

"I've been attending Yedidei Shabbat for two years," she said. "I get a good feeling of spirituality here."

He had difficulty listening. His heart now pounded, and he wondered whether it was too familiar to place his good ear, the one with no hearing aid, so close to her mouth.

He told her he found his first encounter with the group very interesting. He bent forward and whispered in her ear, "I'm glad to find out there are some mature people at the meeting, not only youngsters in their twenties and thirties."

She smiled, amused. Her beautiful eyes, he determined, were cocoa-brown, not black.

Once at home, Sarah processed the evening. "A wonderful experience! So meaningful! Wonderful people! I noticed you talked to Mickey. She told me she's divorced, has two married boys and two grandchildren. Is still doing supply teaching in high school."

"Is that right?" He feigned indifference, but took in every word.

"Are you going back next week?"

He pictured Mickey's thick mane and dark brown eyes. "Sure," he said, "why not?"

Next Monday the Kleins took the subway downtown and bought Birkenstock sandals and brand new, already washed-out jeans, the dress code of the Yedidei Shabbat. On Friday, Harvey urged Sarah to go early to the meeting so that they could get good spots to sit, perhaps even on floor pillows. In his heart he longed for a strategic place to gaze at Mickey.

She arrived shortly after them. During the meeting, he stared at her on and off, and she smiled whenever their eyes met. He interpreted her smiles as evidence that he was being cautious after all, neither intrusive nor insolent. She didn't come across to him as ravishing as he remembered. On the first Friday, he told himself, he had been infatuated, a teenager. Now he felt invigorated, mature. Mickey was just an attractive woman, not a goddess.

That evening's program seemed less long, even tolerable. His buttocks and low back hurt less. During coffee he talked to Mickey about his old Shul and how intrigued Sarah and he were with Yedidei Shabbat.

"Do you think you'll be back next week?" she asked. "Or are you still shopping around for a congregation?"

He furrowed his brows. Shopping around? Going for services somewhere else would be abdicating something he couldn't yet define. "As far as I'm concerned, I'll be here." Three other words tickled the tip of his tongue, "To see you," but it would have felt terrible to utter them. Perhaps he'd never tell her anything like that — a mute, pent up passion.

The week after, a girl of about twelve sat close to Mickey, and throughout the ceremony they held hands. A granddaughter, Harvey inferred with some jealousy. He gazed at both of them and saw little or no physical similarities between them. The girl's eyes, for example, were doe-like, and her cheekbones too high. In this case, he concluded, beauty hadn't been transmitted to a third generation. The girl's age reinforced his initial hunch that Mickey must be in her early sixties.

He didn't talk to her that Friday, and he didn't mind it. Instead, he chatted with other members. For the first time ever he admitted to himself that every week he enjoyed the Friday services a bit more. He now found their songs quite appealing and their presentations reasonably stimulating. Was he falling in love with Mickey?

All his life he had been a rational believer. He thought of God as the creator of all things human and non-human and couldn't even conceive of a world without Him. Many times Harvey had heard of embittered Jews who questioned the relevance of the spirit in a world that included, among others, Hitler and Auschwitz. But he wasn't a deep thinker; he delegated painful questions to sharper, more profound, more committed minds. He was content to sing hymns and pray, as he had done since he was a child. He was, he felt, a musical Jew.

He wasn't kidding himself, he insisted. He was slowly growing fond of Yedidei Shabbat. This, he knew, was taking place primarily because every week he basked in the beauty of Mickey's pretty face. He was so in love with his own consuming attraction that he never questioned the appropriateness of his prolonged gazing in a community of worshippers.

By averting his eyes whenever he felt his staring was becoming excessive, he made sure he wouldn't be rejected. He harboured the fear that Mickey might tell him to cut out the gazing, or tell Sarah about him being childish and inappropriate.

Weeks later, Friday afternoon was so hot that Sarah considered not attending the gathering. Harvey, however, replied that the basement at Aaron's was well air-conditioned, and they ought to go. "Our friends are waiting for us," he said, praying that Mickey would be at the meeting. "Let's not disappoint them. Skipping sessions is like the domino theory. You skip one, and it might become a habit."

Sarah extended her arm across the table and held his hand. "Maz'l tov, Harvey. You're becoming a spiritual Jew!"

He shuddered, feeling guilty and ashamed. His so-called spirituality consisted of an irresistible compulsion to gaze at a beautiful woman. His relationship with Mickey, he felt, was a pure fantasy; nothing real, carnal, would ever come out of it. It embarrassed him that at his age he lived for optical sex. Deep down, he remembered fondly the services at their Shul and wished he had met Mickey there long ago.

Only seven people showed up that Friday. Mickey sat by his side, for the first time ever. He didn't cherish that arrangement, as he'd gaze at her profile, see only her mane, cheek, and an eye. The whole evening he'd miss the lively expression stirring her face. Feeling disappointed, he peered at the floor, and a pleasant surprise electrified him: Mickey was wearing white sandals with thin leather strips. Her pretty feet were small and tanned. They had no traces of bunions or of dry, rough skin. The toes were long and thin – spiritual, he told himself. The unpainted, pinkish toenails curved gracefully, beautifully.

He became so absorbed gazing at Mickey's feet that he tuned out the blessings, the singing, and that night's presentation. The world came to a halt; his mind focused on the sexy sandals and what they enclosed. Unadulterated beauty, he felt, and wished he could perpetuate his excitement and awe in a poem.

"But this is sacrilege," a little voice inside him piped. Still, this awareness of sin didn't stop him from admiring the pristine, girl-like feet, so different from his own bunioned monsters with twisted, overlapping toes and discoloured nails.

At night, he tossed and twisted in bed, hallucinating spiritual toes in the dark, elegant arches, and soft heels. He woke up early and over breakfast announced that he had to attend to an urgent matter at his office.

"What's the matter with you?" asked Sarah. "I'm surprised. Can't you wait till Sunday? Why let your business spoil the spirit of Shabbat?"

He agreed to wait. The entire Saturday he felt anxious, a born-again, young tiger aching to be released from its cage. On Sunday he woke up before dawn. It was torture to wait for breakfast and feign it was just an urgent matter at the office.

Once at work, he locked the door to his office, not to be disturbed by workaholic colleagues coming in early on Sunday. Also, he wanted to concentrate better and to conceal what he was doing. He fished out a pencil and on blank pages of printer paper drew picture after picture of Mickey's beloved feet. Only after furious, ecstatic work and a basket full of balls of crumpled paper, a satisfying drawing sat on his desk. As if driven by demons, he bent over and frantically kissed it, again and again. Heart pounding, he stood up, unzipped his fly, and fondled his erect penis with the picture.

"Mickey, oh Mickey!" he murmured. "Love in the winter of my life!"

Following that Sunday, he made up a clever excuse: he had new and demanding clients that necessitated going to the office every morning. Sarah didn't mind his absences, as in the mornings she worked on her correspondence course on Jewish mysticism, and her afternoons were crammed with alternative therapies for her bad knee. Also, she held money in contempt — all their married life Harvey had brought home the brisket and amassed plenty. She never asked if his increased workload led to a higher income.

Often, it occurred to Harvey to hurry to his office without breakfast. But that might have aroused Sarah's suspicions, as he habitually read the *Report on Business* in the morning, before venturing out. These days, he held the newspaper in his hands, but couldn't concentrate on the news. His mind was fixated on Mickey's feet.

At last, when he felt he had done enough time, he gave Sarah a peck on her cheek and rushed to relieve himself from the added anguish of waiting so long. Once at the office, he engaged in the sweet routine of locking the door, closing the blinds, and turning on the lamp on his desk. He unearthed the drawing from its hiding place. Holding this one-page passport to the lands of fantasy, excitement, and sheer pleasure, with his other hand, he masturbated.

Daily he turned on a private movie of Mickey draped in an elegant black dress to her ankles. Invariably, she came to his office barefoot, and her irresistible feet glowed, two Byzantine icons. Without removing her panties, he fondled her juicy buttocks and thick thighs. Kneeling down, first he kissed and licked her feet. Ever so slowly she sat on his desk, then lay down. His ravenous, rock-hard penis adored his idols for a very long time.

His experiences in sex therapy came in handy. Feverish and breathless, he'd masturbate almost to the "point of inevitability," then abruptly stop. He'd start and stop, postponing orgasm until he ached for relief. Despite repeated efforts, he had miserably failed to transpose his self-control to lovemaking with his wife; but now, with Mickey's feet on his desk, he felt young, confident, potent. He lasted and lasted. He didn't have to put up with angry complaints and demands.

With few variations, every day he returned to the same scenario. In the back of his mind he felt guilty. First, he was using his wife by pretending he was a budding spiritual Jew. How selfish and deceitful could one get? How long would this delirious game last? Then, he felt guilty and ashamed of abusing Mickey's beauty. He barely knew her, beside the basic facts that she was a divorced spiritual believer and taught in high school. He rarely talked to her. Perhaps he didn't need to. Fantasy was sufficient. Their few conversations consisted of small talk related to the Friday services. How little he knew her! This realization contrasted with the passionate, elaborate fantasies about her face and feet.

In his moments of lucidity, his excitement struck him as a perversion, a hopeless infatuation, the work of an aging, disturbed mind. Indeed, he was an old Don Quixote, dreaming in the winter of his life about love without intercourse. What would Mickey think of being the target of his fantasies of foreplay? He smiled wistfully, thinking he wasn't serving main courses, just appetizers.

He considered himself off-track, a neurotic, and felt impotent to control his passions. While in the grip of lust, he saw nothing wrong with what was happening to him. Every weekday he looked forward to his sweet rituals and his share of delights.

"Harvey," said Sarah one Saturday morning, "Mickey will be calling you at the office."

His back went up. He anticipated punishment for illicit pleasures. "What does she want?" He strove to conceal his excitement.

"She's thinking of opening a private school and is worried about tax problems. I said you'd be glad to help."

"I am," he said, heart racing.

He agreed with Mickey to meet him at his office. As usual for work, he wore a blue blazer, white shirt, a sedate tie. She came wearing a smart cream-coloured blouse and a green skirt. He saw her legs for the first time: they were thick and flabby, but it didn't matter. She was wearing the beloved white sandals. He felt like exclaiming Hallelujah. His fantasies had become true.

Though painfully aroused, he managed to understand her issues. In a few moments he explained to her the tax rules and their business implications. He wanted to be helpful and wrote his recommendations on a lined page. A simple matter, he could focus on it even when his heart pounded and his desire reigned supreme. He wondered what they would talk about once they finished with the accounting.

An awkward silence ensued. He drew in a deep breath. Without considering the consequences he said, "I want to show you something." He opened the bottom drawer of his desk and fished out the guide to his fantasy trips. He surprised himself. Never in his long life had he been so forthcoming, so revealing. Intoxicated, he told himself to let the unavoidable take its course.

She put on thick reading glasses and appeared old and professorial. "What's that?" she asked, perplexed. "I don't understand." She removed her eyeglasses and eyed him, suspicious.

He stood up. "Your feet. I love them." She knitted her brow, and he hurried to add, "I love you."

Before she could reply he strode around the desk to her seat. "I'm crazy about you, crazy," he whispered as he knelt down, grabbed her feet by the ankles, kissed and licked them.

She pushed back her chair, and struggled to step backwards out of his embrace of her feet. "What's the matter with you, Harvey? Are you mad? What will Sarah say?"

He remained on his knees, staring at her feet. "I love them . . . and you . . . You're on my mind . . . all the time."

"For God's sake!" she raised her voice. "Stand up! Compose yourself!"

He looked up. "Please, Mickey. Let me kiss you . . . there."

She looked at him, her face red with anger. "You thought you could get away with this filth because I'm a single woman. Is that it?" Before he could reply, she turned on her heels, reached for the door handle, and left his office.

Shocked, he remained on his knees, eyes closed. He feared she'd taken the drawing with her. He opened his eyes, wobbled to his feet, and peered at his desk. The drawing lay flat on his desk. He walked over and stuffed it into the drawer.

Panic overcame him. Would Mickey ever talk to him again? What if she dropped out of Yedidei Shabbat? When would she tell Sarah? How could he explain his conduct? He called himself a jerk, a juvenile, a bastard. He knew he would hear all these and more. Stunned and ashamed, he anticipated a momentous punishment, but couldn't name it. It felt like a foul mixture of doom and disgrace, like the time his mother shrieked when she caught him masturbating. At this moment, he was so fearful of Sarah's anger that he decided to have lunch downtown and see a movie in the afternoon. At dinnertime he would face the music.

When he entered the condo, Sarah was in the kitchen, preparing dinner. "How was your day?" she asked flatly.

"Fine." He had expected a hurricane and now felt puzzled by her cool reception. Could it be that Mickey kept quiet about the incident at the office? He sighed in relief, praying that nothing would happen, at least not that night.

They ate in silence. Harvey felt anxious, waiting for a storm to be unleashed any moment. He wouldn't go to bed unpunished. At any moment Sarah would attack him. He would disintegrate into single cells, a child terrified by his angry mother.

"Mickey called me this morning," Sarah said while they were having coffee. "She was crying. She said you showed her a dirty picture, then assaulted her. What's your version?" She gave him a cold, distant, cutting look.

He put down his cup and cleared his throat. "You could say she was right. I find it hard to explain."

"For me, what's very hard to accept is that you fooled me the entire summer. You pretended to be interested in spiritual matters, when all you cared about was her pretty face. I don't understand the business of kissing her feet."

He didn't answer.

"Another thing," she spoke softly, and that scared him more than if she yelled and cried. "For years you were dysfunctional with me, but turned into a tiger with a younger woman. What am I supposed to make out of that? Answer me, be a man!"

"Give me some time," he begged. "I'm sure we can work it out, go back to where we were before Mickey."

She looked at her watch. "At eight Rachel will pick me up."

He leaned forward, his brow furrowed. "I don't know why you're involving our daughter."

"I'm staying with her until you straighten yourself out."

"Please, Sarah, please, don't. I—"

"Call Aaron Weiss," she lowered her voice. "Ask him to recommend a Jewish psychiatrist for you. I'm not coming back until the therapist tells me you're making progress."

"But Sarah, why not go into counselling together? There's no need for us to split up. Please, Sarah, please!"

She stood up. "No, Harvey. You hurt me enough. Sort out your filth, then we'll see." She doddered toward their bedroom.

After Sarah left, he sat on the couch in the living room, feeling empty, lonely, and devastated. In one day he had alienated the two women he cared about. One was forever out of his life, he was sure, while the other demanded that he get into treatment. He smoothed his bald pate with his palm, skeptical that he'd change a great deal at his age. Sex therapies hadn't helped much, and he doubted that psychiatry would turn him around.

Sure, he regretted he had hurt both women, but he cherished that rejuvenating summer of magic. It had been full of excitement and passionate hours. No matter how hard he and the shrink worked in this new therapy, it would be impossible to dissolve his fond memories.

No doubt, he wanted Sarah back. He'd co-operate with the shrink and talk his heart out until the doctor announced he was making progress. In two and a half years Sarah and he would celebrate their golden anniversary. He looked forward to it. In his eyes, his relationship with her was a thick, steel cable, his passion for Mickey a thin, glittering gold chain. He had a wealth of memories with Sarah, some good, some bad, but she was his swan, a life mate. Mickey, he sighed mournfully, was a flitting dream.

He stood up and looked out the pane. The windows in the high rise across the street were fully lit. Perhaps he hadn't turned into a spiritual Jew, but the glimmering lights against the inky sky brought a flicker of peace to his conflicted soul.

Death by Leisure

Lillian

The morning was cold and overcast as I stepped down from the streetcar. I walked briskly along the blocks of mock-Victorian houses where scores of psychotherapists, including myself, plied our trade — "Angst Alley" a waggish Toronto journalist had called it. Here and there, between chest-high forsythias with sparse flowers, a few green tips had emerged on the scruffy, brown lawns, a promise of renewal still struggling with winter's harshness.

My building's dark hallway was fusty with an odour reminiscent of a funeral home. I unlocked the door to my suite and stepped into the consulting room. All in perfect order. The telephone on my desk, at the back of the room, flashed no messages. For the last two months I had had no referrals for psychotherapy, and the absence of new cases worried me. At sixty-four, I dreaded death by retirement. Besides my darkroom, where on Friday nights I developed films and made black-and-white prints, I had no hobbies. What would I do with my endless leisure once my work life had died down?

I opened the door to the waiting room at the back of the suite and hung my coat on a wooden rack, one of the two pieces of furniture I shared with my patients. All in order in that portion of my castle, too. By the tall, old-fashioned window, I turned on the radio and let classical music flow over my tired body and mind.

Back in the consulting room, I sat down at the desk and studied my appointment book. Friday, April 11, 2003. Only five patients scheduled. I'd finish work by three o'clock, go home, have an early dinner, and watch the news. No darkroom that night. I was too tired from the storms at home of the night before, and a dull headache reminded me of my lack of sleep. I'd tuck in early to relieve my stress.

Eight thirty. Half an hour to kill until Harvey, my first patient of the day. I slid open the bottom drawer, fished out the article on gratitude I was writing with my friend Christine, also a psychologist, and tried to edit the latest paragraphs. After the first few sentences, my lead-heavy head balked. No way.

How could I possibly see patients? I tried to picture myself on my Eames chair, comfortably sitting back, looking relaxed. I wouldn't, I swore, let my eyelids flutter. Squelching my yawns instead, I'd be chatty, supportive, life-affirming. The lessons from thirty-four years in this draining trade would keep me out of trouble.

The evening before, I'd arrived home worn out from convoluted dialogues with five troubled people. In my thirties and forties I'd felt alert and fulfilled after work, ready for a movie or the theatre. But now all I pined for was sweet home routines, such as a candle-lit dinner with my grey-haired, overweight wife, Lillian.

After changing into jeans and a T-shirt, I wandered into the kitchen, which smelled of vegetables, chicken, and spices frying in oil. "How was your day, dear?" I asked her, though twice I'd already called her from work. Despite our bickering, the older we got, the more Lillian and I craved tokens of affection. "Dave called," she said, without swivelling her head away from the wok spluttering on the stove. "He'll come by, to have coffee. He has something to tell us."

"Do you know what?"

She turned to me, puffed-up cheeks almost concealing her lips. "I assume he finally wants to talk about Martha."

I took a deep breath. Dave lived with Martha, his black Jamaican girlfriend — a schwartze, a shikse, Lillian called her behind Dave's back.

"How do you feel about it, Lillian?" I asked.

"C'mon Peter!" She raised her voice. "There you go again, asking how *I* feel, instead of telling me where *you* stand. You're not in your office! I'm not one of your patients!" Whenever we quarrelled, Lillian alluded to my profession.

I reached to caress her shoulder. She squirmed out of reach. I stuffed my hand into my pocket. "You know I've nothing against Martha. It's you that gets uptight about her."

"Why do you ask questions, if you're so smart and know how I feel?"

Blood rushed to my cheeks. "Are you angry with me, Dave, or Martha? I can't help it if you're pissed off at the whole world!"

She removed the wok from the stove. "The stir-fry is ready. Why don't you go set the table?"

We ate without lifting our eyes from our plates. I tried to initiate small talk about my day at the office, then about the violence in Israel. I asked about the rya rug she was weaving in the basement despite her arthritic fingers. She answered each question briefly, then took another mouthful. Lillian was a religious Jew, and for long years had harboured fears that

Dave or Dan, his younger brother, would marry shikses. Martha's being black only made things worse.

My heart pounded. I feared that what she dreaded would come out of Dave's mouth.

"I'm home!" Dave called from the door. Lillian insisted that our sons keep the keys to what would always be their home.

"Dave!" I shouted. "We're just about to have coffee!"

He joined us at the dining room table. A basketball player and a weight-lifter, Dave's chest and upper arms bulged under his bluish shirt. A shock of dark brown hair almost concealed one eyebrow. After a round of talk about his work and the war in Iraq, he cheerfully announced, "Mom, Dad, we've decided. Martha and I will get married this fall in Kingston, Jamaica. She has a lot of family down there, and most of them can't afford a trip to Toronto."

I rose from my seat and hugged him at length, then planted a long kiss on each cheek. "Maz'l tov, son! Maz'l tov! I'm very happy! I wish Martha were here! At any rate, I've a bottle of champagne in the fridge! Let's drink to this great occasion!"

"Hold on there, Dad!" He held up his palm and turned to his stiff-faced mother. "What do you say, Mom?" She perched on her chair, silent.

After a few moments she muttered, "Talk to your dad. I'd better not say anything."

Dave's face fell. "Aren't going to wish me maz'l tov?" He asked.

She stood up. "I'd better soak the wok. The sauce will harden, and it'll be difficult to scrape it clean."

I sat down. "That's all you have to tell him?"

She stared at me, eyes cold. "I told you I'd better keep my mouth shut."

Dave half whispered. "Do you hate her, Mom?"

She shook her head, almost imperceptibly. "You know the custom, Dave. If I'd married a goy, my father would have mourned my death for seven days."

"Your father was a long time ago, Lillian," I butted in. "You're hurting his feelings now that he wants your blessing."

She leaned toward me. "Keep your platitudes to yourself, Peter. Right now we don't need a family therapist. You two know where I stand. I'd better do the dishes."

Dave pushed back his chair. A moist film shone in his eyes. "Will you be coming to the wedding, Mom?"

"I'll have to think about it."

"Think about it?" I smacked my palm on the table. "What's there to think about? He's our son, he's getting married. Are your medieval beliefs going to destroy this family?"

She waddled to the kitchen as if I'd said nothing.

Dave stood up. "I'm going home."

Slowly I rose to my feet. "Stay for a while," I urged him and extended my hand to his shoulder. "Sooner or later she'll get over the initial shock and wish you maz'l tov."

"I don't want anything from her!" He shouted. He strode into the kitchen. "Hear me, Mom? I don't want anything from you! If you reject Martha, you reject me!"

I walked into the kitchen where she was washing dishes with her back to him. "Let's talk about it, guys. There must be a way out!"

"No, Dad. There can be no compromises. Mom can't stop me. I'm getting married in October. Are *you* coming to the wedding?"

"But of course! And I'm pretty sure she will too."

He smiled, mournful. "How many times I've heard you say that in this family everyone speaks for himself?" He turned to his mother. "What do I tell Martha, Mom? Will you be at the wedding?"

She didn't turn around. "You heard me, Dave. I have to think about it."

He strode into the hall. A moment later the door slammed.

I helped Lillian with the dishes, then flopped onto my stuffed chair in front of the television. She made a couple of phone calls, then tramped downstairs to the basement, to weave her rug. After the scene at the dining room table, I couldn't concentrate on the show. My mind wandered. I thought about Dave and Martha, how our grandchildren wouldn't be considered Jewish by rabbinical law and in Lillian's eyes. She must be terribly upset, I thought.

I also trudged downstairs to the basement. Lillian was perched on her weaver's stool by the loom, sliding the shuttle close to the already woven lines. I stopped next to her. "How are you, Lillian?"

She didn't look up. "I don't know what you are doing down here."

I caressed her head, but she didn't respond. "I came to see how you're feeling."

"You know I'm upset. Why add to it?"

I withdrew my hand. "It seems to me you're angry with me too, not only with Dave."

"Right now I'm not angry with Dave, but I'm pissed off with you. I blame you for Dave marrying that schwartze shikse."

"Me?" I barked. I felt the blood rise to my cheeks. "Dave is a happy man. It's *you* that feels miserable. Why drag us into *your* black hole?"

She let go of the shuttle, jumped to her feet, and stood by a basket full of balls of wool, eyes gleaming. "Jerk! Manipulator! You always talk as if you have all the answers."

"I've never implied that!" I shouted. "You passively let me decide, then blame me for the consequences. You know, Lillian, Dave is thirty-two, a lawyer, not a child. He makes his own choices."

"Choices, choices, choices! That's what you've always told me. 'When the kids are adults, they'll make their own choices.' What a crock! You gave me that same bull ten, fifteen, twenty years ago. And what drives me crazy is that I thought that you, a psychologist, were an expert in child-rearing. You never gave them an opportunity to be Jews. You insisted on a secular education, and in your eyes parochial schools were a crime against humanity. What I find out now is that your fucking secular ideas drove a wedge between me and my children. They're neither Jews nor goyim, just some souless citizens of the world."

She stared at me, cheeks frozen, eyes glinting. "Deep down, you were ashamed of being a Jew! No wonder Dave found that schwartze! I hate you!" she bellowed, then bent down, picked up a ball of wool and threw it at my chest.

I hardly felt the impact of the ball, but I jabbed a finger at her and yelled, "Be honest, Lillian, *you'd* like to make the decisions for Dave, yet have the nerve to call *me* a manipulator."

Lime-white, she stepped forward and with her small fist boxed my chest. "It's all your fault. I could gouge your eyes with my nails."

Accusation after accusation! I felt like punching her in the mouth. "You bitch!" I hollered and, grabbing her by the shoulders, shook her, hard.

She pulled back, struggling to free herself. "Let go of me, you bastard!"

"You started it!" For the first time ever, before I realized what I was doing, I took a swing and slugged her across the mouth. She pitched backwards onto her loom, then rolled to the floor.

"Wife beater!" She screamed. Blood trickled down the corner of her mouth. She wiped it away. "In one night, my son rejects me, and then, you asshole, you beat me up."

Shaking, I bent down, inserted my hands under her armpits, and tried to heave her to her feet. She was crying. "I'm sorry," I whispered. "Let's go upstairs and talk."

"Leave me alone!" she screamed. "Get out of my life! From now on I'll sleep in the living room."

"No, you sleep in our bed, and I'll spend the night in the basement."

She wiped her tears with her sleeve. "Do me a big favour. Let me sleep where I want."

That night I tossed on our queen-sized bed. Were my sons Jews, or just generic entities with no firm foundation? Was I to blame, or were my children the product of malls, excessive TV watching, and pop culture? I needed answers right there and then and twisted in bed, anxious and desperate.

Dave's upcoming marriage was the hardest to digest. Despite my outward approval, the idea of him marrying a black woman struck me as a final, irreversible blow. Lillian and I spent a month in Florida every winter and, upon return, boasted a deep, bronze tan. But the notion of my descendants having an indelibly chestnut skin disturbed me. Schwartze? Would they be labelled "black?"

I despised my racist feelings. Still, on my bedraggled bed, I couldn't shake them off. I felt ashamed and swore not to say a word about them to Lillian, lest they exacerbate her anger.

Even more troubling was the guilt about striking her. How in God's name could I have done it? I was usually a reasonable, calm, and patient guy. Behind my back, I was sure, my friends even called me "over-controlled" — a clinical cliché that well described my urge to talk about issues rather than act on them. With Lillian I had failed miserably. Instead of empathizing with her pain, I had let old conflicts get the better of me.

Again and again I pictured my fist slamming across her mouth, and the muted sound of buffeted flesh haunted me.

Wife-beater. That hurtful phrase kept me awake. At last, I must have fallen asleep for a while because I felt Lillian, next to me, tugging at my shoulder. I sat up in bed, surprised, yet gratified. "How do you feel, dear?" I extended my hand to caress her cheek and to redeem myself. Her face was sopping wet.

"Terrible. Lonely. It bothers me that I started it."

"I feel very guilty. I was enraged when you accused me of messing up the boys' lives."

"I'm to blame. I hit you first." She paused. "Were you asleep? Did I wake you up?"

"That's all right. I had a hard time falling asleep." I slid my arm under her head, and she moved toward me, resting it on my shoulder. "I feel awful. Beating you was unforgivable."

"I'm also to blame."

We fell silent for a long while. This was an old pattern: first we fought dirty, then pulled back, hurt and angry, then hurried to make up when the gap between us grew too wide. "I was crying uncontrollably," she said, "thinking about our poor boys. Dave's wedding bothers me to no end. You probably think I'm a bigot and a racist."

"Try to sleep now. Once you calm down, you'll think more clearly."

"Are you going to work tomorrow?"

"Today. It's four fifteen now. It's Friday, and I have five patients booked. Don't worry. I'll manage."

She drew closer. I adjusted the duvet with the other hand. Soon she fell asleep. I was as alert as a sleuth. Though I'd vowed I'd manage at work, I worried. Would I look sleepy and stressed-out? Definitely not a good image for a secular clergyman ministering to a flock of agnostics and non-believers.

Harvey

At nine, Harvey was perched on a chair in my waiting room. "This afternoon I've a meeting with a client," he announced. He looked at me apprehensively, as if checking whether I'd approve of his dressy black pants and white button-down shirt. No jacket. He wore a garish green-and-red necktie, apparently mocking whoever imposed a dress code on him.

Light headed, "Good morning," was all I replied. No need to encourage counterproductive small talk.

He entered my consulting room and eased himself onto the edge of his Eames chair. Contrary to habit, he didn't plunk his feet on the black leather ottoman between us, but strained forward. "You remember Bill?"

"Yes, of course. Your nemesis at the office. At the time, I'd suggested he's an anti-Semite, and you resisted that idea."

"Well, Bill restructured the teams. I'll no longer work with Anette."

Every session he rhapsodized about Anette's shapely legs. She was easy to talk to, he insisted, because she didn't merely listen, but probed his feelings. Like me, she made him feel understood, better than his wife ever did. On more than one occasion he had vociferously rejected my interpretation that he craved an affair, a smoke screen around his conflicts at work and at home.

I lifted my feet and plunked them onto the ottoman. I had two Eames chairs in my office, one for me, one for patients, but only one ottoman. Sharing a piece of furniture forged a feeling of closeness. "I bet you miss her already."

"I do." His big brown eyes looked hurt. He stroked his narrow forehead, as if wiping off sweat. No wonder women liked him: his pointed chin, full lips, and thin nose were handsomely sculpted. "We'll no longer have our chats. But that's not the worst." He wiped his mouth with his palm. "I was assigned a second-rate project. You don't need an architect to do it. A draftsman could handle it."

"How do you feel about it?" That's what I said when I didn't know how to comfort patients.

"Awful," he stared at his knee. "Awful."

"Awful what? Awful resentful, awful angry, awful depressed? What kind of awful? Look me in the eye and tell me." I bustled with authority, to stave off my own distress.

He lifted his head and peered aside. "Awful angry. I could kill him. He always puts me down with snarky remarks. But this time he implied, in front of the others, that I'm incompetent and dispensable." He paused, then looked me in the eye. "This may sound to you like a minor thing, but I feel it's a form of abuse."

"Sure, I agree with you. It's maddening to assign a menial job to an architect. Any idea what you could do about it?"

Silence.

After three years with Harvey, I knew that he found it hard to contemplate action on his conflicts. Instead, he preferred to ruminate about real or imagined slights, or use uncommon words like "dispensable". Was I pressuring him too early in the session to keep myself alert?

He gazed at his knees, as silent as a fish in a tank.

"What are you thinking about, Harvey?" My voice was avuncular, to pierce the Plexiglas shield around him. As a rule, I didn't tolerate long silences. They were simply a waste of time, an uncaring, cold tactic. But that day, the silence made me anxious. I looked at the clock on the wall behind Harvey. Nine after nine. Thirty-six minutes more to get through. A pang of anxiety stabbed me.

"I was thinking about Bill. You said I'm afraid of him because he represents the bullies of my childhood."

"Yes. You were surprised." I was glad I had interpreted Bill accurately. Something to hang on to on a rainy day.

"I was. I hadn't grasped how destructive the bullying was. I thought all kids got teased at school. One of those things."

"It wasn't just teasing. It was abuse. They beat you up and made fun of you on every occasion. It went on for years. Your reaction was typical: you denied the emotional impact of what was going on."

He was staring me in the eye, alert and wide-eyed. Without a word, he lifted both feet and plunked them on the ottoman, unaware that this behaviour might connote something signif-icant. Despite being on a roll, I decided not to comment. Why nip meaningful feelings in the bud? "Doctor Greenberg," he whined. "You always talk to me as if I was in therapy all my life, as if I should have been 'aware' — your word — even in my childhood. One of these days you'll claim I should have been in touch with my feelings while sucking on my mother's breast."

I ignored his sarcasm. After Lillian's painful accusations, a discussion of parent-child relationships was too painful. "Harvey," I instructed, "look what's happening with Anette. You get involved with a woman who gives you a lot of attention, but you deny that you want an affair with her. I had to point out how *she* is giving you the green light."

A brief, odd smile passed his lips. I felt he was getting angry, not amused. "Sometimes I get the impression you *want* me to have an affair. Why is that, eh? Are you craving graphic details of my sex life? If that makes you happy, I can tell you my fantasies while making love to my wife."

I fell silent, of course. Nothing like an expectant silence to stoke cathartic anger. His face would crimson, he'd stammer a bit, he'd get into meaningful material. But he didn't take the bait. To my surprise, he remained stubbornly silent, watching me as intently as I watched him. During the long period of waiting, I began to fantasize about a disgruntled Harvey planting his feet on the floor, standing up, then announcing that he was ending therapy. Other angry patients would dump me. My caseload would shrivel. It wouldn't be financially feasible to keep an office. I'd die emotionally. I pictured my last day at work, mournfully saying goodbye to a couple of faithful patients. I'd go into retirement, having only my darkroom as a meaningful hobby. Bored, white-haired, and overweight, every two hours I'd pester Lillian, "How about a cup of coffee?" Three years after my forced retirement — useless, lonely, forgotten — I'd die of a heart attack.

I eyed Harvey. He looked back as if expecting me to shatter the silence. Fortunately, a streetcar clattered by, and he turned his head toward the window behind him. I calmed down a bit and against all the teachings of my supervisors, decades before, once again I asked him, "What are you thinking about?"

"Bill," he answered more at ease than I felt inside.

How hard, it seemed, when the doctor was shakier than the patient. Out of habit, I bent forward to encourage him to verbalize further. Unless I got control of my agitation, he'd soon realize how disturbed I felt. He'd abandon me and troll for a younger, healthier therapist, a man unencumbered by the terrors of going into retirement. Of course, my successor wouldn't be a wife-beater. My rival would furrow his brow in disbelief as Harvey told him how glaringly dysfunctional I had been at the office. Twice I blinked, anxious to banish my disturbing scenarios. What could I do to keep Harvey in therapy? "Tell me about Bill," I said to him again.

He straightened his spine and sat upright in his chair. "You were right, doctor, when you said that Bill is the condensation of the kids that bullied me in my childhood. He teases me, he throws out snarky remarks, he assigns me second-rate work, he . . . "

No need to worry about Harvey abandoning me. He used words like "condensation", and, the way he was slowly progressing, we'd grow old together. Other patients wouldn't leave me in droves, I consoled myself. "Just stay calm," I preached to myself.

The real problem was Lillian. Her wife-beater had badly hurt her feelings. She slept next to him only because of her agitation. That didn't mean she had forgiven him. The issue was likely to stay with her for years, maybe forever. I thought of calling her after Harvey left. I wouldn't say, "Hi honey." Too familiar, too cheery. Sounded unrepentant . . .

"He's going on vacation next week," Harvey's voice dissolved my reveries.

Grabbing the arms of my chair, I sat up. Who the hell was "he"? What was Harvey talking about? *Pay attention!* I rebuked myself, *and don't get carried away by shame and guilt!* How embarrassing if Harvey realized I was on a separate planet!

"It's going to be relaxed at the office while he's away. A breather." Harvey smiled scampishly.

"How long is Bill going to be away?" I ventured, my heart racing, expecting to be attacked — by Harvey, by the College of Psychologists, by God — for not following him word for word.

"I told you," he said, puzzled and taken aback. "Two weeks."

I'd guessed right. He had been talking about Bill. It was now nine twenty-six. With half a session to go, I had to get into something deep and meaningful that would leave a lasting impression. I raised my forefinger. "It occurred to me that we never talked about the relationship between Bill and your parents."

"What relationship? Why should I upset them with my problems at the office? They've enough to contend with now that my sister and her husband have separated."

"That's the pattern." I said firmly, to inspire confidence in myself. "Just as you didn't tell them about Bill, you never told them about the bullies in your childhood." Exploring that link between past and present would let me off the hook.

"You're on a fishing expedition!" The gap between his eyebrows narrowed as the vertical line between them deepened. "You're going too far, doctor! What happened thirty years ago bears no resemblance to today. I was a child then, and now I've two children. I see no connection!" He pinched his nose. His eyes glittered, he seemed ready to pounce. "I've no idea what you're driving at."

"You sound angry with me."

"Yes! I'm annoyed at your pushing me."

He called it annoyance, but I didn't want to quibble about words. His anger with me confirmed that I'd struck gold. "Harvey," I said softly, "are you aware of your tendency to protect your parents?"

He screwed his face, puzzled and angry. "And why shouldn't a son protect his aging parents?"

"Very Jewish, Harvey," I snorted. "You answer my question with a probing question. But I'll start with today, then probe the past. You feel your parents are frail, and you don't want to burden them. On the surface, you come across as a loyal, devoted son. But we can't ignore how you never said boo to your parents about the abuse at school. You chose to bear the burden on your small shoulders rather than worry them."

"But my mother was so fragile," he flung out his hands. "She was depressed since she left Auschwitz! She had to be hospitalized when her mother died. How could I possibly rock the boat? I know you don't like it when I walk on eggshells, but, believe me, I had no choice, neither then nor now."

We had slid into an argument, and I felt drained. Could I continue with that line of inquiry? Should I tell him I wasn't feeling well and cut short the session? I'd lose one hundred and fifty dollars, but, worse, I feared the loss of face. To my surprise, I said, firmly, "You sacrificed yourself on the altar of loyalty. Your parents, and especially your mother, taught you how fragile they were, and how devastating it would be if you opened up and told it like it was." I looked at the clock, wondering how much longer I could stand dealing with victims of the Holocaust.

"I have the feeling that you want me to be to a callous son. You're suggesting I should have hurt my parents already then."

I cringed. I knew that dealing with an angry patient was the most taxing aspect of my vocation. Though it would have been easier to deny his charge, I chose to stay silent. I felt strongly about the ethics of my trade. Shirking them would only enhance my guilt.

Chin jutting out, he peered at me down his nose. "You're silent, eh? Every time I get really angry with you, you drop out of the argument. I've the feeling you want to get me really angry."

"You're so angry at me that you imply I'm inciting you to hurt your parents. The issue is that you're not relating to your mother as adult to adult," I held my hands straight in front of my chest, to denote an equal relationship. "As in your childhood, you're frightened that if you opened up, your mother would implode and die. But she isn't as fragile as you imagine." I stopped for a while to gather my strength, glad that the conversation had turned into a lecture. "She immigrated from Europe, she married here in Toronto, she started a family, she did much better than — "

"But she had a breakdown!"

"You interrupted me! You didn't want to hear what I had to say! That means I was probably right! But I'll continue anyhow. The breakdown took place when you were nineteen, when her mother died. And she was hospitalized for two nights only. She was stronger than you realized." My chest and belly swelled with anxiety. I wished I could end the session right there and then, but I'd opened Pandora's box and had to continue. "As a child, her anxiety frightened you, and you spared her. You kept secrets, like the abuse by other children."

"My mother really loved me!" He raised his voice, indignant and hurt. "You're implying that she's to blame for my insecurities."

"I'm not blaming her for anything, Harvey." My answer sounded defensive. He had reached the limit of his tolerance, and now that we had only ten minutes to go, I felt like soothing him. It was my duty to calm him down, to make sure he left my office in relatively good shape. (He was as fragile as his mother.) "Think about two tuning forks. When one of them vibrates, the other one will do the same, at the same frequency. It's the same between you and your mother. She was anxious and transmitted her anxiety to you. It was all done unwittingly, unconsciously." I paused for effect and to gather my strength. "You acquired her anxiety early in life, but she is not to blame." This intellectual discussion of anxiety revived me. I thought how much I needed to talk about my own problems to someone, to see a therapist, and vent my stress and guilt.

"Do you think I should tell my parents about Bill?"

"Not a bad idea. Your mother survived Auschwitz. She can deal with your problems at work. She won't fall apart. Opening up might help dissipate your assumption that she's a fragile porcelain doll. You may even enjoy her company, instead of worrying about every word that comes out of your mouth."

He eyed me intently, then let out a thin smile. "You were wrong about Anette. I wasn't setting up an affair with her. It was just a fantasy."

I smiled. I'd managed that session without him detecting my inner restlessness. I leaned forward, and raised my hand, as if about to deliver an eternal verity. "Sometimes fantasies are just fantasies, a pastime."

"I've never been able to figure out whether you're a Freudian, or an eclectic. You like to talk about my mother, but you don't push sex and stuff."

He had a long way to go, I thought. He'd be with me until I retired, then I'd refer him to another therapist. A good, loyal patient who rarely challenged how I felt about him. "I'm not a purist, Harvey. And I don't like to talk with patients about theories. It just takes us away from our feelings. Well, we'll stop for today."

"By the way, next week I can't come. We're going to Montreal, to visit my in-laws."

I hated it when patients cancelled scheduled appointments. It wasn't the money I'd lose that bothered me, but their absence. I missed the scheduled sharing of intimacies, the opportunity to witness the changes they were slowly making. I loved the role of benevolent parent surrogate. "Enjoy your trip. I'll see you in two weeks."

As soon as he left the room, I leaned my head on the doorjamb and heaved a deep sigh. "I managed, I managed," I whispered, elated that I'd fooled Harvey. On the other hand, I also felt drained. How would I deal with four more patients? It was only April, and my vacation was scheduled for the end of July. Three months! How would I handle my work stress. And Lillian, I shook my head. What would become of us?

Slowly, I tramped to my desk, lowered myself onto the chair, and in a few minutes wrote half a page of notes on Harvey's chart. I capitalized on the relationship between Bill and Harvey's parents, as all the rest had been previously documented. I worked fast and without too much deliberation, a mere requirement by the College of Psychologists.

After I put the chart in its place, I sat down again, opened my top desk drawer and fished out my private telephone directory. Friedman, Milton, an analyst well known for seeing mental health practitioners. It was a good time to call, as he probably was on his break between patients. I called, and he picked up the phone. "Dr. Friedman," I said, "I'm Peter Greenberg, a psychologist. I wonder if you could see me."

"Are you in pain?" said a soft, deep baritone.

"Yes. I would appreciate it if you saw me as soon as possible. I was in analysis, some thirty years ago, but now I have to sort out some contemporary stuff."

"How about next Friday, at eight?"

"Perfect."

He gave me his address.

Before Heather, the next patient, I had a few minutes, time enough for a chat with Lillian. I called, and the phone rang and rang. She had probably unplugged the answering machine. She knew well my tendency to apologize profusely the day after a fight. This time she was very angry and apparently wanted me to stew in my juices rather than hear how terribly sorry I was. Frustrated, I'd have to wait until evening — assuming that she didn't dump me and was still at home.

I closed my eyes, focussing on the pain in the pit of my stomach. I deepened my breathing. No need to read my notes on Heather. She was my favourite patient, and I remembered our conversations well.

Heather

At ten o'clock exactly, I opened the door to my waiting room. Where was Heather? More often than not, I heard her open the door from the hallway about ten minutes early. Recently, she was the only patient I saw three times a week, and I enjoyed her appointment more than any other. She not only paid my top fee, but I looked forward to witnessing her peaks and valleys as she slogged along with the novel she was writing.

I left the door to my consulting room open, turned around, and checked my phone. No new patients had called to make an appointment. Too bad. To top it off, Heather had failed to come on time or call. I perched on my chair, my back to the waiting room. No doubt Heather was caught in traffic or didn't find a parking spot. The reassurance lasted only a moment. She had never been late before. Why didn't she notify me about being late?

I remembered how a few sessions before she had pulled out the cell phone out of her purse to switch off a call. So she could have called me if she got caught in traffic. My mind rummaged for reasons why she might be dissatisfied or angry with me, but came up with nothing. Had something happened at home? Her emotionally abusive husband might have interfered with her treatment. But why would that happen now, and not a year ago when she started seeing me? At sixty-five, her health was good, and there seemed no reason for her skipping a session.

Five after ten. Cheeks hot, I started a fantasy of Stan, Heather's husband, calling to announce her death. In the next frame, I stood in my black suit and tie in the funeral home where her tearful son was delivering a eulogy, which mentioned all I had done for his mother. Even in grief, I remembered how I hadn't seen any new patients for months, and how Heather's abandoning me would only hasten my death by leisure. I pictured myself unshaven in a white undershirt and short khaki pants sitting by the computer, working on my memoirs, and I shuddered. I knew nothing about my life worthy of that effort. Teary and bored, I was writing every day only to kill time and stave off a premature heart attack.

In the waiting room, the empty chairs made me think of a desolate baseball field in mid-winter. My anxiety peaked. But what was I panicking about?

I strode back to my desk and lowered myself onto the chair. After riffling through my patient's phone numbers, I called Heather's cell phone. I got her voice mail. I left a brief message, asking her how she was feeling. Despite my panic, the irony didn't escape me: nearing disorganization, I had called about her feelings only to soothe myself.

"Sorry I'm late," I heard Heather pipe at the entrance to my consulting room.

Relieved, I struggled to my feet. My fantasies of doom and gloom almost evaporated. I felt acutely alert, ready to do battle. "Please come in," I said. As she made her way to her chair, I strode to the door and closed it. Then I sat down and peered at her. Her eyes glinted anxiously. I remembered my best asset: even in the worst crisis, in the most awful angst, I kept a poker face, a survival strategy refined by decades of stresses at work.

"Sorry I'm late," she said again, avoiding eye contact. "I just couldn't get going this morning." She lowered her eyes, gazing at her knees.

Usually she came to see me made up and dressed elegantly, as if on her way to the opera or a cocktail party. That Friday she wore a plaid shirt, jeans, and much used running shoes. Despite my monster fear of losing her, I did what I had to do. I asked her if she didn't feel like coming.

"Yes . . . no . . . you're right . . . I didn't feel like coming . . . today. I came because I didn't want you to think I'm copping out."

My God, what a raw transference reaction! I felt like rolling my eyes in mock despair. We would have to explore where we were at in our relationship, her feelings about me, whatever impelled her to come late. But after a panic attack, in my own office, I felt poorly equipped for such intimacies, though in calmer days I was raring to go whenever the fulcrum of therapy made an appearance. "Begin at the beginning," I managed to say in a soothing, gentle voice, "and tell me what you're feeling."

She pushed herself onto the back of her chair. Her alert, dark-brown eyes contrasted sharply with her hoary hair. For the first time ever, she lifted one foot onto the ottoman. The sole of the other foot remained firmly planted on the rya rug. Rhythmically she tapped the floor with her heel. She gazed toward me without maintaining eye contact. "Look, last session, on Wednesday, I tried to open up about my novel, but you were cold and indifferent."

I couldn't tell if she felt hurt, indignant, or both. Still reeling from my end-of-my-life fantasies while I had waited for her, I stared at her. I was determined to get to the bottom of the problem, my anxiety under control now that I had a real, not imagined, crisis on my hands. "Remind me what happened," I said, almost matter-of-factly.

"I was telling you about Marla's love for Ed, and how she felt physically attracted to him. I told you how I wanted to have a scene about them having a tryst, at her invitation. But you looked bored, as if impatient for me to get to the point."

I barely remembered that passage of the novel. "I'm not aware of any boredom at that point. But please continue." I immediately regretted saying "at that point." It might have reinforced the idea that, indeed, I was bored with her novel.

"You know how hard it is for me to talk about sex. It took me months before I told you that Stan loses his erections soon after he penetrates me. In my whole life, I had sex only with him, and I've never had an orgasm from intercourse. You knew all that." She gazed at her knee, and once again was blushing as she broached that topic. "I have orgasms only when I masturbate." She paused a while, then raised her head and stared me in the eye. "You knew how hard it is for me to write about sex! Instead of encouraging me, you looked uninterested, as if hurrying to get it over with. You repeatedly looked at the clock, and that bothered me. Whenever you do it, I get the impression you don't care about me, I'm just another patient who pays your fees, and you can hardly wait for me to leave. I'm sure you enjoy working with young girls. You just tolerate me because I pay you six hundred dollars a week for the privilege of you stealing looks at your clock."

Of course, I did take an interest in her, but I didn't want to sound apologetic, or even worse, too anxious to mend fences before we got to the bottom of her feelings. I removed my feet from the ottoman and planted them on the rug. "You sound very angry right now."

"I'm not *very* angry! You're exaggerating. I'm annoyed. I got disappointed on Wednesday because you failed to support me! I felt I was drowning, but instead of showing under-standing, you were looking at the clock galore. For two days I've been upset. It even occurred to me not to come back. If I can't get support when I feel vulnerable, what do I need you for?"

"You're angry with me because I didn't come through when you needed me."

"Exactly! Here I come three times a week, I share with you all my pain and insecurities, I like you, I depend on you, and you look at the clock when I'm sharing something really painful."

"I was dense and insensitive, a clod," I said, knowing that she had attacked me to the best of her ability and wouldn't dump me.

"And that annoyed me. You usually care about me and point out the psychology of what I'm writing. You suggested that Marla is falling in love with Ed even before I was ready to go there. I was so grateful to you that I felt like dedicating the novel to you. I can't do it because my husband would feel betrayed. Look, he is terribly possessive."

It occurred to me that hysterical women may be charming in their twenties and thirties, but a parody of themselves in their sixties — an observation to share with a colleague, but not with her. Perhaps I could tell Christine about that. With difficulty I tried to refocus on Heather's hurt and anger. "I think you do like me, and you had a hard time getting angry with me."

"That's true. Look, I like it whenever you support me, like when my husband puts me down. I never had a man in my life who really cared about me. My father sold insurance six days a week, and on Sundays he stayed in bed, in pyjamas. He was never there for me . . . "

I thought about Christine. It would be a relief to unburden myself to a fellow psychologist before I talked with Dr. Friedman, just to admit I was having a hard time at work. I would call her right after I saw Heather. Luckily, I knew Christine's habits. We had been working on an article for months and met every two weeks.

" . . . she preferred my sister because she was a charmer, a good ballet dancer, and a good student. I had thick legs, and my grades were average."

Heather must have been talking about her mother. "She also didn't show many signs of caring. Small wonder I left home early and soon fell for my husband who showed me a lot of attention." She paused, deep in thought. "I had no idea Stan would turn into an abuser. He never hit me, but he put me down so many times."

And here she was complaining about her emotionally abusive husband to me, a wife beater! I looked at my hand, the one that had slugged Lillian. There was no blood on it, but it appeared monstrous, the hand of an abusive husband comforting an abuser's wife. I felt as if anyone could see through me and join the chorus of condemnation. Was Heather aware of my hypocrisy? She was talking about falling in love with Stan and failing to realize he had a mean streak until they already had three children.

I would call Lillian again, but omit any requests for forgiveness — they only made her angry. I looked Heather in the eye. "You stayed with Stan because women of your generation didn't break up marriages. They stayed married for the children's sake." I wondered if Lillian would dump me this time. I decided to call her every hour, between patients.

"You're right! I'm sure that Edith, my daughter, wouldn't put up with abuse from any man . . . "

Her words were boring a hole in my heart. With only ten minutes to go, there was no reason to declare I wasn't feeling well. I hated to cut sessions short under the guise of illness. Patients distrust a sickly therapist.

" . . . and that's why Edith left her husband. It hurts me to think that she divorced him even though he never abused her. I feel I'm stupid for staying with an abusive husband." She paused and peered at her wristwatch. She raised her head and gazed at me, pensive.

What a bad day — a wife beater, soothing the pains of an abused woman! What would Christine or my colleagues say about such a paradox? Meanwhile, I would call Lillian before calling Christine.

Heather smiled. "You were right, doctor. The business of me converting to Judaism was just an attempt on my part to get closer to you. You warned me at the time I was acting impulsively by contacting Rabbi Feldman. I initially felt surprised at your comment, but now I can see that I was in a hurry and I was, as you said, taking a major step in life without discussing it with you. 'There are simpler ways of getting close to me,' you said. 'You don't have to convert, you don't have to do something just because you think it will please me.' Those were your words. Now I can see you were right."

"We have just a few minutes left," I said. "You got closer to me today by expressing your anger and disappointment. You rested one foot on the ottoman, a sign of feeling less inhibited with me. It was unfortunate that you chose to come late, but your indignation was loud and clear. You crossed a milestone. You let me know you have negative feelings toward me, like hurt and frustration."

"I feel better than when I entered. I was really distraught then. I feel my head is in good shape," she laughed.

I tried my best to beam a smile at her. "We'll stop for today."

As soon as the door shut behind her, I closed my eyes and slowly let out a deep breath, relieved that Heather had not dumped me, that she was feeling better. I could count on her to see me on Monday. For the first time ever, I felt I could live without being a psychologist, without seeing patients, without the fears of being abandoned into retirement and a leisurely death. That thought was so new and so unexpected that I couldn't digest it. What would become of me now that I had broken a personal taboo? I leaned against the door for a while. Nothing special happened, and I felt cheated for that moment lapsing without even a trace. I lurched to my desk and sat down.

After scrawling a quarter of a page on Heather's chart — I saw her frequently and saw no need to enter into details — I dialled home. The phone rang and rang. Apparently, Lillian had still not plugged in the line. I felt like doing something drastic to allay my anxiety, like calling my twelve-thirty and one-thirty patients to tell them I had an emergency and couldn't see them that day. I would, of course, apologize deeply, then offer make-up appointments on Monday or Tuesday. My idea was to drive home and comfort Lillian. However, when the answering machine at home didn't kick in, I concluded she must be in a rage.

I dialled Christine. I needed to confess my crime, unburden my guilt. Christine's office was across the street, just a minute walk from mine. Her taped message came on, then the beep. "Hi Christine," I said, "it's Peter. It's urgent. Could I come to your office and talk? Please call."

I looked at my watch. Five to twelve. I hoped Christine would be available soon. Heart pounding, I couldn't sit by my desk or on my chair. I stood up and walked and walked around the room like a tiger in a narrow cage. As I glanced at my watch again and again, my restlessness grew. I was about to give up, when the phone rang.

"Hi Peter! How are you?"

"Not too good. When can I talk to you?"

"Today?"

"Please, Christine."

"I finish at four."

"What about now?"

"Right now?" She paused, and I pictured her furrowing her brows. "If you don't mind me eating a sandwich, I'm free until twelve twenty-five. I have to review my notes on the twelve-thirty patient."

"I'll be there in a couple of minutes."

From a drawer in my desk, I pulled out the list of my patients' cell-phone numbers. I called the twelve-thirty patient and, luckily, got his voice mail. I cancelled the appointment and added that I'd call later. Unfortunately, the one-thirty patient answered the phone. "Hi David," I said in as calm a voice as I could muster, "it's Peter Greenberg. I'm sorry to cancel today's appointment."

"Are you okay? I hope it's nothing too serious." He sounded warm and genuinely concerned, and I hated myself for cancelling someone kinder and more empathetic than I was at that moment. How selfish could I get?

"I'll be all right, after the weekend. Can I see you Monday at two-thirty?"

"That's fine. I'll be there. Take good care of yourself, Peter." Despite my hurry, I realized that some patients were as concerned about me as I was about them, at times even more.

I hung up, opened the door to the waiting room, put on my coat, and hurried out. In my rush to cross the street, I remembered that I hadn't locked the doors to my office.

"What the hell! I keep nothing valuable there." I was too eager to confide in Christine to consider my confidential files.

Christine

I had known Christine since graduate school — almost forty years. We were friends then, and shared miseries and triumphs. Weeks before her marriage, she had invited me for dinner in her apartment. I accepted, thinking that she needed distraction from the busyness of orchestrating a wedding. The two of us ate, drank, laughed, and smoked pot. Without preamble, she began fondling my inner thighs. I was surprized, as there had never been anything sexual between us. Was she saying goodbye to a single woman's freedom? Was she angry or disappointed with Brian, her fiance? At the time, I felt no need to explore why we ended up naked in her bed. I even felt flattered that she had chosen me for the occasion.

We flunked that encounter. Harbouring little passion for each other, we went through the motions of foreplay and lovemaking as if following a research protocol, and tried, but in vain, to arouse each other. After the gasping dissipated, we laughed at our botched-up affair.

For a few years, we kept our distance, as if to erase the memory of that arid experience. As again and again we ran into each other at professional conventions, gradually we renewed our friendship. A year before I slugged my wife, I had become interested in gratitude in personality disorders and invited Christine to join me in writing an article. She would review the literature and be the junior author. She agreed, and every two weeks we met in her office to go over our progress. The experiment just before her wedding was never mentioned.

Christine's office was located in a building with a large waiting room by the entrance on the main floor. The receptionist knew me by sight and saw no reason to check with Christine. I walked straight up the stairs and knocked on the door of what must have been a bedroom before the building was converted into therapists' offices. In a moment, Christine opened, holding a bitten sandwich in one hand. Her hair was dyed raven-black, and her unfashionably long mane reached her shoulders. Her eyes were chestnut-brown and her cheeks puffy from gaining weight over the last ten years. She wore a pink blouse, a single strand of fake pearls, and long, black pants. Very professional-looking.

"Please, come in," she said, her tone as semi-formal as her attire. What was I doing in her office, in the middle of a working day, intruding on her lunch break? Was she annoyed by my insistence and impromptu visit? Or was she adopting a listening attitude, honed by decades of tuning in on anxious, disturbed people? Perhaps I shouldn't have come. What could she do for me in twenty-five minutes? I could thank her for being there for me, then swivel on my heels, and go back to my office.

"Thank you," I managed to mutter and headed to one of her two imitation Louis the XV chairs with upholstered arms. Behind the chairs stood a desk. Above the desk, on the wall, hung Christine's five framed diplomas. By the window, stretched an analyst's brown leather couch with an unfolded, large tissue paper where the patient's head rested. The couch was a relic of her training in psychoanalysis, in the seventies. For many years she hadn't had patients in analysis, as she had grown disillusioned by both its theories and practices. "What's up, Peter?" she asked as she sat down and took a bite of her sandwich.

I stared at her thick legs. My lowered gaze must have given away my embarrassment and discomfort. Remembering we had too little time and so much to talk about, I raised my eyes and peered into her expectant face. Was she truly curious and interested in my plight, or just assuming a much-rehearsed professional posture? In her eyes, was I a cipher, a statistic, or a friend? "I'm having problems at work. It's hard for me to concentrate. My mind is wandering when patients talk."

One of her eyebrows went up a bit. "You sounded upset on the phone. Is it some counter-transference to a difficult patient?"

Counter-transference. Already she was jumping to conclusions, dealing with me like a colleague in distress. Where was our friendship? I wondered if I had enough time to explain my torments. I felt I owed her an explanation, having butted into her office and alarmed her. "Sort of. I'm having difficulties with all my patients." I stopped. Was it was wise to go on with that admission of incapacity? Too personal, too shameful. After all, a necessary theorem of the therapy trade is that problems call for solutions. A therapist's hardship at work is something to be dissected, understood, resolved. Sharing personal issues with peers is just a means to that end. I propped my chin on my fist and said, "I'm in trouble. I already made an appointment with Milt Friedman for next Friday. But I had to talk to you. I felt I was freaking out, going into my own problems while my patients were talking to me. I barely kept my cool."

She rested her sandwich on her lap and leaned forward. "Did anybody complain or remark that you're acting out of character?"

"I had no clashes with patients. But I . . . I . . . was afraid I'd flip, tell them I'm not capable of seeing them anymore." Time was precious, yet here I was, beating around the bush. I had only a few minutes to unburden myself. I turned my head and gazed at the couch. "Christine, I had a fight with Lillian. It got out of hand and I . . . I . . . slapped her." Staring at Christine's shoulder allayed the pain of my confession. "I hit her hard, and she fell to the floor." I paused, hoping Christine would say something. "Now Lillian isn't talking to me." Despite Christine's silence I felt relieved. My crime was out in the open. I felt less burdened, less ashamed.

"Did you come here to dump on me that you beat your wife?" She looked stern. "Is that what's bugging you? Well, I too would feel upset if I had to contend with wife beating. I think you're lucky she didn't charge you with assault."

I felt accused, embarrassed, diminished. "I don't find you supportive, Christine. I'm here to dump on you? That's harsh, Christine!" It bothered me that I didn't get any empathy or kind words. Was she annoyed — no, angry — that I'd beaten a woman? I had known for decades how most women are intolerant and vindictive about physical abuse. I felt angry with myself. Why, oh why, did I broadcast my marital hassles, instead of just waiting a week, then calmly sharing them with Milt Friedman? I'd humiliated myself by washing my dirty laundry in public. Christine, on the other hand, was discreet. She would have kept her weakness to herself, shared it only with her analyst, then, years later, shared it with others as a distant memory. Suddenly I envied her deeply: her going through life with seemingly few crises, without my ups and downs.

She eyed her watch. "Our time is limited, Peter. I want you to know you're my friend, but I can't accept your abusing Lillian. For me that's a no-no. I resent it that you came running for support just a few hours after you abused your wife. You're using me."

Her portrayal of me as a sordid wife beater, without even knowing the circumstances, lessened my anxious clinging. I was angry. Demolish her! I barked at myself. "And you? Didn't you use me badly?" I said with clenched teeth. "You set me up to fuck you just before you married Brian."

She stared me in the face, one eye half-closed. "Bringing up stuff from decades ago! That's dirty pool! So are we even now? You got your guilt and anger off your chest. Are you satisfied?"

I wouldn't stoop to a meaner altercation. She meant a lot to me, and her acceptance was crucial. "I got hurt when you rebuffed me," I said in a thin voice. "I shared what's troubling me, and you passed a harsh judgement."

"We go back a long way, Peter, but I can't be your therapist. Also, it didn't look like you wanted to talk to me in particular. You felt lonely and in pain, and you conjured up my name. But if the walls had ears, you'd be talking to them." She peered at her watch. "Excuse me, but I have to go over a chart. Talk to you later."

In slow motion, I stood up. Instead of comforting, she had confronted me, summed me up, labelled me. As I looked at her black mane, another wave of anger swelled. My friend didn't understand me, and I could only turn to a therapist, a designated source of support and empathy. Christine, a professional trained to listen to people in distress, had passed a judgement, carried away by preconceived ideas. Loneliness flooded over me. "At any rate," I finally said, "thank you for your time. I'll see you next week, when we go over the article."

She shook her head, almost imperceptibly. "Sorry, Peter. I need a break, some distance from you. Go ahead! Look for another co-author! I'll understand."

Now she was rejecting me! Not only didn't I get a dollop of affection, but she was dumping me, indignant that I'd slapped Lillian. I put forth my hand, but avoided gazing into her eyes. "It'll be all right. Thank you for your time."

I hurried out to the street. What would I do the next two hours? I had cancelled the one-thirty appointment to recover from the morning's stresses. I crossed the street to my office, took off my coat, and checked the phone. No messages. It worried me that Lillian hadn't called.

I dialled home. Once again, no answer. Hurt and angry, Lillian was shunning me as if I were a leper. Though I had plenty of time on my hands, there was no point in going home. I remembered a movie where a wife uses her lipstick to write a brief goodbye to her husband on their washroom mirror. At least, despite our fights, Lillian had never mentioned a break-up.

Though I had a sandwich and a can of Diet Coke in my briefcase, I walked to a restaurant at Yonge Street, a ten-minute stroll. On the way, I reviewed my clashes with Lillian and Christine. I couldn't help dwelling on my sessions with Harvey and Heather and my failure to provide them with optimal treatment. I feared how I'd cope with Debbie, my last appointment that day.

Where was life leading me? I asked myself as I sipped coffee in the restaurant. In one day, two women had indicated they wanted me at arm's length. Though I was in love with my work — my authentic world, my shelter — I'd been distractible with two patients; the gap between me and death by leisure had grown maddeningly shorter.

I pictured Heather staring at me on Monday, inquisitive and piercing. "Are you okay, doctor?" she'd ask. I'd mumble something evasive. Then she'd probe, "What's on your mind?" I'd try to gain time to compose myself by asking, "Why are you asking me that right now?"

"You acted strange last time," she'd shoot. "I thought something was wrong with you, doctor. But how are you feeling?" the role reversal would go on, "Please tell me."

I reassured myself that I could get away from her probing with, "What did *you* think about last session?" or, even better, "What fantasies did you have about me?"

I shuddered. Being candid would only reveal how impaired I'd been. Trust in therapists is like a match: it can be used only once. Afterward, it's very hard to rekindle the flame.

Back in my office, the phone signalled a message for me. Was it Lillian calling to say she was dumping me? Was Debbie announcing she was cancelling her session? I pushed the right buttons and found out that Paul, my three-thirty patient on Tuesday, had called to cancel. He apologized and asked to rebook. I sighed. Relieved that at least no calamities had come my way, I went over my last week's notes on Debbie.

Debbie

When I opened the door to my waiting room, Debbie was sitting on a chair, absent-mindedly gazing into empty space. As soon as she noticed me standing nearby, she hurried to open her purse and quickly slipped on huge black sunglasses. I wondered what was up, but didn't comment. Her blond hair was a bit dishevelled, and she wore a bluish, un-ironed blouse and scruffy jeans — a bit less groomed than usual. The second patient to show up to her appointment too casually dressed.

"Good afternoon," I said invitingly. "Please, come in." I had been seeing Debbie for thirteen years, since she was at university, and quite often she had something in store to surprise me. Why was she wearing those dark sunglasses indoors? Had she been crying a lot? And why hide it from me?

Without a word, she slowly walked past me and sat on the edge of her chair, feet firmly planted on the rya rug. She wouldn't make use of the ottoman, I reasoned. After I installed myself on my chair, she appeared to be gazing at me, then looked aside. "What's up, Debbie?" I asked, "what are you feeling right now?"

She remained silent. I knew from experience that the changes in her behaviour — black sunglasses, un-ironed blouse, inclining forward at the edge of her chair as if to be closer to me, yet peering aside, in silence — signalled one more crisis in her life. I raised my chin and watched her down my nose, readying myself for her onslaught. Over the years, without warning, she had frightened and worried me, banging out of my office, or throwing the box of Kleenex next to her at the wall. Such bursts of rage had become much less frequent over the years, but she was still prone to fits of temper rather than discussing what upset her. What should her next step be? I remembered how in graduate school one author had referred to borderline patients as "stable instability." That fitted Debbie to a T.

I had to soothe her before she got out of hand. "Debbie," I said, "you and I go back a long way. I have the feeling you're upset today. Let me in, tell me what's cooking."

Silence.

"Debbie," I continued after a pause, "it bothers me that you're not looking in my direction, as if I'm not in the room. Please look at me! I need to feel you're with me, right here, right now, and not miles away, lost in space." Nothing like a borderline to dispel my hang-ups and problems with concentration and put me to work, real work. That's why I liked her. The disturbing vibes she was sending kept me alert and alive despite my own distress. "I'm competent," I told myself. "I'm not about to retire," I smiled inwardly.

Silence.

I raised my voice a bit. "Debbie," I leaned forward, hands cupping my knees. "for God's sake, don't keep me in suspense! Look at me and start from the beginning. What's bugging you?"

She turned in my direction. Her thin lower lip quivered. Was she crying behind the black sunglasses? "My father," she half-whispered, "has a brain tumour. The doctor said he has three to six months to live."

Oh boy! Was she mourning him already? Was she angry? I had to go easy. That was a minefield. One rash step and she would explode. It surprised me that despite my lack of sleep, my guilt, Lillian's and Christine's rejection, and the day's stresses, I felt ready to deal with Debbie's upset, not mine. "I'm very sorry to hear that, Debbie. I didn't know he was ill."

"For months he was complaining of dizziness and headaches. Last Saturday he fainted, and my mother took him to the hospital. They did a lot of tests, and yesterday the doctor told us he's dying."

"Have you been crying? I thought you had sunglasses on because you didn't want me to see your red and puffy eyes."

She went silent, and I almost regretted interpreting the black glasses too soon. What a trap! Her chest heaving up and down showed how anxious she was.

"I've been crying a lot, and my eyes are swollen. But that's not why I'm wearing sunglasses." She stopped, as if searching for words. I eyed the black plastic lenses concealing her eyes from me. Her lip was still quivering. "I'm wearing them because . . . because . . . you're not a religious Jew!" She wiped her mouth with the back of her palm, as if to erase what she'd said.

"Go on," I coaxed her.

"I know you're secular. You come to work on all the Jewish holidays. You even saw me once in Yom Kippur. You don't care about God and religion, so it's hard for me to tell you that I've really forgiven my father!"

I was flabbergasted, but managed to conceal it. "Forgiven your father?" I said, to gain time.

"Yes, first I cried a lot and felt overwhelmed and desperate. When I came home from the hospital I felt calm and decided that I forgave my father."

Another one of her surprises. I wondered if I had enough stamina to deal with her fusion of religion and denial. How I longed to go home, appease Lillian, take a break from people who demanded close attention and left me little room to lick my own wounds. "Just like that? You felt calm and forgave him everything?"

"I knew you'd doubt it! That's why I'm wearing sunglasses. I can look at you without you seeing my eyes. Safer that way. Then I have a measure of control over you." There was a ring of sarcasm in her voice. "Many times you told me that I try to control you."

Debbie would be one of the last to leave me. She couldn't survive without her weekly fix of therapy and would stay until terminal illness or advanced Alzheimer's cut short my career. She'd have a hard time without me, and at the end I'd have to refer her to a young therapist who'd treat her for decades. Christine called such lifers "junkies," and had no patience with them. I, on the other hand, appreciated loyal patients who posed no threat of abandonment. "Debbie," I said firmly, "you're doing it right now!"

"Doing what?"

"Trying to control me! I can't see your eyes and gauge my impact on you. You hide behind the sunglasses and manipulate me by limiting contact between us. If this goes on, you'll defeat me by tying my hands behind my back." I paused to assess the impact of my words.

She responded with pig-headed silence. A streetcar jangled by.

"Debbie," I chided, "please remove your glasses and let's talk, really talk. In all these years you've been with me, I've never assaulted you, and I won't do it now that your father is dying." Knowing that she wouldn't leave me, I could be myself, focus on reaching her rather than brooding about my conflicts.

"Yes," she rushed to reply, "you've been kind to me all these years. But every time I had a change of heart, you cautioned me that I was impulsive. I was supposed to count to eleven every time I got involved with a man. Often you were right, I admit. Yes, I've a tendency to get involved with the wrong kind of guys, and I have to watch out. But this time it's different. I came home and had this epiphany: my father molested me when I was a child, and I'm grateful to you for helping me remember it. When I first came to see you, it was all under the rug. But now I'm a woman of thirty-three, and I can't go on blaming him. I love my father and have to forgive him."

I was only partially surprised. She often got into disturbed relationships and over the years I'd witnessed her falling in and out of love with hurtful misfits and unpublished poets. "It's a step forward for you to recognize positive feelings for your father, but what about the sunglasses, what do these feelings have to do with hiding your eyes from me?"

"I don't want you to tell me that I forgave my father on a whim. You have no idea, Peter, how my whole body, my whole being is in the grip of forgiveness. You're not religious and you don't know what it feels like to be born again. You can't understand what it's like to be ready to resume your life where you left it, in your childhood."

I felt a bit hurt. Was she casting doubt on my ability to empathize with her? I felt like a beginning therapist whose talents were being challenged. I pinched my lips to control my impatience with her epiphany. "But Debbie, only weeks ago you were enraged with your father and repeated that he is the root of your screwy relationships. I'm quoting your own words."

"That's it! That's why I'm wearing sunglasses. Whenever I'm about to win an argument you bring up my anger at my father molesting me. I can't win with you. You must let go of your fucking the-patient-is-always-wrong stance. Part of my epiphany is that I don't want you to harp on my so-called inconsistencies. You have a way of pointing them out whenever I've a new man in my life, or when I feel like moving west. I'm sick and tired of you focussing on my weaknesses. This time I want to be a grown-up, to be taken seriously, not treated like a girl with temper tantrums. I know what I feel, and I don't want you to talk me out of it."

The sunglasses were a new invention, but I'd heard many of her arguments before. I stole a glance at my clock. I had fifteen — no, eighteen — minutes to go. A long, exhausting time. She'd criticize me and all I'd said over the years. But this time I didn't expect her to get enraged. The epiphany about love and forgiveness would keep her in check. I probably looked calm, as usual. That would help her control her temper. "Looks like you feel threatened by me."

"Whenever I try to become independent of you, you say I'm impulsive or that I'm angry with you. But today it's a new tune." She raised her voice. "I don't feel threatened by you today! I'm getting exasperated because you're a fucking atheist who refuses to understand that abused people can forgive their fathers. Yes, it came suddenly, but that's what an epiphany is all about. An idea comes over you and grips you. I put on the sunglasses to protect myself from your bullshit skepticism. To tell you the truth, I even thought of taking a break from therapy."

That comment punched me in the gut. What if she didn't come back the week after? I pictured my appointment book without her name on Fridays, and for the first time ever, I felt that our relationship could come to an end. "Debbie," my brows furrowed, "it's good that you're discussing your plans with me rather than rushing to act on them. Looks like you're afraid I might talk you out of your love for your father. The opposite is true. It's a step forward for you to recognize feelings other than anger for him." I felt flattered: my capacity to come up with therapeutic lines even in the face of fear was intact. Researchers were right: being an experienced therapist is the most important dimension in this absurd process. I could still do battle with my own problems while wrangling with hers.

"Are you all right, Peter?" she lowered her voice.

An awl poked my heart. "I'm fine," I lied. "But what have you noticed?"

"Strange. You seem strange today. Kind of slow, taking time before you talk to me. Did my sunglasses bother you? Or is it . . . " She furrowed her brows, and two lines sprang to life right above the bridge of her glasses. "I mentioned taking a break from therapy, and you winced. It was so subtle that I hardly noticed it initially. Were you upset about it? Please, tell me the truth. Don't give me some cockeyed therapy baloney."

How well borderline patients read their therapist's feelings and motives, better than any other group! "Maybe 'upset' is not the right word. Only concerned about you leaving therapy just when you just began to change attitudes about your father. It's all too new, too raw for you and me."

The lines between her eyebrows gradually vanished. A thin smile pushed back the corners of her mouth. She took her time. In slow motion, she raised her hands, pinched the arms of her sunglasses, and slid them upwards till they rested on her crown. Her green eyes glinted, amused. "So I mentioned quitting, and you squirm. Just like when my boyfriends mention problems in the relationship, and I panic. What's the matter, Peter, why are so anxious about me taking a break, huh? Can't you live without me? Is your caseload so low that you can't make ends meet?"

I gasped and gazed at her shoulder to avoid her piercing eyes. Truth is the best excuse, I preached to myself. "Debbie," I said and looked her in the face, "we've been together a long time, and I like working with you, I like you. The idea of not seeing you bothered me. I don't like Fridays without you. As for my caseload, it's low because I'm close to retirement and no longer advertise that I have openings in my practice. I deal primarily with old patients."

She looked angry. "You want me to stay in therapy because you want to help me, or because you're afraid of losing money?"

Her directness disarmed me. "Money doesn't have a lot to do with it. I wouldn't want to lose you after all these years. I'm not ready to say goodbye." I paused, and she peered at me as if for the first time.

"I'm in a forgiving mood, remember?" She let out a thin smile. "I forgave my father, and I forgive you for clinging to me. I won't leave you right away."

I wanted to express my appreciation. "I feel—"

"Don't worry, Peter. You were there for me all these years. I'll stay with you for a while until you are ready to say goodbye. I know how it feels when somebody dumps you, and I won't do that to you. You helped me, and I'm paying you in kind. You can bill me for all your goodbye sessions. You're worth it."

I felt numb. All my worries of being abandoned by patients condensed into one blunt acknowledgement of my vulnerabilities. I felt no harrowing pain and was perplexed that no anxiety flooded me. A clean, surgical ending to our relationship. "How do you really feel about paying for me to say goodbye to you? Or perhaps you too need to say goodbye to me?"

She laughed. "I spent more than fifty thousand dollars on therapy over the years, and a few dollars more won't tip the balance. And you're right. I also need to say goodbye to you. And, believe me, I'm more insecure about forgiving my father than I initially let on. It's a whole new concept, and I'll need your help with it."

I removed my feet from the ottoman. "Debbie, how do you feel about today's session? We covered a lot of ground, anywhere from forgiveness of your father, forgiving me, and plans for leaving therapy."

"I feel nervous, but elated. I feel I accomplished a lot. By the way, I don't have plans for leaving therapy, I *am* leaving at the end of next month."

"Next month?" The words stabbed me in the gut. "Aren't you in a hurry? Saying goodbye in just a few weeks?"

"I know, I know. I'm impulsive. But that, like the colour of my eyes, will never change. I'm fortunate you helped me recognize it. Besides, I'm on a forgiveness kick, I want to forgive myself, start a new chapter in my life." She stopped, as if to deal with an idea that had just come to her. "Will you see me if I get into trouble? I mean, after next month."

"Of course!" I bellowed. "Are you afraid that I'm angry that you're leaving me and will retaliate?"

"Yes. Well, anyhow, it's reassuring to hear I can come back if things get rough."

"Sure. I'm retiring in twenty years. Until then you can always call me."

She rose to her feet and left the room. I stood by the door and pondered my reaction to her leaving. Flooding, I told myself. As behaviour therapists say, I had been exposed in full force to a situation that scared the hell out of me. But instead of collapsing, as I'd fantasized, it relieved me, rendered me almost calm. It even occurred to me that my fantasies of abandonment by patients were a distorted scenario of the end of the world. It perked me up that despite my agonies I'd coped well with Debbie saying goodbye soon. I even took pride in her ending treatment. I was, after all, a professional committed to changes in people's life. Despite my hang-ups, I derived some pleasure from patients no longer craving my company and moving on.

Even if Debbie had ended her treatment impulsively, it was refreshing that she'd overcome her need to cling to me. She might not be ready to live without therapy altogether, of course, but me treating her one decade longer wouldn't accomplish much more than what we'd done so far. "Better let go of her," I mumbled.

"I'll discuss Debbie with Milt Friedman right after we discuss my marriage," I told myself. By leaving, Debbie had helped me cope with my worst conflicts. I'd miss my work with her, but with a single stroke the patient had nearly cured one of her doctor's symptoms. For that I felt grateful.

Lillian

At four-thirty, after a couple of beers at a bar, I headed home. Slowly I opened the front door and stepped inside. Silence. I roamed through the living room and dining room, through the kitchen, even the washroom. "Lillian?" I bellowed at the end of the survey. No answer.

I padded up the stairs and entered our bedroom. She was lounging on our unmade bed in her red robe and silky white pyjamas. "How are you, Lillian?" I asked. "I called you many times. Did you disconnect the phone?"

She nodded, her face frozen expressionless.

I extended my hand, to fondle hers. She drew back her whole body and sat up in bed, eyes wide but lifeless. "I felt terribly guilty the whole day," I said, despite myself.

"No matter what, you always end up terribly sorry. Guilt comes as easy to you as changing a shirt."

"This time it was different. I hit you hard. I feel horribly ashamed."

"Guilt and shame won't change a thing. You hurt me terribly." She smoothed her hair. "You're a pig, Peter. You beat me up when we talked about Dave marrying that shikseh. Right when I needed your support." She paused. "Please leave me alone. I don't want to see or talk to anyone."

"Lying in bed won't solve a thing. Why don't you get dressed? Let's go out, have a bite, talk things over. Maybe we'll find a way out."

She threw the duvet aside and sat up in bed, her toes on the floor. "Typical Peter! Always rushing to yak problems to pieces. You abused me, and now you expect me to forgive you, right? You hope things will go back to where they were before you beat me up, right? Well, Peter, this time you crossed the line! I'm not forgiving anything!" She took off her robe and threw it on the bed. "I haven't decided yet what I'll do, but I'm not going to take you back just because you're begging me to."

Her rant frightened me. Would she leave me? "I made an appointment with a therapist. I'll see him next Friday and have a look at our marriage. I don't want to slug you ever again."

She shook her head and smiled bitterly. "I bet that therapist is a man! You want to dump your guilt on him and say that your wife is a bitch, right? Why not marriage counselling, with a woman? Dealing with two women, you couldn't get away with that bloody bullshit."

"If it's important to you, we'll see a marriage counsellor of your choice."

"I don't want any talking therapy. All I want is to be alone with my thoughts. Why don't you leave me alone, for God's sake? I want to shower and get dressed."

"Let's have dinner out. We can talk about Dave's marriage."

"No! From now on I'll sleep in Dave's room. And I don't want to hear you, you wife beater. Your voice makes me angry!"

"Please, Lillian. I — "

"Shut the fuck up!" She yelled on top of her voice. "Get out of here! Leave me alone!"

I left the bedroom and perched on my favourite chair in the living room. At least she'd mentioned no plans of leaving me. Sleeping in different rooms — for days or weeks — that was something I could put up with. Perhaps it would be better to stay out of her way for a while.

I heard her showering upstairs. After a few minutes I heard her working in the kitchen, probably fixing something to eat. Later on I heard the sound of the television in Dave's room.

I thought about the start of my second therapy. I imagined a dark consulting room, geared toward recreating the womb.

"Doctor," I'd say, after he took down my name and other vital statistics, "I slugged my wife. I'm a wife beater."

He'd listen attentively. I'd share my anxieties at work. I'd work on Debbie leaving me.

"And," he'd gaze at me, inquisitive, "how did you feel when your wife didn't leave you?"

"Relieved, very relieved." I'd tell him about Christine. "In a way, she was as hard on me as Lillian."

I spent a while conversing in my mind with the analyst, then had dinner. After returning to my favourite chair in the living room, I reviewed the day's events in my office. Except for Debbie's comments about me acting differently, no one had alluded to my crisis. Despite my miseries, I soothed others' pain, even mobilized the strength to challenge them. I'd been far from perfect, of course, but I'd performed acceptably, a disturbed but still competent healer.

If only new referrals called, I smiled ruefully. It would lessen my angst about my work life coming to an end. I remembered the green tips of crocuses rising above the cracked ground by my office and felt a stir of satisfaction about seeing patients on Monday morning.

SONS AND FATHERS

SO FAR, IRWIN GLASBERG REASSURES HIMSELF, Jerry's bar mitzvah is coming along just fine. Not a single glitch. His in-laws and parents have been called to the *bimah*, the Shul's raised platform, to intone the blessings before and after the reading of Torah segments. As a ripple of anxiety rises through his excitement, he forces his eyes to follow the English translation of the holy text. It's the story of Abraham almost slaughtering Isaac, his only beloved son. He shivers. He glances at his own son, sitting to his right. Breathing shallowly, Jerry is fidgeting. Soon he'll be called to the bimah to chant the *maftir*, the last segment of that week's Torah portion.

Grey-haired and dark-skinned, Irwin swells with pride: he's soon to play host to dozens of guests he andbhis red-haired, fair-skinned wife Jennifer have invited to the ceremony. He turns around and decorously inspects the Shul. Gathered behind the Glasberg clan, most women are decked out for the occasion in a rainbow of smart hats and festive dresses. The Glasberg men, their male guests, and some regular Shul-goers, wear dark suits that elegantly clash with their lime-white shirts and silk neckties. Together, they exude pomp and a gratifying, solemn excitement.

At last, it's the loud, manly voice of the hoary master of ceremonies summoning the bar mitzvah to the *bimah*. How hesitantly Jerry walks up the stairs to the Torah's lectern. Why must his voice be so high-pitched as he recites the blessings, so tremulous now that he chants the *maftir*? Look at his eyebrows, as thin and downy as a toddler's. And that small praying shawl, draped over his oversized charcoal suit with such a broad, satiny red-and-blue necktie. It makes him look too young for his age — "a shrimp", that's what his taller few friends call him. Against the silence, with everyone watching, Jerry's reedy voice only intensifies his immaturity. Just get the readings over with, one way or the other, Irwin thinks, and be rid of this nagging anxiety!

Summoned to the *bimah*, in unison with Jennifer, Irwin blesses God for ridding him of the burden of his son. His own bar mitzvah, thirty years before, in this same Shul, comes back. How anxious he had been to please his relatives, especially his father! Then a high-powered corporate lawyer, his father not only insisted that Irwin read the Hebrew texts accurately, but also chant them pleasantly, in a loud voice. Days before the ceremony and the readings, he had slept poorly, afraid of disappointing his family. Yet, he'd performed at the *bimah* very well, exactly what had been expected of him. Afterwards, however, it had been weeks before his anguish could subside.

Now his own Jerry stands on the *bimah* alone. He's intoned the blessings and chanted the *maftir* without a blooper, and now is chanting a passage from Kings, the accompaniment to this week's Torah portion. Not a single mistake! As Jerry recites the final prayers, Irwin feels Jennifer pinch his hand twice. He smiles back at her. Turning to the boy's bearded tutor, he nods knowingly and smiles his thanks. His gaze shifts to his own father. Look at him, proud as a peacock, engrossed in his grandson's praying.

Jerry's chanting ends, and everyone is noisily showering him with the traditional soft, coloured candy. Raising his arm to protect himself, Jerry looks so stiff and unresponsive, even as the children swarm to pick the candy from the floor. He must be worried about his upcoming commentary on the Sabbath's Torah portion, the *Dvar Torah*.

"Come, come," the Rabbi is urging the Glasberg family and members of the congregation to hold hands, dance, and sing around the *bimah*. Slipping beside Jerry, Irwin whispers in his ear, "Dance, son, dance! Relax! Just one hurdle left! You can do it!"

Should he have said that? Why was he always afraid of Jerry screwing up in public? Why couldn't he just bask in Jerry's accomplishments so far? Sit back, relax. Why be so hard on Jerry and on himself?

Once again, Jerry stands alone on the *bimah*. Relax, Irwin tells himself. Just weeks before, he'd helped his son edit his *Dvar Torah*. In a few hours, they will host a reception at home. Jerry will stand by the door and greet family friends, relatives, and his own few guests. Nothing demanding. Nothing potentially embarrassing.

Any moment now, Jerry will slide his hand into his jacket's inner pocket, pull out his speech, and read it. Instead, Jerry's eyes have focused on a point above the heads of the congregation, as if trawling for inspiration. "Today," he finally utters, "we won't deal with Torah *per se*, but with a topic that involves us as Jews."

Irwin shudders. The speech he edited revolves around Abraham, one of the few figures in the Bible whose faith God has tested. In our times, his son had written, divine tests are unnecessary, obsolete. The Holocaust, Jerry asserted, poses spiritual questions that only souls unsoiled by rage can answer. Experiments like Abraham's and Job's were relevant only before the advent of violent anti-Semitism. Today, his son had concluded in the prepared speech, testing of one's faith is an everyday event. As a high school teacher of English inured to inarticulate papers, Irwin had marvelled at his son's depth of thinking. He'd encouraged him to read further on the complex issues raised by his *Dvar Torah*.

Now, Jerry gazes into empty space, as if casting for his next sentence. If only Irwin could go up to him, fish the written speech out of his jacket's pocket, and hand the folded pages to his son. "Don't fool around! Read it!" he wants to whisper, his voice firm and authoritative. "Don't embarrass the family and me in front of the congregation! Read your commentary! Go ahead, just do it!"

In a barely audible voice, Jerry begins. "As practising Jews, we must contemplate the fate of the Palestinian people. Millions of them live in squalid quarters. They're hungry and humiliated."

The congregation is so silent, Irwin can hear them breathing.

Irwin's only son goes on. "The Palestinian refugees . . . " he half-moans, " . . . every honest Jew shares in the responsibility for their misery." Irwin's face flushes. A wave of anger floods him. Why is Jerry preaching pity to the congregation? And what do politics have to do with Torah, with the Sabbath services? Why is Jerry — always so shy, so meek, so unassertive — talking down to adults as if they know nothing about the topic? Where does he summon so much chutzpah?

Jerry halts, as if searching for further arguments about the plight of the Palestinians. White-faced, he stammers, "There are now millions of them, in squalid camps. They — "

A voice from behind Jerry bellows, "At the time, there were almost a million Jewish refugees from Arab countries." Irwin spins around. Who has broken the taboo of never butting in during a *Dvar Torah*? One of the Shul's regulars, with abundant white hair under a colourful skullcap is red-faced, as if he can't wait to get his indignation off his chest.

Jerry stands frozen on the *bimah*. Have all his thoughts abandoned him? He looks hurt and helpless, a little boy dressed in adult clothes. The prayer shawl he wears for the first time ever in Shul is a mockery of grown-ups.

The air in the Shul feels as if it has turned into a membrane. Jerry gazes at the ceiling for a few moments. Regaining composure, he goes on, tears gleaming in his eyes. "The Palestinian people are our brethren," he half whispers. "We must love them, nurture them, treat them as equals. They are poor, landless, they are — "

"The bar mitzvah boy forgot our sources," another voice thunders.

Irwin whirls around. Dr. Jacob Mandel, past-president of the Shul, is standing up, both hands clutching the long fringes of his oversized prayer shawl. His knuckles are white now, his thick cheeks red. He mutters something in Hebrew, then hollers, "Get up early in the morning to kill those that conspire to kill you! The Torah sanctifies life! There can be no pity for murderers!"

People applaud. Irwin is mortified. What a terrible scandal! Jerry clasps his hands, crestfallen and pitiable.

Stocky Rabbi Goldfarb has jumped to his feet. His red, blue, and white prayer shawl swings as his outstretched palms motion to the congregation to calm down. He steps up to the *bimah*, and standing next to Jerry, embraces him. "Jerry's approach to his *Dvar Torah* is seemingly unusual, but not against our traditions." The Rabbi's forefinger pushes his glasses up the bridge of his nose. His balding head shines. "Jerry was talking about *tzedakah* — charity, mercy, from the Hebrew *tzedek*, justice. What Jerry was saying is that we Jews have to spread justice and be charitable, even with our perceived enemies. I know, what he said came across as controversial, but it's still acceptable to us Jews. We can't dismiss it. Sometimes, Torah and politics don't mix."

Still standing up, Dr Mandel looks right and left, then bellows, "I want to go on record as saying that there can be no *hesed*, no mercy, no compassion, for our enemies. The Rabbi and the bar mitzvah boy are appeasing murderers." He sits down, angry and self-righteous. Some people applaud.

"Jerry!" a young man Irwin doesn't know hollers from the back of the Shul, "I swear that tomorrow, between four and five after four, I'll indulge in your Jewish-mother guilt."

Some people are laughing, others chatter loudly. The Shul sounds like a vaudeville, thinks Irwin. What an infuriating, embarrassing commotion his son has created.

Rabbi Goldfarb opens a prayer book. His face is stern. "The services will continue on page four hundred and twenty-five," he announces. The leader of the services climbs the steps into the *bimah* and sings the first prayer. The chattering and whispers stop. Jerry walks to the pew and sits down beside Irwin. Why even dignify that boy with a look? Jennifer, of course, stands up, hugs, and kisses him, but she refrains from praise or congratulations. Her embarrassment and shame are obvious.

The services go on. Irwin dreads the end of the prayers: it'll be time for the *kiddush*, the Sabbath luncheon, and their guests will come up to him and his wife to congratulate them. Will their friends and relatives ignore the embarrassment of the *Dvar Torah*? Will they express only polite, lukewarm congratulations to conceal their indignation? Will they hug their hosts or merely shake hands, cooly?

If only the services could continue indefinitely, but it is time for him to bless the wine, and later on, in the Shul's basement, the braided Sabbath bread. Irwin is mortified. His guests shake his hands, congratulate him on Jerry's readings, but omit any references to the humiliating *Dvar Torah*. He's certain they're pussyfooting, afraid of hurting his feelings. He looks around the room and sees Jerry awkwardly dealing with well wishers.

"Brent," Irwin asks his slim and bearded best friend, "could you pass by my house half an hour before the reception starts?"

Brent tweaks his square chin. He must have trimmed his beard that morning: his smooth upper cheeks shine, and his well-cropped moustache looks thinner. "Certainly," he says, "but are you sure I won't be interfering with last-minute preparations?"

"No, not at all. I must get something off my chest."

"The *Dvar Torah*?"

"Yes. It's bugging me."

"I understand."

Once at home, Jerry hurries to his room, probably afraid of being confronted. Frustrated, Irwin changes into jeans and a sweater and helps Jennifer prepare for the evening's reception. "You look uptight," she remarks.

"Are you surprised?"

"No! I'm also upset about Jerry's speech."

"'Speech' you call it? It was one huge guilt trip. And what a chutzpah! To imply that the congregation knows nothing about the Palestinians, and it's up to Jerry Glasberg, a grade eight kid, to preach justice and fairness to them. He shot off his mouth. It had nothing to do with Torah and learning!"

"Look! The reaction he got was a harrowing experience! He needs our support, not your anger. Calm down! He's a kid, Irwin! He's a loner, you know that, an idealist without the benefit of feedback from peers!"

"I felt stunned, mortified! He embarrassed us in front of our guests. I'm so angry I could kick him!"

"Control yourself! You're the adult!" She peers around the room. "I've a lot of things to do right now and I've no time for your tantrums."

At six-thirty, Irwin sits in the living room, anxiously waiting for Brent and his family to arrive. Brent is fifteen minutes late. What if there isn't enough time to air all his concerns?

"It's about Jerry." Irwin pours his best friend a drink. "I felt terribly humiliated by the commotion."

"Just rebellion, Irwin. He's a teenager now. Hormones are crackling in his veins."

"That's not the issue. Jerry hasn't reached puberty. In the gym, he hides behind a towel. He's hairless down there, a shrimp."

"Irwin! You sound derogatory! I know you're angry, but you can't put your son down."

"This morning I thought about Abraham. He got murderously angry with Isaac and almost slit his throat. Only later, when his rage abated, he made up the tale of God testing him."

"You're going too far, Irwin! My David dropped out of school and is on drugs and isn't working. I'm hurt and disappointed, but I don't feel like killing him."

"Are you sure? You can't deny that our teenagers make us feel murderously angry!"

"Use your head, Irwin! You don't even know why Jerry did what he did. Teenagers can be so callous!" His hand taps Irwin's knee. "You're too angry at the moment."

"The Canaanites sacrificed their firstborn, Brent. The Greeks too were honest. Remember Chronos devouring his children?"

"For God's sake, take it easy! To justify your rage, you're quoting myths alien to us Jews. You attribute filicidal rages to Abraham. What a crock! It isn't even hinted at in Genesis or in any commentary!"

Irwin stands up. "Our guests will be here in a moment. I'll be at the door, with Jerry."

"Okay, Irwin. Call me." Slowly Brent rose from his chair. "We have a lot to talk about."

Friends and relatives pour in. The house gleams from the ceiling lights and candles burning in every corner. The guests are effusive, and no one mentions the services at Shul that morning. Jerry stands at the door, greeting all the well-wishers with equanimity, as if nothing unusual has happened. Struggling to conceal his bad mood, Irwin shakes hands with the men and exchanges pecks with the women. He keeps thinking about his conversation with Brent and despite the busyness of the reception, he can't stop thinking about the word "filicide". To control himself, he hauls another stack of Jerry's presents up to the bedroom.

Jennifer meets him in the upstairs hallway. "I talked to Jerry while you were with Brent," she says.

"What did he say?"

"Almost nothing. I did almost all the talking. He was testy and didn't answer my questions."

"What did you ask?"

"I asked him why he gave a speech about the Palestinians instead of reading his *Dvar Torah*."

"Exactly what I want to find out."

"He doesn't trust us with his feelings, Irwin. My hunch is that he felt indignation about the condition of the refugees and decided to use the *bimah* to draw the attention of the congregation."

"On his bar mitzvah, eh? As someone hollered in Shul, here goes Jewish guilt. How many WASPs," his forefinger pokes the air, "feel guilty about what their ancestors did to Canadian Indians? After the reception, I'll talk to him."

She reaches for his stiffened arm. "Please don't! You look so hurt, so angry. It'll only make things worse. Wait a few days!"

With fewer guests streaming in, Irwin stands in the sunroom, where people congregate around the bar. He doesn't want to think about it, but sooner or later people will go home, and he'll have to face his rebellious son. The prospect feels like re-opening wounds that have barely stopped bleeding. Still, he can't wait. His anger demands straight answers.

At about one in the morning, all the guests have departed. Jennifer is placing the leftover food in plastic containers. Irwin takes off his jacket and tie, then pads up the stairs, to confront Jerry in his bedroom.

His son is sitting at the computer, so absorbed with the game he's playing that he doesn't notice his father standing by the door. Twice Irwin clears his throat. Jerry turns around. He blushes, and his fearful eyes assess him.

"In the afternoon I was busy helping your mom," Irwin says icily. "But now," his lower jaw tightens, "we've plenty of time for a man-to-man. After all, now you're a bar mitzvah. You're supposed to be accountable for the moral consequences of your conduct."

Jerry just sits there, breathing shallowly, his eyes downcast. He says nothing.

Irwin draws closer. His son's forehead is level with his navel. "At the Shul you gave a political speech. How come you didn't read your *Dvar Torah?*"

Jerry pulls back. His eyes are gleaming with fear.

"You're quiet, eh? C'mon! This morning you had a lot to say! I'm asking you, why didn't you read the written stuff?"

Jerry's face is a mask of terror. Twice he shakes his head, like a wet dog ridding itself of excess water. "I just wanted to make a point. We Jews sweep these issues under the rug."

"But why the hell did you have to play prophet from the *bimah?* Why not spray your message on a wall, after the ceremony? Do you want be to be a preacher at the family's expense, at *my* expense? C'mon, let's hear it! Why humiliate your mother and me?"

Jerry just shrugs. Does the question have any relevance for him? Has he nothing to say?

Irwin bends forward, grabs Jerry by his shirt, and lifts the limp body off his chair. Now, it occurs to him, his son is as submissive as Isaac was at the altar, on Mount Moriah. Irwin ignores the insight. "Talk, smart aleck, talk!" he hollers. Don't play games with me! In the morning you were alive and kicking, but at night you want to play dumb?"

Like a big tome being slammed shut, the first slap reverberates as Jerry collapses onto the carpet. Irwin kicks him in the side. The ribs offer little resistance. The next kick, harder, in the stomach, makes almost no sound.

"Uh!" Jerry's muffled gasp doubles him over, like a foetus.

"Talk, shithead, or I'll kill you!"

Irwin feels a yank on his arm. "Stop, Irwin, stop!" screams Jennifer. "What are you doing? Today is his bar mitzvah!" She kneels down and buries Jerry's head in her chest. Jerry is wailing like a frightened toddler.

"The bastard asked for it! The whole day he's been against me!"

"He's just a kid! Instead of showing support, you kick him. What kind of father are you?"

"I'm furious!" Irwin barks. He strides to his bedroom. His blood is boiling; he's too upset to change into his pyjamas. Instead, he perches on the bed and riffles through a magazine, his heart pounding. He can't even concentrate on the captions under the photos. When he catches his breath, in his mind he hears Jennifer barking, "What kind of father are you?"

He closes his eyes. He knows: as soon as he calms down, guilt will replace his rage. Like a puppy, he'll fawn on his son and wife. He'll swallow his pride and apologize: head down, he'll swear he'll never do it again. He'll beg forgiveness, arguing like a lawyer that this was the first time he ever raised his hand against his son, the first time he ever slugged anyone since he fought kids in the schoolyard. He holds his face in his hands. What a father! Why hasn't he just put up with the antics of a teenager, a shrimp?

He wobbles to his feet and begins unbuttoning his shirt. "What," he murmurs, "did Isaac ever do to incur his father's rage?"

To Kill A Buddy

Sergeant Yoshua smoothed his trimmed, black moustache with a forefinger, as he drew up the left eyebrow. He glanced at his wristwatch, then barked at our platoon to hop off the trucks in twelve seconds.

"It's twenty to two!" He yelled.

We froze to attention.

"There!" He turned around, forefinger pointing slightly above his shoulder. "By four thirty I want a perfect training camp *right there!*"

My neck and face were freezing. A clump of tall weeds tickled my thighs; my black boots trampled the green grass underfoot. On the horizon, dead fruit trees and a slim cypress — abandoned in the War of '48, I supposed — dotted the leaden skies. There were no birds in sight; early winter in upper Galilee.

"Soldiers!" Sergeant Yoshua went on, his deafening voice trapped between my helmet and scalp. "This is the Golani brigade! Don't drag your asses around here! Run!" He craned his neck to inspect the third row. "Wear a helmet and always carry your weapons, even when you step out to take a dump!"

Before I caught my breath, Corporal Ehud, our squad commander, barked, "Barak, Guidon, and you, Yuval! Unload the four trucks."

The three of us climbed up the trucks' folding ladders empty-handed and trudged down with wooden boxes, tents, and backpacks. We were in no hurry, of course: there were never shortages of shit work for recruits to do. One assignment out of the way, and on the dot, Ehud dreamt up *something* to keep our hands busy. Yet, despite our systematic stalling, wooden boxes of tomatoes, warty cucumbers, onions, and odourless bread began to carve red, green, and golden islands in the grass. We stacked boxes of ammunition in three piles, as Ehud had specified, and set the folded pup tents on top of each other, neatly. We hauled the guys' huge, green-grey backpacks and kicked them into four straight rows.

Four rows? Why *four* rows?

I didn't ask. Three and a half weeks under Ehud's thumb had taught me to keep "why" to myself.

I had learned it the hard way one late afternoon in our second week of basic training. For undisclosed reasons, our platoon had lazed about for almost half an hour. Just as the nirvana of a second, unhurried cigarette had begun to settle in my veins, without the trace of a smile Ehud had announced, "Platoon! You're all kindly invited to a refreshing, pre-dinner run on the highway!"

"Why lug helmets and weapons?" I quipped.

Ehud stared at his bootlaces, then at mine, mute.

Well, for over an hour our platoon raced in and out of the dark shade of fragrant eucalyptus trees arching above the narrow highway to Acre. Boots beating the ground in unison, and sweat rilling down our necks, we thundered by grove after grove of mostly green, tart-smelling Jaffa oranges dangling from beds of silky leaves. Breathing in and out frantically, we ran without a song. Nobody griped and nobody looked back at me gasping in the last row, but in my heart I knew that the guys were mightily pissed with me: I imagined they blamed and cursed me for the extra miles on the road. Back at the regiment, a scarlet-faced and dripping Ehud had panted, "Yuval, you will whitewash two rows of already whitewashed tree trunks *right away*. At midnight, two, and four a.m., see the sergeant on duty. He'll write down all your comments and questions. You're free to tell him," Ehud exhaled like a horse, "'bout the novels you've been reading."

That same night, at four in the morning, a wickedly smiling sergeant on duty asked me for the third time whether I had any questions or comments.

"No, commander," I shivered, humiliated by the weight of the full combat gear and miserably aching to sleep.

Ehud's message had hit me right in the gut: the instructors expected me to respond like a robot and keep my mouth shut unless directly asked. They would bend my body and mind until I behaved just the way they saw fit. From that night on, I just did what the brass told me. Did it fast. And well. No questions asked.

Now, as Barak, Guidon, and I lumbered in and out of the second truck to be unloaded, the turd-coloured tarpaulin of the first amplified the sound of Guidon's transistor radio. Elvis crooned a drippy, new song.

"You guys like this chicken shit?" I plunked a box of ammunition on top of a pile. "Why aren't they playing the good ones, like 'Jailhouse Rock'?"

Guidon whistled a few bars of one of Elvis' tunes. "For national security reasons, dummy." Guidon had begun to bug me from day one, as our platoon sat on cots under a large tent at Tel Hashomer, the intake centre.

"Lay off, Guidon," I said. "You really think the Syrians look for hidden messages in the army hit parade?"

"Look," Guidon said. "One thing the Syrians do just right." He licked the corner of his moustache. "Every other Thursday they truck hookers to their outposts. Hey," he turned to Barak who had just let go of a backpack. "If the Jewish Army brought us broads for free, d'you think Yuval would go for them?"

"Guidon, Guidon," I teased. "You fart too loud. Night and day."

"Quit bickering like a married couple," Barak snarled. "Give me a hand, will you? Don't just stand there, like two Sabbath candles on a table."

"Like an instructor," Guidon winked at me. "Talking down to us like an instructor. Barak, *khabibi*, is it true that you want to become an officer?"

Some twenty metres away, eight unlucky souls were digging trenches with picks and shovels. Farther away, and in no hurry to finish his cushy job, Yoav, Guidon's high-school buddy, was hammering stakes into the ground and enclosing them with burlap. Outhouses?

Sergeant Yoshua hollered and hollered at the top of his lungs as a detachment helped Maurice, the cook, to set up a field kitchen. The same crew later pitched a large tent, our mess hall, with a corner designated for praying. Except for a cemetery, our platoon had set up almost all amenities of military life by twenty after four.

Later in the evening, the colourless light languished on the darkening hilltops and bushes. Maurice, the cook, ladled a soggy salad onto our mess kits, then minuscule black olives, cream cheese, slices of stale bread, and a carrot-tasting red jam. I wolfed down the chow, lapped up the lukewarm tea, and puffed hard on my cigarette. Moments before, Sergeant Yoshua had brayed, "In thirty minutes I want to see your pup-tents pitched in two straight lines! Night manoeuvres to follow!"

In the darkness, Barak and I speedily pitched our tent, whose taut sides kept our backpacks out of sight, then dug a drain all around. Kneeling inside, with four stones we secured one of my olive-green blankets tight on the ground. I rolled the flaps at the entrance and tied them up.

"What d'you think, Barak?" I asked. "Is our lair in accordance with the army beauty code?"

"There are no stupid answers," he said. "Only stupid questions."

I can't remember whether Barak or I suggested that we share a tent. For eighteen years we'd lived in Ramat Gan, only a stone's throw from each other, but Barak and I went to different schools His parents owned a furniture store and attended Shul on all holidays. They voted for Herut, the right. My father worked for the government, my mother taught in kindergarten, and both of them voted for Mapai, the socialists. Fate had separated Barak and me until we shook hands and smiled at each other inside the truck that shipped recruits from the intake centre to Regiment Twelve, just north of Acre — a long ride, by Israeli standards. We broke the ice by cheerily dropping the names of common acquaintances and favourite hangouts in our hometown.

In preparation for that night's manoeuvres, I spread out old newspapers on the grass, then lit them with a match. In a moment, the burning pages scrolled inward, as though bowing low before the conquering flames. Barak and I palmed the remains of the newspapers, then playfully smeared each other's nose, cheeks, and forehead with ash.

"You look like a coal miner after a long day's work," I said.

He donned his helmet, then slung his Uzi over his shoulder. "I've absolutely no intention of ever burying myself underground."

After Sergeant Yoshua's inspection, three squads filed out of the training camp to practise night patrols and ambushes for the umpteenth time. Ehud — that mother! — marched fast. Ahead of me, Guidon's bayonet bobbed up and down against the steely skies, while I, at the squad's tail end, ran nonstop over black rocks and bushes, lugging my F.N. machine gun.

Sergeant Yoshua had fixed me up with that seven-and-a-half kilo monster the evening he'd lined up our platoon inside a warehouse. Onto a tin-covered counter, unceremoniously he had plunked down Uzis, F.N. rifles, and machine guns one after the other. Barak, ahead of me, got a nifty Uzi. "Hurry up, man!" the sergeant hollered, when, stunned, I wavered before taking into my arms the dinosaur with a folded bipod. Right behind me, Guidon and Yoav got away with light, four-point-two kilogram F.N. rifles. This chain of events reinforced my belief that life in the army was largely determined by fate. Sheer luck could make things tolerable — almost — just as one bad twist could drive you crazy.

That evening, Ehud had halted at the foot of a hill. "No water," he'd whispered.

My face had felt hot and clammy despite the chilly eastern wind blowing. Ehud had told us to take up positions looking mostly over the valley. For a long while the squad rehearsed the art of setting up a murderous ambush. Bellies freezing on the ground, our boots tapped wordless messages to one another, first clockwise, then counter-clockwise. At the end, Ehud squatted by each man to check safety catches and ammunition clips, and to see whether we had planted our legs and elbows on the ground properly. He tapped helmet after helmet to signify *b'seder*.

Exercise over, he sat us up in a half circle. Two sips of water, no smoking. Sitting Buddha-like, Ehud faced the squad, looking stern. He grabbed a dead branch nearby and began to stab the ground by his thigh. "After a whole night of waiting for the enemy," he droned, "you're dead tired and scared shitless inside. Guys," he raised his voice, "you better learn quick to lie awake a whole night without taking a leak." In the darkness, Ehud's boyish, unblackened face glowed like a slab of slate.

"Are you there, Yuval?" Ehud asked.

"Yes, commander," I whispered, firm.

"Can you imagine?" Ehud went on, conspiratorial. "Six guys lying in an ambush and listening to a transistor radio? Well, *fedayeen* came up from behind them, threw grenades, and machine-gunned them. Next morning, guys that had carried the stretchers into ambulances told me that the dead bled like slaughtered cattle. Not one inch of green cloth on the corpses." One by one, he gazed at eight blackened faces.

I peered left and right. Above our helmets, five bayonets pierced a low, grey country sky: no pink halos glowed on the horizon. My frozen hands cradled the even colder bipod of my F.N. I cringed inside.

"Stories like that never make the newspapers." Ehud's branch pounded the ground before his shins. "Fools destroy other people's lives. And their own. In that order."

In daylight, Ehud occasionally peeked at some mimeo-graphed instructions, and his presentations came across precise, at times even elegant. After dark, however, he got off with tales of disaster, incompetence, stupidity, tough luck. His yarns depicted the Golani brigade as dumb as The Three Stooges. Ehud, I suspected, scared us in preparation for the worst, because the worst, he preached, lay in wait behind every rock and tree. I have no idea why one night he set aside his tough-guy front and let us in a bit. Born and bred in Jerusalem. Father a labourer, he added, shrugging. "My Jewish Mom," he chuckled, and I could hardly believe that *Corporal Ehud* had used the word "Mom", "she cried her eyes out the day I dropped out of grade eleven to work as a car mechanic."

Now, in front of my eyes, Ehud glanced at his watch. Face solemn, he straightened his spine and slid the dead branch under his butt. "Why d'you think," his voice rose, didactic, "we need bayonets in modern warfare?"

"Can't do without them," I jumped right in. "In the dark, you really can't tell a Jew from an Arab. The guys with bayonets can approach the shadows; others must be careful before they open fire."

"What else?" Ehud demanded. Barak, Guidon, and Yoav muttered their opinions.

Frankly, I preferred night manoeuvres. Once Ehud had witnessed my alertness, I managed to relax even without a smoke, then turned on my favourite fantasies. That particular night I tuned into a private movie about Greta, a German — no, Danish — tourist. Her long, blond hair didn't have that phoney sheen of Jewish women who bleach theirs. A nurse, twenty-eight, let's say, she'd volunteered to help in a dig — the kind of visitor who in her free time enjoys the Holy Land's cheap hashish.

I picked her up at Café Kassit, on the Dizengoff strip, and on that same gorgeous, end-of-July afternoon we shared her red-and-white towel on the Gordon beach. Every few minutes Greta sat up and rubbed a lime-scented cream on her tomato nose and juicy thighs. I *love* juicy thighs. So I felt her inner thighs. And more. In staccato English Greta moaned, "How 'bout a drink, Yuval? Your place or *my* place?"

I came to with a start. From Ehud's answers to the guys' questions, I anxiously pieced together that tomorrow morning the platoon would march to a training field — somewhere. Squad after squad to storm one of the hills. A live-fire drill.

Half way back to the training camp, Ehud the bastard began to run. When, at last, he dismissed the squad, my heart pounded and my lungs ached.

Moaning, Barak and I stood by our tent and took off the helmets we both hated. As I poured water into Barak's cupped hands, the gurgling of my almost-full canteen played the first notes of a minor scale. Drops showered over his wool jacket as, sighing, he scrubbed the ash off his face. From the chin down I was boiling, but after I, too, had splashed my cheeks with ice-cold water from Barak's gurgling canteen, they froze painfully.

"Keep your boots away from the flaps," I suggested, once we'd unlaced them inside our tent. "It might rain tonight."

"Yuval," Barak's hands rummaged inside his backpack. "From the day I've met you, just about every night you tell me the forecast. Have you thought of a career in meteorology?"

"I have no idea what I'd like to study," I said. "Journalism. Or philosophy, perhaps. I don't know."

"You've got almost three years to make up your mind."

As he did every night, from the depths of his backpack Barak unearthed a flashlight and a bunch of letters from Aviva, his girlfriend. I set my machine gun on the ground between us, and in the diminutive light of his flashlight he laid his Uzi on top. Through the trigger guards of both guns I slid a thin rope, tethering the ends to my ankle and his, lest one of the instructors steal our weapons at night. Winter jackets off, we slipped, shivering, under the three blankets covering our weapons.

Barak slid one blue envelope from under the silvery string fastening Aviva's letters, then unfolded three white pages. After he'd rested them for a time on his nostrils, he trained the flashlight on the first page, lips moving as if he were kissing the cold air.

I lit a cigarette. How I hated all army hassles and, especially, nineteen-year-old instructors ordering me around like a German shepherd. When the daily rigmarole ended, I was so keyed up that it took no less than three butts to calm me down.

As smoke filled our tent, I felt angry with myself for not telling Barak the truth. Chicken shit. My line about studying journalism or philosophy was plain chicken shit. What I hadn't told Barak — or anybody else, for that matter — were my almost uninterrupted daydreams of writing and illustrating storybooks.

Even in the first days of basic drills, as our squad sat under a tree and, blindfolded, the guys took apart, then reassembled rifles, Uzis, hand grenades, and machine guns, plots and phrases competed inside my head. I got high on single words or, more often, whole sentences, but deep down feared being caught editing dialogues in my ever-changing stories. Of course, a recruit in the Golani brigade had neither privacy nor a desk for putting his ideas in writing. No matter what we rehearsed at the time — hand-to-hand combat, bazooka, or marksmanship — sooner or later my free-floating obsessions carried me into faraway worlds. Days before we pitched the training camp with the benefit of Sergeant Yoshua's hollering, my absent-mindedness had gotten me into *real* trouble. I swear I tried my best during that bayonet drill, but Yossi, the brown teddy bear in my best story, wouldn't leave me alone. Midway through that two-hour-long drill, Yossi decided that he would *never* say "Shalom y'ladim" — Hi kids. Too safe a line. Though

I tried to knock some sense into him, he refused to wear Walt Disney blue overalls. Smiling triumphantly, my Yossi announced that he would keep his right eye closed until the kids came up with the correct answers to his clever riddles.

Perfecting Yossi's riddles consumed my mind and soul; but as the drill went on, my feet didn't quite dance in the manner Ehud had trained us. His left eye narrowed to a slit when I didn't yell as loud as the other guys. Worst of all, my bayonet too often failed to pass through the orange-size hoop at the end of Ehud's four-foot pole.

He went ape shit. Raspberry-red and yelling at the top of his voice, Ehud sat the squad under a tree, then asked Guidon for his bayonet. Lowering his voice, he took me a few steps aside. "Shuffle your feet the right way!" he bellowed.

I did what he had ordered, all the while stabbing the empty air again and again, dozens of times. "*Intelliguent!*" Ehud hissed, more scary than a rattlesnake. "Airhead! Space cadet! I've no use for dirty dreamers in my squad!"

With Guidon's bayonet Ehud clobbered my helmet again, and again, and again. "*Where* was I? *Who* was I?" I asked myself, stunned. He kicked my ass hard. I fell forward, and landed on my chin.

"On your feet!" he thundered.

I bolted up.

His bayonet stabbed my side. "Dance! Dance!" he hollered.

I stabbed, hollered, and danced — just the way he wanted. Around me the guys watched in silence. I was mortified.

On my back in the dark tent, I lit a new smoke, anxious to dispel the ghosts of that drill. Barak was reading the first page of another letter. Cold air sneaked from under the flaps and chilled my feet. No rain flogged the sides of the tent. One forearm under the back of my head, I watched the smoke disband under the tent's triangular ceiling. Unperturbed by the smoke, my buddy muttered to himself.

Jealous, and increasingly impatient for Barak's company, I sat up and rearranged his Uzi and my F.N. in the intimate space between us.

"Why," I asked myself, "*why* can't I trust him with my vision? No," I chastised myself, "he wouldn't belittle my illustrated books or think any less of me. What ugly insecurities keep me from telling my best friend what really makes me tick?"

The memory of one night back in the regiment compounded my discomfort and embarrassment. As we lay almost shoulder to shoulder on our beds, Barak had whispered in my ear that he would apply for officers' training as soon as possible.

"How can you give or take orders one day more than necessary?"

"Relax, man." He'd chuckled. "I'm no hero. I've no intentions of dying for the motherland. An officer's rank will look awfully good the day I apply for Business Administration in Jerusalem." In our smoke-filled pup tent, Barak had finally sat up and buried the letters in his backpack. "Yuval," he turned off the flashlight, "you need a girlfriend."

"Is that so?" I shot back. "I've never even thought about it."

"Don't' get so uptight." He laughed. "Does it bother you to sleep in a tent, so close to a man?"

"It's all right. I'm sure I'll survive."

"I'll survive it, too." He sniggered. "I'm not giving you advice, Yuval, but in my experience, once I got laid, some anxieties just vanished."

From scalp to toe I blushed. How the hell did he pick it up that I was still a virgin? In desperation, I searched for words to ease my awkwardness. "I didn't see any female soldiers parading around here today."

"When we're on leave, Aviva will introduce you to her girl friends. I'm positive something will work out." He fell silent; I rolled on my side and faced the bottom of the tent.

"Yuval," he broke the silence, "in my next letter I'm proposing to Aviva." He turned on his flashlight and we sat up. His close-set eyes stared at me. Below his hairline, a thin, black strip of ash still clung to his forehead. His cheekbones jutted out even more than usual.

"You what?"

"Don't play silly games, Yuval." He sounded annoyed. "You heard me. I've been seeing Aviva for a year. I love her. If I have my way, we'll get married as soon as I get my discharge."

"If you become an officer, that's three, four years from now."

"You haven't told me yet how *you* feel about it."

"Scared, man, scared." I pinched my box of matches to soothe my anxiety. "I've been on two dates with the same girl, Barak. That's all. I'm not ready for this kind of responsibility." Not knowing what to say next, I paused. "Are you going to tell the other guys?"

"No." He switched off the light, then stretched under the blankets. "No need for it at the moment."

We lay in silence.

"Yuval," he said in a while, "do me a favour, will you? Stop wiggling your ass! Relax, man. I'm proposing to Aviva, not to you."

In a couple of minutes Barak began to snore and I untied the rope at my ankle. Wearing my unlaced boots, I went out to pee and puff on one last cigarette.

Gleaming like the concave side of a silver spoon, the skies over Canaan hung perfectly still. The bushes and tall grass didn't stir. Wistful, I reflected on my buddy — the first one

— proposing to his girlfriend. Only two months before, we were beardless high-school students, living under our parents' roofs, cramming for matriculation exams, worrying about our grades.

"It's in the cards," I told myself, "that Barak will be a father before I find a publisher for my first book of stories."

I stubbed out my cigarette, then gazed at the unchanging skies. No chance of rain tonight.

Next day, the guards woke us before sunrise. After allowing a minute for a leak on the black, frozen grass, Ehud led our platoon for a silent run and stretch exercises, army-style.

At daybreak the sky shone like a giant canopy of pewter as we sat Buddha-like in front of our tents and cleaned our weapons.

Knee next to Barak's, I disassembled my F.N., making sure that all its parts stayed put on my thighs. First I blew away any visible grains of sand, then my nylon brush chased off all the sneaky particles hiding in the flash suppressor or this end of the barrel, in the bolt or the receiver. My morning prayers for the immaculate cleanliness of my F.N. ended with a square of oily flannel polishing the black-olive steel and the grainy wood to a sheen.

I dreaded morning inspections: a mote of dirt in an innocent nook led, invariably, to several "rendez-vous," as the brass called them, with the sergeant on duty at some odd hours of the night. My heart hammered my breastbone at the mere recollection of Sergeant Yoshua flashing his teeth one chilly morning. He'd ordered me to take three steps forward and stand at attention in front of the platoon. Holding my machine gun, he glowered as if I'd soaked it in an ocean of shit. "M'*tumtam*! Idiot! Imbecile!" he'd brayed words that haunted me for weeks. "Your bipod has so much sand you could grow potatoes!"

On the morning of the fire drill, most guys, as usual, finished polishing their lighter weapons before I did. I rested my glittering gun on its extended bipod, then fondled it back and forth. We'd practised shooting at large, stationary targets before, but that day my baby would give the guys cover, real cover. Six hundred rounds per minute.

"*Khevreh*," yelled Guidon, sitting beside Yoav. "I'm sick and tired of sleeping with a rifle and a man next to me."

"I'm tired of jerking off with a machine gun," I followed up. The intensity of my wish to amuse the guys surprised me.

"We know that," a sneer deformed Guidon's face. "We can smell it all the way to the kitchen."

"You're lucky, Yuval," Yoav shouted. "Your barrel is double thick and the flash suppressor makes your thing three inches longer."

Half our platoon laughed.

"My first evening off," Guidon said, "I hitchhike to Acre and get laid." He licked his upper lip and moustache. "Twice," he added, as if in afterthought. "Hookers are just like flies. You find them everywhere. Coming with me, Yuval?"

"Guidon, Guidon," I faked a deep sigh, "you'll get just the kind of women you deserve."

"Don't we all?" Yoav came to his tent mate's support.

"Where d'you stand?" Guidon turned his face to Barak.

Bored with our banter, Barak looked aside.

After a breakfast without time for a cigarette, Sergeant Yoshua led our platoon north. We marched single file, very fast. The sky had darkened in the west, but it felt at least five degrees warmer than the night before. The bushes and grass underfoot gave off a fresh, spicy odour of mint, leeks, and raw vegetables.

Barak marched ahead of me, the handle of his folded spade swinging up and down. Were it not for the weight of my F.N., the goddamn helmet, and my web-gear crammed with clips of ammunition, I might have written home about our winter hikes being brisk, even enjoyable.

We began climbing a steep hill. From behind me a clear voice rang. Swinging my head back, I caught sight of Yoav's face shining solemnly under his raised helmet, like a cantor's. He sang loudly, and in an instant Barak and others joined him.

> *Here they approach, they come,*
> *Soldiers of a fighting regiment.*
> *With their bodies they will shield you,*
> *Our State.*

I glanced forward, then backward. Voice by voice our platoon ignited into a deafening, exuberant, twenty-metre long, single-file male chorus rending the air and the earth.

> *With bullets and bombs*
> *The young men storm forward*
> *In the name of Golani, the warrior.*

Even I hummed along.

In about an hour we halted by a narrow valley between two greening hills. Lieutenant Avner — a tall, slim man with a fat lower lip — leaned against the side of a Jeep, arms crossed. Once a week our platoon gathered briefly in a classroom to hear that sad-eyed man dump some dinosaur shit about the army, the State of Israel, or both — while the instructors under him toiled night and day, drilling passive-aggressive characters like me. According to one rumour, the officer had no intentions of returning to his Kibbutz' cows, but had, instead, applied to several undergraduate programs in Israel and abroad. Barak swore he'd heard that our commander had been admitted only to evening courses at Tel-Aviv University. "Too dumb," Barak had sniggered, "for a B.A., even in English or Hebrew Literature."

The lieutenant sat our platoon in a half-circle at his feet; apart from Uzis resting across thighs, our hands clutched upright weapons, their butts resting on the ground.

"In a couples of hours," the lieutenant droned, "our artillery, or the air force, could bomb the enemy worse than Hiroshima or Nagasaki in August 1945." He glanced left and right to assess whether we had fathomed the depth of his simile. "But no hill is in Jewish hands," his forefinger punctured the air, "until the black boots of the infantry walk all over it."

The officer crouched. His palm cleared a square on the ground, then his fingers sculpted our first drill on the sand. "Guidon, Yuval. You will give cover from the hill on the west." The lieutenant pointed. "The rest of Ehud's squad and you and you," he pointed, "will storm and capture the outpost to the north."

Seconds later, on Sergeant Yoshua's heels, Guidon and I began to race uphill. We halted near the top and, breathless, took positions. In the west, the horizon resembled a blue-black ribbon pinned to the bottom of a grey skirt. All around me, thousands of spent, greening shells lay on the ground, unburied. How many generations of recruits had fired their weapons on these hills?

The wind brought Ehud's voice barking at his men to stand no less than three meters apart. Yoav and others mounted their bayonets, and, bending forward, Barak gripped his loaded Uzi with both hands. A few meters behind the squad, the lieutenant watched the scene.

Ehud inserted a clip into his Uzi and, swinging his left arm clockwise, bellowed "*Akharai!*" — after me. The guys began walking up the hill, every few steps kneeling for cover behind rocks.

Halfway up Ehud yelled "*Esh!*" — fire — and darted forward. Rifles popped shots, Uzis pattered like toys, leaving behind a thin cloud of grey-blue smoke.

"*Esh!*" Sergeant Yoshua thundered next to me. "*Esh!*" I unlocked my safety catch and, after aiming, squeezed the trigger. My F.N. stuttered and a row of dust puffs rose on the hill across. The peppery scents of gunpowder flared my nostrils. My bipod had recoiled, so I aimed again. The excitement, it seemed, was shredding my windpipe and the pit of my stomach. I could barely breath.

"*Esh! Esh!*" the sergeant hollered.

"My F.N. is stuck!" Guidon yelled.

"*Esh*, Yuval! Keep firing!" The sergeant ordered. "Your boot, Guidon! Cock the rifle with your boot!"

I inserted a new clip and kept firing ahead of the squad storming the hilltop across.

"Stop fire!" Sergeant Yoshua trumpeted.

I raised my head. On the hill to the north the squad began to congregate in a circle.

In an instant the sergeant, Guidon, and I raced down our hill. Climbing up the next one, we didn't slow down much either. "What happened?" I asked myself with foreboding, skipping over bushes and rocks. On all sides, the rest of our platoon ran towards Ehud and his men.

Breathless, I halted at the top of the northern hill. Most guys huddled in a clump, while the brass conferred some steps away.

"What happened?" I asked Yoav who'd just parted from the crowd.

"You and your fucking questions!" He rumbled. "Why don't you see for yourself?"

Lest I scratch the guys' hands, I folded in my upright F.N.'s bipod. I pushed my shoulder into the knot: helmet off, and one hand still grabbing his Uzi, Barak lay on the ground. His face betrayed no feelings; the head and winter jacket swam in a pool of blood. Who had closed his eyes?

Like fractured candles, Barak's contorted left hand and fingers clutched the grass as if in desperation, while his twisted legs seemed much too small for the rest of his body. "What happened?" I asked in terror.

"Don't you see?" Guidon hissed. "He got shot in the head and neck. Died instantly."

My helmet off, I wanted to cry, vent the overwhelming grief taking hold of my being. I blinked and blinked, feeling giddy and helpless, inwardly praying to be able to pray.

Sergeant Yoshua grabbed Barak by the ankles, and Ehud lifted him by the wrists. The instructors rushed downhill, the bleeding body rocking back and forth like a hammock, the bum scrubbing bushes and rocks. Shaking, on the verge of vomiting, I watched the brass stuff Barak's head, arms, and boots into the back of the Jeep. The sergeant hurried to the driver's seat; in a moment the engine roared to life and he took off.

Ehud raced back up our hill. Moments later, in a hoarse voice he told his squad — Guidon and I included — to stand in line, take off clips, and present our weapons for inspection.

Slowly Ehud strode from man to man, his little finger burrowing the guns' innards, searching for bullets. I must have been the fourth in line. Ehud's tan, hairless face looked even more boyish as he checked out my F.N. at great length.

"How many clips did you fire?" he asked, eyes dim.

"One and a half, commander," I answered, wondering in terror, was he singling me out? My knees quivered; a cold sweat came over me. Only the fantasy of fainting as the whole platoon watched prevented me from collapsing to the ground.

"Wipe your face," Ehud said as if in deep thought. "It's black from gun-powder."

"Platoon!" He barked at the end of his inspection, "Lieutenant Avner wants to talk to you."

The platoon sat on the ground, Ehud standing behind us. The officer wore no web-gear, and his green beret, daintily tilted to the right, looked cute, almost obscene. His tightly laced black boots shone against the grass.

"Soldiers!" The officer spoke. "Today, one of us, Barak, got killed. I'm sure all of you are upset; I feel upset, too." He sniffed, stolid. "You've seen a buddy's blood drench this land." He removed his beret and, after wiping his forehead, donned it again and smoothed it with one palm. "This is very unfortunate, of course, but wars are made for men, tough men who understand why lives are being sacrificed for our state!" He gazed at the darkening skies.

My eyes closed. I gasped, astounded to harbour so much rage inside: the lieutenant's speech had killed Barak a second time. I pictured myself clicking a twenty-round clip of ammunition into my F.N. and, at close range, machine gunning the torso of the grimacing lieutenant.

"Son of a bitch!" I yelled and leaped to my feet; lime-white, the officer took a few steps backward. "This is just mind-fucking chicken shit! It won't bring Barak back." Right fingers frantically searching for a loaded clip in the web-gear, I cradled the machine gun in my left arm.

"Yuval!" yelled Ehud, who'd run from behind the platoon and now blocked the space between me and the officer. "Hand me the gun, Yuval!" Ehud hollered. "It's an order!" He hopped forward to grab my F.N., but my feet danced backward, better than in any bayonet drill.

"I'll kill this motherfucker!" I screamed.

"The gun, Yuval, the gun!" Ehud hollered. "*It's an order!*" He lunged forward and grabbed the barrel of my F.N. We tussled back and forth. Ehud yelled into my ear, "*B'seder*, Yuval. I'll talk to you in private."

Wavering, I handed him the machine gun. Immediately Ehud started away from our platoon, his own Uzi slung on one shoulder, my F.N., with the flash suppressor down, on the other. For a while he marched very fast, and I followed him, almost dazed. He halted by the remnants of a wall, only meters away from an almost grey cypress and two atrophied fig trees. From three sides, patches of powder-covered cacti enclosed the trees and the broken wall. "Not long ago," I told myself, "some Arabs called these stones and trees 'home'."

"Sit down." Ehud leaned his Uzi and my F.N. against the wall, then squatted.

It bothered me no end to stare at moist soot soiling my F.N.'s flash-suppressor and barrel. Unless I stole gasoline from one of the trucks, I would spend more than an hour scrubbing it clean. "Do you mind if I smoke?" I asked, sitting down.

"Yuval," Ehud searched for words, "there will be an inquiry into the accident." He paused. "But nobody thinks Barak got killed . . . out of . . . negligence."

I gazed skyward. A cold wind from the north was chasing away the few remaining grey clouds hovering since dawn. Low-lying, dark clouds scudded above our heads, making me think of gunpowder and soot. In minutes it would rain.

"I killed Barak, right?" I hooted. "Is that what you're trying to tell me?"

"No," Ehud answered, calm. "It's not up to me to determine who's responsible. But right now, you're out of control. I can't trust you with a gun. Are you listening, Yuval?"

"Not really." I stared at my dirty boots: mud and blades of grass had got stuck between the heels and soles. I thought of Barak's burial, probably next day. My finger and thumb snuffed out my burning cigarette. I felt nothing.

"Your buddy is killed and you have nothing to say?"

"He's dead." I said, lighting a new cigarette. "You can't help him, I can't help him, God can't help him. Personally, Ehud, I do like you in a weird sort of way." I turned my left palm up. "But tell me, what's the point of talking? It's all one big machine."

"Is there nothing I can do for you?"

"Not really, *Corporal Ehud*," I hissed. "I really don't wish to feel any better than what I feel right now."

He stood up and, after shouldering the weapons, began marching fast. Some twenty feet behind I followed, eyes fixated on my F.N.'s flash suppressor bobbing up and down above rocks, bushes, and grass. Ehud stopped once and waited for me to close the gap between us.

As soon as we arrived at the training camp, Ehud told me to help Maurice in the kitchen. The cook, a Moroccan Jew living in Israel less than four years, still spoke Hebrew as if it were a French dialect. I'd worked for him before and knew that he had done at least two things that we, Sabras, would never do: getting married while still in the army and, incomprehensibly, living in some godforsaken hick town called Kiriat Shmonah.

I'd never blamed Maurice for the brown or grey grub he'd ladled onto our mess kits every day; instead, I toyed with fantasies of an underground, dimly lit bunker with profusely sweating high-ranking officers toiling to design the Army's repulsive menus. Wednesdays, by decree, were days of chicken and rice; if scents of beans cooked in canned tomatoes and little meat wafted down the chow line, you could bet your sausage it was Thursday. Ultimately, no one was responsible for what happened in the kitchen. Officers, cooks, and helping hands were all in the same boat: we just carried out orders from above.

Maurice sat me on a wooden box inside the kitchen tent. Chain-smoking, he and I peeled potatoes. Though Maurice smoked like Humphrey Bogart, he never once coughed and he peeled three times faster than I did. Rangy and bent-over, Maurice wore a three-day-old beard and his bushy mustache looked as if it hadn't been trimmed for weeks. He seemed to float inside an oversized shirt and green trousers held by a dirty rope; he wore no standard black boots, but unlaced, disintegrating running shoes. Either the Israeli ethos of male toughness had somehow bypassed Maurice, or the cook had swapped the ugly "glories" of combat duty for the security of his kitchen.

My face boiled. I dared not say *his* name, but pictured *him* supine, floating on a lake of warm blood atop a volcano. The smell of slaughtered chickens and plucked feathers haunted me. "His belly is bloated," I confided in myself, "the swollen cheeks conceal his eyes. But who closed his eyes?" I tortured myself.

"Who closed his eyes?"

Unable to bear my thoughts, I stopped peeling. "Maurice, how long have you been in the army?"

"I'm getting discharged in two weeks." He smiled, proud.

"Two weeks?" I must have looked awe-struck and jealous, as if the cook, like a figure from the Bible, had lived for hundreds of years. "What will you do for the rest of your life, Maurice?"

"Well, Miriam, my wife, and I will operate a steak and hamburger stand. Slowly we'll save some money to buy a small restaurant."

"A restaurant?" I asked, sincerely surprised. "Are there enough people in Kiriat Shmonah to support a restaurant?"

He looked annoyed. "The problem with you, Israeli-born, is that you think Tel Aviv is the capital of the world and everything else is a black hole."

For a while we peeled in silence. Then he looked up. "Ehud sent you to help in the kitchen. Why, Yuval?"

"I don't want to talk about it." I flung my cigarette on the ground, mashing it with my muddy boot.

With a running shoe Maurice snuffed his cigarette, then balanced his knife on one thigh. "Barak," he uttered it like a French name, "got killed. I —"

"I don't want to talk about him!" I screamed.

A cold wind whistled in under the walls of the tent. In silence we hauled the pot heavy with water and potatoes into a dark corner. After we'd perched again on our wooden boxes, we resumed peeling. The wind rocked the tent's ceiling back and forth, while the flaps at the entrance blew in and out. I thought of a black, abandoned house.

He offered me one of his cigarettes; I lit his, then mine. "Yuval," his accent pierced the silence, "my mother died of cancer." A potato plopped into the water, and he eyed me softly. "I was twelve years old. It still hurts quite a lot to picture her face and hands. But," he paused, "I've been feeling much better after I met my wife." He drew on his cigarette and exhaled through his nose slowly. "Life," he closed his eyes for a moment, "lasts longer than death."

For a while I stared at him, my gut fretting. I stood up and, after making for the tent's entrance, peeked out at a grey and black world. "I'm going for a short walk before it starts raining."

"I'll be here when you come back." Maurice said.

After scrubbing the dinner's pots and pans clean, Maurice and I lounged on his mattress while soft, melancholy Arabic music floated out of his transistor radio. On and off our cigarettes gleamed inside the black kitchen tent, calling to mind bleeding fireflies."Yuval!" At the tent's entrance, Ehud rent my reveries of blood, fractured fingers, oddly twisted legs. "No need to get up. This evening you're staying at camp."

"What are the guys doing?"

"Night patrol."

Hours later, when the platoon returned to the training camp, Maurice was stretched on his mattress, snoring. From a distance of twenty metres, I longed to be one of the guys again. I watched them remove their helmets, scrub the ash off their faces and necks, then crawl headlong into their pup tents. In an instant, flashlights glowed orange under the tents' sides. Some guys, I fancied, dipped their hands into their backpacks to set their small private world in order. Others, I supposed, reread old letters.

"Aren't you going to sleep, Yuval?" It was Guidon, with Yoav, on first guard duty, passing by the kitchen tent.

"Just one last cigarette," I explained.

In a while I tottered to our dark pup tent. The thought of spending the night where *he* and I had shared secrets filled me with unspeakable dread. Yet, I crept in on all fours and, sitting inside, unlaced my boots. My blanket stretched tight on the ground, almost as tight as in the morning. His winter coat, at the far end of our improvised home, lay neatly folded. Where were his Uzi and helmet? I shut my eyes for fear of hallucinating his face, flashlight, and Aviva's letters.

Perfectly still I lay in the cold space under our blankets. After several minutes I opened my eyes and gazed at the tent's side. It felt almost unnatural not to have the cusps of my F.N.'s bipod chafing my arm. Convinced that I would shake uncontrollably or cry like a baby and wake up the guys, I wouldn't move my limbs. No one would ever forget, or forgive me, for crying in the middle of the night when hours upon hours of drills awaited us. I tossed onto my back and vowed to rid myself of all unpleasant thoughts. But the gaunt face of Benny, my father's cousin, flashed and flashed in front of my eyes. Years before, Benny's wife had died of cancer and, the last I'd heard, he still slept on a sofa in his living room. "A man fights the Nazis in Poland's forests," I shook my head understandingly, "then the Jordanians in '48 and the Egyptians in '56. But in his personal life, he's like a child, afraid of sleeping in his own dark bed."

Maurice, I guessed, wouldn't have minded if I'd slept in his tent. The brass wouldn't have minded it either — how could *that* possibly interfere with their training schedules?

I felt paralyzed under the blankets. Would I fall asleep only when I stopped blaming myself for the accident?

"Accident?" A male chorus thundered. "What accident? This was negligence, irresponsible behaviour, the work of a fucking bastard! Instead of aiming your F.N. right, you spend your life obsessing about stupid little stories!"

I counted from fifty down to one. It didn't soothe me at all. "Buddy killer," I called myself. "You're a buddy killer."

I sat up. "But accidents happen. Don't get carried away. Stay rational."

No good. I felt even more alert, lonely, and afraid of the darkness and silence.

"Where is my F.N.?" I asked and reached for my weapon. How could I, a feeling person, a pacifist, and a young intellectual who wished to read Kafka, Camus, and Sartre one day, have been so brainwashed to miss the damned machine gun as if it were my third hand?

From my shirt pocket I hooked out a crumpled cigarette pack. "Empty?" In terror I began to tear the pack, when my quaking fingers came across a crooked one hiding in a corner. I breathed out. I smoothed the cigarette, then clamped it with my lips. Patting all my pockets, I searched in vain for a box of matches.

I turned around. "Barak, d'you have a light?" I reached for his shoulder. But my hand plunged into cold, woollen blankets and the ground hard underneath. I'd been firing questions at a dead man, a hunk of nothingness!

Biting my lower lip, I crawled headlong through the tent flaps. Once outside, I leaped to my feet and raced across the icy grass until my face and chest froze. My panic subsided, but my feet hurt from trampling shrubs and thorns.

A rock caught my foot. Down I fell, flat on my chest, banging my left arm. Jaw chattering, I slowly sat up. No wind was blowing. The earth, the grass, and the bushes seemed at peace with the overcast skies. Were it not for my aching, hide-stiff arm, the solitude would soothe me. Soon I would freeze to death, free of my obsessions.

But my arm and chest hurt worse and worse. I wobbled up to my feet and, stumping on frozen socks, headed back in the direction of the training camp. To stop shaking, I hugged myself, scared of dying of exposure.

"Stop! Password!" The order brought me back to my senses. Blue Bears? That was the week before.

"Don't shoot!" I begged. "I'm a Jew. Can't you hear? I speak Hebrew."

"Password!" The voice rose, harsher.

"It's me, Yuval. Don't shoot!"

Their bayonetted rifles still horizontal, the guards drew near. Guidon and Yoav.

"Yuval," Guidon raised his rifle, "what the hell are you doing barefoot, almost naked, in the middle of the night?" He shook his head. "What's your problem now?"

"Guidon," I paused. "Be a man, tell me. D'you think I did it?"

"Did what?" He sounded angry.

"Kill Barak?"

He took his time. "My rifle jammed, Yuval. In the meanwhile, he got a volley from the side."

"Yuval," Yoav butted in. "Why don't you get some sleep? It was an accident. Nobody knows what really happened. Nobody is blaming you."

Lowering my head, I whispered to the earth, "I am."

At next morning's inspection I shivered, ignominiously standing at attention without a weapon.

"Trucks will drive you to the regiment," Sergeant Yoshua told us, his voice a bit softer than usual. "There, you'll shine your boots, shower, and change into clean winter attire." He turned his head left, then right. "Barak's funeral is at three. Yuval," the sergeant's head toss indicated that he wanted me to step aside, "I want to talk to you." He lowered his voice. "You're staying behind to help in the kitchen and guard the camp."

"I must be at the funeral," my grief blurted out. "He was my best friend." Inwardly, I told myself to keep cool: Sergeant Yoshua might, perhaps, understand.

"I know." He averted my eyes. "But you're acting weird. I can't have you at a military funeral."

"You guys can't fucking do that to me!" I yelled.

"Oh, yes, soldier! We can! We will!" Incisors flashing, he stared me in the eye. "You're not going to the funeral, man. It's an order!" He hissed, very angry. "You're out of control. You openly threatened to kill an officer! A Jew!"

Panting, the sergeant stared at me with hatred. "*His* parents will be there," he yelled, and I shuddered at the thought of the guys hearing him shout. "They already have a hell of a lot on their plate. *I*, do you hear me? *I* will make damn sure that his funeral takes place without a hitch. Now, beat it!"

Minutes later, I stared in disbelief: weapons resting by their thighs, the guys departed in two trucks.

Maurice lent me two packs of cigarettes. We lazed about in his tent until early afternoon, when we began to prepare the late evening meal for the guys. The skies remained melancholy grey the whole day, as if Yoshua — the one from the Bible, I mean — had ordered the rain to wait. I felt numb, empty, my flour-dry eyes and lids burning.

Late that night, after we'd cleaned the pots and vessels, I told Maurice, "I'm leaving." The platoon was back from the funeral, on manoeuvres.

"And where are you going?" He sounded worried, like a parent.

"Don't worry. I'm hitchhiking."

"Don't, Yuval. You're playing with fire."

"Believe me," I tried my best to sound reasonable, "but I feel I *have to* do what I'm doing, Maurice."

"'Have to' you said?" He raised his voice, ironic. "What's that? Middle Eastern fatalism?"

"No. Believe me, Maurice. I made a choice. I'm taking matters into my own hands, rebelling against my fate."

"Listen, Yuval, when the military police lay hands on you, it won't be a barrel of fun."

"I know that," I shot back, raring to go. "Thought about all the possibilities the whole day. My mind is made up. I have to do what I chose to do, Maurice. Bye, and thank you for the cigarettes and everything else."

"You're not telling where you're going?"

"Good night, Maurice," I intoned, feeling determined inside.

In my tent I spread the contents of my backpack on the ground and, covering my belongings with three blankets, made the lair look as if I was sleeping underneath. Winter coat on, bent down, I padded along, fingertips brushing the grass to avoid the searching eyes of the night guards.

For a time I followed the path the trucks took to arrive at the training camp, but soon stumbled upon knee-high weeds. Panting, I stopped to search for bearings. Under the overcast skies, bushes shot up every way I looked; only the silhouettes of lone, faraway trees dotted the landscape. I walked uphill, stopping only at the top. A pink and golden halo glowed on the horizon. Acre? Haifa?

With my left sleeve I wiped my running nose and decided to walk in the direction of the lights. Up and down the hills I walked, perhaps a couple of hours. Abruptly, I stepped onto a narrow highway.

Where was I? Taking a chance, I veered left — or south, I assumed — and marched down the road. As in an eerie dream, black, lone, twisted olive trees watched as I passed by.

In a while, a light shone from behind me. Turning, I stretched out my arm, thumb up.

"Where are you going, soldier?" The truck driver threw the cab door wide open. A dim light glowed inside.

"Haifa, then Tel-Aviv."

"Step in. I'll drop you off after Haifa."

The truck smelled of live chickens, onions, and fresh milk. In the dim light sat a slim, mustachioed man of about thirty-five wearing professorial horn-rimmed glasses and a wedding band. I started a fantasy about a patriotic Kibbutz member who survived at least two wars and never griped when called up for six weeks of military reserve duty, but donned his army fatigues and green beret. Then, sad-eyed, he muttered to his wife and two young daughters at the door, "See you soon."

I dreaded the moment my hero would bombard me with questions, and watched in silence as the headlights cast an advancing white swath up the black highway.

"D'you smoke?" He offered me a fine, filter cigarette.

"Thanks." I lit his, then mine, and looked out my window at the telephone poles racing by.

"Soldier," he peered at me, "why are you hitchhiking in the middle of the night?"

I got totally paranoid: my hero would drive me to the nearest police station, crank down the window, then yell, "Get him! A deserter! A traitor!"

"Got a special leave," I half shrugged, "to attend a funeral."

"Sorry to hear." He stared ahead.

I couldn't help myself. "My brother. He died in an accident." Inhaling deeply, I enjoyed his aromatic tobacco, grateful that he didn't wish to know any more.

"Soldier," someone was shaking my left arm. "You get off here."

"Where? Where are we?" I asked, dazed. The driver had pulled the truck over. On the other side of the highway, headlight after headlight flashed by.

"Haifa-Tel Aviv Road." The truck driver said. "I'm turning right."

I ducked toward the floor of the truck to pick up a machine gun that wasn't there.

"Thank you," I saluted from the road.

About an hour later, a car dropped me off at the corner of Arlozorov Street and Haifa Road. A cold, bleak day. The ugly, low apartment buildings typical of Tel Aviv squatted under a dull sky of tin. Would rain fall, at last?

Seven twenty. I'd promised myself not to knock on *his* parents's door before nine o'clock. (Seized by a morbid superstition, I still dared not say his name.) Groggy, I staggered up Arlozorov Street. Stumbling upon an open kiosk, I bought a newspaper, three packs of cigarettes, matches, and a candy bar. The kiosk owner lent me his telephone directory, where I checked if I had the right address. Outside the kiosk, for over an hour I perched on a stone fence, pretending to read the newspaper while worrying about military policemen asking for my papers. Now that I stayed put in one place, my heart raced madly and my lungs and breastbone ached. I chain-smoked, and my muddy heels mashed butt after butt into blobs of brown paste.

At eight thirty I took the 61 bus to Ramat Gan. Knowing my hometown as well as the hollows in my hands, in a few minutes I stood by the entrance to his parents' building. An empty mail slot with the name "Avinoam" stared at me. I drew a deep breath and pushed in the switch glowing on the wall. The light went on. With firm strides I climbed one flight of well-lit stairs. In the short corridor, on one of the brown doors, was a chrome-plated sign engraved with the name "Avinoam". My stomach fluttered. Should I? After, there would be no escape. With a sense of inevitability, I pushed the doorbell button.

I waited and waited. Slowly, a plump, short woman in black slowly opened the door. Bloated cheeks, swollen red eyes. A grey curl had slipped from under her black scarf and flattened on her forehead. I couldn't stop staring at her dark brown, closely-set eyes. The high cheekbones also reminded me of *him.*

I took off my beret. "Mrs. Avinoam?"

"Yes, soldier?" She muttered.

"I'm Yuval, his friend." Though embarrassed to my veins, I couldn't utter his name. "I'm sorry I couldn't attend the funeral."

"Please, come in." His mother fell back one step.

I bent down, unlaced my muddy boots, and, inhaling anxiously, tugged them off. Without a word, she hung my coat on a hook by the entrance. Tiptoeing, she led me through a short narrow corridor. As I trod on the off-white tiles, the cold seeped through my green army socks. An odour of kerosene burning in a heater hung in the air.

She showed me into a living room with a three-seat green sofa and several chairs staking out an uneven circle around the walls. "A *shivah*," I commented to myself, scratching my day-old beard.

"Please, sit down," she said softly.

"I'd better sit on a newspaper," I said. "My fatigues are dirty. I really don't want to soil your furniture."

Mrs. Avinoam left the room, and I looked around. At one end was a sliding glass door beyond which spread a large balcony with potted plants and white folding chairs.

In an instant she returned with a stack of newspapers. "Have you had breakfast, Yuval? We're expecting some people. My husband and Yaron will soon be back with fresh rolls."

Yaron? Yes, of course. His baby brother. "No, thank you, Mrs. Avinoam." I swallowed spittle. "I'm staying just a couple of minutes. Have to get back to the regiment."

After covering a chair with newspapers, I perched on its edge. She sat on the sofa, but soon leaned forward. "Did you know Barak from high school?"

"No, from the army." I said. Her overwhelmingly sad eyes drove me into silence, but despite my anxiety I managed to maintain a fragile eye-contact with her. After a while I said, "This is really very hard on me, Mrs. Avinoam. Usually, I'm good with words. The guys say I talk a lot, perhaps even too much. But this . . . I don't know." I halted.

"Well," my forefinger wiped away my tears, "it's really hard to talk about certain things . . . like . . . like me . . . writing . . . " I held my breath, "writing . . . children stories."

Overcome by tears, I stopped. "Well, the night before he . . . got killed . . . he told me of writing to Aviva and proposing to her."

With her upper sleeve she wiped her cheeks dry. "I didn't know that." Her voice rolled out from the depths of a cave. "We couldn't get hold of Aviva. She wasn't at the funeral either."

"Something else I need to tell you." I mustered all my courage. "It was an accident . . . he got a volley . . . from his left . . . some people think *I* did it."

She stood up and doddered to the sliding door. Her back to me, she looked out for a long while. Abruptly, she slewed around on her heels. "You must be feeling guilty, Yuval. Is that why you came here? To tell me how guilty you feel?" Her voice cracked. I couldn't gauge whether I'd hurt her, or whether she was angry with me.

"Guilty?" I snorted back my tears. "How could I not feel guilty, Mrs. Avinoam? He was my buddy, we slept side by side. Now they are suggesting that I did it." I badly felt like smoking, but sensed it would not be right to ask for an ashtray. "But not only guilt brought me here, Mrs. Avinoam." I raised my voice. "I feel *ashamed*, yes, *terribly ashamed* of living in a world where someone may mow down his best friend."

"But weren't both of you in the line of duty?" Dim, her eyes begged me to agree with her.

I leaped to my feet and began to shout. "You see, Mrs. Avinoam, I really don't want to be a soldier. I don't feel like shooting anybody, Jew or Arab." I cleared my throat. "All I wish is to write and illustrate children books. But one day they handed me a machine gun and told me to give the guys cover. So I obeyed, and will remember that miserable day for the rest of my life."

Choking with tears I stopped, then sobbed. "But I want you to know . . . Mrs. Avinoam . . . that I . . . loved him . . . deeply . . . like . . . like Jonathan . . . in the Bible . . . loved King David."

Buried in thoughts, she stared blankly at me. Then she said, "Where do your parents live, Yuval?"

"Oh, two blocks away." I wiped my cheeks and chin with a sleeve.

"Would you like me to call your mother?"

"My mother?" I choked. "No, Mrs. Avinoam. Thank you." I shook my head. "Not my mother, or anybody else, can help me with my suffering. I want to bear my pain alone."

Her left eye narrowed to a line. "That's enough!" She yelled, as if I had trampled everything dear to her. "Now go, Yuval. Go!"

I loped into the hallway and took my coat off the rack. She stayed behind, in the living room. "Good-bye!" I called.

An hour later, under pewter skies, I stood by the highway to Haifa, arm stretched out, thumb up. Back to Regiment Twelve, of course. Where else could I go? Jordan? Egypt? Syria? Though I loathed drills and militaristic jabber, the idea of becoming a deserter in an Arab country didn't even cross my mind. I dreaded being tortured and couldn't rid myself of what my parents, teachers, and the likes of Mrs. Avinoam had rubbed in so deeply: that my army stint would be the zenith of my noble youth, that there were no reasons to shirk my obligations to my country.

Late in the afternoon, I marched into the sergeant-major's office at the regiment and saluted the paunchy, balding man. He listened to my story, twisting his Salvador Dali moustache. After I finished my account, he said, "Tomorrow afternoon you'll stand trial. Shine your boots and wear a clean, ironed shirt under your winter attire."

At one o'clock next day, on the wooden porch of the regiment's office, the sergeant-major barked, "Ten-hut! March!" Into a dark, musty room I strode.

The wooden floor quaked as, behind my back, the sergeant stamped and clicked his boots. "Yuval Tamir!" he barked. "There are charges against you!" Anxious and disoriented, I couldn't take in my crimes.

Facing me, a lieutenant colonel — the regiment's commander, I assumed —sat behind a desk littered with khaki-coloured files. Wreathed in greying hair, his pate glowed like a pink billiard ball. Up and down the officer scanned me, then put on his horn-rimmed glasses. As if I were not in the room, he riffled through my open file.

The lieutenant colonel knitted his thick eyebrows. "Do you have anything to say?"

"Yes, commander." My pulse fired like a pistol. "Barak," I forced myself to say his name, "was my best friend." I raised my voice. "Sergeant Yoshua told me that I couldn't attend his funeral. An injustice, commander. An injustice without precedent!"

The officer leaned forward, as if about to share a secret. "Listen, soldier. *You* left the training camp without permission, not sergeant Yoshua. You're the one on trial, not the army!" He took off his glasses and set them upside down on his desk. Leaning back in his chair, he sentenced me to thirty-five days in jail and loss of two week-long leaves.

As soon as we stepped outside the office, the sergeant-major brayed, "To the garage!"

Marching briskly, I glanced at the skies growing pallid against the rheumy raindrops. It brought me relief to think of my trial being over and, after days of painful suspense, to see that the rain had finally come.

Aching to smoke, I pondered how would I ever repay Maurice for the packs of cigarettes I'd borrowed from him. The cook's lips whispered in my ears, "Life lasts longer than death." I wished I could cry and cry for Barak — and for myself, too.

"But what's Maurice's last name?" I asked myself with a start. I vowed to find out his surname and address as soon as I got out of jail. Hurt and angry at the whole world, I put off my gratitude until a more opportune time.

In the regiment's garage, Sergeant Yoshua and a corporal with a loaded Uzi were sitting inside an empty stall. The sergeant-major whispered instructions in their ears. I stood by, listening to the rain's gentle fingers drumming on the tin roof overhead.

Sergeant Yoshua stood up. With a toss of his chin he pointed. "Hop into the back of the Jeep, man! Jailhouse Number Six!"

Pushing me aside, the corporal with the loaded Uzi forced me to share the slim rear seat. It rained and rained while we drove south, the Jeep's short, stiff wipers working the windshields back and forth. I peered out the blurred plastic window: one black telephone pole raced after another; under the flogging rain the houses had turned dark grey.

AKHMAD'S FATE

The desert wind coloured the sky red. In the tea and spices market, closed-eyed merchants perched on round stools by their stores, drawing afternoon dreams from coiled water pipes.

Ibrahim and his oldest son, Akhmad, stood in front of the family store. Ibrahim cocked his chin and, after clearing his throat, clapped his hands three times.

"Listen, oh dealers in tea and spices," Ibrahim bellowed. "For thirty years I've been in business in Baghdad. You all know, I've spoiled my six sons as little as I've praised the competition." While he pondered what to say next, his forefinger and thumb tweaked his square chin.

The merchants eased themselves up from their stools and huddled around Ibrahim and his son.

The father resumed. "Akhmad, a man of few words, returned last week from a journey to India. There he signed scores of contracts with British merchants." Ibrahim lent his friends time for a good look at his son, who, marble-faced and hands knotted behind his back, brushed Ibrahim's right sleeve with his upper arm.

"British ships," the father's moist eyes shone, "will haul tea and precious spices from India and Ceylon into Shatt-al-Arab.

My younger sons's caravans will carry the goods all the way down to Yemen!"

The stunned audience watched Ibrahim take off his black fez. One hand shaking in the air, he danced a few jolly steps forward. "Akhmad," the father hitched up his loose pants, "has his eyes on a large house with tall, lovely date trees in the back yard. After sunset," Ibrahim winked, "the clever matchmakers of Baghdad are welcome to my home!"

The older merchants applauded and young people whistled while Ibrahim patted his moist face with a red, rumpled handkerchief. He gave Akhmad a long, tight hug, and kissed him on both cheeks. The merchants took turns hugging and kissing Ibrahim, then shook hands with his son.

The Almighty had not blessed Ibrahim's firstborn with good looks. In pain, Akhmad had watched three of his brothers grow taller, straighter, more handsome than him. At only twenty-five, his balding head glowed as sickly as an old piano's keys, and Akhmad seldom removed his red fez in the street. With the back of his hand he often wiped his hulking nose: inexplicable droplets clung close to its tip, in defiance of winds and winter frosts.

After two weeks of bargaining, Ibrahim gave his son permission to pay ten thousand pounds of coffee beans for the hand of Fatima, the youngest daughter of Farid, a prosperous, God-fearing merchant of rice and dates. "Fatima's beautiful face shines like a full moon on the Tigris," swore the few women who had cast their eyes on the unveiled bride. "And her arms," they added, "are plump, but firm."

The wedding was meant to last only three days, for the bridegroom's urgent business could not wait a whole week. Under huge cotton tents, hundreds of guests feasted on roasted lamb, steamed rice, fresh dates, halvah, and pistachio nuts from Haleb, while musicians strummed lutes, and poets read odes to the bride's beauty and to Akhmad's mercantile genius. Ibrahim and Farid took turns visiting tent after tent, to make sure that no guests imbibed a single drop of arak or other spirits.

On the third evening, Fatima and Akhmad strolled about, thanking their families and friends for the lovely wedding gifts. The young couple's last stop was the main tent, where men stood chatting in groups, mature women congregated in their own knots, and young women sat on floor rugs, playing with their children. The newlyweds basked in the light of tall torches by the tent's main pole. Akhmad smiled, his hand fondling Fatima's shoulder. "Why is no one else smiling?" The bridegroom asked himself. The conversation died down, the musicians stopped playing, and, to Akhmad's chagrin, dozens, perhaps hundreds, of eyes converged on his. "My guests expect a goodbye speech," he told himself, and, wrinkling his eyebrows, searched for kind words of gratitude. In the charged silence, he made up his mind to start by asking, "Is it at all worthwhile to amass wealth in the absence of friends?" But before the first syllable left his lips, two young women slapped their mouths, and a young man guffawed, loudly.

"Akhmad!" Ibrahim's voice thundered, his forefinger pointing at his son's feet.

Bunched in a pile, Akhmad's white silk pants and underwear lay at his ankles. His erect penis jutted out: pink, apparently, but pathetically smaller than he'd remembered. "When did my pants slide down," Akhmad asked himself in terror, a red-hot knife twisting and twisting in the pit of his stomach.

He closed his eyes like a blindfolded criminal before a firing squad. His whole life thundered in his mind. Once again he heard girls with black, long pigtails chirping, "Akhmad? How ugly! And his brothers?" The teasing voices rose, "How good-looking!" Paralyzed, tears boiling under his eyelids, Akhmad relived the tortures of telling himself, "What a disgusting pig!"

Akhmad's lifelong fears spilled into the open. The entire world, he felt, was watching him at his worst: half-naked, vulnerable, hopelessly awkward. From scalp to toes, ocean after ocean of shame and humiliation washed over him, and the disgusting, sweet odour of charred flesh flared his nostrils.

At long last Akhmad opened his eyes. Breathless, he bent over and his trembling fingers hitched up his pants. The tent quaked with the uproar. Men and women clutched their bellies and rocked up and down with laughter. On the floor, children squealed and pointed their little forefingers at him. He glanced at Fatima, and saw tears shining on his wife's cheeks. Was she laughing or crying? His father had vanished from the tent.

Akhmad sprinted to the house he had bought only two weeks before. Gasping, he darted upstairs to his room and crammed a small suitcase with clothes and books. Back in the dark, empty streets, the bridegroom ran without ever looking over his shoulders. A while later Akhmad arrived at a square, where drivers and carriages waited all night long.

By degrees he caught his breath and made out a turbaned man, who squatted by a nearby carriage, warming his hands on a kerosene lamp between his knees. As Akhmad drew near, the driver rose. Though the flame from the lamp threw almost no light, Akhmad caught sight of a black patch on the man's left eye. The right scanned Akhmad's face and suitcase, as if gauging the depth of his character.

"Driver," Akhmad panted, "we're going south and then east."

"And where are you heading, sir?" The driver bent his head down, as if to hear Akhmad better.

"Shatt-al-Arab. I want to get there as soon as possible."

"It's a very long journey, sir." The driver shook his head, in disapproval. "We'll change horses, several times. It'll cost you an arm and a leg."

"Do as you're told, driver." One by one Akhmad handed four gold coins. "And remember! Don't spare the whip!"

"A lot of people run away at night, sir. It's really none of my business, but I wonder, what are you trying to escape?"

Caught by surprise, Akhmad answered without thinking, "My own shadow, I suppose."

"But sir," the driver shook his head again, "almost every day is a sunny day around Shatt-al-Arab, and the blistering sun casts black shadows on the ground. At night, in their huts, the fishermen light candles, and huge shadows dance on the walls."

"Yes, yes, I know all that, driver. I've been in Shatt-al-Arab, not long ago. Let's go!"

The entire night they raced, but shortly after dawn the brown horse collapsed. Akhmad helped the driver pull the carriage to the nearest collection of small mud huts, a village whose only horse was chomping straw so slowly that Akhmad's heart sank in despair.

"This horse is old and very frail." The panting driver wiped his forehead with the tail of his turban. "I can't imagine it pulling a carriage. Let's wait until we find a fresh one." "No!" Akhmad yelled back. "I'm going on."

The driver's eye roved, in mockery. "The earth must be burning under your feet."

Akhmad muttered to himself, "Being laughed at and taunted in public are the meanest flames in hell."

Less than an hour later Akhmad straddled a nodding donkey and left the village, his pointed, elegant shoes scraping the rocky ground. A second, even more sleepy donkey lugged loaves of bread, water skins, and dry dates. Day and night Akhmad took turns riding one animal or the other, but on the third morning, both creatures dug in their heels. Though Akhmad pleaded, cursed, and whipped the beasts savagely, they would not budge.

He stuffed dates into his pockets, shouldered two water skins, and wandered in the wilderness until several days later the water ran out. Exhausted, Akhmad lay under a thorny bush and prayed to die. As he agonized, a caravan passed by. Akhmad moaned, and was given water and food. For two gold coins the Bedouins drove him to a fishing village not three days ride away. In the village, Akhmad made arrangements to board a ship sailing for Calcutta in three days. He rented a room in a fisherman's hut and, for the first time in many days, ate and drank, unhurried. Next morning he woke up disoriented, but feeling stronger inside, as though a chain of nightmares had been interrupted at last.

A mirror on the wall showed a muddy beard and a caked, thicker moustache. His much thinner face had tanned, almost to the colour of tea. Sighing in relief, he wiped droplets of sweat off his nose with the back of his hand.

Akhmad whistled, almost content, his shaving brush working a thick lather on his cheeks and neck. Left and right he glanced, and merrily began to shave one cheek, then the other. After the razor scraped off the moustache he had worn for seven years, Akhmad studied his baby-smooth face in the mirror. His glowing appearance pleased him. On the spot he decided to change his name into Yusuf.

He stuck out his tongue, then piped, "Yu-suf", "Yu-suf", "Yu-suf". But even as he pronounced his new name, a queer taste lingered in his mouth; for a time his thumb and forefinger fondled the void left by the shaven moustache. "It'll be a while," he bent over and kissed the mirror, "before the sights and sounds of my new identity fall into place."

Weeks later, Yusuf opened a large store in Calcutta. Unlike his father, he not only dealt in tea and spices, but also imported and distributed cheap English goods. Soon, his impassive face, refined manners, and cold blood while negotiating a deal's details endeared Yusuf to English businessmen. Aspiring Hindu merchants began to imitate the newcomer's Baghdadi accent, even wiped their noses with the back of their hands.

Like ivy thriving on a wall, Yusuf's business sprawled into the neighbouring warehouses; within months his stores occupied most buildings across the street. So lucrative were his enterprises that after a couple of years he bought a red-tiled, white house many times larger than his matrimonial home in Baghdad. A meticulously trimmed English-style garden occupied most of the lot, but in the back yard palm leaves rocked rhythmically in the wind.

Three years later Yusuf employed more than one hundred people; after a decade in India he owned scores of branches in Bombay, Delhi, Madras — even half a dozen outlets in Karachi. Five years afterward, before Yusuf turned forty, he heard of Muslim mothers nagging their children to work harder at English and Mathematics. "Students that do well in those subjects," the mothers preached, "will one day become as wealthy as Yusuf."

But Yusuf changed: his riches set him above the others. Without warning, he laid off a third of his experienced store managers at unpredictable times: time and again, he set the dates for the lay-offs by consulting tables of random numbers. Written by scribes, but always signed by Yusuf himself, the letters of dismissal stated, "In the long run, it is to your own advantage, and in the company's best interests, that you make use of your talents elsewhere. We wish you good luck." Without hints or warnings, heads of families lost their jobs, and younger, panic-ridden men toiled day and night hours, just to keep up with the accelerating demands of Yusuf's company. Behind their boss' back, his underlings sniggered, "On his tombstone they'll carve: 'Here lies the first man to manipulate mass anxiety to generate huge profits'".

One night at home, after dessert, Harun, Yusuf's turbaned, coffee-coloured servant and personal secretary stood, as usual, pillar-stiff and arms crossed by his master's right. The flat-nosed Harun closed his eyes and moved his purple lips as if rehearsing a speech. "Sir," he intoned at last, "one of your competitors has been trying to imitate your strategies. The chap failed miserably, like the others, before him." Harun opened his eyes and handed Yusuf a folded-back local newspaper.

Twice Yusuf read the story. Pensively he sipped sweet tea and, after setting his white cup on the saucer, drew up one corner of his mouth in glee.

Some newspapermen in Calcutta who, Harun observed, spent most waking hours reading other newspapermen, wrote exalted editorials about Yusuf's practices. "His company will annihilate India's business ethics," wrote one editor. "The reclusive foreigner," another writer fumed, "is the harbinger of a rapacious philosophy, not only in business, but life in general. For a shilling or two," the columnist warned, "the likes of Yusuf trample all traditions and human values."

"Amateurs!" Yusuf roared. After rolling the newspaper into a narrow cylinder, he handed it to his wide-eyed secretary. "Fools! These sentimental pen pushers have no idea how to run a profitable business!"

Later in his study, Yusuf muttered to himself, "Incompetents! Imbeciles! These news-hounds know *nothing* about me. And their research is so poor, they haven't even found out my real name is not Yusuf."

∽

In his office, Yusuf toiled from dawn until after the sky turned ebony. When he sat down to dinner, Harun recited the news and gossip about town. After a conversation about Harun's family and household matters, Yusuf riffled through the newspapers. Though fond and trusting enough of his servant to seek his advice from time to time, Yusuf never shared anything about his life in Baghdad.

Later in the evening Yusuf perched cross-legged on an ottoman in his study upstairs and resumed the hard game of chess he had been playing for weeks with — or, he often felt, against himself. Before blowing out the kerosene lamp, he read in bed a few pages from his favourite authors: Herodotus or Thucydides, in translation. Though the characters in these books had been dead for over twenty-three hundred years, Yusuf felt closer to them than to his contemporaries in Calcutta.

He shunned the company of all people, even businessmen who sincerely admired his talents and wished to share his wisdom. With no friends at all, he quelled his occasional bouts of loneliness by mocking himself, "Lonely? Yes! But only some of the time." Acting on orders not to make any changes in his master's personal life, Harun barred all matchmakers at the garden gate. Yusuf no longer prayed either — not because he scorned his father's teachings, but because even the *thought* of personal involvements with any divine or human beings gave him goosebumps. Fearful of all bonds of affection, cold-hearted

Yusuf could not even for a moment fancy prostrating himself in passion before the Almighty.

After decades in India Yusuf still dwelt from time to time on his third wedding night. "Did I imply," he chewed his lower lip, "that single-handedly I would make my family the richest in the Middle East? Was I unduly proud? Or arrogant?" He brooded, sometimes even at his desk. "Were my shame and humiliation a test of my mettle? Or did my talents," he shuddered at his own audacity, "rouse the Almighty's anger and envy?"

The daily dread of being exposed in Calcutta, too, reinforced the deepest of Yusuf's convictions: whether by the name of Akhmad, or by his adopted name, he alone had been writing the story of his life. He despised himself when in moments of weakness he blamed the world, the Almighty, or other people for some boring chapters or awkward turns in the plot. "Keep writing, Yusuf," he chanted, to harden himself, "keep writing, even if at the moment you can't edit your tale or fathom its moral."

"But what about your fate?" A condescending baritone boomed inside Yusuf's head. "Tell us, Yusuf, why did your life turn out the way it did? And when, Yusuf, will you accept the fact that you were the victim of bad luck?"

"Come on," Yusuf smirked back. "An impersonal destiny in charge of my life? *Bad luck?*" He pitched his voice higher to drown out the hoots and catcalls of an invisible audience. "So-called 'fate' is the religion of mediocrities who dread *my* kind of hard work. Fate," he waved, "is the self-pity of lazybones soothing themselves for their shortage of talent."

Any conjectures of a faulty belt buckle, for example, being responsible for his pants sliding down were fiercely rejected.

Yusuf believed in his capacity to make choices, free choices, just as piously as he believed that in his stores, at least, supply created demand. Whenever whispers urged him to forgive himself for a day or two, he scoffed at them with a loud, "Is that so?"

"You might enjoy it, Yusuf," the sweet voices tempted him.

"I like the way I live." Yusuf hooted back.

These and other ruminations receded into the background as he pored over contracts at his desk; they hardly perturbed him while at work.

Still, his *memories* haunted him. Yusuf's heart ached, sweetly, whenever he recalled his father painstakingly, lovingly, introducing his sons to the art of transmuting one dinar into three. Pining, Yusuf smiled every time he pictured his mother's bleary eyes, weeks before his first journey to the east. "Who," she had anxiously fondled his arm," *who* will prepare my Akhmad's hot meals? And who will do his laundry?"

On sleepless nights on his bed, shivers streamed down Yusuf's spine, as he watched the gloom. His hands, mostly against his will, caressed his perspiring chest, as he wistfully recalled the tenderness of his two-nights marriage. His mouth relived his wife's supple skin, as cool as spring water. Moaning, he writhed in pleasure and in pain as Fatima's fragrances tickled his nostrils. But in a few moments, the bedroom walls and ceiling flashed scenes of his last wedding night; deafened by the abominable uproar in the large tent, he stared at pictures of himself naked from the navel down.

When at last the phantoms faded, a young girls' chorus lilted in his native tongue. "Akhmad, dear Akhmad! You can conceal, but you can't hide!"

For almost three decades Yusuf's habits remained as constant and predictable as the minuscule, child-like signatures he affixed on thousands of contracts. After lunch, however, his eyelids felt heavier than lead, though he ate little and appeared slimmer than his father at middle age. Unless he took naps, the fine details of transactions began to blur in the late afternoon, and, grudgingly, Yusuf returned home one hour after sunset. His nightly games of chess with himself became longer, less exciting. He no longer read ancient history before falling asleep in his bed. The inevitable encounters with the mirror now yielded a sallow pate with brown, ugly stains embedded in a wreath of white hair. A flabby neck and deep furrows at the corners of his dim eyes made Yusuf's sad heart sink. Though he gave little thought to the meaning of the droplets on his nose, only they and his handwriting remained unchanged from his youth.

One morning Yusuf woke to light filtering through the shades of his window. To his surprise, he saw no tray with tea and cold milk on his bedside table. Twice he clapped his hands. Nobody came. After pondering these unusual events, the master strode to the servants' quarters, where Harun's wife, her children and grandchildren were sobbing softly. Harun had passed away the night before, and his grieving family had neglected to serve breakfast. Stunned, Yusuf turned on his heels and hobbled to his bed. Moments later he yelled that he wished not to be disturbed.

Flat on his back and immobile, Yusuf brooded and studied the ceiling. He missed Harun badly. His dense, iron ball heart feared that something monstrous, terrifying, irreversible had taken place. For the first time ever Yusuf felt weak and pitiable — "Like an abandoned, blind puppy," he commented.

These new thoughts frightened him so much that he jerked up in bed and gazed for hours at the horizontal strips of light travelling clockwise with agonizing slowness from one wall to the next. The light in the room became keener and keener as the day went by, but hours later it died away, almost imperceptibly. Still awake, Yusuf watched transfixed the dawn drawing faint lines on the window shades. Nevertheless, his eyes remained thorn dry. "One day I'll die, too," Yusuf muttered again and again, as if unable to let go of a childhood prayer. "Just like my servant."

He stayed in bed for days, his skin swelling in the dark, stale air, upper chest aching from dry-eyed loneliness. When anxiety tormented him, Yusuf tossed or dozed, waking up to find a bowl of fresh soup or a cup of tea by his bedside table. Despite his anger, he could not muster enough strength to bray at Harun's wife or her children for disobeying his orders. Though embarrassed to the bone, Yusuf admitted he even looked forward to their modest shows of concern.

Day and night, nasty questions startled him out of his light sleep. "What are you living for, Yusuf? What's the point?" Unrelenting, the interrogators kept torturing him until he pounded and pounded his head on the bedstead to obtain some relief. But soon, the prosecutors came back to cross-examine him even harder. "Get rich, Yusuf? Is that it? Richer than Croesus? How many millions do you need before you calm down?"

Every so often a reedy soprano trilled in the Calcutta dialect, "India, Yusuf? What the hell are you doing in India, where so many people hate you?"

Desperate, he strained to move his arms and legs, but his soft-as-pillows limbs barely obeyed him. Yusuf wrung his cold hands. He had to warm up his mercury-heavy blood and feel real!

When the pain hit even harder, he covered his head with his blanket. Eyes pinched tight, he prayed like a child who fears he'll be flogged, "May my past, my present and my future vanish, as if they were never meant to be." These words brought no relief; instead, a dreadful feeling of emptiness took hold of him. He flung away his bedcover and murmured in terror, "Unless my mind stays clear, I'll slash my wrists. Or hang myself."

The intense fears of killing himself drove a blinking Yusuf out of bed. Still dazed, he bathed and shaved his silvery beard — but not the hoary moustache that had sprouted while he grieved. He put on clean clothes and summoned his chief accountants and lawyers.

Sitting in a half circle about their master's desk, the underlings glanced at each other in disbelief. How could they possibly draw up an inventory of all Yusuf's assets *in one month*?

"It can't be done," a senior lawyer finally took a risk.

"Do it anyhow!" Yusuf yelled in a rare display of emotion. His cowering aides jumped to their feet and one by one scuttled out of the room.

In less than five weeks the inventory of Yusuf's business and properties appeared to be in reasonable order. He bequeathed his house and all its contents to Harun's widow, and after saying goodbye to her, but to no one else, boarded an English steamship. Luggage and suite inspected, Yusuf climbed the stairs to the ship's upper aft deck. He leaned his back and forearms on a varnished wooden rail, and admired the ship's tall chimney glowing in the early afternoon light. Unlike old sailboats that depended on favourable winds, this ship would be cruising Shatt-al-Arab in about a week or so!

Yusuf's thumb and forefinger fondled his five-week-old moustache. "With boats like this," he thought, "the world will soon become a smaller place. And canny merchants," he winked at the chimney, "will make millions of pounds by shipping inexpensive goods from continent to continent. The average person," he concluded, "and not only explorers or outcasts like myself, will feast their senses on the wonders of the globe.

"Progress!" Yusuf summed up his ideas, as the ship slid away from its pier, and Calcutta's warehouses grew smaller and smaller. A foghorn startled him with its long moan. Panting, Yusuf struggled to recover his optimistic mood. "The world is changing," he said aloud to himself. "And, for the better, perhaps. Human beings might change a little too."

He spread his right hand on his chest and made a solemn vow: "I'll settle down for good in Baghdad," he whispered. "Yes! Baghdad! Despite what happened, I'll get into business, buy some properties, stop living like a hermit. I promise," he raised his voice, "to spend some of my free time with new and old friends."

The shores of India disappeared before sunset. Though the amber flames of kerosene lamps on the ship's rails shed a sweet light, the deck turned dark. Yusuf felt lonely and empty; doubts began to gnaw his entrails. "Will I, or my life, change for the better by resettling in my home town?" He found no relief by biting one thumbnail, then the other. "The best I can hope for," he reckoned, "is an opportunity to tell my family what terrors made me flee the way I did.

"Dinner, dinner." A blond, young sailor marched by, striking a cymbal.

In the ship's well-lit dining room, Yusuf chose to sit by himself at a small table. The entire meal — poached fish, vegetable soup, roast, and boiled potatoes — smelled fresh and delicately spiced, but he managed to swallow only a few spoons of soup. "Am I depressed again," he worried, "or just terrified of all the changes in my life?" Furtively he slid his right fingers under his shirt. Moments later he concluded, almost serene, that there was no reason to panic: his heart was not beating faster than usual. "Mere excitement," he pronounced. Nonetheless, he dismissed the waiter and began to sip tea with cold milk.

"My life has been a string of spectacular deals," Yusuf reassured himself, adjusting his black bow tie. "I've amassed one hundred million pounds. *Sterling*! And it's not really *my* problem," he chuckled, caustically, "if many of my competitors retired into *very* modest bungalows in the countryside.

"How many millions of Muslims and Hindus envy me?" Yusuf swung to his right, as if Harun stood cross-armed and ready to answer. But instead of his loyal servant, he caught sight of passengers at their dinner tables. A tide of grief welled in Yusuf's chest.

Later, while smoking a cigar by the bow, and watching the ship's wake, he murmured, "Father and mother, too, must have passed away." The pitch-black sea had swollen, and the moist air smelled of salt and fresh fish. "Long ago," he added.

Yusuf pictured his parents' old home, five handsome boys and himself sitting around the room. "What happened to my brothers?" Twice he cleared his throat.

"The first thing I'll do back home," Yusuf pinched his eyes shut, "is throw myself at my brothers' feet. I'll beg them to understand how ashamed I've felt all these years."

One by one he imagined his five brothers, a row of grey-haired men in red robes, perched stiffly on tall, black leather chairs. His brothers' immobile eyes watched him from under their bushy eye-brows — Ibrahim's black, bushy eye-brows — until Yusuf finished the account of his life in Calcutta.

"You're right, brothers," Yusuf pleaded, eyes glued to the puny red carpet under his knees. "I've not written a single letter in almost thirty years, out of sheer cowardice, I confess. But *please*, forgive me, so I may live my last years in peace."

In desperation, Yusuf raised his head to face Salah, his baby brother, a teenager at the time Yusuf ran away. "Salah," he begged with all his heart, "please, intercede with your brothers!" Blood rushed to Yusuf's face, but, still, he gazed into Salah's eyes. "I may not deserve it, brother, but please, *please*, be kind, and perhaps the others will forgive me, too."

Yusuf paced the ship's deck and gazed overhead, where millions of silver points glittered against the black velvet sky. Were it not for the disturbing memories of his wife, he would have said his heart felt lighter, a little purged of guilt.

"I wish," Yusuf told the cold, distant stars, "that Fatima has remarried, borne children, and no longer despises her first husband. Once settled in Baghdad," he swore, "I'll write Fatima a letter, inviting her to listen to *my* version of my innermost thoughts as a young man."

He shut his eyes, and imagined himself in Fatima's flower garden, smiling almost effortlessly at a plump, grey-haired, still very attractive woman. Fatima did not smile back, but showed him the way to a white, wrought iron table. They sat on cane chairs, sipped sweet tea, and talked, in whispers.

"After twenty-nine years," Yusuf sighed at the end of his story, "I stopped pretending that all I needed was my servant's devotion."

Briefly, Fatima told him of her sons and daughters.

"No!" Yusuf chastised himself inwardly, and resisted the temptation to take her sons into his business. "No!" He bit his tongue, "an offer like that might be viewed as a bribe. I might offend her again."

He bent forward, and asked Fatima, "Do you remember, perhaps, how awkward I was? I almost never looked people in the eye. I still don't, Fatima." He peered aside, and chuckled.

"You were fond of me at the time, and even if you just look at me and don't say a word, I'm grateful you've listened to the end of my tale."

On the ship's deck, Yusuf blew his nose in his handkerchief, eyes still dry.

Yusuf alighted in what stood in his memory as a fishing village. A new pier thrust a long, slim finger into Shatt-al-Arab, and massive warehouses with thatched roofs lined the pebbled shore. The village now boasted its own horse-drawn carriage, and the driver he hired, a bald man with a moustache as white as lambs wool, wore a black eyepatch on his left.

"Driver," asked Yusuf, who loathed coincidences even more than he hated surprises, "where are you from?"

"Born and raised in Baghdad, sir." The driver's eye roved. "But, like the angel of death, I ply my trade everywhere."

"Do you remember," asked Yusuf, "a frantic young man who left Baghdad for Shatt-al-Arab one night almost thirty years ago?"

"I can't possibly remember all the people who run away at night, sir. Only special cases."

"Pardon me!" said Yusuf.

"Oh," sighed the driver, "like the heavyset poet from Baghdad, who dreamt of the angel of death striking him the day he became famous. In a panic, the man hired me after midnight and told me to race all the way to Damascus. Well, we arrived four days later at noon, and my passenger stepped out of the cab in a terrible hurry. But an old scribe in the market recognized him and trumpeted, 'Damascus is proud to welcome Baghdad's most noble voice.' Sir, I'm telling you the truth: my paunchy poet lumbered a few steps into the street and dropped dead. He had only a few coins on him, so the authorities made me pay for the balance of his funeral."

"Yes, yes, I remember," Yusuf sniffed. "Of course, your story made the Calcutta newspapers years ago. Driver!" he shouted before stepping into the cab. "We have a long journey ahead. Let's go!"

They crossed stretches of desert, rested under the shade of date trees, drank putrid water, slept in mud huts. The blue, cloudless skies over the wilderness brought back to Yusuf the sights and sounds of carefree games in the streets of his childhood. He recalled the smells of Baghdad's sprawling bazaar: spices, teas, rugs, rice, and dried-up dung. On the third morning, Yusuf began to fidget in his seat, more excited than he had dreamt possible at his age.

A few afternoons later the carriage trundled over the crest of a hill. Looking out the window, Yusuf recognized some of Baghdad's minarets and mosques on the horizon. He bade the driver to halt, and stepped down from the carriage. For a long while he stood mesmerized by the view of his hometown bathing in golden light.

"Driver," Yusuf pointed, "when did they build the white stone bridge to the left?"

"A magnificent bridge, isn't it, sir? Well, they finished it some ten years after Akhmad's wedding."

"Akhmad?" A dagger pierced Yusuf's stomach and remained lodged. "What . . . what do you know about Akhmad's wedding?"

The driver chortled, as if unable to hold back. "In Baghdad, sir, any child knows about Akhmad's wedding." He laughed louder. "On the third evening, right in the middle of the party, Akhmad ran for dear life, without saying goodbye. You see, he was caught with his pants down."

Images flashed before Yusuf's open eyes: his youth, twenty-nine years in India, grieving Harun, his prayers to renew life in Baghdad.

Ashamed from scalp to toes, Yusuf took a few steps backwards. He cocked his head toward the blue, indifferent sky and hissed between his teeth, "Is this my fate? To become a landmark, a living joke in my hometown?" Oblivious to the driver, he squatted by the carriage like a tired old man.

"Twenty-nine years!" Yusuf mumbled. "And nothing, almost nothing at all has changed!" He hung his head, and closed his eyes.

"Are you all right?" the driver asked. "Please, have a sip of water, sir."

Yusuf waved to dismiss the intruder. Moments later he opened his eyes, and staggered up. He glanced at the sky above, then swivelled on his heel. One thought after another exploded inside his head. "Order the carriage around! Race, nonstop, back to Shatt-al-Arab! Take the first boat to . . . "

Pictures of Cairo, Singapore and London blinded him, though he knew of them only from the research for his endless contracts. He would, once again, make brilliant deals, leave his competitors agape.

"Driver," Yusuf turned about, "what would children and parents do if there were no Akhmads they could taunt?"

The driver waited before he whistled. "There would be fewer stories to swap, sir."

The passenger gritted his teeth. Where in the world would he settle down?

"Yusuf, Yusuf," a fluty soprano teased him. "*Again?* Are you *running?* All over again?"

Yusuf bit his lower lip, then slapped his cheeks until his mind cleared. "No," he muttered, shaking his head, "it's not true! My life has not been in vain! Without help whatsoever,

I became a very rich man. I've learned a couple of things about life and death — and about myself, too. And before I die," he lowered his voice, tears scalding his cheeks, "I want to see the glint of forgiveness in the eyes of a few people."

Yusuf loped to the carriage and flung its door ajar. "Climb into your seat, driver!" he bellowed, his forefinger pointing at his hometown, "and don't stop until you come to the tea and spices market! There, you'll trumpet that *Akhmad, son of Ibrahim* , is back in Baghdad. And his nose is still moist, much of the time."

"What? Akhmad? *The* Akhmad?" The driver's eye swelled in disbelief. "Sir," he pleaded after a while, "in Damascus, they made me pay for the poet's funeral. And you," the driver stepped forward, the palms of both hands turned up, "you seem very upset. Forgive me for saying, sir, but you're not a young man. I'm afraid . . . "

Akhmad dug into his pocket, cupped two coins, and one by one flung them into the air. The driver's one eye rolled high. Smiling, he caught the gold.

"Pass it on, driver." The passenger flexed his left eyebrow. "Akhmad is no starving bard. Next time you brag about your work, tell the children of Baghdad you've been in the service of the wealthiest Muslim in India."

LUNCH BREAK

I hate this warehouse. The intense, milky light from the water-stained, low ceiling blinds me, makes me sick. In desperation I gaze at the turd-brown floor to ignore the yellow, windowless walls.

The door is closed, and customers can't see me chewing my egg salad sandwich. I perch on an orange plastic box, hemmed in by bags of coffee and pink packages of sweeteners in an open grey box.

I'm the manager of five dumb girls right out of high school, and they work for one dollar above minimum wage. They brew espressos, serve hot and cold coffees. All day they flash smiles, even when the customers mouth complaints. Looking happy is company policy, and it's up to me to enforce it. When too few customers are having coffee, my kids sweep the franchise's floors, wipe counters, shine the chrome, throw the garbage out.

I don't drink coffee. I know the taste of my chocolate milk in the fridge is just chemicals, but, on the whole, healthier. One day they'll "discover" that coffee, like cigarettes, is poison. The white men who saw the Indians smoking, thought it was an apple a day. Even before, Bedouins noticed how goats hopped after munching on coffee beans. A new stimulant descended upon the world. One thing led to the other, and here I am, managing a Second Cup.

Jews my age are doctors, lawyers, accountants. The older ones went into business right after high school, made piles of money.

"Buy it cheap, then sell it with a huge mark up." That's Dad, word for word. His hardware store was chaotic. When I gave him a hand on Saturdays, I barely found my way through the poorly-lit maze of narrow aisles with ceiling-to-floor, wobbly shelves crowded with tools, pots and pans, paints, every imaginable screw. All his life Dad dreamed of a white Cadillac to drive Mom and him to properties in Florida and the Muskokas. Never made it. Is that what turned him into the only alcoholic in our shul?

The old man finished half a bottle of scotch after dinner, but got stewed only a few times a year. While he moaned in bed, Mom minded the store. She told the regulars that Dad suffered from severe migraines. Not a lie, really.

How small was our bungalow, especially when almost every night they bickered about money. Dad hollered, "I'm no Rotschild! You better put up or shut up!" Mom complained, "We don't have enough money to buy me a decent fur coat." She was lazy, never looked for a paying job, showing up at the store only when Dad was hungover. She always got back at his drinking and our too-small bungalow. She watched soap operas, then went for coffee klatches in girlfriends' homes. Small wonder I'm allergic to coffee.

Sundays were the worst. The store closed, Dad drank to distraction and picked fight after fight with Mom. I gripe about Dad and his boozy outbursts, but he still lives in his own house. I don't.

"Norm?"

Long-haired Kate is at the door. What does my assistant want now?

"We have a problem at the coffee beans counter, Norm."

"Be right in."

A problem. Kate and the girls always call me. Scared of confrontations. The girls and I are on first-name basis. At the office, my staff called me "Mr. Berg." As Vice President, my management style was expertise above, hard work below. But now, *Norm, you have a crisis at the counter.*

By the counter, Kate tosses her head towards a woman in a black angora coat. Holt Renfrew. I remember the store, just half a block from my old office.

Hair done, lots of makeup. Gold glitters on her fingers and wrists.

I beam a policies-and-procedures smile. "How can I help you?"

She looks me in the eye. "We tried the mocha. It's way too weak." She hands me a brown paper bag.

My hand feels the coffee beans. I open the bag, peer inside. Half a pound of roasted beans left. Weigh it? If Mrs. Renfrew takes offence, she'll ask, "Your full name, and the owner's name, and his number, please." She'll call head office. I'll lose my job. For months I'll wait for phone calls that never materialize.

"Do you want a refund for what's left in the bag?" I ask.

"Yes, of course," she says, glaring.

"Do you remember how much coffee you bought?"

Mrs. Renfrew cocks her chin. "Two pounds!" She fires back.

Liar.

I turn my face away and pound the cash register buttons. The drawer beeps, slides back. I hand her a ten-dollar bill and coins. The girls are watching. The paper tiger blinks.

"Thank you."

"Oh, you're welcome."

My throat burns.

"Kate!" I say. "I'm going out on an errand. Be back in twenty minutes."

"That's fine, Norm," an edge of sarcasm in her voice. No wonder.

If Jerry heard about the incident, his mouth would twitch. He's the owner, but he never criticizes me openly. The worst thing would be to go on unemployment again, stay home, reading all the ads, the editorials, the obituaries.

At seventy-five, Jerry still has thick, salt-and-pepper hair parted to the right. He wears no glasses or hearing aid, but brand-new cardigans and matching Harry Rosen pants. Last winter he called me from Florida on Mondays and Thursdays to check up. Meanwhile, I work extremely hard, making sure nothing ever goes wrong. The washrooms are squeaky clean. Surgeons could carve patients there.

Jerry still deals in commercial real estate. Owns half a dozen franchises. Smart Jew, Jerry. Made it big. He hugs the girls, kisses them on the lips, sighs as if all the time they were on his mind. "You've pretty legs," he winks, "you should be in Hollywood. What the hell are you doing here? Looking for Mister Right? At Second Cup? Loosen up! Spiffy up your make-up and hairdo."

They giggle into their cupped hands.

That charmer pays me and the girls peanuts. If we all resigned, he'd fill our positions next day. The impotence of today's underpaid working class!

"You've changed, Norm," Shirley said days ago. "The day you left the Board you turned into a worry-wart."

Small wonder.

Cold. Should have worn my vest. I forgot how the staff's faces turn pink with the espresso and coffee machines on.

The sky is ground-pepper grey. A few yellow-brown leaves still dangle in the branches. At forty-five, I'm minus a house, renting in Don Mills, carping about my job. Even Shirley stopped listening. After dessert she stands up, "Sorry, there's a lot of work in the kitchen."

"Shirley," I try to say, "I *can't* go back to my pre-Black-Friday days."

She yells, her eyes glitter, cold and hostile. "Get hold of yourself! Behave like the vice president you used to be."

I shouldn't be going out, but I am. Just one drink, one scotch.

Déclassé? I'm not even sure what it means. Up one day, then bottom of the barrel the next? I waste my talents, my management skills.

Management skills? Since my layoff, the cupboard has been bare. It took four years to get my Bachelor of Commerce degree. In days — no, hours — I was out of a job, no self-respect left. From one interview to the next, I spun tales about the re-organizations I'd headed. Talvest was the last corporation to consider me for a management position. I was interviewed by the Vice Prez of H.R. He asked about work experience outside government. He hadn't even read my resume!

So many leaves have fallen. As Vice President for Special Projects, I made ninety thousand a year, had a private secretary, a three-washroom house in Pickering. On the commuter train, I paged through the *Business Report*. I thought I had it all.

At four fifteen, as I looked out my window at the mansions of Rosedale and Moore Park, the sudden call from Fred intrigued me: he asked me to drop everything.

Once inside his office, he introduced me to Jim, a bulldog if I ever saw one. The first stab of anxiety. On the other side of his desk, Fred cleared his throat. I thought of Dad, who was such a heavy smoker. Even in his sleep he coughed and wheezed, waking up my mother.

"Norm," Fred cocked his square chin, "we are re-structuring. I regret to say that as of today, your position is terminated."

My mind evaporated. Fred had praised my good work over the years. More than once he said "sorry." "Terminated," and "castrated" rang in my ears.

Fred stood up. He said that Jim The Bulldog would escort me to my office. At the door he vigorously shook my limp, sweaty hand.

My corner office, its oak desk and state of the art computer. In the corridors and elevator, unfamiliar faces, snatches of a nightmare, stared. I heard malicious voices whispering, "Norm Berg has been fired. Was given *three minutes* to clear his desk."

"One drink," I thought, "just one drink to get hold of myself, muster enough courage to break the news to Shirley."

Now, the manager-in-chief of a Second Cup gazes at the entrance to Beaver Bar and Restaurant. I push the heavy door with bevelled glass open. Inside are tables with bluish marble tops and white upholstered chairs with tall backs. A couple of suits are gesticulating, five-inch-thick brown briefcases beside their chairs. Three more perch by the counter.

Three fat-assed guys sit on high stools by the smoky bar. What *are* they doing here this time of the day?

"What would you like to have?"

A pretty smile. "Double scotch on the rocks," I mutter.

Could I market myself? I think of careers I could have pursued: surgery, management consultant, owner of a chain of stores. Booze makes it easy to write and edit the scripts. The faster the scenarios flash by, the more stable they become.

I stare at a burgundy maple leaf. Everywhere, the tawny or reddish mementos of the fall show up, even on this varnished counter.

Shirley says I'm living in a cave, excluding her. "I want family life," she hisses, even in front of the girls. "I want to be included, have a husband who talks, helps the girls with their homework. I'm not looking for a roommate."

"Roommate" sums it up pretty well. She cooks dinner, I wash the dishes. She prepares the sandwiches, I stick labels on the brown bags, then stuff the fruit and food inside. Since Black Friday my good wife twice tried to cheer me up in bed. But my nasty moods are not a flu that dissipates in days.

Side by side we lie on our queen-size bed, and passion never happens. Often, after the lights are out, I hear our girls twisting in their beds. I think of beds creaking to the rhythm of a slow metronome, of lovers moaning, groaning, sweating, swooning. Only Shirley and I gaze at the darkness — passive, lonely, alone.

I've been through stages: first I turned into a scaly lizard. Soon I dried up, became a dust ball under the bed. The day the vacuum cleaner sucks me in, I won't put up a fight. Who am I to put up a fight? Instead, I'll twist and twirl inside the disposable bag. I'll disintegrate, lose my fragile identity. Come Thursday, Shirley or one of the girls will dump on the curb the black garbage bag with my thready remains.

Shirley's right. I don't open my mouth, don't defend myself when she berates me. I just hang my head, and that irritates her even more. Later, after I dry the dishes, I plop myself on the couch with my rye. I pretend I'm watching the show and acknowledge her presence with monosyllables. Up and down my brain bobs, travelling in timeless, rarefied spaces. Light-headed, perspiring, I watch private movies about becoming a Director or Vice President of a multinational. Marketing new software. Hours-long meetings in boardrooms.

But it's hard to picture the details of meetings with sales managers. I'd rather live in the cozy world of glamorous scenarios. I make up new, adventurous lives packed with hilarious punch lines I share with Shirley and my few remaining friends. Like potters, I mould revolving hunks of moist clay into fleeting identities. Whenever the trance slows down, I sip my rye.

Later in the evening, Shirley helps me to bed. In the dead of night I wake up alarmed, temples throbbing. Writhing, I mess up the blankets, study the short-lived swaths of light cars cast on the ceiling.

"Here it is."

Now the girl sets my glass with the amber liquid on the counter's colour-by-Technicolor leaves. The first drink is always the best, it pleasantly sears my throat and stomach. In seconds the blessed liquid warms my innards, straightens up a self-confident spine. A drink a day keeps the shrink away. What rhymes with "lunch break?" Even if I thought long and hard I'd end up with nothing. Rhyming? Me? Like small talk and dancing, it makes me feel I'm a sick cell under a microscope.

At bar mitzvahs and weddings, Shirley insists that we dance. My mortifying, bamboo-stiff feet step on her toes. When I open my eyes, the disc jockey's lights daze me. People are staring. "Norm was a Vice Prez," they whisper, "but, poor guy, he fell on hard times. Managing a franchise, wears a gaudy vest. Brings home peanuts."

A monstrous necktie is strangling me. Breathless, face and hands sweating, I'm going haywire. The insane cloth will separate my soul from my body. Should I ask forgiveness? I must be going crazy: beg forgiveness from a tie I don't even wear? Maybe Shirley is right. I should see the shrink Dr. Doyle referred me to.

Come to think of it, why not beg forgiveness? It might bring relief, end the pain. It might not help, but it has no side effects.

By now I've acquired such tolerance of lousy moods, I've learned to live with them — almost. What I dread is physical pain. It reminds me of poorly-lit, smoky emergency rooms with filthy washrooms where Mom and I waited for hours. When the young doctors in white coats to their knees finally examined me, the sadists inserted ultra-thin, curved icepicks into my ear. More often than not I fainted.

How miserable was my childhood! In dread I waited for infections to explode my inner ear. Lived in fear of shaming myself, screaming in the classroom. Had I known then what I know now about booze, I would have medicated myself by swilling from Dad's bottles. He lacked finesse, his treasures stood on kitchen counters, even on the bathroom window sills.

How many sluggish, sleepy doctors inspected my ears through black, conical tips of thin, chrome flashlights? I remember a screwball lady doc who blinked nervously. She wore a floating, unbuttoned white coat that suggested early pregnancy. That irritating witch too often cleared her throat. After poking into my ear's innards, she recited, "Don't worry, Mrs. Berg. It's a minor infection. With penicillin, he'll be all right in a week."

That fridge-cold bitch didn't even mention my torture. How would the earache go away when no doctor ever brought it up in conversation? I already knew that covering my ear with a cupped hand stopped the pain only for a minute. Have ear infections predisposed me to the agonies of my forties?

Why try to get off the hook? For twenty years you toiled, a goody two-shoes. When the going got tough, you hoisted a white flag. Others gallantly braced themselves for the fierce wars of attrition. Why did Baby Norm lie in bed till noon? Now he hates himself, concocts historical-hysterical excuses for his misery. Amateur psychologist, eh?

Is there anything easier than self-contempt? To indulge in it I spit at myself without even opening my mouth! I pray, instead, for the day my eyes close for good. Sweet, blessed darkness. I'll see and hear nothing. Hallelujah!

"Hi Norm!"

Annoyed, I turn around in my bar stool. Who but Dave Weiss is smiling, strained? He removes his Navy trench coat, neatly folds it, lays it on the stool next to mine. His black leather briefcase remains on the marble floor. He's dressed for a boardroom meeting: chestnut suit, white shirt, a striped wide tie. His brown brogues shine. Gee, am I glad I took off the Second Cup vest. How embarrassing: to wear an eye-popping *shmate* while having a drink! The yellow nylon windbreaker beside me is humiliating enough.

I wish I could bury my tawny boots deep in the ground. Unpolished for years, the leather uppers seem velvety. In the past I wore them only when I worked around the backyard. Now I go through the motions of being alive in my work boots. Who was the phoney philosopher that said life begins at forty?

"Long time no see, Dave. What brings you to Beaver, of all places?" Yeah, I'm curious to hear what he's doing here at two p.m. Commercial real estate? Guys in this line of business just love to cut deals while drinking and smoking.

"Have a meeting at four. Felt like a beer. How about you?"

Two hours to kill in the middle of the day? Perhaps he doesn't wear a suit the whole day, only before a business meeting or an interview. Poor Dave, still "in transition," still bobbing up and down elevators. Reads year-old magazines in waiting rooms, tries hard to sell himself.

"Having a drink. I'm on my break."

"What kind of work do you do, Norm?"

A blow below the belt. My nostrils flare, a lump swells in the throat, sweat explodes in my face and neck. "I'm in transition. Looking for something new."

"I see."

"What would you like to have?" The cute waitress gets me off the hook. Perhaps I won't answer mortifying questions about my fall from grace.

Fall from grace? Not a bad phrase, after all. It captures my work clothes, the girls that make me feel dumber by the hour, the owner that pays me peanuts. These hassles drive me around the bend, but I'm past whining. All I want is to relax with a drink or two.

"A Molson 50." He says and eyes me, bemused. Has he heard about me, or do my shirt and boots tell all he needs to know?

"I'll have another scotch," I let out, as if in afterthought.

"Single or double?" The waitress asks, smiling.

"A double, please," I mumble and blood rushes to the roots of my hair. Where could I bury my sweaty, monstrous palms? Dave, no doubt, sees my empty glass on the counter. And now, another double. How mortifying!

Dad's drinking was common knowledge. But I'm in khaki clothes, drinking early in the afternoon, tongue-tied, face flushed, heart pounding my ribcage. Why don't I get over my awkwardness and enjoy shmoozing with a pal from the old neighbourhood? Does he still go to Shul? At the time we took tonnes of pictures of the kids and showed them off to each other.

What's happening?" I squeeze out a smile. Better scour his terrain before he assails me with questions. Please, almighty God, keep my trap shut. I don't want to broadcast how we lost our house and live in a curry apartment.

"Not much," he nods. "Some consulting, some work out of the house." He chuckles. "No complaints. I make a living."

Liar! People who "consult" or "work out of the house" don't kill time in bars. They make cold calls, track accounts, rewrite brochures. It's macabre to see how Dave, a Vice Prez only three years ago, has also fallen from grace. But he's a self-respecting, decent déclassé. He swings his briefcase like a pendulum as he marches from revolving doors to elevators. One by one he crosses off items on his What To Do list.

"I'm glad to hear. How're Bev and the boys?"

He shrugs. "Fine, fine," Dave says. "Do you meet any guys from the Board?" He gulps down half a glass.

"Haven't come across anybody." He too has nothing to tell. We'll mumble monosyllables about the past, finish our drinks, say good-bye, exchange regards to Bev and Shirley. In our zenith, the four musketeers went to movies and, afterward, to light bites. We elbowed each other's navels at the jokes' punch lines. Old school friends, not just acquaintances. Now that I've become a hermit, Dave and I are like ships: every two years we pass by each other, letting out brief foghorn wails. I bet that his life, like mine, is a measly, unending worry about credit cards.

"I don't quite get it, Norm." He eyes my work clothes and boots, then, sideways, glances at my face. "Are you . . . " he pauses, polite, " . . . working at all?"

The humiliation gives my chin a jolt. Deep down, what am I doing with my life? Wasn't I a good student, a bright Jewish boy that made Mom and Dad proud? Before finals I helped Dave with statistics and economic theory. Twenty-some years later I'm a has-been. No longer a go-getter, I can't even confess I'm managing a Second Cup. Like Dad, I need booze to keep my nose above water. I flop my head back, finish my drink, set my glass on one of the counters' maple leaves. "Oh, just managing a place. Did a few things before, now I'm doing that."

I pinch the same phoney smirk I beam at my dentist. No response in Dave's eyes. He's racking his brain, searching for words that won't hurt me. I know, I know: he won't kick me when I'm down! Still, I feel I'm sending awful vibes.

He furrows his eyebrows, not knowing what to say. We men are not good at trading words of comfort, the way Shirley soothes the girls and her friends, even on the phone.

"I know how you must feel," he says in a monotone. "Had rough times too. For six months I climbed the walls, waiting for the phone to ring."

"That bad, eh?"

Thank you, dear Dave. More than two decades ago you and I started as adjudicators, seduced by the iron-clad "security" of a government job, a great pension plan, good dental benefits. But our asses grew fat. With high mortgages, we were afraid to leave, take a plunge, start our own business. Too goddamn comfortable, we ignored the digital world skulking in this side of the horizon. We sat in day-long board meetings, pretending that something momentous was going on. Two-bit bureaucrats.

"Mmh," he mumbles. "How's Susan?"

"Not bad, not bad. She and her husband took over Dad's store after he retired."

"I see."

Susan, my sister, my parents' old-age pride! Susan, who graduated from grade twelve with a C average, and wouldn't even hear of legal-secretary courses. Just parked her fat ass by

Dad's cash register, bagged the merchandise, smiled, took cash, Visa, and Master Card. How broken-hearted Mom and Dad were when she began to date Ian! A part-timer, he helped Dad assemble gas barbecues and fix broken windows. Poor Mom. I really felt sorry for her. Lost so much weight when Susan and Ian moved in together! It must have torn her apart to see her daughter living with a *sheyguetz*. But now, with the kids in Hebrew school and the store booming, has Mom dropped her snide remarks about *goyishe* drop-outs.

I wonder how Mom and Dad feel about their Joe York University going downhill. I bet they rarely bring up my name in conversation and, if they do, they lay guilt and shame trips on each other. What's there to talk about? That I've fallen into bad times? Who but *shleppers* don't get back on their own feet after two years? Two years! These days, that's one and a half eternity.

They must have heard about my drinking. How do you keep secrets in a family? Yes, yes, I'm worse off than my dad. He drank every evening, binged from time to time, but he managed! Didn't drink at lunch break or procrastinate making cold calls; he would have slept well even before job interviews. To this day enjoys good food, and his eyes still glint whenever he comes across a shapely pair of legs. Even in the worst of times he looked straight ahead, a man. Didn't gaze at the sidewalks as if looking for twenty-dollar bills.

"Dave!" I put an end to the harrowing silence. It's terrifying to think that after four decades Dave and I have nothing to say. Just two jalopies sitting at a bar, trying to forget the race, ignoring the fumes. "I've to get back to work."

I set a ten-dollar bill on the counter. Let the cute waitress enjoy a fat tip. I put my hand out.

"I'll hang around for a while," he says.

Hang around. Well put. It's how we'll be spending twenty years, waiting for our pensions to kick in. Then we'll worry about new worries.

Ambitions? Holy Moses! Who am I to dream of changes? Can't even picture them! What I really need most is to fall asleep as soon as my head hits the pillow. Not to remember, not to dread, not to dream. One day at a time. No regrets. A lizard basking in the sun, a plant. Hopes? What hopes? They might turn out to be false.

"Take care."

"You too."

My windbreaker on, I tread the floor with phoney precision, to mask I'm under the influence. Back in the franchise I'll pretend I'm back from the bank. With a Certs under my tongue, no one will notice booze on my breath. A solid, respectable citizen.

The keen grey light outdoors blinds me. Blinking, I watch the depressing office buildings and orient myself toward the franchise. Come to think of it, why are bars so poorly lit? Somebody must have done marketing research. These days, nothing is done only because it feels right. Everything, including one's self, must be researched in depth, then marketed systematically. Otherwise, at forty-five, you become a has-been.

The tree trunks and branches glow black against the steely sky. The icy wind has blown away most leaves; on anorexic twigs only dead leaves still dangle like victims of a lynching. Whenever I think of victims I pity myself, too.

I'm uptight. For twenty years I resented being on first-name basis with subordinates. I instructed my first secretary to answer the phone with "Mr. Berg's office," even when I expected a call from home. Always voted for the Tories, and

Survival Of The Fittest was my favourite song. Believed in the bottomless wisdom of the market place.

My face feels warmer. Did a couple of drinks do the trick, or has the wind calmed down? I'm too anxious, too hesitant to take a stand, even on the weather. I need a break, like spending a few weeks by the sea. If Shirley and I tightened the belt, we could afford a couple of weeks in New Brunswick.

I love the sea, especially the breeze at dusk. The grainy, pearly sand soothes the toes, the heels sink and rise, the smell of airborne salt, fish, and algae invigorates me. It's great to take a walk in the beach — barefoot, of course. Just walk and walk for hours, stare at the line where frothy waves and the gentle slope of wet sand meet. I'll pick up intact shells to bring home.

Seagulls have such a haunting, mournful cry. How different from the timid wails of Toronto's fat, sociable gulls. The lazy rascals crave breadcrumbs and shake their heads, then stare, pretending to trust.

For months Mom and Dad planned their Florida vacation. At night they studied books and guides, as if the trip was about saving money, not the beaches down south. They argued about closing the store for three weeks. Dad couldn't wait to hit the road. Mom urged him to chill out. "What's the hurry? After so many years, we can wait."

But my old man loved the sea. He couldn't wait. He ached to sit on the beach, sip beer after beer, listen to the seagulls at dusk. He taught me that summer how to immerse myself in their unnerving, painfully nostalgic singing.

I listened once to a recording of seagulls shrieking. The cheesy "environmental" cassette captured only faraway echoes of seagulls. Where was the sun setting behind the mountains, the inebriating sand, sea, and salt?

If we save enough, we'll camp for a couple of weeks. Every evening, before dinner, I'll take a walk, alone. I love to be with my own thoughts. Strolling barefoot, I'll listen to the seagulls screeching, gaze at faraway sailboats, study the rocks and the sea. Before it's too dark, I'll turn around to walk back to our pup tents. Dry-eyed, I'll shrill my contempt and hatred at the sky and cresting waves. "I believed in the system, but it fucked me over, real good. Now I feel down, a defeated man! When I'm back in Toronto I'll clamp a phoney smile to my lips to signal I'm happy, always happy at work."

Hovering, circling, the seagulls will understand it all.

FIRST DATE

Is that the alarm clock shrieking? His dream dissolves into a pitch-black universe. His dick is steely, almost painful. He smiles, gets up, staggers toward the washroom. He flips the switch. The ceiling's light explodes into his eyes.

A tortured face in the mirror. Last night was too excited, jerked off to sleep. Tonight it'll be a dinner date. Too many after-work drinks.

What enormous gapped teeth! The orthodontist wants five thousand bucks to fix his yellowing Chicklets. Even his best acquaintances say he's too cheap to spend on his smile. He hides his sallow piano keys often by wiping the corners of his mouth while he eats. A simple trick. It works.

He pees, farts, shaves, showers. Once again, he studies his incisors, his too-long head, his untrimmed brown moustache, and the pink cheeks glistening now. What if Annette notices his skinny, drum-tight neck?

At the end of the date he'll escort her to the door of her apartment building. She'll mutter, "Thank you for the lovely evening." If he's relaxed, he'll peck her on the cheek. He'd feel mortified if the tip of her tongue brushed his monster teeth. Even he knows that cosmetic dentistry could do a lot of good.

A toasted bagel and instant coffee for breakfast. No butter, no cream. Has to save now because of the new made-in-China suit for Singles Gourmet events.

Chicks hate cheap guys. So, after dessert and coffee, he'll be the first to plunk down his credit card on the waiter's black plastic tray. But what if she doesn't go Dutch? What a drag! He hates to throw money at a date that might dissipate like morning mists.

His bachelor apartment is within walking distance from work, a saving of eight hundred bucks and change a year. That buys two summer suits on sale.

Pewter skies. Frozen needles pierce his cheeks and forehead. It must have been brutally cold overnight. On weighed-down trees, branches and twigs glitter, enveloped by crystalline membranes. Pedestrians in black or dark-green hooded coats tread gingerly, heads down, as if looking for twenty-dollar bills. The salt-and-pepper slush on the sidewalks and street has almost iced. His galoshes squelch the filthy sorbet underfoot.

Inside the office, the odours of wet, salted leather, drying wool, and moribund perfumes nauseate him. Too many women in black or grey sweaters, not a single skirt in sight. The guys dress too casually, some even in faded jeans. He's the only one in a blue suit, white shirt, silk necktie. Bet ten to one that behind his back they gossip about his work clothes, too. How infuriating! One day he might lose control, even punch someone in the mouth.

At thirty-three, he has never had a girlfriend. No hobbies, nothing to share on the weekend. The bastards swap sickening rumours: Howard is a loner, a virgin, no guts to fuck a hooker, get it over with. Walls around him are porous, the jerks know all about his problems.

Weeks ago he'd asked his family doctor to prescribe sleeping pills. Rambling for a long while, he'd told Doc West about his shame of sleeping alone.

"People talk about me all the time, doctor. They get together by the cooler. They gossip and giggle."

"How do you know it's about you?"

"They're jealous. I've got a Western MBA. Started out not too bad, managed a small business. But everywhere . . . others . . . especially the guys . . . said I'm gay." To his surprise, he'd begun to sob. "Always had enemies . . . got fired, went down the ladder." He snorted back his tears, wiped his tear-streaked cheeks with the hem of his jacket. "A glorified clerk . . . a high-school graduate could replace me. I have no friends . . . only acquaintances that come and go. Please, doctor, please help me! On Saturday nights I think of taking a hot bath and slashing my wrists."

"Has it occurred to you that you *want* others to talk about you? It would feel less lonely, wouldn't it?"

The doctor prescribed two Loxapac at bedtime. "Call me if you develop side effects. Please come back in two weeks."

Loxapac. The printed page at the pharmacy said that the drug was an anti-schizophrenic. Crazy, bonkers, *meshuguene*. Others can't hear the voices talking about him, eh? The hypocrite didn't tell him to his face, "Listen, you're badly off." Why play games? He, too, has pride.

At dinner time, he bet, the doctor-shmoctor would tell his curious wife all about him. The wife and the doctor would shake their heads, pity him.

How can you trust anyone? Even a doctor betrays you the moment you open up. From then on, he just calls the pharmacist to renew his prescription. Bet a loony to a louse that the two white coats swap gossip, "He's down in the dumps, sick, eh?"

He's terrified one day he'll blow up, thump the phoney doctor, the pharmacist, his nasty co-workers. Get himself into trouble.

Lunch time. Every day a sandwich and a soft drink from home. Much cheaper this way. They've long ago stopped inviting him to go to the cafeteria. Once in a blue moon a married woman invites him, wants to fix him up with a girlfriend. But he needs no help, no advice. He'd be just fine if others stopped staring, analyzing, undressing him in their minds.

He comes to work swinging his vinyl briefcase like a pendulum. Clothes maketh the man, make him feel safe. No reading between the lines, nothing between periods and capital letters.

A persona, a front, a mask? Who cares? Much better than slugs with cracked shells dragging themselves naked, exposed.

At two p.m. he plays back his calls. He recognizes *her* voice. His heart whams. He knows he's blushing. She's cancelling the date. The unwanted child in him feels humiliated. Like fine sand, his last chance is slipping away between his clenched fists.

Be honest, man! You barely know each other. Met at a Singles Gourmet party. She'd sat to his left at a round table during salad. Despite palpitations and paralysis, eventually he'd gathered enough courage to say, "Hi, I'm Howard Bloom." Faked a smile, worried about his gapped incisors. "I'm in transition, looking for a challenging position."

Lousy rhyme. Blood had flooded his cheeks and scalp. "What's your name?"

"Annette."

No last name. Didn't mention what she did for a living. Nothing personal. Avoiding him. Intimating she has more important things to do, like meeting good-looking, interesting guys.

She'd turned left and talked to a black blazer with an off-white mock turtleneck. Chic, expensive stuff. His own buttoned-down shirt and necktie were suffocating him. No wonder she'd ignored an out-of-place, grotesque character.

Before the main course the facilitator had announced, "Time to change places, guys!"

People had milled about, sashayed to other tables. Next, he'd sat by Maria White, an overweight tax lawyer. Maria? A *goyishe* name, and a bore to boot. Thirty-five. Biological clock ticking, she's desperate, frantic, wants to grab somebody. Even a Loxapac with gapped teeth will do.

Dancing after dessert. Most guys had leapt to their feet, invited the girls. Couples shook and boogied, chests just one foot apart. Annette had perched by a table nearby, her search-light eyes longing for a partner. He'd loosened his necktie and stood by her. "Hi, Annette. May I invite you to dance?"

How awkward! Why not, "How about a dance?"

She'd headed to the razzle-dazzle without looking back. A revolving globe cast indigo and lip-pink lights on the ceiling. Walls and contorting couples shone ghost-like.

She'd kicked her feet to the rhythm, swung her head, arms, hips. Her shoulders swayed back and forth, knees gavelling up and down. He tried, but their eyes never met. He *loved* her almost pretty head, long neck, tiny tits. He detested his own limbs, felt grateful this was not a slow, cheek-to-cheek dance. Would have missed beat after beat, stepped on her toes. Hell was inside his body, his legs a torture chamber.

The dance had ended. He'd given her his card. Three days later she'd called, left a brief message. Despite devouring anxiety, he waited, called back only the next day. Two days later they connected. As if by miracle, he managed to gab, courageous enough to invite her for a drink, after work.

They'd met in a bar. She'd brought up skiing, Celine Dion, Stephen King.

"I like hockey," he'd mumbled, already feeling rejected. "A couch potato," he'd snickered.

She was just out of a relationship, not ready to get involved. "How about you?"

His hot cheeks, he thought, must be glimmering like a tomato. "I'm in transition in this department too. Jinny got a job in Calgary," he lied.

"Did you live together?"

"Spent weekends together," he lied again, staring at his drink. He panicked. How long will he keep up the bullshit?

"How old are you?" he broke a long silence.

The corners of her eyes measured him. "Does it matter?"

He shuddered, embarrassed to his cells. "No! Just asking."

She agreed to have dinner in a week.

"Hi, Howard." He recognizes Anette's voice. "Something came up. I won't be able to see you tonight. Talk to you soon."

He bites his upper lip. Could stab her. His anger frightens him. Better get hold of himself. The whole office might notice. People will talk.

How will they ever connect again? She may not answer his calls. A flirt, a teaser. Leading him on, cancelling a date, no apologies. Someone better came up. And now it's up to him to wait and wait, though her message may never materialize. But if they talk again, he'll forgive and forget, a nice Jewish guy. Went to services for years after his bar mitzvah. Never rebelled. Listened to advice. Otherwise would have felt very guilty. Only these days, when he's lonely, he tries *goyishe* girls. His father doesn't know, and he's not about to tell him.

Six o'clock. He'll head to Café Select, splurge on himself, have a Belgian beer on tap. What the hell, he saved on a dinner for two.

The streetcar to Spadina and Queen sways and clatters. Once inside the barely-lit restaurant, he hangs his coat on a brass hook, heads for the varnished, narrow bar. Butt atop a high stool, he studies the dining tables, the smoking area, the entrance.

The bartender wears a white apron to his ankles. A guy with a long dress! Ridiculous! If he wore one, they'd whisper he was gay. Just thinking about it makes him feel self-conscious, scared, dry-mouthed. He's shy and uptight, can't even picture a guy sucking another's cock.

He sips from the thick, bowl-shaped glass. Great stuff. Even the froth tastes like clove. He already feels hungry. Dinner in front of the TV will save ten bucks.

But he's feeling sorry for himself. She'd too dumped him. He's a baby, will bawl soon. When Mom died, he'd cried and cried for weeks. No wonder. She'd been diagnosed with leukemia on a Friday and passed away on a Monday afternoon. Father didn't allow him to visit her on the ward. "That's the rule. You're only six years old."

After dusk he waited and waited across the street from the hospital. One by one the windowpanes turned on. "Which room is Mom's" he sobbed, too frightened even to pray.

Father showed up at the funeral scandalously drunk. Paid no attention to his abandoned only son. Abandoned by Mom and by Father, in that order.

In the evenings Father had drunk rye after rye. Soon found an excuse to throw a slap or two. The pain had scorched his cheek and chin. His whole head had felt numb.

Father remarried, but the beatings stopped only at grade ten. Now with blinding shame, he hates his old man. Never calls him.

The door to the café flings open. If it isn't Annette, followed by a not-bad-looking guy in a bomber jacket. The waiter shows them to a white, marble-top table not twenty feet away from where he sits at the bar. She drapes her red coat over the back of her chair. The guy unzips his jacket. She sits facing the street. He can see the date's face and chest in full view.

Howard's saliva boils. A steaming iron frizzles his cheeks. He grits his teeth, bites his lower lip. A rich kid stole a poor man's lamb. How mortifying! Robbed just when he was about to have his first real date, feel better about himself, announce to the mirror, "Here I am! A man!" Her date will stare, instead, at an inveterate virgin. And now the robber is enjoying his spoils!

The enemy bends over, whispers close to her ear. She laughs. What's so funny? Isn't his torturer aware how he, Howard, is falling apart?

Howard stands up. "A bottle of red wine, please."

The bartender looks surprised. "At the counter?"

Nodding, he asks for the bill, hands him a credit card, signs the slip. Clutching the bottle neck behind his back, he strides to their table and barks, "Good evening."

She looks up. She blushes.

"Who's he?"

"Just a friend," she murmurs.

"Is that right?" he turns to her date, his foe.

"Listen, buddy. I don't owe you any explanations."

Howard half closes one eye. "You owe me a lot! Let's have it out."

He aims a clenched fist at the date's nose. He misses. The date pushes back his chair, stands up, grabs his arm. Swinging out the wine bottle, Howard hammers it over his rival's head. Something cracks. The skull? The date crumples to the floor.

"Help, help!" She pushes her chair back and leaps up.

With one hand he chokes the bottle. With the other he grabs her arm. "I can explain . . . I just . . . "

"Let go of me," she screams, pulling her arm back. "Coward! Nut! Murderer!"

She grabs her coat. With a long, ear-piercing scream she runs to the door. He sprints after her.

On the sidewalk, outside the café, she's nowhere, vanished into the crowd. Only a black shoe lies askew on the snow. Hers? Where is she then? Her foot is freezing, she can't be too far. She'll come back to get the shoe. His heart is about to implode. He turns around.

A streetcar rattles by. The shoe is still there.

Back inside Café Select he pushes past the crowd huddled around the man on the floor. He sets the wine bottle on the bar's counter. He picks up his coat, folds it neatly, places it on a high stool. As an afterthought, he perches on the next one. His face and neck are cold and cardboard-stiff. Tears well in his eyes.

In the bartender's wide-open eyes he reads the terror. "Why . . . why did you come back? For the coat?"

"Don't you see? I've done . . . something awful. But I'm not a bad person! I know what's right . . . I know what's wrong." His hands cover his face. He sobs. "You guys don't know me . . . I could escape. But I know I can't run away. She'll be there to remind me. I wanted to love her . . . wanted her to love me." He lifts his head, looks the bartender in the eye. "Did you call an ambulance?"

A cruiser arrives first. He lets the two cops lead him to the car. He spends the night at the station. Next morning he's fingerprinted, mug shots are taken, he's charged with aggravated assault. "I won't plead not guilty by reason of temporary insanity," he tells a cop. "It's my doing. I know the consequences. I'll pay."

SHALOM CAMENIETZKI was born in Rio de Janeiro, Brazil, raised in Israel, educated in the US, and now resides in Canada. He earned a doctorate of psychology and currently works out of his private office in Toronto, Ontario, where he makes his home. Inspired by writers such as Chekhov and the Brazilian writer Graciliano Ramos, Camenietzki studied creative writing at the University of Toronto. *The Atheist's Bible* is his first collection of stories.